on thin ice

jamie bastedo

Red Deer PRESS

Published by
Red Deer Press
A Fitzhenry & Whiteside Company
1512, 1800–4 Street S.W.
Calgary, Alberta, Canada T2S 2S5
www.reddeerpress.com

Credits
Edited for the Press by Peter Carver
Copyedited by Kirstin Morrell
Cover and text design by Erin Woodward
Cover image courtesy iStock.
Printed and bound in Canada by Friesens for Red Deer Press

Acknowledgments
Financial support provided by the Canada
Council, and the Government of Canada
through the Book Publishing Industry
Development Program (BPIDP).

National Library of Canada Cataloguing in Publication
Bastedo, Jamie, 1955–
    On thin ice / Jamie Bastedo.
ISBN 0-88995-337-6
    I. Title.
PS8553.A82418O5 2006   jC813'.6   C2006-901291-1

Printed on 100% post consumer recycled paper

For all the proud sons and daughters
of the Arctic.

The great sea moves me!
The great sea sets me adrift!
The mighty weather storms through my soul.
– Uvavnuk, *Northern Voices*

. . . I carried my grandfather to a rock that faced the sea
And I felt his calmness and joy.
I looked at the sights that drew his eyes:
The land, the sky, the sea.
I heard a soft melody that grew with strength and pride.
From this song, his body moved and our world surged with life.
I listened to my grandfather and felt the song deep within my soul.
I stood next to my grandfather
And we moved to the ancient rhythms, the sound of the chant
And we embraced our youth.
– "Song of Spring", *Inuuqatigiit*

Some days you have to work hard to save the bear.
Some days the bear will save you.
– Barbara Kingsolver, *Small Wonder*

Acknowledgements

Thank you, Darren Keith and the Hunters and Trappers Organization of Gjoa Haven, for your book, *Inuit Qaujimaningit Nanurnut—Inuit knowledge of polar bears.* It was absolutely crucial in shaping this story. Thanks also, Darren and Peter Irniq, for your help in finding just the right Inuktitut words. Thank you, former Kugluktuk resident Mindy Willett and my teenage daughter Jaya, for your fine-tooth reviews of an early manuscript. Your suggestions were hugely helpful. I thank my daughter Nimisha, for your help with the French text. Thank you, Rosemary Lundrigan, for inviting me to Tuktoyaktuk and helping me find the key to the underground community freezer which became Nanurtalik's "Icehouse." Thank you, Maureen Gruben, for sharing your Tuktoyaktuk home, your stories of the land and your wonderful collection of Inuit artifacts gathered from the real Spit. Thank you, Myrna Pokiak, for your amazingly detailed story of your first polar bear hunt. I could not have painted Ashley's hunt without your help. Thank you, Mitch Taylor, for your early guidance on polar bear studies and stories. Thank you, Rosemary Kuptana, for helping me see the on-the-ground face of Arctic climate change while developing the *Sila* project. Thank you, Jean Lauriault of the Canadian Museum of Nature and Environment Canada's Earl Blacklock, for enabling me, through our work together, to learn so much about Arctic climate change. And a very big thanks to all the staff at Red Deer Press, particularly Dennis Johnson for encouraging me to "find the magic" in this book, Kirstin Morrell and Erin Woodward for shepherding it through production, Stephanie Stewart, and Peter Carver whose editorial prowess and indefatigable support helped me find the story's fire. Finally, and as always, thank you Brenda, for supporting my writing habit in so many ways.

Foreword

Inuit have a special relationship with the polar bear. We both fear and respect *nanuit*. When a young hunter got his first polar bear, he would share the meat with the Elders in the community, and this was considered a very high honour.

My father made his living as a hunter, and spent his entire life on the land. When I was young, he taught me many things, including the uses of the polar bear. However, many of the things I learned from my parents are not true anymore. For example, we cannot predict our weather. We see our ice getting thinner and this poses a great challenge to the bears, as they do not have the space to hunt. They are coming into our communities, which is dangerous for people and for the bears. Inuit have long been telling the rest of the world that the climate is changing.

I hope that the people who read this book will begin to understand the impact of climate change on Inuit culture. Everyone needs to be concerned, not only us Inuit and the polar bears, but the entire global community. We must act soon before it is too late.

Enjoy the book. I did.

Peter Irniq
Inuit Cultural Activist
Former Nunavut Commissioner

Author's Foreword

This book is a work of pure fiction. I made the whole thing up and had a lot of fun doing it. The truth is, though, that Ashley Anowiak's journey is a real journey. The lives of all Arctic people are unpredictable adventures played out against a backdrop of timeless cultural values, a rapidly changing climate, and the meeting of many worlds.

Though all the adventures in this novel are imaginary, they are based on well documented events that occur in today's Arctic. A freak blizzard that lasts almost a week (Rankin Inlet, Nunavut). A catastrophic flood that devastates a coastal town (Barrow, Alaska). An explosive ice sheet or *ivu* that moves as fast as a man can run (Beaufort Sea). A polar bear half-starved by bizarre weather and sea ice patterns (Churchill, Manitoba). Whole hillsides torn open by melting permafrost (Sachs Harbor, Northwest Territories). A huge, frozen catacomb carved deep below an Arctic town (Tuktoyaktuk, Northwest Territories). An Inuit hunter slashed and scalped by a polar bear (Kimmirut, Nunavut). A shaman who strides easily in and out of dreams (Iglulik, Nunavut). All these dramatic threads are woven into the novel from real-life places, stories and experiences of Arctic people.

Even Ashley's magical journey through the "sea tunnel" is adapted from well-documented experiences of traditional Inuit shamans, like the one from Iglulik recorded in 1928 by the great anthropologist Knud Rasmussen who, like Ashley, was half Inuit by birth.

For the very greatest shamans, a way opens right from the house whence they invoke their helping spirits; a road down through the earth or down through the sea below the sea ice, and by this route the shaman is led down without encountering any obstacle. He almost glides as if falling through a tube so fitted to his body that he can check his progress by pressing against the sides, and need not actually fall down with a rush. This tube is kept open for him by all the souls of his name-sakes, until he returns on his way back to earth.

Ashley's inner world undergoes a hurricane of change even as her outer world is rocked by the stresses and storms of climate change. This global threat is an abstract concept to many people living in temperate climates. Not so in the far north where, among all the citizens of this planet, Arctic people are being hit "first and worst" by its insidious impacts. Ashley's story presents a stirring picture of climate change in the flesh.

It is my hope that this book will transport you to a fast-changing Arctic world where darkness and light, fragility and endurance, co-exist in a perpetual state of creative tension—as revealed in the two faces of *Nanurluk,* the mysterious, giant bear that haunted Ashley's dreams.

– Jamie Bastedo
Yellowknife, March 2006

The Bear Shaman's Song

Part I
Searching for the Bear

Watching the ground for her tracks,
I search for the bear.
Nameless rivers, distant mountains,
My search seems endless.
With strength drained and mind exhausted,
I cannot find her.
There is only the song of the sea—*Ha-jai-jaa, ha-jai-jaa!*
And the thunder of crashing waves.

Goodbye Nanurtalik

ASHLEY'S DREAM JOURNAL

SUNDAY, SEPTEMBER 4TH 3:48 A.M.

I trudge through the center of Nanurtalik, leaning into a hot, angry wind. It's so strong, my lips are flapping. I force both hands to my face. Layers of skin seem to blow away, revealing another face below my own.

I reach back and touch my dream-hair. It's braided in long loops like the kind Inuit women wore a long time ago. I pull one in front of my nose. My red hair has turned jet black!

The water on Crab Bay is pure froth. Huge waves crash on the Spit, raking house-sized hunks of dirt into the sea. I struggle against the wind. I have to get to the Spit. There's someone waiting for me there. Someone who can tell me who I am.

Near the edge of town I see shadowy figures hunkered down with their backs to the wind. Nobody looks at me. I feel like a total stranger in this town. A stranger even to myself.

I hear yapping above the wind. A pack of sled dogs tears past me with blood lust in their eyes, headed straight for the Spit.

All kinds of junk whiz past my head—garbage cans, plywood doghouses, razor-sharp metal siding. I'm in a bloody hurricane.

My legs feel like cement. I look down at my feet. I'm wearing beautiful sealskin kamiiks. *I wiggle my toes and my feet disappear, swallowed by a road that's turned to quicksand. I realize with horror that the permafrost under the whole town is melting. People, telephone poles, houses—everything sinks out of sight. The last thing to vanish is the big white church. It goes down like a sinking ship, with the bell tower disappearing into a geyser of black muck.*

I'm up to my waist in cold, wet ground, madly thrashing my legs like a seal escaping from an ice hole. The more I struggle, the faster I sink.

I spot what looks like a piece of driftwood caught up in the swirling muck. With all my might I wade forward and wrap two fingers around the stick. The instant I touch it, a flood of warmth surges through my arm. I stop sinking. I lean on the stick and step onto a round patch of solid ground just big enough to stand on. I yank the stick out and gasp.

It's a huge narwhal tusk harpoon. Its spiraled shaft takes on a purple glow around my hands. That tingly warmth flows up my spine. And another feeling. How can I describe it? It's like I've found something precious that I didn't even know I'd lost. With junk still zinging past my head, I inspect the spear-point, carved from a brilliant, reddish orange soapstone that any Inuk carver would die for.

Above the roar of the wind I catch faint pulsations that sound like a drumming song. I look up to see a strange figure dancing where the Spit drops into the sea. At first I think: polar bear—and my stomach fills with ice. I squint my dream-eyes. It's a tall man dressed head to toe in polar bear skins except for a weird striped hood. A knife-shaped point sticks out the top. Some skinny, white thing spins around this as he dances. A belt of polar bear claws hangs from his waist.

The bear-man slowly turns towards me, his face hidden by the Qilauti he's beating. Shreds of his drumming song break through the wind like daggers, cutting a fiery hole in my chest.

I'm so stunned by his song I don't notice the dogs returning until they're almost on top of me. They run full-tilt, tails between their legs, and a green terror in their eyes. They're escaping from a rising sea that's already swallowed the Spit. I raise the harpoon as if I'd done it a thousand times before. But the dogs ignore my threat and knock me down like a bowling pin. The harpoon flies from my fingers and disappears *into the seething muck. My tiny island of firm ground instantly collapses and I fall back into quicksand.*

The last thing I see before my head goes under is the bear-man plunging headfirst into the sea. The last thing I hear is his haunting song and the muffled thunder of waves crashing over my head.

Uitajuq

ASHLEY'S HOUSE
SUNDAY, SEPTEMBER 4TH 12:55 P.M.

I spent Sunday morning drawing scenes from my hurricane dream. I filled my sketchbook with sinking churches, glowing harpoons, freaked-out dogs, and that strange dude on the Spit dressed in polar bear skins and a crazy hat.

When I'd woken up I could still feel that burning ache in my chest ignited by the bear-man's song. I knew right away it wasn't my asthma. This ache went deeper, like a stab wound that turned my insides out. I lay with my eyes closed, rubbing my chest, but the ache wouldn't go away. Floating in that limbo-land between sleeping and waking, I sensed that the only way to heal this wound was to get back into my dream-girl's head and find whatever she was looking for.

After two hours of white-knuckle sketching, I had a sudden urge to look up from my drafting table to the full-length mirror on my door. I studied my reflection. I held my chin at different angles. I raised my arm above my head as if to spear something. I wanted to see past my red hair and pale complexion to the black-haired, harpoon-slinging girl who seemed to hide just under my skin. I tried to sketch her face from the dim memory of my dream-fingers touching her cheeks, her nose, her brow. But it was all a blur and my pencil froze on the page.

I gave my head a quick shake. "Get real, space cadet," I said to my reflection. "There's no one else in there."

The smell of fresh baking finally lured me downstairs. Aana, my grandmother, was sitting at the dining table, sewing as usual. I snorted when I saw what she was working on. My mishmash coat. That's what Mom called it. She'd plucked it out of the path of a bulldozer at the Inniturliq dump. She'd washed it, patched it as best as she could, then presented it to me on my sixteenth birthday.

It was the weirdest fur coat I'd ever seen, made from a zoo's worth of animals from all over the map. The chest and back were all *siksik,* the sleeves were beaver, the cuffs and hem were embroidered sealskin, the hood wolf, and the ruff was made from raccoon of all things. Everything had been cut and sewn together in wavy lines, giving the coat a kind of weather-beaten look.

"It's a good match, don't you think, Ash?" Mom had said when she gave it to me. "Just like you, eh? A real mishmash."

It was hate at first sight. That coat was like a loudspeaker that blared everything about me that didn't fit in—my minestrone blood concocted from an Irish grandfather, a French Canadian mother, and an Inuk father. My quirky artwork. My stormy moods. Besides, it was strangely uncomfortable. Too loose here, too tight there.

Mom knew I hated the coat but insisted we bring it from Inniturliq when we moved here. I'd torn a pocket when I yanked it out of a moving box. Aana's always scrounged for things to sew and must have found it after I'd chucked it deep into my closet.

I pretended not to see my mishmash coat as I headed to the kitchen to check out Mom's latest goodies. Ahh. Fresh bearberry muffins. She must have taken some over to Dad who, as usual, had been working all weekend at the radio station.

My little brother Pauloosie and his buddy Lewis sat in front of the idiot box, racing stock cars with a pair of joystick controllers in their laps. Above the digital roar of revving motors and screeching tires, I could hear Gabe, my older adopted brother, practicing "Flop-eared Mule" on his fiddle.

"Hey, can you throttle back a bit there, Pauloosie?" I shouted.

"It's *boring* without the sound," he yelled, his eyes still glued to the screen.

"Not off," I said, "just *down!*"

I ended up standing in front of the TV until he knocked a few decibels off the racetrack racket. A moment later I heard what sounded like thunder. Aana turned briefly to the living room window, then back to her sewing.

I sat down across from Aana with a couple of muffins and a stack of math homework. I was hardly thrilled with my new school. I couldn't believe what they'd already dumped on us after just two days.

"Muffin, Aana?" I asked.

She stopped humming along with Gabe's fiddle.

"No thanks, *Uitajuq.*"

"Why do you always call me that? *Uitajuq,* Big Eyes."

"*Auka,*" chirped Aana. "Not big eyes. Open Eyes. When you were a baby you always used to sleep with your eyes half open."

"Keeping an eye on the door probably. Lots of scary stuff going on in Inniturliq. What exactly do you think I was scared of?"

"*Auka.* Not scared. Watching. You were always watching. Waiting."

"Waiting for what?"

Aana carefully slipped a needle into her sealskin pincushion and looked up at me. Through her bifocals, her eyes were as big as a beluga's. "Just like *Anaana.* She was always watching."

"You mean your mother—and Uncle Jonah's?"

Aana nodded slowly.

"The great grandmother I'm supposedly named after?"

"Also *Uitajuq*. I gave you her name. Now she's in you."

I could hold my own at Inuit sports like the high kick, leg-wrestle, and knuckle-hop. I liked eating *maktaaq*, raw whale blubber. I'd even developed a taste for *igunaq*, fermented walrus meat. But thanks to my no-nonsense Irish blood—or maybe my "French skepticism," as Mom called it—I could never swallow the Stone Age belief that spirits jumped from the grave to the cradle just because you happened to be named after somebody. How could I be anybody but *me?*

"Thanks, Aana. It's an okay name, I guess. But you still haven't told me what she kept watching for."

Aana looked at me like she was sizing me up. "How old are you now?"

"Sixteen last May, remember? That's when Mom gave me that ridiculous—I mean, that wonderful coat."

Aana motioned for me to lean closer, then pulled my sweatshirt down below my collarbone to reveal my peculiar birthmark. About the size of a loonie, it was a cluster of five dark squiggly lines. "You know who made this?" she asked, tapping my chest with a bony finger.

"Dad likes to say it was a polar bear," I said, straining to look over my chin. "Very funny," I added.

"That's what *Uitajuq* was always looking for."

"Polar bears?"

Aana said yes with her raised eyebrows. "And you too, little *Uitajuq*. Watch out."

"You're telling me that's what I was watching for in my *crib?*"

Aana chuckled softly, making her round chest jiggle. "All that watching paid off, I guess."

"What's that supposed to mean?"

"You see things. That's why you draw good. Nice bear pictures anyway."

Aana tied the last stitch on the coat pocket. "*Taima.* Good for another five years."

"It's nice, Aana," I lied. "Thanks."

"It's a good coat. Made just for you." Aana grabbed my hand and placed it on the coat. "Feel it, *Uitajuq.* Close your eyes and feel it. Sometimes you see better with closed eyes."

I started to pull my hand away but she grabbed it again and pressed my long fingers against the coat. Mom called them "*les doigts d'une artiste,*" artist fingers, a throwback to my toddler days when she only spoke to me in French. I gave the fur a couple of token strokes. There was no magic here for me. "Real nice, Aana." I reached over and spread the coat on her shoulders. "But I think it would look much better on you."

She sniffed while carefully folding the coat in front of her. "*Tiiturumaviit?*"

"What, Aana?" I always got flustered when she fired Inuktitut at me like I'd spoken it forever. My French was way better.

"Tea. Tea. You want some tea?"

"Oh yes, Aana. Please."

"Then make some for me." Aana snatched a needle from her mouth and pretended to lunge at me as if brandishing a harpoon. I dodged her assault, barking like a scared seal, and fled into the kitchen.

"Any new drawings to show me?" Aana called as she pulled my sketchbook out of my stack of homework.

A full cup of tea slipped from my hands and crashed to the floor.

Pauloosie started clapping and whistling. "Hooray! The Kitchen Klutz strikes again!"

"Stuff it, Pauloosie!" I snapped.

I must have scooped my sketchbook off my desk by mistake. My dream pictures were too hot, too confusing to show anybody yet—even Aana who was the only one who seemed to take my artwork seriously.

"Maybe later," I yelled while frantically wiping up my mess. By the time I raced back to her it was too late. She had opened my sketchbook and was staring wide-eyed at my bear guy with the crazy hat.

Sometimes Aana was like my personal dream dictionary. I got the feeling this was one of those times.

"*Angakkuq,*" is all she said.

"What, Aana?"

"Where did you see him?"

"Last night, Aana. It was a pretty wild dream. Who's . . . Angah-cook?"

"Lucky *Uitajuq.* You had a good visitor in your sleep. *Angakkuq.* This man is a shaman. A sorcerer. He can teach you." She pushed her glasses against her nose and studied my sketch. "You see good, little *Uitajuq.* You draw good. He's wearing polar bear skins, right?"

"Uh-huh," I said, peering over her shoulder at the strange dancer of my dreams.

"*Nanjrmikangakkuq.* A bear shaman."

For some reason this floored me. Something hot jumped in my chest. "So . . . what makes him a shaman?"

Aana softly clicked her tongue. "That belt. Those are bear claws, right?"

Part of me was drifting back into the dream. I could almost hear fragments of his drumming song. "Uh-huh."

"Hmmm." Aana leaned forward. "And look at his cap. A shaman's cap."

"What's that pointy thing sticking out of it?"

"*Tuullik* beak."

"What, Aana?"

"Loon. Loon. It's a loon-skin cap."

"And that white flag thingy? It spun around his head in the wind."

"Not flag. *Tiriaq.*"

I was getting impatient. "Please, Aana, you know I don't speak—"

"Weasel. *Angakkuq* dances. The weasel spins." She twisted around to look at me. "You say even in the wind it was spinning?"

"Yep. It was a bloody hurricane."

Aana pinched her chin. She was breathing hard. "Hmmm. This is a very powerful bear shaman. Strong medicine. Your Uncle Jonah would like to see this."

Why was a bear shaman dancing around in my head? And why was Aana so worked up about him? Whoever he was, I knew I'd never show my sketches to Uncle Jonah. "Ah . . . I don't think so, Aana. He might get all upset and throw one of his—"

An agonized scream erupted from Uncle Jonah's bedroom. "*Najak! Najak!*"

"Speak of the devil," I muttered. "Time for our daily emergency."

Tizzy Fit

UNCLE JONAH'S ROOM

SUNDAY, SEPTEMBER 4TH 1:05 P.M.

I hunched over and leaned on an invisible cane. "*Najak! Najak!*" I cried in a cranky old man voice. "My baby sister, help me! Help me!"

Aana pushed her sewing kit aside, tightened her flowered kerchief, and waddled as fast as she could to Uncle Jonah's door.

"He's sure got you well trained, Aana," I said, hobbling along behind her.

Wiggins, our pet macaw, got all charged up by the sudden commotion and joined in the screaming.

Gabe's "Flop-eared Mule" stopped in mid-gallop. His door flew open. "Aana! Aana! Uncle Jonah's calling again! Aana! Go see Uncle!"

Pauloosie turned up the racetrack sound effects until I could almost smell burning rubber.

"*Ana banana! Ana banana!*" shrieked Wiggins.

"What a waste of life," I said as I reluctantly fell in step behind Aana. "All he does is eat, sleep, and scream."

Aana turned right around. "He's a dreamer like you, *Uitajuq,*" she said sternly. "Sometimes he has bad dreams, that's all."

Wiggins piped in with a new tune. "*Shit-in-the fan! Shit-in-the fan!*"

I shot Pauloosie a mock look of horror. "What *have* you been whispering in that bird's ear?"

"It was Gabe. Honest!" said Pauloosie, giggling to his friend.

As Aana swung Uncle Jonah's door open, my nostrils flinched with the smell of dirty socks, homemade cigarettes, and cheap wine. His ratty old polar bear rug was all bunched up and half flipped over like he'd been wrestling with it. Uncle Jonah had fallen out of bed again. His good arm thrashed the air like a drowning man. He made weird gurgling noises like he was swallowing seawater.

Another five-star performance. "Not again," I grumbled. I really should have worked on being more sympathetic to Uncle Jonah. If it had been Gabe sputtering on the floor like that, I'd have been running.

Aana went right to work, calling him *Ikuma*—fireman—and making soft clucking sounds as she tried to lift him off the floor. She shot a glance at me and hissed, "*Uitajuq,* help."

In spite of my disgust, I grabbed Uncle's withered right arm and wrapped it around my shoulders. Aana stooped under his other arm. Together we hoisted him to his feet and flopped him on the bed. I couldn't tell if his eyes were open or closed. As soon as his head hit the pillow his body went all tense like driftwood. His back curved and lifted off the bed. He started smacking his lips real loud. His tongue shot out and whipped back and forth like it was trying to escape. Mom called this a tizzy fit.

Mary Jane, the nurse in town, claimed Uncle Jonah suffered from mild epileptic seizures. "They're nothing at all to worry about," she'd say in her thick Scottish accent. "Just so long as he takes his nerve pills."

Aana stroked his sweating brow and hummed what sounded like a thousand-year-old lullaby. As his body unwound, he started mumbling something in Inuktitut and making awful gurgles in the back of his throat. He stopped for a moment, then scrunched his face as if straining to hear someone in another world. Throughout this routine, Aana continued her haunting song and gently stroked her older brother's forehead.

We knew his tizzy fit was almost over when his arms and legs shot up from the bed like he'd stuck his big toe in a light socket. Then, as quickly, his body fell limp as a wet rag. Everything relaxed except his face. It stayed locked in a listening pose, eyes squeezed shut and lips curled back, revealing his few remaining teeth, as yellow as dog pee on snow.

It wasn't long before he was snoring like a bear. Aana grunted for help. We rolled him over on his side and tucked up his legs as we had countless times before.

"Big baby," Aana said as she closed his door behind her.

Sila

I always felt stirred up after witnessing one of Uncle Jonah's tizzy fits. The weird energy that tied his body in knots seemed to leak out of him into my hands, my lungs, my brain. To shake it off there was only one solution. Go outside. With Wiggins of course.

Wiggins had adjusted to our new life in Nanurtalik much better than I. All he needed to feel at home was me. Mom had brought him up in a box from Montreal soon after he'd lost his baby feathers. I'd been his sole trainer ever since—that is, when Pauloosie or Gabe weren't spicing up his vocabulary with a few choice words. When we moved here in June, I heard mutterings about how Wiggins might bring the town bad luck, how he belonged in a zoo, or how we should have at least kept him indoors. I ignored all opinions and advice. Wiggins was part of our kooky family and that was that. A scarlet macaw zooming over the bald Arctic tundra made perfect sense to me.

Wiggins seemed especially restless on this particular Sunday afternoon. It must have been the weather. Although the sky was clear, there was an eerie static in the air like it was about to ignite. One minute Wiggins would swoop low over the tundra with outspread wings like a short-eared owl hunting for lemmings. The next he'd rocket skyward, cart-wheeling high in the air like some cockamamie crow.

In spite of the fast rising wind, we made the usual circuit, wandering down to the Spit to see what had washed up on the beach, then circling back along the base of Anirniq Hill until we came to the church.

Ever since we got here, Wiggins had always loved the church, probably because it stands head and shoulders above any other building in town. Once he got bored with all his crazy swooping and soaring, he started circling the bell tower, faster and faster, until he was nothing but a streak of red, blue, and yellow. The whole time he squawked bloody murder. I'd never seen Wiggins act so freaky.

When we first moved to Nanurtalik, I couldn't figure out who this "Our Lady" chick was that everybody talked about. Then I learned the official name of the church: Our Lady of the Sea. Mom called it *La maison du bon Dieu*—the good Lord's house. Dad said when he was growing up here, all the kids knew it as the Haunted House. I once asked Aana about this but she just shut me up with one of her royal sniffs.

Except for weddings and funerals Our Lady didn't see much action. The doors were always open though, as Father Ungali often liked to remind us. He was the new priest here, fresh off the boat from Nigeria. He'd been on the plane that flew us to Nanurtalik last June. Father Ungali did a lot of praying on that flight, but then who wouldn't, growing up in steamy Africa and moving to the frozen Arctic? He must have felt as much a fish out of water as I did living in this town. It didn't surprise me that he always took off on what he called "errands of mercy" to God knows where.

"Game over!" I shouted and tried to wolf-whistle Wiggins to my shoulder. I'd never taken him inside before and I thought he might enjoy bombing around the belfry while I chilled out in the church. Usually he'd obey after a couple of whistles but he was in some kind of mad spell and kept strafing the bell tower. "Game over, Wiggins!" I yelled again.

Wiggins let out a crazy squawk and landed on the tower's cross, the highest thing in town. "*Game ovah! Game ovah!*" he shouted defiantly.

"Brat!" I said and yanked open the big oak door.

Mom liked to think I came here to pray. No harm in that, I guess. But it was the ceiling I came for, the closest thing I'd found in this town to what I could call real art. Way back when, some French priest turned the church ceiling into a home-grown planetarium. His very own vault of heaven.

I took my usual seat in a center pew and looked up. All of the bullet-shaped windows were framed by whalebone ribs that pointed to a Gothic ceiling painted lavender blue. Silver stars were scattered like pearls across this indoor sky in amazingly accurate constellations. W-shaped Cassiopeia, the queen whose beauty raised floods and monsters from the deep. Orion, the sword-wielding hunter from the east. And the Big Dipper which forms the tail and torso of Ursa Major, the Big Bear. Dancing in front of these stars was a rainbow veil of northern lights that stretched across the entire church ceiling.

Awesome.

I tilted my head back and squinted. The ceiling disappeared and the infinite sky opened above me. Worries about fitting in at a new school, my burning itch to be a better artist, and that nagging sense of being lost—all my troubles seemed to drift upwards like smoke and dissolve into the welcoming sky. Last to melt away were the weird vibes left by Uncle Jonah's tizzy fit.

I could stare at that ceiling for hours. Like the winter stars that rotated above the church roof, it seemed to change every time I looked. I wondered what I would do with a canvas and colors this grand. Probably much the same. Of course, I'd have to stick a polar bear or two in the sky. They'd popped up in most of my drawings lately—and my dreams, though I couldn't for the life of me figure out why.

"*Game ovah! Game ovah!*" Wiggins's voice came storming down from the heavens.

"Coming!" I yelled to the stars. I bounded for the door. That bird had me well trained.

Below Wiggins's squawking I heard a deep rumble like the echo from a giant drum.

"Thunder?" I said to the flower-shaped doorknob.

As I opened the church door, a blast of hot wind slapped my face. It almost burned. Unbelievably warm for late August.

Seconds later Wiggins fell from the sky and landed on my shoulder. He pecked at the polar bear toe bone that hung around my neck from a cord of caribou hide. He started chomping on it, as he did sometimes when he was upset.

"Hey, cut it out, boy," I said, nudging his head away from the bone. I'd worn that thing since I was a toddler. It was strangely precious to me and I didn't want any of Wiggins's graffiti on it.

He flicked his black tongue in my face and started nibbling on my right ear. Though Wiggins's beak could probably crack open a small coconut he could be amazingly gentle. Still, I wasn't in the mood for a grooming session and slipped him a honey stick from my pocket. We were good for each other, Wiggins and me. Both fish out of water in this crazy little town.

"Don't sweat it boy. I'm here, okay? I'm—"

Something about the sky looked all wrong. In the few minutes I'd been in the church, a towering bank of dark clouds had rolled in from the southwest. They were backlit by a blotted-out sun that gave them a shining edge as white and hard as a walrus tusk. The clouds were moving towards us and, in the deepening gloom, I thought I detected a distant flicker of lightning.

I heard a creaking sound behind me and turned to see a white plastered Madonna and child staring back at me. She wore the sun and twelve stars for her crown and stood on the moon. Our Lady of the Sea. Aana called her the Sila Lady for the spirit who ruled our weather. The baby Jesus had one arm tenderly wrapped around her neck. His other arm had broken off a long time ago and hung from a rusty wire now creaking in the wind.

I felt a growing hole in my chest and the rising wind seemed to blow right through it. For some reason Wiggins refused to fly and rode the whole way home on my shoulder. By the time we reached the back steps, the temperature had dropped by ten degrees and I had to cover Wiggins's head with my hand to protect him from a brutal volley of hailstones.

Sky Noise

A BEACH EAST OF NANURTALIK
SUNDAY, SEPTEMBER 4TH 2:30 P.M.

You have been lying like this most of the afternoon, with your four legs spread wide in the shallow waters of this pebble beach. You don't mind the waves crashing on your head. Anything is better than this heat. You idly watch dark clouds moving in from the south. You scratch at some matted fur clinging to your butt. You roll on your back and blow bubbles upside down. You try not to think about food.

Now and then you push away from shore with your hind feet and plunge into deeper water to scratch around on the bottom for some kelp or a starfish to eat. But mostly you just lie there, half awake, daydreaming about winter and the promise of ice.

The wind suddenly dies. You prop your chin on a flat stone just above the water and let the swells rock your colossal body to sleep.

You wake to a splattering of raindrops on your face. It's safe to get out of the water. The air is cooler now, much cooler. There's no danger of overheating. Seawater pours off your body as you lumber onto the beach. You shake, creating a giant spiral of spray all around you.

You lift your head and sniff. Something in the sky catches your eye. A distant flash of light. A few seconds later, the fur along your spine bristles to a low rumbling boom you've rarely heard. You snort at the sound and gallop off in the opposite direction.

Soon the clouds close in above you and open up. You've never seen rain like this. It comes down so hard that it blurs your vision and you have to stop to avoid stumbling into the tall boulders that line the shore. The sea and rocks and tundra hiss with rain. That rumbling sound follows you. The temperature keeps dropping. Raindrops turn to hail. The land turns white with jagged balls of ice. A deafening clatter drowns out all but the loudest blasts from the sky. Some of the hailstones are as big as duck eggs and one strikes you squarely on the nose. A stabbing pain floods your head. You crouch down, as if stalking a seal, and crawl behind a leaning rock to wait out the storm.

A blinding flash of light from the sky makes you grunt like a startled cub. A split second later, a gigantic boom shatters the air. You cover your eyes with your paws. All you can do is wait.

But you don't have to wait long. The storm ends as quickly as it began. You stick your broad head around the rock and peer up at a sky that is almost black with clouds. You sniff the air. Your nose tells you that more rain and high winds are coming. The rumbling has stopped for now. You spring up on your hind legs to survey the work of the storm.

The land is covered in a gleaming coat of hailstones as thick as your paw. The birch shrubs have been stripped of their flaming fall colors. A crippled, rough-legged hawk perches unsteadily on top of a boulder, its drooping wing broken by the hail. Three eider ducks lie belly up on a nearby pond. The storm has brought you something good.

What's that floating behind the ducks? A large brown lump. You drop to all fours and angle closer to catch a scent from the rising wind that blows in your face. You stand again and sniff deeply. Yes. That lump is some kind of animal. But what? You sniff again. A dim memory stirs. In your long life you have seen this animal only once before. Browsing in the tall willows beside the river of eagles. Now you know this is a moose. Maybe it was struck dead by that blinding flash or that horrible sound. It doesn't matter to you. What matters is that as long as the sky stays quiet, you will eat well.

Uncle Jonah's Cup

ASHLEY'S HOUSE

SUNDAY, SEPTEMBER 4TH 4:10 P.M.

By the time I got back from my Wiggins walk, Uncle Jonah's latest emergency was forgotten. The hailstorm only lasted a few minutes, almost like I'd dreamed it. The weather show was over for now and I grudgingly settled back into my math homework.

In spite of the grand size of our log house, all life seemed to revolve within an arm's length of the dining table. "All cozied up together," as Mom would say, "just like when everyone lived in iglus." The first thing she ordered when we moved here was the longest, widest table she could find in the Northern Store catalogs. In the end she chose the "Pioneer Special," a huge, farm-style table made from three shining slabs of oak. Dad was not impressed with the price or the fact that it took him a weekend to put the thing together. Mom just primed him with praise and sweet cappuccinos while reminding him that we never knew just who might drop in. From day one, she'd labeled our house a safe haven for the lost and lonely and saw that table as a place where anybody was welcome to come and lick their wounds.

Sunday was officially baking day at our house and Mom had been sifting through a pile of French cookbooks for hidden treasures—some new mouthwatering recipe for sweetbreads, cakes, cookies, or deliciously decadent buns. Last week it was frosted Belgian cinnamon rolls. "Keeps the morale up," she liked to say as she eased the latest masterpiece out of her beloved wood-fueled oven.

That bout with Uncle Jonah had taken the wind out of Aana's sails and she was snoring softly in the Lazy-boy chair. Pauloosie had tired of crashing stock cars and now lay belly down in front of the woodstove with his nose buried in a Spiderman comic book. The TV was on and Gabe was stretched out on the couch with his back to the screen. As usual, he had his headphones plugged into the TV doing as well as any blind guy could to follow the show. Today it was a retread World War II movie. The headphone arrangement was Mom's idea, "to help keep the peace," she'd said, even if he happened to be listening to people blow each other up.

Dad was stooped over a dismantled chainsaw that had died on him while bucking up driftwood along on the Spit. He had a huge workshop downstairs, complete with sprawling benches and enough power tools to open a hardware store. But Dad complained that it was always too cold and drafty down there and his fingers just didn't work right. So he'd spread a plastic tarp or chunk of old plywood over the Pioneer Special and plunk down his latest project. That was Dad. He liked to fix things. Mom liked to fix people. Both kinds of projects happened around that table.

You could tell Mom was bummed over this. Dad worked crazy hours trying to keep his dog and pony station on the airwaves. That's what he called it. Understaffed, underpowered, underfunded, that station kept Dad busy eight days a week. So, if sharing Dad's company meant putting up with oily pieces of chainsaw on her precious table, Mom did her best to bite her tongue. When she occasionally went ballistic over some grease or scratch on the table, Dad would just grunt and say something like, "Well, we want to get our money's worth out of this fancy furniture, don't we?" It was a regular source of squabbling between them, but way easier to live with than the knockout brawls I'd seen at Rosie's house.

I was getting lost in my math homework—I mean *really* lost—when I heard the squeak of Uncle Jonah's door. Without a word or a glance, he shuffled over to the far end of the table and hammered down his old cup. I leaned away. I'd been infected enough today by the cloud of dark energy that hung around him. Mom sprang up like a jack-in-the-box and grabbed the teapot from the back of the woodstove. Though we'd only lived here a couple of months he already had her pretty well trained. She filled his cup to the brim. "Black as sin, Uncle," she said. "Just the way you like it."

Uncle Jonah frowned and aimed his skinny, white beard at the cup.

"And sweet as a kiss. *Bien sur,* Uncle. I added your regular cup of sugar to your teapot. It's no wonder you're losing your teeth. But don't blame me." Mom tried to give him a French peck on the cheek but he recoiled as if she'd come at him with a pitchfork.

Uncle Jonah then slowly leaned forward, like his cup might blow up in his face. His back curved into a pretzel. His shoulders hunched forward like he'd been wounded in the chest. He blew over his tea, making hollow wind noises. His gammy right arm hung limp at his side. His other arm snaked across the table and he carefully wrapped his crooked fingers around the cup. He unpretzeled his body, leaned back in his chair, then downed his scalding tea in a few quick gulps.

I shook my head in disbelief. "Is that why they call you *Ikuma*, Uncle? Fireman?"

"It's from all the firewater he drinks!" hooted Gabe during a lull between bomb raids.

Uncle Jonah's eyes widened slightly but he said nothing.

There was only one cup in the universe like Uncle Jonah's. It was carved from a reddish orange soapstone I'd never seen before. Lightning shaped streaks of yellow quartz sliced through the stone. I tried once to capture its strange color and texture with pastels but I couldn't seem to get it right.

Set like raised gems in the soapstone were ten diamond-shaped splotches that looked like volcanic glass. They lined up, five on each side, forming two perfect curves just like a pair of bear claws poised for attack. The edges were so sharp I wondered sometimes if that was where Uncle Jonah got all the scars on his hands, clutching his cup like it was part of him.

Uncle Jonah never let anyone touch his cup, let alone wash it. "That old thing probably hasn't been cleaned in fifty years," Mom said. It seemed to glow on the outside. But inside it looked like a long forgotten toilet bowl. Dark, oily stains lined up in wavy lines like layers of silt trapped in permafrost. That was Uncle Jonah's life to me: blurred, muddy streaks frozen deep out of sight.

Dad told me that Uncle Jonah carved that cup himself but I didn't believe him. With that gimpy arm of his? Impossible.

"Did you really carve that crazy bear cup?" I asked him, just for a joke of course.

Honestly, that was the first time in the two months I'd lived with him that he'd ever looked me in the eye. He raised his wide bear-like nose and flared his nostrils, almost like he was sniffing. Then he slowly widened his eyes and I was shocked to see how dark they were, as black as coal. I knew instantly that there was more going on between Uncle's big, hairy ears than I'd ever thought. His gaze trapped me. I couldn't speak. I couldn't move. His eyes got wider, darker. I felt like I was falling into them. Then, behind the darkness, I caught a flash of something molten, throwing sparks of restless light. Like the guy had a regular thunderstorm going off in his head.

My jaw dropped when I heard a booming, kettle-drum sound. I realized I was hearing real thunder outside. It was like he triggered it. I blinked hard and managed to unclamp my eyes from his. The spell broke.

What the hell was *that* all about? I'd made a little crack about some dumb old cup and my mild-mannered great uncle almost swallowed me with one look.

I glanced out the living room window. Dark clouds churned overhead, squeezing light from the sky.

I looked back at Uncle Jonah. He was twirling his bear cup on the table like nothing happened between us.

Caged Bear

Ashley's house
Sunday, September 4th 5:05 p.m.

We knew Uncle's teatime was over when he started playing with his cup, aimlessly spinning it around, making a grating sound on the polished tabletop like fingernails on slate.

That look of his had stirred me up. I felt angry, rebellious, like he was testing me. I couldn't hack his games a second longer.

I almost pounced on his cup. "Here, Uncle, let me wash that for you."

He snatched it away with amazing speed, I mean, given how old he was—ninety next June. He grabbed that old cup like he was afraid I'd see all the poison he'd put in there over the years. A few drops of muddy tea landed on his wide nose. It dribbled there for a few moments, like old blood, until Aana reached across the table and wiped it off with a checkered hankie.

Another rumble of thunder brought everyone's heads up, even Uncle Jonah's. I'd heard thunder maybe a half dozen times in my life, seen lightning even less, but never this time of year.

"Probably Vince practicing on the D-8 dozer again," Dad said. "I wonder what he's plowed into this time."

Dad seemed unusually chatty. Maybe because it was Sunday and he'd forced himself to take a rare day off. I wished he'd do that more often.

"Sounds like a gust of wind gave the old tin shed a wallop," Mom said. "It's really picking up out there."

I looked out the living room window just in time to see a plywood doghouse rolling down the street. My neck hairs bristled. The sight sparked memories of my hurricane dream. Garbage cans and shingles flying through the air. Running dogs and crashing waves. A bear shaman dancing on the Spit. "Something's brewing all right," I muttered.

I stood up and clapped my hands, trying to disperse the gathering storm inside me. "How about a cup of hot cocoa, Mom?" Wiggins was jogging back and forth on his perch above the woodstove, making odd raspy sounds and getting twitchier by the minute.

My hand froze on the cupboard door while going for some mugs. More rumbling outside. A deep, distant tremor like a nuclear bomb going off a hundred miles away. Mom's stained glass polar bear rattled against the kitchen window.

Uncle Jonah turned to the window and stretched his neck out like a sea turtle coming up for air. He stopped spinning his cup and inspected the clouds through scrunched-up eyes. "Humph," he croaked, then gave a quick nod.

Mom wouldn't let Uncle Jonah smoke near the kitchen so he never lasted long with us. As he shuffled back to his room, cup in hand, I realized he hadn't said boo to anybody. Grunts, whines, and hisses were his specialty, the vocabulary you'd expect from a wolverine.

While I busied myself preparing cocoa—it was the one thing I could make—my brain grappled, once again, with the riddle of this man called Jonah. To me he was mostly a crack of light under the door, interrupted now and then by half-hour coughing fits caused by seventy-five years of chain-smoking. Or by emergency visits from nurse Mary Jane when he slipped into one of his comas. Or by screaming fits for Aana, his baby sister. How his body held up was beyond me. As for his mind, I never knew what went on there. He spoke mostly with his eyes and I didn't like it when he aimed them at me.

All I knew was that Uncle Jonah had lived here always. Born in a sod house framed with whale ribs, he was here long before Nanurtalik was even a village. Back then, when people spoke of Nanurtalik, they meant a long, curvy stretch of coastline dotted with hunting and fishing camps. Nanurtalik, the place with polar bears. Good fishing year-round. Good sealing along the area's many cracks and open leads in the sea ice. And lots of seals meant lots of good polar bear hunting—at least, while Uncle Jonah was growing up. By the time he was in his fifties, polar bears had mysteriously vanished from these parts. As much as I loved sketching bears—like they were roaring to escape from my head—I had none to draw on from the outside world. They prowled only in my dreams. Mom once joked that I should switch to ground squirrels. "Lots of *siksiks* around here," she said.

Why polar bears up and left long ago was an ongoing detective story all the Nanurtalik Elders still talked about. The ice was nothing like it used to be, they'd say. You had to go farther for seals. Most blamed the weather. Uncle Jonah never talked about bears. If he knew what happened to them, he wasn't telling.

Uncle Jonah was the main reason we moved to Nanurtalik. He'd lived with Aana most of his life, but when she got cancer fifteen years ago, when I was a baby, she moved into our Inniturliq home where she could get better medical care. After a year of chemotherapy she made it through. By then she'd taken a liking to life in a bigger community and decided to stay.

Uncle Jonah wouldn't budge even after he couldn't live alone any more. "I was born here and I'll damn well die here," he told Dad when he packed him off to the Singing Drum Elders' Home in Nanurtalik. Uncle seemed to settle in okay at first, mostly sleeping, smoking, and drinking tea. But Mom wanted the family together and told Dad to go and "have a little talk" with Uncle Jonah.

Over loud complaints about the cost, Dad finally agreed to fly to Nanurtalik just to see. He tried to negotiate with Uncle, saying he would be a lot happier in Inniturliq, living with Aana, being pampered by Mom's cooking, seeing me and Pauloosie grow up

Uncle Jonah never said a word. He just scrunched his nose at Dad in that age-old Inuk gesture that more or less meant, "Forget it." The day after Dad returned, we started getting calls from the Elders' home. Uncle Jonah had thrown a chair through his bedroom window. They called again a few days later to say he'd lit a fire in the bathtub. Then he started knocking tables over in the cafeteria. "He's like a bloody caged bear!" the head nurse told Dad in a moment of desperation. He made so much trouble in the Elders' home they finally kicked him out.

And so, with Uncle Jonah's heels dug deep into the frozen ground and nobody else willing to look after him, Dad found a job at the Nanurtalik ABC station—that's Arctic Broadcasting Corporation—and opened our new home to his dear old uncle.

I hardly knew Uncle Jonah existed until we moved here. Now his life and mine had become grudgingly woven together like two taut threads stretched from opposite ends of the earth. Him, a burned-out, Inuk hunter in his late eighties and me, a misfit, mixed blood, teenage artist who knew way more French than Inuktitut.

"Uncle Jonah's your own flesh and blood," Mom liked to remind me, especially when I seemed to care less and less for his daily emergencies.

"Now *that's* a stretch," I'd say. Still, something above and beyond my storm-tossed mind listened to her words. There was so much I didn't know about his life. So much I didn't *want* to know. Yet I had to love the old guy in spite of his disgusting habits and wasted life. There was something in the thunderstorm behind his eyes that I recognized as my own.

If Uncle Jonah had nine lives, I figured he'd already spent most of them by the time he moved in with us. By my calculations, he must have been on number eight when the Labor Day storm hit. After what that did to him, he surely had only one more life to go.

Tempête

All hell broke loose when a bolt of lightning hit the church bell tower. It struck seconds after I'd tapped Mom's fancy French barometer and watched the needle fall well below "*Tempète*"—stormy. There was no gap between the thunder and the flash that seemed to fill the whole house with white light. I ran to the huge living room window. My stomach tightened when I saw it bulge in like it was being punched by the wind. I noticed a new crack, probably from the afternoon's hail storm, and it seemed to be growing as I watched. My view of the church was blurred by pellets of sleet that already greased the glass in a crawling veil. But there was no doubt. The bell tower was on fire.

"It nailed the church, Mom. Quick! Call Dad at the station."

"Lord t'underin'!" shouted Gabe, running for his bedroom. "The sky's about to fall!"

Wiggins flew circles above my head.

Jacques, our black Labradoodle, was jumping around on his spring-loaded legs, barking at Wiggins.

Mom had her ear to the phone, yelling at me. "Keep it down in the barnyard, will you, Ash? It's ringing and I can't—Damn! He's got his phone on call-forward. Where *is* that workaholic?"

Dad was one of a handful of deputy fire chiefs in Nanurtalik, none of whom seemed to know who had the master key to the fire hall. It was Dad's job to trigger the siren whenever a fire broke out. No key meant no siren, and no siren meant no volunteers to fight the fire. Another great example of how things worked—or don't work—in this crazy town. It was no surprise there was a burned-out house on just about every street. But this church had stood for more than eighty years and now tongues of wind-whipped flames crept down the bell tower and were licking the sanctuary roof. It was the only building in town I cared about.

Luckily Mom had made an extra fire hall key and stashed it in a sugar bowl on top of the bread box. She reached for it and pressed the key into my hand. "Here. Give this to Dad. He might be napping on his office couch. If you can't find him, go to the fire hall yourself and get that siren going."

"Right," I said as I crammed into my raincoat and gumboots.

"You sure you know how to work that thing?" asked Mom.

"No sweat. Dad let me blast it last month to kick off Caribou Carnival. I've been looking for another chance ever since."

"Good. I'll start phoning around to see if I can scrounge up other firefighters." She gave me a token hug. "Be careful, Ash. And don't lose that key."

"Sure, Mom."

Before I could slam the door behind me, a small gumboot burst through the crack.

"No way I'm staying here," Pauloosie said. "A bonfire in a hurricane. That's definitely worth checking out."

"Forget the marshmallows," I said. "Let's go."

I couldn't believe the force of the wind when we stepped off the back deck. Pauloosie yelled something and pointed down the road behind me but he might as well have been a mile away for all I could hear above the roar. Then he grabbed my arm and yanked me into the ditch. I was about to shriek a couple of choice words at him when I saw another plywood doghouse sail past the spot where I'd stood seconds before.

I watched it bounce down the street. "Thanks, Paulie!" I yelled.

He shrugged and dragged me to my feet. We held hands to keep each other from blowing into the sea. The wind felt like a predatory animal out to get us.

The direct hit on the church turned out to be just the opening act of a blockbusting storm that lasted all night. We never did find Dad. By the time Pauloosie and I got to the fire hall, after dodging a barrage of flying junk, the sleet had turned into driving rain and snuffed out the bell tower fire. Pauloosie was dying to blast the siren anyway but I wouldn't let him. "Ask Dad on New Year's Eve," I yelled as we carved our way home through shuddering walls of wind.

A couple of hours into the storm we could hear a new sound above the pounding wind and lashing rain. It was a harsh rhythmic roar that seemed to rise every minute.

The power had gone out long ago and Aana, Mom, Pauloosie, and I sat around some candles at the table pretending to play cards. Uncle Jonah had locked himself in his bedroom. Gabe had left his regular post on the TV couch and sat cross-legged on the floor against the windward wall. He was unfazed by the darkness in which he always lived but was obviously troubled by something else. His fingers formed two rigid cages on the hardwood floor. He looked like a contorted Buddha, sitting very still but with his back wrenched against the log wall. He seemed to be reading the vibrations carried by the wind and coming up through the ground.

"It's the sea," he said in a wavering voice.

"What's that, Gabe?" Mom said, walking over to him.

Gabe thrust his arm out for her and she sat down beside him, holding his hand.

"It's the s-s-s-ea," he said again. "That sound. It's c-c-oming closer."

"It's just some big waves, Gabe," Mom said in unconvincing tones.

"The sea's movin' in, Carole."

Mom looked at me with questioning eyes that he couldn't see. "We're safe up here, Gabe."

"I tell you there's g-gonna be a flood of t-t-tears tonight. This town's gonna sink outta sight, Carole. Can't you hear it c-c-comin'? Can't you *feel* it? It's the sea, Carole. The s-sea!"

Gabe's stuttering was a good barometer of how worked up he was. I went over and took his other hand while looking at Mom. "They just beefed up the seawall in July, Gabe. Piled a bunch of cement blocks and boulders along the shore."

Gabe's hand was cold and shaking. I wrapped my other hand around it.

"A bunch of r-r-r-rocks aren't gonna hold back the Arctic O-Ocean, Ash. My eyes aren't worth b-bettin' on. But sure as sh-sh-shootin' you better believe my ears. And they're telling me there's trouble in p-p-paradise tonight."

"Don't worry, Gabe," I said. "I know last fall they lost the curling rink to a storm," I said. "Even the school got a bit flooded. But that was before they raised the seawall."

"Ash is right," Mom said. "It's a sturdy seawall built to hold up to the worst—"

"You go d-d-down there and j-j-just see for yourself. Go s-see for yourself!"

A sudden flicker in the candlelight made me look up at Aana. With her cards still in hand, she was leaning over her chair, staring down at the floor as if some beast was about to burst through it. Her eyes were in shadow but her whole body was tense with apprehension. Mom's stained glass polar bear rattled against the kitchen window in time with the thudding waves.

"It's the s-sea, I tell you," shouted Gabe. "It's t-t-taking over the t-t-town!"

As much as I loved storms, there was a hard edge to this one that rubbed me the wrong way. The bizarre thunder. The way I felt running through the streets with Pauloosie, like we were mice and the wind was a hungry cat. The way Aana stared at the trembling floor. And that dream where the whole town sank out of sight.

Déjà Vu

ASHLEY'S ROOM
MONDAY, SEPTEMBER 5TH 7:48 A.M.

I hardly slept a wink that night. I can't say whether I dreamed or not. As I tossed around in bed, wind and waves seemed to pound right through me as much as around me. The veil between my conscious and unconscious worlds seemed especially thin. Through both, I had the dim feeling that a restless polar bear prowled just out of view.

A big fist of wind against my wall knocked the cobwebs out of me and I sat up to look out my bedside window. Broken raindrops darted across it. The sky seemed bruised by the storm. A grimy blanket of clouds lurched close overhead. I rubbed the sleep from my eyes and grabbed my binoculars.

I could hardly recognize the town.

Fresh Lake, where Nanurtalik got its water, was almost empty. It must have drained into the sea through a new breach in the shoreline. A fishing boat floated sideways in a new lake that yesterday had been the schoolyard. The green Quonset warehouse, once parked behind the Northern Store, now floated in the middle of Crab Bay. Row after row of houses were surrounded by muddy water that seemed dotted with meringue foam.

I adjusted the focus. "Holy—whitecaps flying down Fox Street!"

Most of the runway and airport buildings had almost disappeared. The radio tower had bent in two and now shook in the wind like a giant finger aimed accusingly at the ground. Beyond the Spit—or at least, where it used to be—I could see churning white lines, one after another, that looked like an army of waves preparing to assault the town. I'd seen enough nasty coastal weather to know this meant the storm surge was far from over.

I swung the binoculars around and picked out Rosie Toonoo's house. She was the only real friend I'd made in this town and my calls to her after supper had gone unanswered. I'd worried about her most of the night. Seeing waves knocking on her front door this morning sure didn't help. I could see somebody out front, running back and forth, to dump things in a pickup truck. It was a red one just like ours.

Then it struck me. "Dad?"

He must have been out there all night, helping people evacuate their homes and save what they could from the rising waters. Most of the Spit was already underwater.

I lowered the binoculars, my brain swamped by a sudden wave of *déjà vu*.

I'd seen this all before.

Saving the Drum

ROSIE TOONOO'S FLOODED HOUSE
MONDAY, SEPTEMBER 5TH 8:55 A.M.
Minutes later Pauloosie and I were beside Dad, stuffing clothes and food and blankets into garbage bags.

"Anything that's not nailed down!" shouted Rosie, carrying an armload of photo albums from her flooded house to Dad's truck.

The water had risen since I'd taken a bird's-eye view of town from my bedroom roost. It seemed to be higher after each round-trip to the truck. It was already up to our ankles in the living room. The water had a real current to it, as if there was a river flowing right through Rosie's house. Every now and then, a gust of wind would steal through the front door and create waves right before our eyes.

I didn't bother asking where the rest of Rosie's family was. They're never around much at the best of times and this certainly wasn't one of them. But somehow Rosie found her old spark even as her world drowned around her. "This ain't natural, Ash," she said, pausing to watch her bed float off the floor of her bedroom. "There's something *definitely* wrong with this picture."

That's when I heard Dad leaning on the horn and somebody splashing towards us through the living room.

"Get outta here quick!" yelled Pauloosie with a glint of terror in his eyes. "Dad says sumpin' big's coming."

Pauloosie grabbed my hand and I grabbed Rosie's.

We were almost out the front door when Rosie yanked her arm away. "Wait!" she said. "One more thing," and she sloshed her way back to her bedroom.

I heard serious splashing outside. I stuck my head out the door to see waves crashing against the front wall. The water had risen to the truck's tailgate and there were bubbles coming up from the exhaust pipe.

Dad swung out of the cab window and poked his head above the roof. "Get the hell in here. Now!"

Pauloosie waded out to the truck while I hung back at the door. "Rosie's just gone in for something," I yelled, my voice shredded by the wind.

"Forget it!" yelled Dad. "There's another surge coming!"

I clung to the doorframe and swung my head back into the house. "ROSIE! FORGET IT!"

The force of the current had pushed the bedroom door closed behind her. A hump of water began to curl and grow against the door. She was trapped in her bedroom as an angry sea tried to bulldoze her house.

"ROSIE!"

I looked down at my knees. They were underwater. I looked back at the truck. Dad was shouting something at me but all I heard was the wind and the waves. I couldn't tell if he was fuming mad or stinking scared. I waved for help but by now the water was up to the truck door and he was struggling to open it. Stuff that we'd carefully rescued from the house was beginning to float away from the back of the pickup.

I had no choice but to rescue Rosie myself. I thought I heard screaming above the rush of water pouring into the house. I knew she was okay because her door kept cracking open as she tried to escape, but the water kept slamming it shut. I almost mashed my face against the door because of the current. As soon as I touched the doorknob a big wave came marching through the living room and knocked Rosie's door flat.

It was an odd sensation, swimming in muddy, ice-cold seawater in your best friend's bedroom. My first thought was, *Did the door flatten Rosie when it caved in?* My second thought was, *Which way is up?* Then I felt Rosie's hand under my armpit. She jerked me to my feet as the water swirled around our waists. We were both pinned against the back wall of her bedroom. I felt like we were going down with the *Titanic*. Rosie still held me tight while holding her other arm high above the water. In her hand was a beat-up old *qilauti*, a traditional Inuit drum.

"I got it!" she yelled.

"Marvelous. Let's get out of here!"

I knew we weren't out of the woods yet. Though the water had stopped rising, the current seemed to be gaining power. I didn't know how much abuse those flimsy walls would take before the whole house caved in. We leaned into the current and thrashed our way back through the living room. The house seemed half full of water but somehow we made it out the front door alive and kicking.

Five minutes later, Rosie's house was gone. It collapsed gently, without a big sploosh or puff of steam. Sitting on the roof of Dad's pickup, the four of us watched books, bottles, and boots pour out of its broken windows like blood from a hunter's prey.

Uncle Jonah's Swim

DAD'S TRUCK SURROUNDED BY FLOODWATERS
MONDAY, SEPTEMBER 5TH 9:35 A.M.

Uncle Jonah didn't get out much. When he wasn't locked in his room—which was most of the time—he'd be banging the dining table for tea or bannock or a rib of caribou to chew on. When, in his more lucid moments, he did leave the house, we had no idea where he went. Uncle's little disappearing acts drove Mom bananas.

After an hour, she'd start phoning around to a few neighbors. "Have you seen Uncle Jonah wandering around?" she'd ask. "He's gone for one of his famous jaunts." After two hours, it was the RCMP. "You didn't happen to arrest Uncle Jonah by any chance?" After three hours, the Coast Guard. "He could be washed out to sea by now, the poor dear." Once, Mom even twisted Dad's arm to set off the fire hall siren and rally some volunteers to comb the town. But nobody could ever find him.

Uncle Jonah was the furthest thing from my mind when the Arctic Ocean swallowed Rosie's house. When the final wall fell, all she said was, "Goodbye, home sweet home." She didn't exactly sound broken up about it. No weeping or gnashing of teeth. I got the feeling she hoped the blackest memories from that house—the drinking, the shouting, the fights—would all be swept away by the water like everything else.

Dad wasn't about to get philosophical about what all this meant. At the moment, saving our lives seemed more important. "Hop in!" he yelled. "We're gonna try for the church. It should be dry there." We slipped off the roof of the truck and squatted inside. There were tons of water already sloshing around in the truck, almost up to the seats, but somehow the engine hadn't drowned yet. Dad was going to make a run for it. He managed to back up the truck into the rushing water and had started inching forward when he spotted someone in his rearview mirror. It was Uncle Jonah.

"What in hell's name is *he* doing down here?" Dad said.

With all eyes on Rosie's house, none of us saw Uncle Jonah even though he was only a few car lengths away. He was keeled over with his face almost in the water and his good arm wrapped loosely around a telephone pole. He leaned heavily on his narwhal cane with his gammy arm. The pole tilted away from the floodwaters and, if it toppled, would pretty much flatten Dad's truck and us with it. Broken power lines snapped in the wind just above Uncle's head.

Before Dad could muscle his door open, Uncle Jonah was knocked over by a big wave. The current caught him and he started rolling over and over, face down, face up, face down. The swirling water played with his body like it was a hunk of driftwood on a wave-battered beach.

"He's going to crash into the truck!" I shouted. "Can't you open that door, Dad?"

"The water—it's too strong—I can't get the damn—"

The current caught the bottom of the door. It swung forward and jackknifed like it had been hit by a bus. I could see Uncle Jonah rolling towards us. Just before he rammed the truck, the current split around the tailgate like rapids parting above a boulder. Uncle Jonah sailed right past Dad's open door. Dad stuck his arm out just in time, picked him up with one hand, and dragged his limp body into the truck.

Damage Report

DAD'S TRUCK SURROUNDED BY FLOODWATERS
MONDAY, SEPTEMBER 5TH 10:05 A.M.

It came to be known as the Labor Day storm. Fifteen homes, including Rosie's, were destroyed, with another seventeen seriously damaged. The mayor estimated the total damage to the town to be around five million dollars with the hardest hit being the Northern Store, airport, power plant, RCMP station, coastal road, and—aw shucks—the school. Two of the town's oil tanks ruptured from the force of the waves, spilling so much fuel all over the place that people were urged not to smoke outside since no one knew what might catch fire—the road, your front yard, even the sewage lagoon.

In ten hours, the bluffs on the north end of town were beaten back by almost twenty feet, exposing huge underground ice masses that later melted, causing even more ground to collapse. The north shore was a total mess, like somebody had used it as a missile target range. The biggest hit, as far as the Elders were concerned, was the erosion of a long-abandoned cemetery parked above one of the highest bluffs. For days after the storm, whole skeletons popped out of the hill as it melted and slid into the sea.

At the other end of town, a D-6 Caterpillar and a Bombardier sank out of sight trying to rescue one wolf, two wolverines, and three red foxes that got stranded on a tiny patch of high ground. All the animals drowned. Amazingly no humans died. Not the guys driving those machines. Not the people whose houses washed away. Not even Uncle Jonah.

After vomiting a few pailfuls of seawater all over us in Dad's truck, he had a few good bloodcurdling coughs, then opened his eyes. I'd never seen him without his coke bottle glasses on—which a seal might have been wearing by this time. He somehow looked younger, kinder, not at all the burned-out curmudgeon I'd unwillingly moved in with. It was as if we'd caught him out of costume and some other personality was leaking out. With amazing strength, he pushed himself up on his good elbow to look out the truck's back window, like he'd left a pot of gold back there or something. His elbow dug into my lap but I didn't say anything. There was a strange longing in his eyes as he pressed his wet, wrinkled forehead against the glass.

"Relax, Uncle," I said. "You're not going to see anything out there without your glasses."

His body suddenly went limp and his head fell onto my lap.

"Heart attack!" shouted Rosie.

His eyes were closed but I noticed his lips were moving. "No, not yet at least," I said, bending over him. I couldn't hear anything above the roar of wind and water all around us. "What's he saying?"

Dad leaned over and put his ear against Uncle Jonah's mouth. "Something about the Spit, I think. Something he lost out there."

Dad glanced out the back window and shrugged. "Even if he could see, there's nothing much to look at out there. The whole thing's underwater."

Exactly like my dream. I impulsively squeezed out the window of the truck and twisted around to look over the cab roof. I was trying to spot the church, half expecting to see it sink out of sight. There it was, its bell tower scorched by lightning, but still standing after the freakiest storm I'd ever seen. Not everything in my nightmares came true.

A bulldozer ended up towing us out of that mess. Rosie and about thirty other refugees from the storm spent the night in our warm, dry house. After a few days of serious coddling from Mom and Aana, Uncle Jonah sprang back to his lively, ever-cheerful, sourpuss self.

Caribou Song

ROCKY TUNDRA SOUTH OF NANURTALIK
SATURDAY, SEPTEMBER 10TH, 1:35 P.M.

Once the floodwaters receded, most of the people who lost their homes moved into Rainbow Ridge. It was an abandoned neighborhood of multi-colored shacks that the government had barged in back in the sixties to lure people off the land. Most of the shacks had been condemned years ago, but none of them got flooded and each had a woodstove that more or less worked. Until the mop-up was finished and reconstruction got rolling, people figured life on the Ridge was better than moving back into sod huts and iglus. Rosie's family got a pink shack which she immediately dubbed the Pink Palace.

The idea for Rosie's drumming circle started a few days after the Labor Day storm. She and I were wandering the boulder fields south of town to see what kind of junk the Labor Day storm had tossed out on the tundra. We'd enjoyed occasional shopping trips to the local dump. It was a popular Saturday afternoon pastime in Nanurtalik. We'd found all kinds of treasures—goofy hats, CDs, a new TV for Gabe, a perfectly good drafting table that I now used for all my sketching. On Mom's birthday, Rosie and I dragged an old rowboat all the way home, knocked the bottom out of it, and framed it around our front door. Mom liked it so much she started hanging other dump treasures on it, including a thorny bust of Jesus and a discarded church plaque that read: "He maketh the storms to cease."

We figured we'd use our dump sifting skills to see what gifts the latest storm had sprinkled on the land.

Just beyond the edge of town we found the usual crap: rusted fuel drums and twisted hulks of metal dumped by the army boys years ago, countless pop cans, Styrofoam cups, plastic bags dangling from every rock and bush. Things got more interesting farther out.

"Man, that was some crazy wind!" Rosie said when she stumbled on an acoustic guitar parked on a cushion of Labrador tea. It had suffered only two broken strings but was otherwise unscratched. Rosie picked it up and strummed. "Incredible. The thing's still in tune."

I shrugged. "If you say so, Rosie."

I'm tone-deaf. My voice was so *not* appreciated in elementary school that, after a Christmas concert rehearsal, my grade four teacher politely told me to mouth the words. I'd barely sung a note since, unless of course Gabe was around to drown me out.

Rosie examined the guitar's body, stroking it like an injured bird. "It's clean. No unsightly blemishes." She hugged it to her hips and broke into "I'm a Believer."

"I thought love was more or less a given thing . . . But the more I gave, the less I got, oh yeah . . . What's the use in trying? . . . All you get is pain . . . When I wanted sunshine I got rain. . . ."

"Then I saw your face!" I crooned and gave Rosie a friendly smack on the cheek. "The thing works already." I tugged at her sleeve. "Come on, there must be more good stuff out here."

We found four doghouses, all in pretty good shape; fourteen garbage cans, all without lids; eight TV satellite dishes; three high chairs, none with babies in them; and enough shingles to cover a barn roof. Except for the guitar, we left everything where it lay. It was all junk to us. But it was always fun to look. For me, the real treasure from that afternoon's hunt was the caribou song.

We were walking back on one of the countless ATV trails that radiate from town. Rosie had the guitar over her shoulder in true gypsy style. Then it happened.

The caribou showed up.

She spotted them while I had my head down, soaking in the tundra's last fall colors. Two cows and a calf had been watching us from the shoulder of Anirniq Hill. They were amazingly close to town, just a few hundred yards from the church. Since we heard no gunshots, we figured nobody but us had spotted them. Another cow and calf pranced into view, stole a look at us, then trotted away behind the hill. It was then that Rosie sat down on the moss and started singing.

"What are you . . ." I started to speak but her closed eyes and the soft look on her face made my mouth snap shut. I froze, floored by the lovely, lilting melody sung in Inuktitut. Rosie had a habit of busting out into song, but I'd never heard *anything* like this from her lips. The caribou cows and calves reappeared from behind the hill. They too seemed frozen in their tracks. Rosie's audience was growing.

Her song began softly, almost carried away by the breeze. As she gained volume, her body began to sway to a steady beat. Soon she

on thin ice

was up on her feet, her whole torso rocking from side to side while she beat an imaginary skin drum. I had no idea what she was singing about but I knew, from the first note, that her song belonged to this land as much as the rocks and the cranberries and the caribou now darting across the hill.

Rosie's song reached a jumping climax and she opened her eyes as if coming out of a deep trance. I might as well have been a dead willow stick for all she looked at me. She smiled at the caribou.

"What *have* you been smoking, Rosie?"

"Look, it works."

I glanced at the caribou. They were trotting towards us. Then four more cows, all with calves, appeared from behind the hill and tailed the others.

"What works?"

"That old song. I was calling the caribou, inviting them to come closer."

"Oh."

"My ancestors used this trick when their stomachs got grumbling. It's what they always did when they saw caribou. *Ittuq* taught it to me when I was just a little kid." Rosie looked at me with a rascally grin, her trance now pretty much evaporated. "Did you bring your harpoon, Ash?"

More caribou streamed over the shoulder of the hill. A trickle of animals had turned into a flood. "*Ittuq*. You mean your rock star grandfather?"

"Yeah, the drummer."

"Did he teach you those fancy dance steps?"

"He taught me a bit of drumming. He used to say the drum teaches you how to dance. Hard to sit still when that thing's in your hand."

"Even if it's invisible?"

Rosie looked at her empty hands and laughed. "I guess so."

In spite of my minestrone blood, some part of me got all stirred up by Rosie's surprise performance. I wanted a piece of this action, this magic. I knew I'd never learn to sing. As for dancing, I could take it or leave it. I didn't know why but it was the drum I wanted, the drum that wasn't even there.

"I take it you've got a *real* drum at home?" I asked.

"A couple, actually. It beats slamming doors or breaking windows when things get crazy in my house. You can basically drown out the world. Sometimes Courtney comes over and we really raise hell."

Drown out the world. That sounded good to me. Courtney was her favorite cousin, same age, same lean build. They could have been twin sisters. "So . . . ah . . . do you think I could join you guys sometime and maybe learn a few ditties on that drum?"

Rosie looked at me like I'd asked her for skydiving lessons. "Hmm . . . I don't know, Ash. It might not be your cup of tea."

She knew I had no real culture to hang my hat on. And anything musical was hardly in my teacup.

"I'm serious, Rosie. Could be fun. I promise I won't sing."

"If you insist." Rosie picked up her new guitar and gave it a brisk flamenco strum. "But I warn you, Ash. It could be addictive."

As we walked back to town I felt a tingly glow spread over me, like a snake must feel before it sheds old skin. I could hardly wait to get my hands on a drum.

The Bear Shaman's Song

Part II
Finding the Bear's Tracks

Along the jagged coast,
Leaning against the wind,
I find her tracks!
My warm snow-house far behind me,
I study her claw marks—*Aja! Aja-wa!* So huge!
Nanurluk's tracks,
Suddenly as clear as young ice,
Lead me down the endless shore.
There is no place to hide.

Face of Dust

It's him again, the bear shaman. He's standing behind the church at the base of Anirniq Hill—Angel Hill. He holds his drum high as if guiding me to the summit. Like in my hurricane dream, his song is shredded by the wind. I get the feeling he's trying to teach me something. Like I'm his apprentice.

I try to climb but keep slipping on wet rocks. I can't find the trail.

I slow down, concentrate on my feet—I'm wearing those beautiful sealskin kamiiks *again—and let them find each step on their own. The rocks seem to part beneath my feet revealing a moss-lined trail. I see fresh tracks on it. Polar bear tracks!*

My heart thumps. My throat closes like I'm being choked. But my feet take me higher. They move at a lightning pace even as a heavy fog swallows the hill.

In no time, I break through to the summit and look down on a giant doughnut of fog. A dark inuksuk *crowns the hill. Its rocky arms stretch out above short stumpy legs. Its head is remarkably round and topped with stringy black lichen that could pass for human hair. We face each other like two gunslingers poised for a shootout. But I sense no danger. Instead I feel a strange fondness for this stone figure, like we're old friends.*

An air of expectancy, thicker than the fog, hangs over the hilltop. A raven swoops out of nowhere and lands on the inuksuk's *shoulder. It raises its wings, tucks in its beak, and lets go a bellowing croak. It stares at me, then fixes its unblinking eyes on the figure's head which imme-*

diately starts wobbling. I lunge forward waving my arms at the raven. It croaks again and plunges into the fog.

I look back to see a giant polar bear standing behind the inuksuk. *Its massive paws are wrapped around the* inuksuk's *head. I detect a devilish look in its eye, like it wants to make sure I'm watching before—*

"NO!" I shout.

For some reason, saving that inuksuk *becomes terribly important. But I stand helplessly, watching the bear pick up the head and hurl it at me like a cannonball. It lands with a loud crack at my feet.*

"NO, NO!" I shout again.

The bear seems energized by my reaction and throws its whole body against the headless figure. Its stone arms, legs, and torso burst apart and rocks scatter in all directions. I scream as if it was me the bear was smashing into tiny pieces.

When the dust settles, the bear is gone. The stone head lies face down with only the stringy black lichen showing. I drop to my knees and cautiously turn it over.

At first, I see only the white and purple stains of bird droppings, weathered cracks, and tiny colonies of lichens. I slowly turn the head in my hands. The random colors and textures change into a mouth, a nose, two shining eyes. I can distinctly see a face in this rock.

A human face.

My face!

The instant I recognize myself, it begins to crack open. In seconds it changes from solid rock, to gravel, to dust. A gust of wind streaks out of the sky like a missile and sweeps my shattered face from the hilltop and down into the fog.

No Tricks

As usual, your stomach is grumbling. You remember catching seals along this coastline many years ago, but the feel of ice beneath your paws tells you something is very different now. There are no cracks, no leads, no pressure ridges, not an iceberg in sight. Nowhere for a seal to break through to breathe—and risk a deadly wallop from your claws. Something is wrong. Where are the seals?

What's that?

Fast scratching on the ice. Squealing. Strange vibrations flood your fat hairy paws.

You spring to a stand. Your forelegs hang in a begging pose. You lift your head and sniff. You wave your head slowly, back and forth, dissecting the frigid air with your sharp nose. You squint towards a patch of orange sky above the sleeping sun, towards that squealing sound.

There, standing out against the blue-white frozen sea, a black shape prowls. A thick fountain of snow curls up from the beast's pointy nose.

The beast is downwind and you catch no scent even as it comes closer. But now you recognize it—a round-foot. Trouble. Distant memories of ear-splitting blasts over your head and some stinging thing in your butt send you running for cover behind a high snowdrift.

You slowly lift your head and you watch the beast pass. As it moves upwind you catch the stink of oil and smoke and plastic. Humans. You spot two of them behind the beast's big clear eyes.

The beast follows a trail of thin snow and greenish blue ice. Drifts stretch across the trail like long white claws. The beast seems to be eating them as it roars along. Very strange.

The squealing fades. Then, new sounds: a dull thud, a snap, a splash. Seconds later a shock wave rushes through the ice below your paws.

No more curling snow. No more squealing.

There is a new smell, a good smell. Salt water. Now the seals can come. Now you can hunt. You can eat.

The smell of open water drives out your fear and you leap to your hind legs.

The beast is hunting. Its pointy nose is perched on the ice, at the end of a long rip that is widening fast. Its rear end is tilted down into the water where bubbles of blue smoke pop on the surface. This is a strange way to hunt seals. They will rise only when everything is quiet.

You wish the beast would go away. But you are glad for the open water. You duck back behind the drift. You are good at waiting.

There is no need to wait long. Human mouth sounds. You lift your head in time to see the beast plunge backwards into the wide gash of open water. How odd.

One human smashes an eye of the beast with a long metal stick. He squirms out into the water and starts flapping its forelegs. The other human tries to escape through the broken eye. The beast dives fast and takes the second human with it. Its shrill mouth sounds are swallowed by ice water. With a final plop, both beast and human are gone.

The flapping human claws for solid ice while making softer, whining noises. You lift your head a little higher, feeling a stab of hunger. This human reminds you of a young snow goose trying to fly.

Flap, flapflap.

It is slowing down, barely moving. With a final cry, it lunges forward, throwing its forelegs ahead and clamping its naked paws onto the ice.

Whining, groaning, it pulls itself out of the water. It starts jumping in one spot, hugging itself, spinning around, maybe looking for other humans. It seems weak and helpless. If it were a caribou or musk ox, you would chase it down. Eat it.

But you keep out of sight, with only your sharp nose and small eyes above the drift. Humans mean trouble. Humans play tricks. Luckily, this one has no dogs.

The human starts pounding its forelegs against its sides and back. It rubs the top of its head with its little paws. It spins around and around like a spiral of snow. It hops down the trail towards the sleeping sun. Its frail mouth sounds are swallowed by the wind.

The human falls on its naked face.

It goes to sleep.

You lower your head. You close your eyes against a gust of prickly snow. You feel safe behind this snowdrift. You can outwait anything, even this human.

You wake up to an urgent squeeze in your stomach. Even before you open your eyes, your nose is twitching. You remember that crack of open water but now there is no salt in the air. You open your eyes. The sun has fallen deeper into sleep. The sky is the color of ripe blueberries. You stretch your limbs, first pulling back into a long bow, then pressing forward, your head to the stars and a pink smear of northern lights.

Hunger gnaws on your brain. You raise your nose and probe the air for the scent of saltwater, the breath of seal, the sweet stench of something dead to eat. The wind carries nothing but a hint of oil from the round-footed beast. It must have swum far away under the ice.

The human must still be sleeping. You leap over the drift and gallop to the spot where the beast went down. You snort and shake your great muzzle as the smell of oil grows stronger. There is light enough to see the dark triangle of new ice where the beast disappeared. You spring to a stand, flip your hind legs behind you, and plunge onto the ice. Three times you throw yourself against the ice without making a crack. It is already too thick. You must have slept long.

No seals will come to this place.

As you turn your back on the beast's frozen hole you catch a faint ribbon of scent from the sleeping human. Hunger clouds your usual caution around humans and, with your nose to the ice, you walk steadily along its scent trail.

You peer ahead through the dim purplish light. There. A long, dark hind leg sticks out from a fresh drift of wind-packed snow. You stop and crouch, as if stalking a seal. A swirling mix of fear and hunger courses through your belly. Humans mean trouble. Why is this one sleeping under a blanket of snow? It must be a trick.

You let out a weak grunt. No response. A husky bark. Nothing. You stand and release a full-throated roar. The long hind leg doesn't move. No human head pops out of the snowdrift.

You slowly circle around the half-buried human. This close, you should be able to see the purple glow of life around it. You spot a naked paw poking out of the drift. Its light has gone out.

This human is not sleeping. You are certain now. No tricks here.

This human is safe to eat.

Rumors

TUKTU HALL

THURSDAY, NOVEMBER 10TH, 8:35 P.M.

The rumors started flying the day two of my classmates died on the Inniturlik ice road. They found Jimmy's body—at least, what was left of it—about sixty miles east of town. Everyone seemed to know perfectly well how he died.

He obviously succumbed to hypothermia; then the foxes tore his frozen body apart.

There's no doubt he was killed by a pack of starving wolves.

It had to be a wolverine. It'll take a man when he's lying down.

Oh, and then this rumor, the biggest stretch of all. For sure it was a polar bear. Jimmy was attacked by a rogue polar bear and didn't stand a chance. I just couldn't believe this one, or wouldn't let myself. Everyone knew polar bears didn't hang out anywhere near Nanurtalik. Grandpa Eddy led the community's last polar bear hunt back in the mid-seventies. Dad was about my age then and went with him to help bash a trail through the pressure ridges. He described that hunt as the longest journey of his life.

Then there were all the theories about why Angus's truck went through the ice.

The sea ice froze too quickly this fall, making it weak and brittle.

The huge dump of snow we had a couple weeks back insulated the ice and slowed its growth.

The underwater currents had gone all screwy making unpredictable weak spots in the ice. That made sense to me. No one could trust the ice anymore, anywhere, anytime.

Everybody loved Jimmy and Angus. Who couldn't? The whole town was pretty broken up about the accident but nobody could agree on how it happened. So Mayor Gordon Jacobs organized a community meeting in Tuktu Hall to, like he said, "hash it over and hasten the healing." Gord talked kind of flowery like that. Everyone called him Lord Gord, even the Roman Catholic priest, Father Ungali, who never showed up at the meeting. He was probably off on one of his errands of mercy down south. A lot of people were tied up in knots over this and could have used his services.

But the press came. They loved this kind of stuff. Teenage disasters in a faraway Arctic community, half-eaten bodies in the wilderness, mysterious ice conditions caused by climate change. Perfect for the 6:00 P.M. boob tube news. And thanks to all the press we got over the Labor Day storm, Nanurtalik must've been a household word across North America, at least for those who could pronounce it.

So many outsiders wanted to come to Lord Gord's meeting they had to charter a special plane from Inniturliq. It was stuffed with southern government types, biologists, and weather scientists. A small army of media crews showed up, including a reporter from the *Los Angeles Times.* The Kiq Ass Inn was overflowing. Some people were making three hundred bucks a night to billet and feed visitors who got left out in the cold. If there was one thing Lord Gord had, it was connections. He could invite people to a press conference about a volleyball bake sale and they'd cross the continent for a piece of the action.

I didn't know Angus that well but I liked him from the start. He was a pretty smart guy but didn't flash his marks around. He saved my bacon once by helping me with some thorny math before a big mid-term I'd been sweating over. He'd made an animated movie in media studies class about a dog musher who took a wrong turn and ended up in New York City. I almost peed myself watching it. Angus had a fondness for whipped cream pies and used to plant them on teachers' chairs. He was smart enough to never get caught.

As for Jimmy, I'd taken a liking to him. His locker was two down from mine and sometimes he'd hang around after last period and tell me about his latest hockey game or ask me about some friends we both knew in Inniturliq. We'd eaten lunch together several times, including the day he died. As the buzzer rang for class, I'd casually asked him if he was going to the Halloween dance that night.

He looked away and tugged on his single gold earring.

I think I held my breath.

"Halloween dance, eh?" Jimmy said, sounding genuinely disappointed. "I wish you'd asked me . . . I mean, we should've talked about this sooner." He shrugged. "Angus and I already made plans to go plowin'." He leaned across the lunch table and spooked his eyes at me. "Should be a *howling* good time. You want to come with us?"

"A tad early to be driving all over the sea ice, isn't it?"

"It's okay, really. We had a quick freeze this fall and they've checked the whole route. Lots of ice. A couple of graders pulled in from Inniturliq on Thursday. We're just going to polish it up a bit. Could be fun."

Those were the last words he spoke to me.

I turned him down. Jimmy Kikpak was a nice guy. I would've trusted him. Next to Rosie, I'd probably talked to him more than anybody in the whole school. Mom said he was a cousin of mine, but she said that about every kid in town she happened to like so I didn't believe her. I almost said yes. I really did. I would have ended up with Angus at the bottom of the Arctic Ocean. Or been torn apart like Jimmy. Like in my *inuksuk* dream.

Those two guys were special. Jimmy, the star hockey player, captain of the Kik Ass Komatiks, who brought his home team fame on ice rinks as far south as Edmonton and Winnipeg with his winning slapshots and phenomenal skating. On the ice they called him

Caribou Man, the way he moved like a caribou dodging a wolf's snapping jaws.

And Angus, the skateboard idol of the Arctic. He taught himself to skateboard in the Northern Store parking lot, the only patch of pavement in town. It was one of Mayor Jacobs' grand experiments that totally flopped, thanks to the permafrost underneath that melted as soon as they paved it over. But as far as Angus was concerned, the parking lot was a smashing success, full of rolling gullies and dips that just begged for skateboard wheels.

Pauloosie, who, thanks to Angus, was nuts about skateboarding, burst into tears when he heard the bad news. "Who's gonna finish the skateboard park now?" he'd asked as he ran into his room and slammed the door.

Angus dreamed of bringing year-round skateboarding to Nanurtalik. Some people laughed at his idea but he ignored them. Last summer he spent countless hours shaping junked plywood and plastic into curving ramps and handrail slides in an abandoned warehouse down by the Spit. Of course, Jimmy joined him most of the time and, some nights, you could hear those guys hammering and sawing in there while their buddies booze-cruised the town under the midnight sun. That was another thing about those two guys: they were inseparable, I guess even unto death.

I had seen Jimmy and Angus on TV long before we moved here. They were already media celebrities. In last spring's iglu building contest, they'd scored first prize, constructing a rock-hard iglu in half an hour, then standing on it, arm in arm, for a national TV camera. After that they became known across Canada as "The Iglu Brothers," even though they were only third cousins. When we moved here, I learned that Jimmy and Angus were a two-man team, playing hockey, hunting seals, aiming high in school, or plowing the ice road one dark Halloween night.

Jimmy and Angus were the poster boys of Nanurtalik. They had everything going for them. Everybody loved them. Jimmy and Angus belonged here. And now they were dead.

Lord Gord had got the word out pretty good and Tuktu Hall was packed. More than for a drum dance. More than for a wedding or even a jackpot bingo night. Standing room only. Even Aunty Emma showed up. At 97 she was the oldest person in Nanurtalik, wheeled across the street from the Singing Drum Elders' Home. Couldn't see, couldn't hear, couldn't speak. But there she was, like everybody else, out for Lord Gord's special meeting to clear up, once and for all, what really happened to Jimmy and Angus.

I stood on the sidelines with Rosie Toonoo. A handful of familiar faces from school were strung out along one side of Tuktu Hall. In true high school style, we kept our jackets, hats, and mitts on, even though it must have been eighty degrees in there with all the people and bright lights. Everyone, that is, except Rosie. She yanked her hat off the minute we entered the hall to show off her new doo. The day before she'd dyed her black Inuk hair strawberry blonde. A week earlier, I'd dyed my Irish red hair black. She did it to stand out. I did it to blend in.

I pretended to be aloof but, inside, I was all stirred up. I'd hardly known Jimmy and Angus but somehow their deaths had reopened that deep chest wound inflicted in a dream by the bear shaman's song. It oozed not blood, but a creeping darkness that wanted to dissolve anything solid beneath my feet.

I tried to shake it off as an asthma attack. I reached into my pack for my puffer, turned to face the wall, and inhaled the chilly fumes. The pain in my chest lifted. But the feeling of fragility didn't. I snapped open a pop and took a few quick sips. What I really needed was air and that seemed to be dwindling fast in the rising heat and hubbub of the crowd.

The TV crews had already set up by the time we got there and Lord Gord was at the podium banging on the microphone like he was slapping the nose of a rowdy dog. Each tap sent a booming thump through the hall.

"Okay, okay, Gordie baby," Rosie said, loud enough for him to hear. "It *works* already!" Some called Rosie a loudmouth. I called her fearless. Rosie feared no one—no teacher, no Elder, not even the great Mayor Gordon Jacobs. She wasn't a pig about it, never really disrespectful. She just wasn't afraid to be herself around anybody. In Mom-ese she was "self-possessed." Rosie was at home anywhere with anyone. That was what I liked most about her. We'd become pretty good buds. That night in Tuktu Hall I was almost sitting on her lap without realizing it.

"Hey, Ash, how's about moving your ass off me," she said.

We giggled, in spite of the heavy vibes around us. I did a quick scan of the crowd and spotted Mom and Pauloosie in the front row. Pauloosie usually hung out with his buddies near the hall entrance during events like this. Not tonight. I leaned forward to see what he was clutching between his knees—it was the skateboard Angus had built for him. I saw Dad and Gabe sitting on a table at the back. Gabe loved a crowd and was grinning from ear to ear, rocking his head back and forth in his Gabe-ish way. Something seemed odd about Dad until I realized he'd taken off his Red Power ball cap and parked it on his knee, like it was a funeral or something.

But this wasn't a funeral. Angus was still missing. The coroner in Edmonton hadn't released Jimmy's body until just this afternoon, ten days after the accident. When Annie—the post office lady—and I went out to the airport to get the mail, I watched them unload Jimmy's cherry-wood coffin from the Twin Otter. The official funeral was still a couple days away. But you'd think this was a funeral by the way Lord Gord talked.

After slapping the microphone long enough to raise the dead, Lord Gord lifted his arms to the roof—like he was running for the pope's chair, not the mayor's. He cleared his throat loudly and began. "Dearly beloved . . ."

He actually started like that.

"Dearly beloved, we are gathered here tonight to mourn the loss of the best and the brightest of our youth and to learn what we can about the true circumstances of their deaths."

Already the news reporters were filling Lord Gord's waxy face with camera flash. A couple of TV cameramen jostled each other for the best shot of his pointy nose. With his arms still raised, Lord Gord stole a glance at the cameras and tilted his head back just a notch. I'd heard this was supposed to be a closed community event, but it seemed Lord Gord had invited the whole world to join us and, as usual, he was eating up the attention with a big spoon.

"Before we begin, I've invited Tuurngaq to sanctify our discussion this evening with a drum song."

Tuurngaq was Nanurtalik's oldest drummer. Nobody knew his full name. It was always just Tuurngaq—the ghost. He was an unusually tall man for an eighty-four year old Inuk. He wore a black cloak, fringed with white fur from an Arctic fox, that waved back and forth as he danced. He held a huge, flat drum made from black nylon stretched over a thin, wooden hoop. On the outside of the drumhead, embroidered in white thread, was a dancing polar bear, also holding a drum.

In traditional style Tuurngaq slowly spun his drum back and forth while hitting its rim with a bone mallet. Rumor had it that Uncle Jonah had taught him how to drum like that years ago, back in his "power time," as Aana called it, when Jonah Anowiak was an *Inullarik*—a true Inuk. Of course, I could never swallow that.

With the first whack of his drum, all the cameras swung around and reporters moved in with their microphones. Tuurngaq suddenly stopped drumming and stared at them through cobalt blue eyes he'd inherited from some Danish sailor. At first the southern media guys thought he was posing for them and shot away like a firing squad. Then, one by one, they got the message and lowered their cameras. Ghost Man was telling them to cool it. They had no place in the magic space he was building with his drum.

With each drumbeat decades seemed to peel off Tuurngaq's bony body and soon he was jumping around like a teenage rocker. I didn't have a clue what his song was about, but it was beginning to knock the stuffing out of my cool-as-a-cucumber masquerade.

A few of the Elder women up front joined in Tuurngaq's song. Their thin, wavering voices played over the audience like kites dancing in the wind. I couldn't keep my eyes off Tuurngaq's drum.

His voice wrapped my brain in fog. Above his joyful song, I thought I heard another voice calling my Inuktitut name. *Uitajuq! Uitajuq!* Each blow of his mallet struck against my chest as if trying to bust it open. I slumped against the wall like someone was beating me up.

Through it all, my eyes never strayed from his drum. The polar bear on Tuurngaq's drumhead had come alive. It danced and swayed, following Tuurngaq's subtlest movements. It beat the drum within the drum in time with Tuurngaq's swinging mallet. The bear and Tuurngaq became one.

Rosie had her arm around me and was saying something, but the drum, which seemed louder with every beat, swept her words away. I felt like I was going to black out.

Tuurngaq ended his song with one ecstatic shout. "*Ha-jai-jaa!*"

I looked up from the drum to Tuurngaq's face. He was looking right at me, flashing me an eerie, toothless smile. His icy eyes told me he knew exactly what his drumming had done to my head, to my chest. He knew I'd seen his dancing bear. I had to lower my eyes. It was then that I noticed a shaman's belt of bear claws hanging from his waist.

Time stopped as the ripple of drumbeats echoed through every cell of my body.

Listening

On the sea ice east of Nanurtalik
Thursday, November 10th, 9:12 p.m.

You are walking toward the star that doesn't move. You hope there is rough ice below it where cracks and open water might lure some seals.

You stop with one forepaw still raised above the wind-packed snow. Something makes you lift your head and listen. Something far away, towards the skyline where the sun goes to sleep. It is not the scent of saltwater, the breath of seal, the tempting stench of a dead caribou. It is nothing carried by the wind.

It is a sound. A human mouth sound. You don't hear it with your ears. It enters and fills your giant body like a second pulse in your veins.

It is calling you.

You turn toward that special sound you had almost forgotten. The call of a human with power like your own. A power you can't resist. It warms your chest and makes you run.

Bear Talk

Thursday, November 10th, 9:15 p.m.

I snapped out of it as Rosie's words finally connected with my brain. ". . . looking at you funny, Ash."

"Huh?" I said, straightening up.

"Everybody's looking at you pretty funny. What *have* you been smoking?"

It was true. Except for Gabe and a couple of blind Elders, everyone in Tuktu Hall had followed Tuurngaq's gaze to me. "Ah, nothing, Rosie," I said, retrieving my public mask as fast as I could. "I mean, nothing you haven't tried."

Lord Gord's gravelly voice saved me from the spotlight. "Thank you, Tuurngaq." He made a big show of clearing his throat and pulled out a scribbled recipe card. "Jimmy Kikpak and Angus Oniak were the pride of the Elders, the envy of their peers, the hope for the future. Now, I know there are a lot of stories going around town about what actually happened to these boys. I've invited Bobby Niego up to the mike so we can get an eyewitness account from the first person to arrive at the scene of the accident. Could you please tell us, Bobby, exactly what you saw out there on the ice road on the morning of November 1st?"

Lord Gord had switched from pope to high court judge. The man wore many hats and could throw them on and off in the blink of an eye.

Bobby came up to the podium, shook Gord's hand, then slapped the microphone a few times as if that's what everyone was supposed to do. Bobby was almost as old as Uncle Jonah but he was one of those tough old Inuk guys who had decided long ago never to grow old. I'd seen him out shoveling snow in a blizzard or lugging armloads of groceries halfway across town from the Northern Store. He'd still be out there wrestling polar bears with his snow knife if there were any left around to hunt.

"Well, since we heard the ice road was open, me and the wife was on our way to Inniturliq to do a little shopping," Bobby said. "It must have been around nine in the morning. Yeah, I remember now. The sky was just beginning to brighten up a bit." Bobby's wife, Flossie, sat a few rows back, nodding and giving him encouraging looks between snorts into her pink hanky. I thought she was crying. "We was about sixty miles out when—"

"For the record, Bobby, precisely how far were you from town?"

"Hell, Gord, I don't know *pree-cise-ly*. Ask them cops that went out there to sniff around."

"Fine, Bobby. Go on."

"Anyways, as I was saying, we were sixty miles east of here, give or take, when we seen a big flock 'a ravens hopping all over the ice road. As we got closer, a couple of Arctic foxes took off over the south bank. I could see red all over their muzzles. Obviously chewin' on something."

At this, Flossie buckled forward in her chair and blew her nose.

Bobby looked back and wiped his own nose on his sleeve as if to help her. "As we got closer, I saw some kind of carcass half dragged up the other bank. I thought it might've been a road-killed wolverine or something. But then I spotted Jimmy's ripped up boots. They were covered in frozen blood. I slammed on the brakes so damned hard I almost spun my truck right into him."

Lord Gord slowly took off his Empire Oil ball cap and rested it on the podium like it was made of glass. "What did you do then, Bobby?"

"I wasn't about to leave the kid out there to get mowed down by the next snowplow. So I picked up whatever pieces I could, bundled 'em up in a tarp so the ravens wouldn't peck at 'em no more, then headed home, straight for the cop shop."

"And, in your opinion, Bobby, what do you think happened to Jimmy?"

"Well now, that's none of my business, is it, Gord? That's up to the cops to figure out."

"You and Flossie are the only witnesses to the scene of the accident. Any ideas you can offer would be—"

Bobby looked back at Flossie who had buried her face in her hands. Mom had her arm around her and was gently rubbing her back. "Well, if you're putting a gun to my head over this, Gord, I'd have to say there's only one animal that could'a done that to him. It had to be a polar bear. Fifty foxes couldn't 'a pulled Jimmy apart like that."

Everybody shifted in their chairs. I saw one reporter lift his head and stop writing, like he had to let Bobby's words sink in.

"Hmmm," said the mayor.

"I'm telling you, Gordon, polar bears are going farther for seals, roaming around more. And who couldn't blame this crazy weather, especially the way it's been messing up our ice? We used to be able to read ice like a book. Chapter 1, dark ice, good and thick. Go straight. Like that. Chapter 2, fuzzy gray ice, too mushy. Go around. Chapter 3, *sikuliaq*, new ice. Relax, cross later, at night when it's colder. Chapter 4, *illaujaq*, junk ice, rotten stuff, turn back. We used to be able to read the ice like that. But not any more, can we, Gordon?"

The mayor just shook his head.

"And neither can the bears. Sure, they can read the ice a lot better than us. I've watched them poking the ice with their paws, staring at it from different angles, sniffing it, scratching it, doing their own little tests so they can figure it out—how thick it is, how easy they can smash it, where the cracks are for seals."

Lord Gord leaned over the podium. "Where have you seen this, Bobby?"

"Way east of here, past Suluk River. But now it's tough even for polar bears to read the ice. They're coming east. That's what we've said for years. They'll come back to Nanurtalik from the east. So, honestly, Gordon, I wasn't surprised when I saw it was a bear that chewed on Jimmy. That's what I think anyways."

"Very interesting, Bobby. *Nakurmiik.*"

"Excuse me, Mayor Jacobs," said Raymond Arseneau from one of the floor mikes. He was the new wildlife officer in town. As always, he wore his official camo ball cap, green army pants, and a crisp, khaki shirt trimmed with brass buttons and badges. Slung on his government-issue belt were about ten pounds of mysterious leather pouches, a .45 magnum pistol, and a big, black billy stick. In five months I'd never seen Raymond out of uniform. It was like he was on duty 24–7.

"Pssst, hey, Ash," whispered Rosie.

My mind was playing a videotape, over and over, of a polar bear chomping on Jimmy. "Huh?"

"Tell me something. Is he supposed to use that big stick on people or bears?"

"Shut up, Rosie," I said, in the friendliest tone possible.

"Yes, Raymond?" Lord Gord said.

"Mr. Mayor, we all know it's been over thirty years since anyone's spotted a bear within a hundred miles of Nanurtalik, let alone hunted one. With all respect to Elder Bob, I wonder if he might be jumping the gun here, so to speak."

Bobby had already sat down and was holding Flossie's hand. Without looking at Raymond, he gave his other hand a slight flip in Raymond's direction as if shooing away a pesky fly.

Before Lord Gord could craft a response, a tall, skinny man I'd never seen before stepped up to the other floor mike. He adjusted his gold-rimmed glasses, gave Bobby a friendly nod, then turned to the mayor. "If I may, Mr. Jacobs, I'd like to offer scientific support to Mr. Niego's suggestion that polar bears may be returning to this region."

"*Excuse* me," said Lord Gord, in a polite who-the-hell-are-you? voice. "Have we been introduced?"

"Cripes, Gordy," whispered Rosie, "give the guy a chance!"

"Oh, I'm sorry," the stranger said. "Lyons. Dr. Barney Lyons. I'm a biologist temporarily based at the CRI in Inniturliq."

"You mean the Circumpolar Research Institute?"

Lord Gord knew damn well what he meant. He just liked to be the only one speaking the secret language of acronyms so he could sound like he was in the know.

"That's correct. I'm conducting a study on—"

"You say *temporarily*. Where are you really from?"

Lord Gord put the guy on trial before he barely opened his mouth. At first I couldn't figure out why.

"Corvallis, actually. OSU campus."

Gord arched an eyebrow at the biologist. "OSU?"

"Oregon State University."

"A little far from home, aren't you, professor?" said Gord with feigned sympathy.

"I love the Arctic," Lyons said. "It's been my home away from home for over thirty years. I get up here every chance I can."

"But not to Nanurtalik, apparently."

"True. I've done most of my fieldwork farther east, and some in Greenland and Russia." He stroked his steel-wool beard.

"On bears then, is it?"

"Primarily yes. I'm conducting a long-term study on the effects of Arctic climate change on polar bear distribution—"

Gord kept cutting him off. "Come to think of it, I think I've seen some of your papers. Might've even reviewed one or two before they got published."

"Perhaps so," Lyons said, faintly shrugging.

"Sure, Gordy," Rosie said, scuffing the wooden floor with her runners. "All you read are girlie magazines and bank statements."

I lay into her with my shoulder.

Lyons carried on, "When I heard about your bear sighting related to the boys' death, I thought I might help resolve the question of—"

"Our *presumed* sighting, you mean. Nobody actually *saw* a polar bear."

"Of course. From what I've heard so far tonight, we have no conclusive evidence that a polar bear was involved in this unfortunate incident. However—"

Raymond chose this moment to jump back in. "You've listened well, Dr. Linus—"

"Ah, it's Lyons actually. Like the cat, only with a 'y'."

At this Rosie buried her face in my parka hood, filling it with snorts of laughter.

"Right. Dr. *Lyons,*" said Raymond. "Ah, much to the dismay of many local hunters, Nanurtalik has been what you might call a polar bear-free zone on the Arctic map for the past two or three decades. But from a biological perspective, I don't believe this is a big concern since bears tend to move around in response to natural cycles that science can't explain."

I thought of all the polar bear toe bones Mom and I had collected while beachcombing along the Spit. A few would poke out of the sand after every good storm, like the Spit was a polar bear graveyard. But no skulls or leg bones or anything like that. It was weird, just toe bones. Every time we found one, I'd hand wash it and put it in a big canning jar. We'd collected over a hundred of them, some bleached white, some golden brown, and a few the color of red grapes. When the sun hit them a certain way, those bear bones seemed to glow from within. Mom figured those bones represented at least fifty polar bears that marched right past Nanurtalik over the years—until they disappeared.

"The decline of polar bears in this region is certainly a mystery," said Dr. Lyons. "I would agree with Mr. Niego that changing climate and ice conditions are major factors. Of course there are hunting pressures to consider and—"

This struck a sour note with Lord Gord.

"I don't know what kind of data you've collected," he said, "but I'm sure if you interviewed any of our Elders you'd learn that we've always been responsible hunters, including the days when polar bears were common around here."

Bobby sat up straight and gave Dr. Lyons a long, blank stare.

Rosie tugged my left ear and whispered right into it, "Gordy would have been in diapers the last time a polar bear walked through town."

I burst out laughing but choked it back when I noticed Uncle Jonah shuffling into the gym, arm and arm with Aana, his little sister. It was months since I last saw *him* at a community meeting. Some big gathering for Inuit drummers soon after we got here. Drumming and polar bears. These seemed to be the only things that could drag Uncle Jonah out of his gloomy world.

Before he sat down he shot me a laser look clear across the hall. He'd been doing that a lot more lately, catching me off guard with those coal-black eyes, and it always stirred me up.

The chess game continued.

"I wasn't suggesting that over-hunting was solely responsible," the professor said. "But it has to be figured into the mix when we're looking at the big picture of polar bear declines—"

"You keep using the word *decline*," said Raymond. "Who's to say the bears just didn't go somewhere else?"

This got Dr. Lyons tugging on his beard. "Well, that's the problem, Raymond, isn't it?"

"Uh-huh, Raymond Arseneau." He said his name slowly and directly into the microphone to make sure everybody else got it. Most people around town thought Raymond was still pretty green around the gills.

"Yes, ah, with all respect," continued Lyons, "I think that's one thing we *can* be sure of, Raymond, that the world is quickly running out of *somewhere elses*. And polar bears are no exception to this trend."

Raymond pulled up his belt and took a firm hold of his billy stick like he was getting ready to whip it out. The crowd hushed as if settling into a court case—another favorite pastime for this community. "That may well be, sir, but how can we get too upset about their numbers when some Arctic settlements are ass-deep in polar bears? Look at Amaruq Point, for instance. Or MacPherson Harbor. Every other week a sled dog is eaten as bear bait at the edge of town. Or somebody gets mauled in their own front yard while taking out the garbage. We don't want that to happen around here."

Jimmy's truck went down just sixty miles away. Somebody chewed him up pretty good. If it was a polar bear, it could have waltzed into town the very next day. Or tomorrow maybe. So much for my dreamy walks on the Spit.

"It's true, bear safety is a growing concern for some Arctic communities," Lyons said. "But more bear sightings don't necessarily mean more bears. In fact some climate change models predict an increase in so-called nuisance bears around settlements even as their numbers decline."

"How would you explain *that*?"

"It may be that these bears are hungrier than ever and may be turning to human food sources as a last resort."

"But polar bears are pretty smart animals. They're adaptable, just like us."

"Who's *us*, Raymo?" asked Rosie. I elbowed her again, harder this time.

"Ouch!"

"Yes, they are extraordinarily intelligent, but I would suggest that adapting to sled dogs and garbage cans as a food source is not a very promising survival strategy. Unfortunately, continued warming of the Arctic may soon give them no choice."

"How do you think polar bears managed to live up here for so long?" asked Raymond. "They've *weathered* all this before—if you'll pardon the pun."

He was trying to lighten things up but nobody laughed. The town jury was still out on Raymond. "What about all those fossil redwood trees and crocodiles and flying lemurs up in the Arctic islands? There couldn't have been a heck of a lot of sea ice around in those days."

"That was somewhat earlier, Raymond. Actually about *fifty million years* earlier. Back then it was a very different landscape up here. Polar bears didn't exist."

Clearly Raymond was a bit out to lunch on this point. His public score card did not look good.

"In fact polar bears and humans appear in the fossil record about the same time," Lyons said, "roughly two million years ago. Their lives have been bound together ever since, as reflected in your stories and songs."

As he said this last bit, Dr. Lyons looked away from Raymond and gestured to the Elders in the first couple of rows. Like him, Raymond's bloodlines had nothing to do with sea ice or seals, northern lights or polar bears. Raymond was a southerner and always would be. I sure wouldn't want his job.

"In all that time," Dr. Lyons continued, "neither humans nor polar bears have ever experienced anything like this. As far as we know, the rapid rates of carbon dioxide output, temperature rise, and sea ice shrinkage could be unprecedented in the history of this *planet.* This time around, as smart as polar bears are, they may not be able to keep up to this pace of environmental change."

"And then?" asked Raymond, a big chip on his shoulder.

"Some climate models predict the total extinction of polar bears within as few as forty years."

"But that's just computer hocus-pocus isn't it? I mean, nobody really knows how many polar bears are out there."

"I guess that's all the more reason for studies like mine."

They went on like this for some time, Raymond saying the bears were just fine, thank you, and the southern professor saying the sky would soon fall on their furry heads. I didn't take sides. Besides, my chest was still churning from Ghost Man's drumming. Dreams, drumming, or a change in the weather. They seemed to dig at the same space in my chest. And right now that space throbbed. I felt suddenly exhausted. I leaned on Rosie and she gave me a good push which woke me up a bit. I heard a rising drone of snoring. People were losing interest in the great polar bear debate.

Uncle Jonah had joined the snorers. I watched him stir a bit when a new voice filled the hall. It belonged to Vince Nokusigak.

"Well, just who's to say there couldn't be a polar bear roaming around near here right now?" Vince asked, stretching his crooked lips towards Raymond's microphone.

I couldn't believe it. Vince was the last guy I'd expect to see at a public meeting like this, let alone say anything. He was pointing a limp arm at the professor.

"What he said about the weather changing and all. With the way things have gone bananas lately, you never know what's gonna show up next. You just watch. We'll have moose knocking on our doors pretty soon."

Lord Gord gave his eyes a teensy roll. "That might be a bit of a stretch, Vince."

Vince did not have a lot of credibility in this town, even at his soberest.

"If you don't believe me, go ask the moose I saw two days back."

"Where, Vince?" asked Gord, checking the trim of his fingernails.

"Coming back from Inniturliq."

"You saw a *moose* on your way back from Inniturliq?" asked Gord, who had fixed his gaze at some distant spot on the ceiling.

Vince straightened himself up and flashed a weak grin over his shoulder at everybody. "Yep. Crossing the ice road. It was a big bull. Looked pretty healthy too." Vince forced a laugh. "Next time I'll shoot him for you, Gord, if you don't believe me."

"Oh, we *want* to believe you, Vince," Gord said, as if humoring some lying brat. "It's just that—"

"I saw him too," said a voice from the back. It was Dad. Gabe started rocking from side to side and madly rubbing his hands together.

Lord Gord gave his head a little shake and leaned over the podium. "You're joking, Moise."

Even though Dad ran a radio and TV station, you'd never catch him near a microphone. He just stood up and took a couple steps forward. "Nope. Same day. I was going the other way, headed to Inniturliq to pick up some new computers for the station. I'd just come around that sharp curve past Suluk Crossing and saw this big brown thing hopping over the snow bank."

Vince nodded slowly and inched his lips towards the microphone. "That's about where I saw him too."

"It was snowing pretty heavy," Dad said. "At first I thought it might be a big grizz. But when I drove by, the moose lifted its head above the bank and looked me right in the eye."

"Right in the eye!" shouted Gabe. His whole body was now rocking back and forth, like he was dancing. This was big news to him. Dad was usually too busy to tell stories. Even a whacky moose story like this.

Raymond stepped back to the mike. "I suppose it's conceivable that a moose could find its way down the Suluk River to the Arctic coast."

"If I may, Mr. Jacobs," Lyons said, "my vegetation studies over the past twenty years indicate a pronounced increase in the productivity of willow shrubs along many Arctic river valleys. It makes sense that moose would follow that growth north."

"You might have a point there, doctor," said Gord, "but I'm sure Moise knows the difference between a grizzly bear and a moose. So we'll just have to take his word for it."

At this, Vince's shoulders went up and his head went down. He pulled his ratty tweed cap almost over his eyes. Lord Gord can be such a jerk.

"That's the first moose I've heard about in a long while," said Gord, "but it confirms something I've been thinking about for some time."

Dr. Lyons jumped in. "Actually there are numerous papers, from Alaska to Labrador, which document the recent spread of moose into Arctic habitats. And our own field studies suggest that grizzly bears are making a similar northern advance. In fact we've observed them far out on the sea ice, hunting seals in the exact manner as polar bears."

Lord Gord cleared his throat as if he'd swallowed something awful. He'd had quite enough of Dr. Lyons' highbrow science.

There was something important he wanted to say and at this point he wasn't going to let anyone get in his way. "All right, professor. So why *are* moose and grizzlies and polar bears showing up in weird places like never before? I'll tell you why. Sure, we've all seen some changes in the weather lately. Ice conditions too. But these animals aren't wandering around more because climate change is screwing up their habitat. It's because there are a heck of a lot *more* of them out there than ever before! Warmer weather means there're lots more plants and animals being supported out there. Why do you think they like to trap heat in a greenhouse? To grow *more* tomatoes. To grow *fatter* tomatoes! It's the same with the land and polar bears are, as you say, no exception."

When Lord Gord got worked up about something, he had this habit of rubbing the back of his neck with one hand like he was trying to light his hair on fire. I could almost see smoke rising above his head as he spoke. He had wrapped one leg around the podium and I could see that he was on his tiptoes. The press liked these gymnastics and started flashing away with their cameras.

"And when those bears come back this way," he said, bopping the podium with his fist, "I'm going to do everything in my power to bring the polar bear hunt back to our town. Like you say, professor, these are smart animals. They're adaptable. We've been happily co-existing together for—what did you say?"

"Roughly two million years."

"Right. So after that many years of living side by side in relative harmony, a little extra hunting pressure in the name of tourism and a healthy economy isn't going to bring the sky falling down on them."

"Interesting points, Mr. Mayor," Lyons said, twiddling his beard again. "However, I'm afraid I may have led our discussion a little astray. These are indeed important issues, but wasn't the focus of tonight's meeting to address what exactly happened to Jimmy Kikpak and Angus Oniak out on the ice road?"

The mayor slapped his chest like a gorilla looking for matches. As if he'd been waiting for the perfect moment, he ceremoniously pulled a brown, unmarked envelope out of his sealskin vest. "I'm glad you reminded me. I happen to have some solid evidence here that addresses this very question." Then, without another look at the professor, Lord Gord broke into Inuktitut for about ten minutes, speaking in low tones to the Elders up front. I caught a few words here and there—*sila,* weather, *siku,* ice, and of course *nanuq,* polar bear—plus lots about Jimmy. All the time he kept waving the envelope around in the air like a fly swatter.

The effect on the Elders was electrifying. Even Uncle Jonah woke up and leaned so far foward that Aana had to grab him before he fell over.

Lord Gord finished addressing the Elders, straightened up, and slowly opened the envelope like he was hosting an Academy Awards ceremony. "I have here some privileged information that I know everyone in the community will be *most* interested in."

"Talk about theatrics!" Rosie said. "What's he got up his sleeve this time?"

I shushed her. At this point I was as sucked into Lord Gord's performance as anyone else.

"This seems like an opportune moment to share with you the coroner's report on Jimmy's death," said Gord, slipping on his drug store reading glasses.

A ripple of murmurs swept through the crowd.

"Allow me to read the summary. 'The deceased, Jimmy J. Kikpak, was a seventeen-year-old Inuk male with no prior medical history of significance. He was a non-smoker, needed no prescription medications, and did not use illicit drugs or alcohol. He was last seen by his mother, Rosemary Kikpak, at 4:30 P.M. on October 31st as he and Angus Oniak left Jimmy's home to plow the Inniturliq ice road from Nanurtalik to the Suluk River crossing. Jimmy's frozen body was discovered early the next morning by Robert and Flossie Niego on their way to Inniturliq.'"

Lord Gord looked up from the coroner's letter. He seemed pleased with the effect on his audience which sat in rapt silence.

"'RCMP constable Michael Wrigley, who inspected the site, reported no signs of Angus Oniak or his pick-up truck in the vicinity of Jimmy's body. However, fresh cracks leading to a V-shaped patch of new ice strongly suggest that the truck fell through an unstable area with Angus still inside. To date, no efforts have been made to recover the body in water that may exceed three hundred feet in depth.

"'The exact time and manner of Jimmy Kikpak's death remain unknown. Given the lightness of his clothing, which was saturated with ice, it is presumed that he died of hypothermia after being submersed in open water associated with the truck breaking through. His body was found approximately one hundred yards west of the patch of new ice, suggesting that he had set out on foot towards Nanurtalik before he succumbed to the cold. Multiple tooth and claw marks on his body and its partially dismembered state indicate that he was later scavenged upon by several animals, most likely foxes, wolverines, and ravens.'"

Lord Gord injected a dramatic pause. "'In addition, a subsequent veterinary examination confirmed that massive breakages in Jimmy's left femur could only have been inflicted by a polar bear.'"

A chorus of chatter cut the audience like a gust of wind on a still pond.

Lord Gord finished his show by carefully folding the coroner's letter and tucking it back into his sealskin vest. "Well, there you have it, my friends. Clearly polar bears have returned to our region. We must enhance bear safety around the community while taking advantage of this new economic opportunity. I'm quite sure that's what Jimmy and Angus would have wanted."

Before anyone could ask more questions the mayor turned off the podium light and walked away.

I couldn't believe my ears. "Why the hell did he let everyone go on like that if he knew damn well how Jimmy died?"

"Lord Gord's a pro at turning any issue into a political football," Rosie said with disgust.

"Even a bummer like this?"

"Yeah. It's an old Hollywood pitch."

"What do you mean?"

"You know." Rosie twirled a hand over her head like she was swinging a rope. "Lasso the hottest issue in town. Paint everything black and white. Get everybody worked up. Then pull a card out of your sleeve and make it look like you've solved everybody's problems."

"But to toy with Jimmy and Angus's death like that?"

"Yeah, really. Just so he can bring back the polar bear hunt."

"And make a quick bundle, I suppose."

"You got it. A.S.A.P. He knows there's tons of money in polar bears. And I guess that's fine and dandy for the town—"

"But before the guy's even buried?"

Rosie shrugged. "Business is business. Welcome to Lord Gord's kingdom."

I shook my head as I watched the mayor duck out a side exit. "All I can say is, when I'm old enough to vote, Lord Gord is so *not* getting an *X* on my ballot."

A Place to Hide

Over the past five months since we'd moved here, I'd walked the Spit probably a hundred times. The feeling I got out there was as close to anything I could call home in a community where I basically felt like an alien. In summer, the beach was cleansed daily by the waves and wind, sometimes unearthing ancient bone tools, a copper spear point, or maybe more polar bear toe bones. In winter the snow was reshaped by the wind almost every day, erasing the past forever. The Spit had a cleansing effect on me, dissolving my artistic frustrations, my bouts of loneliness, or the nagging feeling that my true home was light-years away.

But something had changed. On the Spit I now felt watched, even as I became more watchful. It was less welcoming after Lord Gord's polar bear powwow, which he'd disguised as a memorial service for Jimmy and Angus. That meeting had toppled a wall in me and polar bears now wandered freely between my inner and outer worlds.

Jimmy had been ripped apart by a polar bear exactly as I had been in my *inuksuk* dream. Bobby Niego had collected all the bits and pieces of Jimmy's body and bundled them together in a tarp. Mine still felt thrown to the wind.

As I kicked at the rock-hard drifts lining the Spit, Lord Gord's slippery words invaded my brain. What had he called Jimmy and Angus? "The pride of the Elders, the envy of their peers, the hope for the future." Next to Rosie, those guys were about the only people I could half relate to at school. "The best and the brightest" had been snuffed out. My outer world seemed to be shrinking fast. I needed a place to hide.

At first I thought of the church, but somehow sitting on an oak pew under a burned-out bell tower was not what I craved at the moment. Some cocoon-like place, away from everybody, safe from the wind, close to the earth. I needed a cave where no bear could follow me.

I spun around and faced the town. "The icehouse," I whispered. "Now's as good a time as any."

Ice Bear

THE ICEHOUSE

SATURDAY, NOVEMBER 12TH, 4:50 P.M.

I'd heard a bit about the community icehouse, mostly from Rosie who'd never actually been down there. She had a touch of claustrophobia and, as daring as she was, she drew the line on exploring "frozen catacombs," as she called it. I knew that the icehouse was some kind of mega freezer carved deep into the permafrost where people stored stuff. I also knew how to find it. Beyond that, it was a mystery I'd always wanted to check out.

It was getting dusky by the time I reached the gas station. Right across the road was a little white shack not much bigger than an outhouse, which supposedly covered the icehouse tunnel. The road was empty and I could see the gas station guy blabbing on the phone, so I marched right up to the shack and tugged on the door. It was locked. Fortunately Rosie had told me where the key was hidden. An empty forty-five-gallon drum sat beside the shack and, after giving it a couple of swift boots, I rocked it free of the snow and found the key underneath. At first the key wouldn't turn in the frozen lock. I blew warm breath into it for a minute or two, then turned the key and yanked. I was in.

There was enough light from the gas station streetlight for me to see that I'd wasted my time coming here. Instead of a giant hole in the ground I found a solid plywood floor. A coil of old rope hung from the ceiling and a few white plastic buckets were stashed in a corner. That was it. At this point I figured the community ice-house was a local rumor spread for suckers like me.

I was surprised at how disappointed I felt. But as I was stepping back outside, I tripped on something that lay hidden in the shadows. I flew through the door like somebody had kicked me and did a whopping good face plant into a snowbank. Through snow-caked eyes I saw the gas station guy squinting out the window. I lay still for a few minutes until he turned around, then crawled back over the door threshold. I took off my wolf mitts and felt around on the floor for whatever tripped me up. My fingers stopped on a wooden handle. There was a short length of frayed rope attached to it.

I stood up, walked to the center of the floor, and jumped up and down. I heard a hollow, booming sound. I tugged on the hanging rope above me and discovered it was on a pulley. I felt along the far edge of the floor and found a long, metal hinge.

"Aha," I said out loud.

I drew out one end of the ceiling rope and tied it to the handle on the floor. Then I grabbed the other end and pulled while standing in the doorway. The rope snapped. I examined the frayed end. It was pretty ratty but it was all I had. I tied it off again and pulled more gently this time. At first nothing moved. Then, with a tinkling of frost crystals, the whole floor popped open.

I stared down at a hole about four feet square. Propped on one side was a makeshift wooden ladder that led down to utter blackness. What I would've given for a flashlight. The tunnel mouth was rimmed in jagged clumps of hoarfrost that gave it the appearance of a giant, gaping mouth.

A shiver ran up my spine, as much from the cold as from the prospect before me. Still, the whiff of adventure egged me on. I found a cleat on the wall beside me and tied the rope off. This was obviously part of the procedure. So far, so good.

I left the door open just enough to avoid attracting attention, letting a shaft of streetlight shine on the top of the ladder. I swung my legs into the tunnel mouth and dropped, rung by rickety rung. I had no idea how deep it was to the bottom. Rosie had said the tunnel went straight to hell. That tidbit didn't help me much right now. Once my eyes adjusted, I was amazed at how well I could see as the frost crystals lining the tunnel bent and bounced the glow from above. I reached out to touch an extra big crystal and slipped off the ladder.

Even as I hurtled into darkness I had visions of catching a foot in the ladder and snapping a leg in half or cracking my head open on rock solid ice. I managed to keep my legs down and head up but my face kept bonking the side of the tunnel on the way down like someone was punching me with frosty fists.

I must have blacked out. The next thing I remember was a low, rhythmic tapping noise. I couldn't tell whether it rang in my aching head or leaked from the frozen earth all around me. My arms and legs were in a tangle and my face was pressed against dry, cold crystals. I tried moving each limb. They still worked. I lifted my head and craned my neck around. I could see the top of the tunnel, about thirty feet up, still rimmed with its frosted teeth. It was like a farewell look out the throat of some beast that had swallowed me.

I'd never experienced such darkness but, oddly, I felt no fear. My body seemed in one piece and the way out was clear enough. I'd landed on a soft mound of broken frost crystals that must have sloughed off the tunnel walls. I felt pretty good actually, like I'd

on thin ice

returned to some long forgotten, personal power spot. I had found a place to hide.

I felt safe, invisible, embraced by the darkness. The air was moister down here and warmer. I had to chuckle at my fall. I'd have paid to see it played back in slow motion.

I stood up and leaned against the bottom of the ladder. I brushed the snow crystals from my face and felt a warm wetness on my cheek. I tasted it. Blood. Wouldn't I have a story to tell! On second thought, maybe not. I decided that whatever my face looked like, I wouldn't tell anyone but Rosie what happened. I didn't want to give up this place. I knew there was much more to explore. If only I had a light.

Just as I'd decided to come back another time with a flashlight, my foot struck against something hard beside the foot of the ladder. It was a square, plastic thing with a folding handle and some buttons on the top. My heart leapt. I pressed a button. There was a flicker, a flash, then the space around me filled with a feeble orange glow. Somebody's portable fluorescent lamp.

"All right!"

I held it above my head and peered around. I stood at the end of a long arched corridor carved into the permafrost. The corridor walls consisted of pearly ice mixed with layers of fine sand. A thick coating of feathery frost crystals began halfway up the wall and continued across the entire ceiling. I scuffed some shattered crystals off the floor with my boot. Locked in the ice were brightly colored rocks. I held the lamp up close. They were reddish orange streaked with lightning-shaped flecks. I'd seen this kind of rock only one place before: Uncle Jonah's soapstone cup.

"Hmm . . . weird," I said under my breath.

I took a few steps into the corridor and spotted a narrow door with a big, black number one painted on it. I shuffled ahead, being careful not to knock off any of the beautiful crystals that sparkled in my lamplight. There was door number two. This went on, every ten feet or so. I found twenty-one doors in all. These were the catacombs that Rosie had talked about. To me, the glittering corridor with its dwarf-sized doors and red cobbled floor looked like an after-hours scene from Santa's workshop. I was falling in love with the place.

The only thing that spooked me just a little was that tapping noise. It went on for a few minutes, stopped for a while, then started up again, getting louder as I walked down the corridor. That didn't stop me from poking my nose into whatever was behind those doors.

I had noticed padlocks on a few doors but most were crudely latched with wooden pegs. Door number ten was already ajar, so I took a deep breath and went in. My lamp, which was beginning to fade, shone on an ice chamber about the size of a small bedroom. As in the corridor, frost crystals hung from the ceiling like a million chandeliers. On the floor was a small pile of frozen Arctic char, nothing more. I tried the next door. It was locked. I tried number twelve. This chamber contained a tidy pile of caribou legs in one corner and caribou heads in another. Dog food and soup. It all made sense to me.

The tapping noise had started up again and was beginning to rattle my nerves. I must have knocked my head harder than I thought and it was beginning to throb, almost in time to the tapping. The light was flickering, like a candle sputtering out. But I thought I'd try just one more door, number thirteen. It was jammed on a thick wedge of ice but I managed to yank it open with both arms. I figured no one had been in here for years.

The light was fading fast as I thrust it into the ice chamber. Unlike the other chambers, the floor in this one was uneven and some big thing sloped out of it like the back of a surfacing whale. I moved closer. It was a bedrock outcrop showing the same fiery color as the ones locked in the corridor floor. There were deep chiseled gouges in the outcrop and a pile of big chunks beside it, suggesting that this was some kind of soapstone quarry deep underground. Strange . . .

Then I saw it.

In the far corner of the chamber was a gigantic figure that had been stripped of its skin. It was propped against the wall in a semi-standing position with its face turned towards the door. A harpoon and a rifle hung above its head like the crossbones on a pirate's flag. In the dim light of my flickering lamp I made out the massive muscles of its legs, its arms, even the six-pack covering its bloated stomach. Where it wasn't encrusted with frost crystals, the flesh was so old it was almost black. The figure looked remarkably human in all respects, except for the claws and massive head which could belong to no other animal than a polar bear.

The giant bear's teeth seemed to glow yellow against the dark flesh of its staring face. With a short willow stick, someone had propped the mouth open in a roaring pose. The eyes were half open and reflected the dying orange glow from my lamp.

I froze, watching the terrible apparition disappear as my lamp finally flickered out. All that was left was that tapping—in the walls, in the floor, in my brain—and the sound of heavy breaths even as I held my own.

I spun around and bolted for where I thought the door should be. I smacked my whole body against a frozen wall. I threw off my wolf mitts and felt along the wall. I couldn't tell if I was going towards or away from the ice bear. I got my answer when my fingers landed on a set of long, cold claws.

I don't know if I screamed. Somehow I scrambled out of chamber thirteen and down the corridor to the foot of the ladder. I stopped to catch my breath. My heart was doing its best to jump out of my chest. I looked up to see the well-toothed edge of the tunnel mouth. Then I remember thinking, *Wait a minute! It's just a dead bear.* With that very thought, I heard a tremendous crash above me. The tunnel mouth vanished and a powerful gust of air knocked me off my feet.

In the total darkness, the tapping seemed louder than ever. I struggled to get my bearings as I wiped frozen silt and frost from my mouth. I groped around, again on all fours, and found a wall, a door, the sloping mound of broken crystals, the foot of the ladder.

I'd never climbed a ladder so fast. I could feel warm moist air at my heels, down my neck. The tiny shred of reason left to me said, *It's only the earth's heat coming up through the floor.* But my legs weren't convinced and I didn't stop climbing until I bashed my head against the heavy trapdoor.

I pressed my shoulder against it and heaved. The beast's mouth had snapped shut and I was mincemeat. The trapdoor refused to budge. It must have got jammed by all the frost when it slammed shut. The tapping got louder. The air thicker, hotter. I heaved again and again and again. I was crying like a six-year-old. I pounded against the trapdoor with my fist, my boot, my head. Shattered frost crystals fell like razor blades into my weeping eyes.

The trapdoor suddenly gave, as if someone had been standing on it and nonchalantly stepped off. I held it open against my back as I squirmed into the shed and out the shack door. I noticed the rope dangling over the door sill, all frayed to bits. A couple of snowmobiles were gassing up across the street, so I rolled back into the shed to pull myself together, something I'd been trying to do a lot lately.

Candles

I discovered what all the tapping was about on my way home. I could hear it as soon as I stepped away from the shack. Outside it had a higher pitch and a kind of metallic ring to it. At first I thought it was coming from the church. My adventure meter read zero at the moment, so I walked right on past.

The tapping got louder, then quit. It had come from behind the church.

Vince Nokusigak's pickup truck was parked out front with a portable compressor machine attached to his hitch. A thick rubber hose led from the compressor to the cemetery. White wooden crosses stuck above the snow at every angle imaginable. I could see a couple of guys in polar bear pants and down parkas swinging pickaxes into the frozen ground. They'd built a high wall of snow blocks behind them to break the north wind. They must have been working there a long time. Then one of them picked up a big tool and the tapping noise started again. It was a jackhammer.

I glanced at the church. The light from what looked like a hundred candles flickered through the purple stained glass windows. There'd been enough deaths in this tiny town—seven just since we'd moved here—for me to know that nobody leaves that many candles burning in there unless there's a coffin parked in the sanctuary.

It all came together. Those guys were digging Jimmy Kikpak's grave. I clapped my hands over my ears and ran home.

Losing Yoshi

After the community finally said goodbye to Jimmy and Angus, I had a strong urge to sink my teeth into something I could really call my own. Something to remind me who I was before my inner and outer worlds started blurring. In a way, I felt like I was doing it for Jimmy. I wanted to be counted among the best and the brightest. I wanted to belong.

Naturally, I turned to art.

I first heard about the on-line video art course from the most unlikely source: Dad. He was testing out a new high-speed Internet connection that he'd rigged up at the station. He'd duct-taped a fish-eye camera to our TV and was trying to link up, eyeball to eyeball, with the Arctic Broadcasting station in Inniturliq. "If I can pull it off from our house, we can do it from any home or business in Nanurtalik," he'd said as he started playing with a remote controller that must have had a hundred buttons on it. Dad liked playing with this kind of technology, especially when it connected him to the outside world.

Dad had pulled up a long menu of video-linked destinations on the information highway. Near the top of the list I caught the words, *Art courses*. He was scrolling down to *Broadcast Networks* when I interrupted.

"No! Wait, Dad. Can you click the art course one?"

"What for?"

"Well, there might be something interesting there for me. Like, what kind of art instruction am I going to get in a place like this?"

"Who says you need art instruction? Everybody seems to like your stuff."

"Everybody but *you.*"

Dad frowned. "This hookup time costs money, you know."

"Let's just have a peek. You're test-driving this thing, aren't you? Besides, the station's paying for it."

"Yeah, but . . ."

I plucked the remote out his hand and scrolled back up the list to *Art Courses*. "Anyway, you have to make sure that techno-dummies like me know how to work the system." I pressed *Enter* and a new list of web destinations flashed up on the TV. I quickly selected one before Dad could grab the remote back. "Here's a good one. The Boston Academy of Armchair Art."

Dad's new system worked great and within a day I had signed up as the academy's first Arctic student. Dad made a lot of grumbling noises, but Mom seemed to catch fire with the idea of an interactive art course and helped me talk him into it.

"It's just what Ashley needs, Moise," she'd said. "Can't you see she's feeling a bit lost here and this could *draw* her out, so to speak."

I chose a course called Webinar in Transformative Sketching. The teacher's name was Yoshi Suzuki, a Japanese woman who could have easily blended into a crowd of Nanurtalikians. I took to her course like a seal to seawater. I never knew just how starved I'd been for artistic company until that first class. Three weeks later I was still eating up her every word—at least, the ones I could understand.

At the end of each class, Yoshi liked to get philosophical and ask us something deep about art. The week before it was, "As an ahtist, what is your gleatest slength?" I didn't have to think much about that one. When it was my turn, I told her my greatest strength was the ability to pull images out of nowhere, especially my bears. They were just waiting there inside of me, ready to leap out. Some artists have to open their eyes wide and stare at things for a long time before they get inspired. All I had to do was close mine and up popped a bear just begging to be drawn.

This week's question was a lot tougher. "Okay evleyone. What does it feel like when you're leally in the gloove, dlawing at your vely best."

It took my brain a few moments to translate her "Lice-A-Loni" English. That's what Gabe called it. He liked to listen in on my art classes. Here was a guy born blind who said he drew pictures in his head. Whatever.

So, what did it feel like when I was really into it, lost in my bear pictures? I looked away from the fish-eye camera. I felt like I'd been caught in class without a scrap of homework done. You know that feeling. Maybe she'd forget I existed for the moment.

Nobody said anything. I peeked at the screen and saw that all the other students were dodging Yoshi's electronic eye, shuffling papers, pretending to pick up dropped pencils, looking intently at their latest masterpiece. She'd struck a raw nerve here, hit on something pretty private that I for one had never really put into thoughts, let alone words.

Yoshi giggled sweetly. "What about you, Ashley? I can seeeee youuuuu, Ashley." I heard giggles from around the continent. Everyone else seemed to relax.

I knew I absolutely *had* to draw. I had only to stop drawing for a few days to feel my inner eye go dim, to feel somehow starved, bankrupt. Drawing was my breath, my food, my heartbeat. It was a crutch I could lean on when I klutzed my way through the so-called normal world. It was a boat to carry me safely across the stormy waters of this crazy town. It was a fire extinguisher to douse the flaming dreams that seared through my mind at night. It was a map that pulled me forward—though

I didn't have a clue where it was leading me. In short, my honorable Yoshi, drawing was simply a matter of life and death. But of course I didn't say that.

"What's it feel like?" I said. "I don't know. Like, well it's like the world fades away. All the junk in my life, all the worries and stuff, they just dry up and blow away. It's . . . it's like I can get lost in a drawing, in a good way I mean, and pretty soon I sort of dissolve into thin air. You know, poof! Dust in the wind. And all that's left is . . ." I was getting pretty dreamy here. The word factory side of my brain had shut down.

"What's left, Ashley?" I looked back at the TV and saw my fellow students, floating in little boxes on the screen, all staring at me, with Yoshi's smiling face in the center.

"Huh?"

"What's left after you disappear?"

Everyone except Yoshi seemed to freeze, like they were in a movie and somebody had hit the pause button. They were all staring at their own TVs, staring at me. Fred, the retired Navy admiral in California. Erin, the young art teacher in Alberta. Max, the hippie guy from British Columbia. And nine-year-old Amy down in Florida who Yoshi called her "child plodigy"—all gaping at me, hanging on my next brilliant word.

I stared back. It struck me that maybe these budding artists, scattered across North America, might know what I was getting at here. "Well, all that's left is the drawing," and I held up my latest bear portrait, the one knocking over the *inuksuk*. "Nothing but the drawing and this weird kind of fire, sort of like electricity. Yeah, that's it, electricity."

There was a long expensive pause. Dad liked to drop frequent reminders about how much he was paying a minute for my "fancy-dancy art course," as he called it.

Then Amy piped in. "That's awesome, Ashley. Same for me. *Exactly* the same."

"Sounds like high voltage stuff, Ashley," said Admiral Fred. "Can you tell me where I might plug in to some of that electricity? We're experiencing a bit of an energy crisis here in California and my artwork could really use a boost."

"Right on, Ashley," said Max. "Right on. You spoke my mind, kid."

These strangers understood. They'd been in that zone. I felt less alone. Less of a freak. Yoshi smiled and opened her tiny mouth to say something when I heard a shrill, crunching sound outside and the screen went blank.

Mom shot up from the table and pressed her nose against the kitchen window.

Gabe ran out of his room, tripped over Mom's chair, and landed in a heap on the floor. "What kind of half-baked, half-cocked, half-wit is driving that thing now?" he shouted.

"*Game ovah! Game ovah!*" shrieked Wiggins.

I'd normally help Gabe. It's automatic. But I had to find Yoshi. I fiddled with the TV remote, trying every button.

"Who's at the wheel, Carole?" asked Gabe. "Who's at the wheel?"

The TV crackled then lit up again but instead of Yoshi and her band of merry art students, I saw five stiff-looking business types in black suits sitting around a big wooden table.

"Looks like Vincent," Mom said, still glued to the window. "And it looks bad."

I moved closer to the TV. "Who are you?" asked a silver-haired guy sitting at the head of the table.

I'd never tell. "I'm, ah, I'm Judy lost in a tornado. Who are *you?*"

"Sunrite Insurance brokers. We're supposed to be connecting with our partners in New York."

I had to laugh in his video face. Whatever crashed outside must have crossed some wires in Dad's studio. "Well, I hate to tell you, folks, but this sure ain't New York. I'm afraid you must've dialed a wrong number. Welcome to Nanurtalik."

"That Vincent should be hung out to dry," Gabe said, reaching for the tabletop to pull himself up.

I had to find Yoshi. However hard I squeezed those buttons, I couldn't ditch those men in black suits. They seemed really interested in what was going on at my end.

"Where?" asked the old guy who'd pilfered my TV screen.

"Nanurtalik, way up in the Arctic."

"You mean way up there in polar bear country?"

"Yes . . . well . . . no . . . I mean . . . there's none around here anymore . . . nobody seems to know why."

"Do you folks really live in iglus?"

"No . . . well, yes, now and then . . . when we're out on the land sometimes . . . oh, forget it!"

This was a waste of time—and Dad's money. "Hey, have you guys seen any art teachers hanging around your building? A nice Japanese lady named Yoshi? Maybe she's just down the hall or something."

"I'm sorry, miss, but there're no art teachers here," said the old guy. The other men all shook their heads like they were at a funeral. "But tell us," he went on, "who's Vincent and what's he done?"

"You wouldn't want to know," I said.

"Oh-oh," Mom said. "Here comes Moise. He doesn't look too amused."

"Time to pay the piper, Vince," shouted Gabe. "When Moise gets hot under the collar you better run for the hills!"

I threw down the remote and turned my back on the men in black suits. I could hear Dad's voice through the thick log walls of our house. Every now and then Vince made a low, whining reply but Dad walked right over him.

"Must be taking a strip off Vince's hide," Gabe said.

I joined Mom by the kitchen window. "Whoah!" I said, not believing what I saw.

Vince had backed the water truck into the station's giant satellite dish.

Gabe ran up beside me and felt for my back. "What? What?"

"It's the dish, Gabe," Mom said.

"It's toast," I said.

"Somebody declare a state of emergency!" Gabe yelled.

I could tell by Dad's rising voice and his flapping arms that he was boiling over. Everyone in town knew about Dad's temper, Vince included. After a few more whines, Vince threw the truck keys at Dad's feet and beetled down the street. Dad walked behind the truck to inspect the damage. The lower rim of the dish was bent backwards like an umbrella in a hurricane. Fat blue and yellow wires oozed like toothpaste from a cracked pipe under the water truck's rear tire.

Dad let out a rip-snorting stream of rude words, then hopped in the water truck. As he eased it forward, the mangled satellite dish popped back into shape.

I pumped a fist. "All right!"

As Dad slowly disengaged the water truck, the dish split open from top to bottom. The whole thing lunged off its metal cradle and collapsed to the ground like a caribou shot through the heart.

I stole a glance at the TV. The men in black had vanished. The screen was blank.

Vince had done a pretty thorough job on that dish. Dad had finished it off trying to save it. My lifeline to the rest of the world was basically totaled.

I heard the truck door slam.

"Look out," Mom said. "Here comes Mr. Rhino."

"Time to cut and run, fellas," shouted Gabe, dashing for his room. "Hell hath no fury like a scorned station manager." He ducked into his room and tore into a flaming fast version of "Turkey in the Straw" on his fiddle. Art was my escape hatch. Music was Gabe's.

Aana looked up from her sewing for a second when the front door flew open. I caught a flicker of fear in her eyes.

Dad stormed in and slammed the door. By the look on his face you'd think *he'd* been run over, not the dish. At first he said nothing. He just stood in the middle of the kitchen, rubbing his temple and rocking from side to side on his heels, almost like Gabe. For a few seconds he could have been ten years old. Like the world had ganged up on him and he didn't know what to think, say, or do.

Mom knew what to do. "Coffee, Moise?" she asked, like everything was normal.

The explosion never came. Or maybe it went off deep inside him and I missed it. Mom should work for the police bomb squad.

Dad looked up at her, blinking like he just woke up after a huge bender. "Huh? Yeah. Some of that Frenchie roast stuff."

"With maple syrup?"

Dad sighed and mumbled something to Aana in Inuktitut as he pulled a chair up to the table. Aana covered her mouth and chuckled. "Yeah," he said. "That Frenchie syrupy stuff."

Gabe's "Turkey in the Straw" stopped in mid-flight. He stuck his head out the door, waving his fiddle bow towards the kitchen. "Make it two, Carole." Then the turkey took off again.

Dad tore off his grimy Red Power ball cap and threw it on the table. He started raking back his hair like he does when he's really uptight. It seemed grayer than the last time I saw his cap off. Last week, when Gabe blew a gasket over something and threw a chair through his window.

Mom set a steaming cup of coffee under his nose. "There you go, *mon amour.*"

Mom always threw in a bit of French cooing when she was trying to soften him up.

"That Vince," he said, "What a horse's ass."

"A real broncobuster," Gabe said, sidling cautiously up to the table with his nose high. "That coffee sure smells good."

"*Et pour toi,*" said Carole, and out came another liquid soother for her boys.

"Mercy buckets, Carole," Gabe said.

There were enough people mollycoddling Dad. I got right to the point. "So, that dish. It's busted pretty bad, eh, Dad?"

"It's history." Dad took a long sip of coffee. "I knew I shouldn't have left that gate open."

"Vince would've sailed right through there even with the gate locked tight as a drum," Gabe said. "There's nothing stopping that guy, all right. Nothing stopping ol' Vincent when he gets drinking and driving."

"He smelled sober to me," Dad said. "Has been since the Labor Day storm." He shook his head. "That's what he told me anyways."

"That's a mighty long hangover then," Gabe said.

"Must've had another boxing match with Myrna," Mom said. "You can tell when that dark cloud follows him around. And you don't see her for days."

Most of the talk in this town was about what's wrong with who and how to fix them. Everybody wanted to change everybody. Everybody seemed to have a crystal clear idea how other people should lead their lives but no idea how to fix their own.

"The hell with Vince," I said. "What about that dish? When can you fix it, Dad? I've got another art class next—"

"The hell with your art class, Ash," Dad said. "And the Internet."

"*And TV?*" asked Gabe.

Dad just nodded slowly, forgetting Gabe's blindness for a moment.

"Time to break out the checkers, Gabe," Mom said. She'd given him a special set of brailled checkers and a board a couple of birthdays ago and he still hadn't tried them. "Time to explore life after TV."

"Oh, that's just dandy," Gabe said as he dropped his chin to his chest, started swaying his head back and forth, and hummed softly. He did that when he got really bored.

I was looking at Mom when some heavy thought invaded her brain. She jerked backwards like she'd been struck between the eyes. "Wait a minute, did you say the Internet was down too?"

Mom spent an awful lot of time on the computer searching New Age websites for the latest in miracle cures and apocalyptic prophecies. When she worked with Arctic Air as a stewardess, she used to fly regularly to Montreal where she had a band of freaky friends who used to hold séances and palm readings and who knows what other weird stuff. Mom would come home sounding like a walking New Age encyclopedia. She had to give all that up when we moved to Nanurtalik since very few flights came through here. Now she depended on mysterious chat groups and Web sites to plug into her New Age network. Her passion for this stuff had turned her into a hard-core Internet addict. I saw that I wouldn't be the only one suffering from cold turkey if we got cut off from the outside world. Dad confirmed our worst fears.

"The whole community's down. All we got left is phones. Hard to run a radio and TV station over a phone line."

"But I was just getting rolling on that course. There're a lot of budding artists out there who know what I'm going through and we were just beginning to gel. I'll fail the course for sure if you can't get that—"

"The whole damned dish will have to be replaced and we can't get another one in here until the barge comes in next July, maybe August, depending on the ice."

"August! That's over eight months from now. The course ends by—"

"Forget it, Ash."

"What about trucking one down the ice road?"

"The dish is too wide for most flatbeds." Dad pushed his cap back. "I could maybe look into bumming a ride with an Empire Oil truck. But there's fat chance of that."

"Can't you fly one in?"

"Too big. Wouldn't fit in the cargo hold of any plane that could land on our puny runway. Unless you know someone who's got a spare Hercules. Both Hercs based in Inniturliq are over in China helping to mop up after that mother earthquake. There's nothing I can do in the meantime, Ash."

Dad took a big gulp of hot coffee, scalding most of his throat. "Damn!" he shouted, slamming his cup on Mom's precious table.

There was a reason Dad's dish was so enormous—and so vital to everyone's sanity around here. Sure, we were light-years from anything. But how come people in other Arctic communities, even farther north than Nanurtalik, could pull in fifty TV stations plus wireless Internet with only a rooftop dish hammered on their house? The way Dad told it, when personal satellite dishes first came out, they sold like hotcakes at our Northern Store. But reception was always iffy, and eight or nine so-so channels never seemed to be enough for people. Dad figured there must be something in the ground around Nanurtalik that screwed up the air waves. He called it some kind of "geomagnetic anomaly." So it was Dad's brain wave to set up one monster dish to "cut through the crap," as he said, and feed cables, door to door, to everyone in town. The first thing he did when he took over the station was to squeak a big dish on the last barge north. Dad got the whole system up and running a few weeks later. When he flipped the switch on the master cable, it seemed like the whole world flooded into town. My father, the overnight hero. Thanks to him, Nanurtalik became the only high Arctic community with cable TV and twenty-four-seven high-speed Internet. We were spoiled. We could now cruise the global information highway as easily as stepping onto a dogsled. The big dish worked like a charm. It even survived the Labor Day storm. I found Yoshi. Then Vince backed the water truck down the wrong alley.

Mom stepped towards me and brushed the hair from my eyes. "My, your hair *is* dark," she said. "You didn't like red?"

I jerked away. I hated when she changed the subject just to make peace.

"Looks like you're on your own again, Ash," she said. "But that doesn't mean you have to stop drawing your bears."

I didn't feel like drawing much of anything. I just wanted Yoshi back.

Dad scowled at the blank TV screen. "Maybe you could write Miss Cherry Blossom and tell her what happened. Say you live in the boonies where people drink all night, then drive over buildings and stuff. Maybe you could ask for a refund." He glanced out the kitchen window at the crumpled pile that was once his famous satellite dish. He started nodding to himself. "Yeah, for sure. Do that. Ask for a refund. Looks like we could use the money now that Vince has mothballed the station." Dad sucked back the last drops of maple syrup from the bottom of his cup. "That course was a dumb idea in the first place. We can't afford it."

"I paid for it myself, from my post office job!"

"Well, the way things are crumbling around here, it might be better to stir that kind of money back into the family coffers."

"What?"

"And *more* of it too, if we ever hope to pay off this log mansion."

"You didn't have to buy such a big place," I shouted, knowing this was a sore spot for him.

Dad plucked his ball cap off the table and squeezed its rim far beyond the regulation curve. "You know this was your grandfather's house. He wanted me to look after it."

Dad kicked himself every day for turning down this house when Grandpa Eddy offered it to him just before he died. Instead, Dad chose to move to Inniturliq to pursue his dream of being a big time ABC station manager. When Uncle Jonah basically forced him to move back to Nanurtalik, Dad wanted this house so bad that he made a sky-high offer to the next owner who gladly moved out while laughing all the way to the bank. Dad had been paying through the nose for this place ever since. Everybody in town, including me, still called it "Eddy's Place." It would always be that to me, someone else's home, not mine.

"I suggest you go out and tell Annie at the post office that you'd like to work more hours. You won't have time for any of your artsy bears for a while. Art's a luxury we just can't afford right now."

I felt like a shipwrecked sailor in a leaky lifeboat. And I was sinking fast.

The Bear Shaman's Song

Part III
Glimpsing the Bear

The cry of the raven
Echoes off the mountains.
I follow *Nanurluk's* tracks across the sea ice.
Here no bear can hide.
Look!
On an iceberg!
What artist can draw her proud head,
those massive paws?

Tracks

I trudge head down into a blizzard. Ice crystals bombard my eyes. I tumble face-first onto rock hard snow. I feel lost, alone, small.

I punch at the snow in frustration and catch my caribou-skin mitt on a hump of snow. I peer through a screaming wall of flying crystals. I discover more humps lined up just like tracks. Polar bear tracks! I must have shouted in my sleep, almost waking myself up.

I crouch above the tracks. I can make out the wide, kidney-shaped paw pad, the deep imprint of toes, faint nicks in the snow made by heavily furred claws. Like a bear, I spring to a stand, sniff the air, then run. Not away from the bear but towards it. My guts swirl with a mix of fear and fascination. I know this path leads to danger. But what I fear most is never seeing the bear that made these tracks.

The blizzard breaks in front of me like the parting of a sea, then lifts completely, leaving an eerie calm in its wake. Looming above the horizon is an iceberg locked in the sea ice. The tracks lead directly to a white figure standing below it. A bear? A man dressed in polar bear skins? I can't tell. I click into overdrive and reach the iceberg in what seems like seconds. This must be what my dream book calls "fast-tracking."

But no figure. No tracks.

The iceberg towers above me, like a closed hand with one finger pointing to the sky. I frantically search for tracks.

There! Very fresh.

The tracks are different here, all stretched out like . . . like they were half bear, half human. They spiral up the iceberg. I take a deep breath of frigid air and climb.

Something long and skinny angles out from the finger. My heart leaps at the sight of my narwhal tusk harpoon. I greedily lunge for it, almost losing my balance and sailing over the side. I reach out again, more carefully, and clutch my prize. Even through my mitts I can feel that familiar warm glow flooding my body. I move my hands along the shaft which throws out a soft purple light around them.

I stare at the exquisite soapstone spear-point, enjoying its flaming hues. But even as I cradle the harpoon in my arms, something terrible happens.

It starts shrinking.

I throw off my mitts and grab it with both hands, squeezing until my knuckles hurt. I can't stop it.

The shaft grows darker as it shrinks, eventually becoming black and powdery. Now I know what it's become: a charcoal pencil. But not an ordinary one. Like the original spear-point, its tip still glows with an eerie orange light. And it's hot, as if all the energy in the full-size harpoon got concentrated into its fiery tip. I can barely hold the pencil in my shaking hands.

I look up. I've forgotten the bear. Its strange tracks led to this spot— so where is it? I'm suddenly frantic to see it, like my life depends on it.

I'll draw it, I think. I'll bring it out of hiding with my magic pencil. But what to draw on?

Snow. I squat down and try to dash off the profile of a polar bear as I have hundreds of times. The pencil is so hot all I get is slush. I try drawing on my sealskin kamiiks. *They smoke and stink and I get nothing but a dark smears. I try my caribou pants and parka. More smears and smoke.*

What else?

My skin!

I flick the pencil against the top of my hand as if striking a match. My skin burns but the pencil leaves clear marks. I decide it's worth the pain.

At first the lines are thin and distinct, like tattoo patterns I've seen on the faces of Inuit women photographed a century ago. My drawing hand blurs. The lines change from reddish orange to snow white. In the wake of my flying pencil, my skin erupts into white fur.

Polar bear fur.

I watch with a sense of relief, as if freeing some long-hidden identity lying just under my skin. I roll back my sleeve. My hand sweeps up and down my arm, creating a forest of lines that sprout more fur behind them. It slows at my fingertips, making careful strokes that turn into black curving claws.

My caribou-skin clothes get in the way. I tear them all off and fling them over the side of the iceberg. Between the warmth of my pencil and my sprouting fur, I feel protected. I take a moment to enjoy the cold air on my naked body, half girl, half bear.

The wind rises. I hurry to finish the transformation. I set to work on my other arm, my torso, my legs. As more fur emerges behind my magic pencil, I feel the bones and muscles in my body growing and shifting to adjust to the polar bear's form. After finishing my toes—now claws—I flop myself down on my furry belly and start drawing all over my back. There are a few tricky spots to reach but my pencil knows where to go and, by passing it from hand to hand—I mean, paw to paw!—I manage to cover all of my body from the neck down.

Next: my mystery face. A flash of doubt stops my hand for an instant. As I hesitantly lift the pencil to my cheeks, it slips from my fingers and falls down a narrow crack of ice.

The sound that comes out of my mouth is half scream, half roar.

The blizzard drops from the sky as quickly as it lifted. It returns with a vengeance, engulfing me in stinging snow, almost blowing me over the edge. I drop to all fours and cling to the iceberg. I shield my unfinished face from the angry wind, feeling utterly lost and defeated.

Then, through the blinding snow, I spot the crack that swallowed my pencil. I desperately peer down and see it just out of reach. With my new strength I manage to pry the crack open and touch it. With fingers I might be able to pick it up, but my claws are useless.

I heave again.

Things only get worse. The green walls of ice fracture all around me. The whole iceberg is falling apart.

I dive headfirst into the crack, hoping to grab the pencil in my teeth. Over the howl of the blizzard I hear the iceberg splitting and groaning like a sinking ship. Something crashes above me, sending chunks of green ice down the crack. The finger has fallen. The ice walls close in on me. My new body is ready to burst.

I wake up with a splitting headache and a burning pain in my chest. Before I even open my eyes, my drawing hand is still roving around, now checking my teeth for fangs and my face for a long wide muzzle.

Weather Change

WALKING JACQUES ON THE SPIT
SUNDAY, JANUARY 8TH, 12:45 P.M.

It took a few dull days and dreamless nights for me to screw my head back on after drawing myself into a bear. I could still feel the burning tip of that magic pencil against my human skin, and then . . . well, it was almost too weird—even for a dream.

I managed to whip off one half-assed sketch as soon as I'd woken up. Drawing always had a healing effect after some mega-dream turned me inside out. It was a portrait of myself—or who-ever—standing on top of the iceberg, defiant forepaws in the air with a blizzard brewing in the background. It was a view from behind, all polar bear except for the head. Long dark braids spilled down over the bear's massive shoulders. Somehow my hand could-n't bring itself to try the face.

Luckily, something came along to distract my mind from the gnawing confusion of that dream. Something very big. Another record-busting storm.

If you ever happen to drop in on Nanurtalik, you could visit the Northern Store and pick up a postcard for your grandmother that showed a bunch of kids snowboarding down the roof of a house. You can't really see the house. The only clues that tell you there's a house under there are a small tunnel carved out for the front door, a couple of power lines disappearing into the snow, and, barely visible above a giant curlicue drift, a chimney that one of the snowboarders is sitting on while waiting his turn. At the bottom of the postcard, in puffy white letters, are the words, *Nanurtalik—Blizzard Capital of North America!* Your grandmother would probably be impressed to receive such a card—that is, as long as you didn't tell her that you can buy the exact same card in Inniturliq and a bunch of other Arctic towns. All they do is change the name.

I hadn't lived in Nanurtalik long enough to tell you which town got the wildest blizzards. All I know is I'd never seen anything like this. Even the Elders said it was a freak storm. It wasn't the power of the storm that got everyone talking. Winds over sixty miles per hour were no big deal in the Arctic. What made this storm so bizarre was how long it lasted. Almost six days. Talk about cabin fever!

Don't get me wrong. I loved blizzards. They were a perfect antidote to the winter blahs that seemed to hang over this town like a suffocating shroud, slinking in through your front door, settling into every corner of your house, seeping into your very bones. Like a spreading cancer, the winter blahs infected a house or two at first, then, after a string of sunless days and moonless nights, they silently took over the whole town. The blahs fed on the droning voice of half-awake teachers, the burning itch of idle muscles, the blare of video games, the smell of empty beer bottles and secondhand smoke.

With the first whiff of a blizzard, the blahs unraveled and fled.

My first clue that a blizzard was headed our way came the day before when I casually tapped my knuckle against the barometer as I do every morning before breakfast. The needle dropped so fast and so far I thought it was going to fall off. I stepped outside. I saw thick stratus clouds stretching from above my head all the way to the northwest horizon. The clouds seemed to be fast filling with lead. There was a heaviness in the air, a strange lightness in my head.

Walking on the Spit with Jacques, I noticed a few peculiar flecks of snow falling straight down from clouds which now looked positively black. All seemed innocent enough. No tempest here. But I could tell a bomb was about to go off. I stuck out my mitt to catch a dusting of snow crystals and brought them close to my nose. The crystals were small hard pellets, rounded and packed together by some kind of turmoil overhead. A gentle, southeast breeze washed over the town, carrying with it an unreal warmth and false hopes of spring.

Circling

ON THE SEA ICE EAST OF NANURTALIK
MONDAY, JANUARY 9TH, 7:10 A.M.

You've been circling around the orange lights for almost two moons, hoping to hear that special mouth sound again.

The calling sound.

This is where it came from. Somewhere in those strange lights is at least one human, maybe more, with power like your own.

The ice is restless here and forms new cracks and ridges after every big wind. Some seals have found them but not many. You can't wait much longer. You need to find a better place to hunt. You are more restless every day.

But this is where the calling sound came from.

You can't resist any longer.

When the storm arrives, you decide to look for its source. You walk towards the lights even as they disappear in sideways snow.

Blizzard

ASHLEY'S HOUSE
MONDAY, JANUARY 9TH, 9:05 A.M.

That night, while I dreamed of tundra flowers and returning geese, the tide turned, the tantrum began. Professor Lyons, who had set up a research base here soon after Lord Gord's town hall meeting, later told me that things started going crazy around 1:00 A.M. The wind swung 180 degrees, blowing from the northwest with gusts up to seventy-five miles an hour. The temperature plunged by ten degrees every hour until it bottomed out at minus fifty-three. "And that's not counting windchill," he said.

I woke up to a wailing, scraping noise that sounded like everything around me was tearing itself apart. I must've really slept in. It was already light out, sort of. I sat bolt upright and looked out my bedside window. I discovered a world gone mad with whiteness and wind.

I pumped my fist. "*Yesss!*"

The ABC station building across the street had disappeared. Besides a couple of leaning power poles and an overturned snowmobile, I couldn't make out one sign of human civilization. It might as well have been a bad day on Pluto.

It didn't take much wind to get my bedside window whistling. The drafts never bothered me much as long as I had enough blankets to dive under. But this I'd never seen before. Every few seconds, tiny particles of ice would shoot over my bed with the velocity of bullets, whizzing through cracks between the logs. Blasts of wind slammed against the outside corner of my room like huge waves breaching against the bow of Dad's fishing boat. I felt a cold sting on my hand. I had to laugh out loud. "Some palace," I said to the four walls.

I grabbed some duct tape from my bookshelf and used half a roll to seal up the leaks around the window and the logs. I stood still and put my ear to the wall. The wind screamed and howled with an almost human sound. I took another look out the window. Through shredded veils of sideways snow I caught the shape of some large animal moving out there. I pressed my nose against the cold glass which instantly steamed up. I hurriedly wiped it clear but saw nothing more. Must have been a loose dog, probably one of Vince's rogue malamutes. A dog like that would eventually tuck into a ball with its back to the wailing wind, then promptly vanish under a thick blanket of snow. That was okay for a dog or a fox. But this was the kind of day when, without a guiding rope, you could risk your life on the way to the outhouse.

Of course I had to go outside.

Mom opened her mouth when she saw me barrel down the stairs but I ran right past her. Wearing only my polar bear pajamas and Aana's slippers, I stumbled across the street and ducked behind what was left of the giant satellite dish Vince had wrecked. My cheeks tingled as I felt the winter blahs leak out from every pore of my skin. The wind had a purging effect on me, shooing away all the shadows left over from my crazy iceberg dream. I just stood there, enjoying the blizzard, until my bare ankles went numb.

"For heaven's sake, Ash," Mom said, as I stomped back indoors with a dizzy smile on my face. "Get some clothes on!"

Without a word I grabbed a banana and fresh baked croissant off the kitchen counter and ran up to my room. I felt quite content to be alone. I didn't need to listen to the radio to know that school was cancelled. We had no tests coming up, no homework due. It seemed like a good day to go into my hermit mode and catch up on some sketching. My drawing table had been beckoning me ever since that dream. Though I couldn't yet see them clearly, I knew I had a lot more sizzling images stacked in my brain and they wanted out.

I pulled out a crisp sheet of Grumbacher number eight sketch paper and anchored it to the table with masking tape. I sharpened my best charcoal pencil, smiling at the memory of my dream pencil and its magical powers. I flicked on my full spectrum desk lamp, adjusted the angle of the drawing surface, and sat to draw.

I never knew what my hand would create. When it came to deciding on the subject matter, my brain took a back seat to my hand. Yoshi once said that starting a sketch should be like working a Ouija board. I knew exactly what she meant. My fingers felt nimble but relaxed. My pencil barely touched the paper. My wrist and arm offered no resistance to the cosmic puppeteer that moved them. I became a silent witness, waiting eagerly to see what came next.

I was hungry to draw. I wanted nothing more than to draw. And at last, as the storm raged outside, I found some quality time to sit back and watch my favorite art show.

Such were my thoughts when the power went out.

"Crap." I flicked my best charcoal pencil into a corner.

I pressed the light button on my watch. Though it was almost noon, the only daylight that filtered into my room was a pale, bluish glow. The art show would have to wait.

I did a belly flop onto my bed and closed my eyes. I could always catch up on my sleep. Maybe dreams would give me back that magic pencil and I could draw up a storm.

"Hey, Ash!" It was Gabe yelling up the stairs. I put a pillow over my head. "Rosie for ya' on line one!"

Apparently the phones still worked.

"Ash! It's Rosie for you. Rosie, Rosie! Hey, Ash!"

Gabe's world spun at a different warp speed than mine. The only French he knew was *Toute de suite! Toute de suite!* He had the frustration threshold of an ant. Watch what happens when you put your toe in its path and you'll know what I mean. It goes mental.

I heard him pounding up the stairs.

"Get in the groove, Ash, the phone's for you. There's a typhoon out there, girl. Time to pull your head out of the sand and save our troops."

Gabe never knocked. I'm not sure he knew how. I threw my pillow at him as he barged in.

"Easy now, sister. Hold your horses." He straight-armed Mom's cell phone in front of him and waved it around as if I too was blind. "It's Rosie. She sounds like all wind and piss this morning."

I grabbed the phone. "*What?*"

"Something about snow to the rafters. You might have to rescue her, Ash. Rescue her!"

Gabe slammed the door.

"Thanks, Gabe!" I yelled after him. I could hear Rosie's horsey laugh on the other end of the phone.

"You sniffing nitrous oxide again," I asked.

"What's all this talk of wind and piss?"

"Ask Gabe. Maybe he'll translate for you. What's up?"

"There's a lot of wind going to waste out there and it's time to hit the slopes."

Power or not, Rosie was not going to let me do any swoony sketches today, as she called them. She had already phoned around to a bunch of her cousins and friends and organized a blizzard walk up Heartbreak Hill. It was the same story in Inniturliq. When a winter storm hit and the school doors were locked, anyone under twenty years old exploded out onto the land to play in the wind.

Rosie called it blizz-bopping. You found a high spot, faced the wind, opened your arms, and leaned. The trick was to find that magic angle of repose where the forces of gravity and wind pressure were in perfect balance. At that point you started jumping. With a stiff wind and the right tilt of your body you soared backwards by a yard or more. Open your parka or stretch out a tarp between you and a partner and you'd double that distance. I was convinced that this was the closest thing to human-powered flight that our species had yet to invent. The only rule was that we stayed in sight of each other, which meant moving through the blinding snow like a tightly knit herd of caribou. Blizz-bopping alone would be suicidal. You could literally get blown clear out of town and they'd never find your body until spring melt. Blizz-bopping in a gang is a blast.

on thin ice

There were only four buildings on Heartbreak Hill, the ABC station, Lord Gord's double-wide trailer, another fancy trailer owned by Empire Oil—which was usually empty—and our house, Eddy's Place, parked on the hill's knobby crown. Without asking me, Rosie had told everyone that this would be today's launch pad. By the end of the phone call I'd thrown myself into the plan. Rosie always seemed to know how to kick my butt.

"Tell your mom to get something going in that woodstove of hers. We'll be over in a jiff."

"Right."

"Oh, and pull out some extra tarps. Mine blew away in the last blizzard."

A mixed flock of Toonoos, Akavaks, and Onaliks showed up at our door a half hour later. We caught some good air. Had some good laughs. Didn't break any bones. It was clean, wholesome fun for everyone.

The party ended when the shooting began.

Phantom Bear

ASHLEY'S HOUSE
MONDAY, JANUARY 9TH, 1:48 P.M.

Raymond Arseneau had never visited Eddy's Place before. He must have felt pretty bad about firing six bullets into our home, one of which made a clean bull's-eye in the east-facing picture window. Another bullet whizzed between two logs, just like the ice pellets in my room, and blew up the TV. At that moment Gabe had been watching a *Star Wars* video, *Episode V, The Empire Strikes Back*—or at least *listening* to it—and he figured the explosion was part of the show. Once the shooting stopped, Pauloosie ran outside with a pair of pliers and yanked them, one by one, out of the log wall. Then he stuck the mashed slugs from the four bullets in a bar of soap and displayed them on the coffee table.

Raymond had already called to apologize and said he would be right over to explain everything. Mom was sweeping up the last of the mess when he knocked on the door. The way she clutched that broom I thought for sure she would club him over the head with it.

As usual, Raymond was in full uniform, all buttons and badges, with his pistol and billy stick ever-ready at his side.

Mom went as far as opening the door but made no gesture to invite him in even though fingers of snow were already reaching across the kitchen floor. She must have been really steamed. Normally she would welcome a band of lepers with open arms. She leaned toward him and sniffed. "Do I detect a smoking gun?"

"Let me explain, Ms. LeBeau. I was only trying protect the community from—"

"And tell me, just who is going to protect us from *you?*"

Pauloosie trotted up beside Mom and proudly held up his slug collection. "Do you want your bullets back? Four direct hits to the side of the house."

Raymond stared at them like they were road-killed toads. "Only four, eh? All outside? Thank goodness for—"

"Hey, cowboy, tell that to my poor TV!" piped in Gabe who was rocking back and forth on the couch. "What do you think this is? Yoda's mud hut or something? We happen to like a little techno-tainment around here. So why don't you just keep your bullets to yourself! Keep 'em to yourself, cowboy! Better yet, why don't you just *stick 'em,* cowboy! Yeah, stick 'em where the sun don't shine!"

A bit of ice melted from Mom's face. "It's okay, Gabe. Moise will get you another TV from the station." She finally stepped aside for Raymond to enter. "I think you should see this, Raymond."

Raymond's jaw dropped when he saw the splintered picture window.

"Nice bulls-eye, Raymond," Mom said with her hands on her hips.

"I'm awfully sorry about this," said Raymond. Then he straightened his shoulders and cleared his throat. "Our department will of course pay for all damages." His voice always seemed to have a formal tone, as if he were talking to you on the phone back in his office with his army boots on his desk. "I admit that the blizzard may have had a disorienting effect on my aim . . ."

I heard a giggle from the table where Aana sat sipping tea. Even she found this funny. It's a good thing Dad was at the station. After what Raymond did to our house, Dad probably would have punched him in the face for saying something so stupid.

"When the target became obscured by snow, I shot high in the air. As a deterrent of course. Unfortunately I must have got turned around in the wind—"

"And our house jumped into your line of fire?" Mom said.

"It was a calculated risk," said Raymond flatly. "But the fact remains that we had a marauding polar bear in our midst and the consequences for everyone could have been much, much worse."

"A bear!" shouted Gabe. "Have you flipped your wig?"

"Did you actually *see* a bear?" I asked.

Raymond looked more intently at Mom as if she had asked the question. "Without question, it was a bear."

"Who says it wasn't a loose dog?" I said as calmly as I could. "I saw one earlier running for cover."

"Yeah!" shouted Gabe. "And isn't hunting a polar bear in a snow-storm a bit like finding a needle in a haystack? Isn't it, cowboy? Are you listening to me, *cowboy?*" Gabe was really rocking now. I went over and sat beside him so he wouldn't fall off the couch.

Raymond ignored Gabe. "Certainly the tracks were far too big to be a dog."

I wouldn't let up. "So you saw tracks. But did you see the *bear?* Like, what were you actually taking aim at?"

"As I said, I shot into the air when my view of the animal was obscured."

"You mean, into our house," said Pauloosie holding up his soap art again.

"So it's an *animal* now?" asked Mom. "Not a bear or a dog?"

"It was a polar bear, I can assure you."

"Where did you see these so-called bear tracks?" I asked.

"I first spotted them behind my house actually, while bringing my dogs indoors out of the wind. I followed them on foot to the base of your hill and that's where I spotted the bear."

Mom gestured for him to sit down at the table. "What was it doing? Where was it headed?" Mom drew Pauloosie close to her side. "Towards the kids playing on the hill?"

Raymond glanced at his watch and kept standing. "Like I say, it was difficult to tell exactly with all the blowing snow. I lost sight of it behind Gordon's place."

"So did you fill the mayor's house full of lead too?" asked Pauloosie.

Raymond shot him a tight smile that more or less said: *Why don't you go jump headfirst in a snow bank, little boy?* Then he turned back to Mom. "Today's sighting confirms what Dr. Lyons has observed ever since he set up camp here a few weeks ago."

"And that would be . . ." I said.

"That polar bears east of here are on the move, generally head-ed towards us along the coast."

Aana clicked her tongue at Raymond. "Our Elders could have saved him a lot of trouble. We knew they'd come back that way. Just a matter of time."

"With all respect," Raymond said, "whichever information source you prefer, the upshot is the same. We can't be complacent any longer about the presence of polar bears. We have to take extra precautions. Daily bear patrols. More efficient garbage handling. Restrictions on the movement of children."

"What do ya mean?" asked Pauloosie. "You gonna chain us up every time there's a bear less than a hundred miles from here?"

"Yeah, what do ya mean?" demanded Gabe. "What do ya mean, mister sharpshooter cowboy?"

Wiggins had been extra flappy ever since Raymond walked in. He couldn't resist this one. "*Wahduyah meen! Wahduyah meen! Wahduyah meen!*"

Raymond looked over his shoulder as if to make sure the door was still there. He was planning his escape.

Mom had other plans for him. "Would you like some tea? I'd like to hear more about these bear movements."

Raymond snugged down the flaps on his muskrat hat and zipped up his official Fish and Wildlife Department parka. "You might want to invite the professor over sometime and let him tell you himself. I really should get back to my office and file my report."

"Well, don't forget to include the bit about you taking pot shots at the mayor's house," shouted Gabe.

Raymond acknowledged Gabe's existence with a slight lift of his hand. "I did *not* take aim at the mayor's house. I was—"

"Oh, I *seeeee,*" Gabe said. I love the way my blind stepbrother says that word. "You were only aiming at *our* house."

"I took aim at a polar bear. A very dangerous animal to have traipsing around town."

"You mean the bear you didn't really see."

Gabe must have been a lawyer in a past life. In his more lucid moments he can speak with the tongue of a fox.

Raymond grunted. "This could well be the same bear that killed Jimmy Kikpak last Halloween."

"We don't know that it killed Jimmy," I said. "Didn't the coroner's report say he probably froze to death a long time before the bear got him?"

"Regardless, once a bear has tasted human flesh . . . well . . . we don't want to think about *that*, do we." Before putting his mitts back on, Raymond unsnapped the brass button on his pistol holster. "Thank you for your hospitality, Ms. LeBeau."

"*What* hospitality?" she said with a shrug. "You didn't even take your coat off."

I grabbed my parka from a hook by the door. There was still snow caked on it from our blizz-bopping party. I had a thing for bear tracks and wanted Raymond to show them to me. "So at least we have the tracks to prove that your bear was here. I'd really like to see them."

Raymond frowned. "Ah, I'm afraid they'd be all blown over by now," he said, as if he'd made the whole story up. "I couldn't see any sign of the bear on my way up the hill. To be honest, I couldn't see much of anything."

Mom can't stay mad for very long and made one final overture for him to stay. "Now really, Raymond. We know it was an accident." She cast a pained eye at the window. "And we know you'll fix all the damage. Nobody should be out in that blizzard alone. You talk about safety. Wouldn't it be safer to stay here for a while and wait till things lift a bit? I have some fresh croissants and—"

"I'm sorry, Ms. LeBeau—"

"It's Carole, please."

"I'm sorry . . . Carole, but we can't take any chances with that bear around. I must file my report. I'll be meeting with the Hunters and Trappers Council later this afternoon to discuss a polar bear safety program for the community."

Raymond gave a perfunctory nod to Aana, who stared blankly back, then made a quick escape. I hung up my parka and clicked the door tight behind him. With my back against the door I called out to the room at large. "Don't you find it just a little ironic? I mean, to feel so unsafe around Joe Safety himself?"

Steven

ASHLEY'S HOUSE
MONDAY, JANUARY 9TH, 8:25 P.M.

Raymond Arseneau was the first of many visitors to Eddy's Place over the next four days. Dr. Lyons and a young Inuk guy I'd never seen before dropped in soon after Raymond left. All the stories coming out of Nanurtalik about vagrant polar bears and moose, weird ice conditions and storms, had inspired Lyons to set up a research base here. Lord Gord first opposed the idea. "We already know what we need to know about the land," he told a *Tundra Times* reporter after rejecting Lyons' research application. "My people are resilient," he was quoted as saying. "We can handle anything climate change might throw at us without help from a bunch of southern scientists hoodwinked by fancy computer models that predict the end of the world."

Lyons was quoted in the same article. "My aim is to build bridges, not walls, between conventional science and

Qaujimajatuqangit—traditional Inuit knowledge. There's so much we can learn from each other about Arctic climate change. My proposed research base would provide a keystone to help build that bridge."

After several weeks of gritty negotiation, Lyons finally got approval for his base camp after promising Lord Gord that he would dish out big bucks to hire locals as research assistants and to pay for any local knowledge used in his studies. Lord Gord had a knack for pumping money into the community, even from people he didn't like. The trouble is nobody, except maybe Lord Gord, knew exactly where all the money ended up.

Lyons called his base camp the Arctic STRESS Center, STRESS being short for Scientific and Traditional knowledge Research on Environmental and Storm-related Systems. Having agreed to pay a monthly rental rate that would make even the Kiq Ass Inn look cheap, he set up shop in a corner of the warehouse down by the Spit where Jimmy and Angus had built their skateboard park. It amounted to one small laboratory, three bunk beds, and a couple of picnic tables. In a gesture of public goodwill, Lyons had even designed a logo showing an iglu with a satellite dish sticking out the top and a stressed-out polar bear drifting by on a melting ice pan. At his open house party, he handed out a bunch of free T-shirts and ball caps with the logo on it. He wore one of the caps when he paid us a visit on day one of the blizzard. He and his Inuk assistant had been out looking for polar bear tracks in the blinding snow.

"I'm not exactly sure what Officer Arseneau was shooting at," said Dr. Lyons, casting a quizzical eye at the splintered window, "but whatever it was, it left no tracks."

"Perhaps you could have a better look when the blizzard dies down tomorrow," Mom said, placing a plate of hot-buttered cheese croissants in front of him on the table.

Dr. Lyons' eyes widened at the sight of them. "Wow. I haven't seen baked treats like this since my last trip to Portland."

The Inuk stranger who sat beside him reached over and plucked a croissant off the plate. He glanced at Mom, then wolfed it down in three bites like he hadn't eaten for a week. The guy looked somehow familiar. He was about my age, maybe a little older. His face was friendly enough but he chewed everything sideways, having lost all his front teeth, which gave him a peculiar grin while he ate. He had walked in wearing a traditional, wolverine-rimmed parka with a Suluk Delta braid around the cuffs and lower hem. When Mom hung it up I'd noticed it was all stained with blood and motor oil.

"There's not a snowball's chance in hell that you'll find tracks out there!" yelled Gabe from the sidelines.

Lyons looked at the stranger like he was very curious about how he'd respond.

The guy reached for another croissant and ate it in silence. He wiped his mouth on a denim sleeve and turned to Gabe like he could see him. "Maybe so, Gabe, maybe not. Bears don't like wind any better than me or you. We might find some tracks tucked behind a rock where the snow's softer."

"How do you know Gabe?" I asked.

"I listen to KBRA sometimes," he said, still looking at Gabe. "What do you call it? Kick Butt and Rule the Arctic?"

"Yeah, something like that," Gabe said defensively.

"I can even handle fiddle music in small doses."

"No sense buttering me up along with those croissants," Gabe said as he raised his nose high in the air. One good sniff and Gabe could tell what kind of jam I was putting on my toast at forty paces. "I still think you're wasting your time looking for any old bear tracks in this hurricane," he said, searching the table with both hands.

"I'm sorry," Lyons said, placing a croissant in Gabe's hand. "I assumed everybody knew everybody around here. This is Steven Allooloo, one of my new research assistants."

"Steven Allooloo!" Mom said. She gave my hand a light tap. "Another cousin, Ash."

"Right, Mom. Him and every Inuk in the phone book."

Mom stared at Steven for a moment like he was a museum specimen. "My, my. The prodigal cousin has returned. I thought your family moved to MacPherson Harbor years ago."

Steven looked down at his empty plate and shrugged. "I move around a bit. Don't know where my folks are."

"You seem to know a lot about polar bears for someone from Nanurtalik," I said.

"I seen a few."

"I flew Steven in from Suluk River," Lyons said, giving him a cheery look. I could see they were obviously on buddy-buddy terms.

"Cappuccino, professor?" asked Mom.

"I don't believe it," Lyons said. "How could I refuse a cappuccino during a storm like this? Please, thank you."

"Steven?"

Steven tightened his lips into a thin smile and gave his head a polite shake. I don't think he knew what a cappuccino was.

"I'd heard that Steven had proven himself quite useful on a few bear hunts out of Suluk River," Lyons said. "Most of them were very traditional hunts, dog-sledding right from town and using only harpoons for the kill."

I almost choked on my croissant as my glowing dream-harpoon sprang to mind. "Harpoons?"

Steven stuck his knife into another croissant as if spearing it. "Yep," he said. "Like in the good old days."

"But I thought harpoon hunts were illegal," I said.

"Not over in Suluk," Steven said.

"So," Lyons continued, "I thought Steven would make a perfect addition to our research team."

"Besides, he's a local boy," Mom said. "Mayor Jacobs must be pleased you reeled him back home. He's been desperately trying to organize a tourist hunt out of Nanurtalik."

I knew that if any place up here was ass-deep in polar bears, as Raymond would say, it's got to be Suluk River. "So . . . why harpoon hunts?"

"Those rich guys seem to like the old-fashioned way," Steven said. "The tougher the hunt, the more they pay."

"Ass-deep in bears, eh?" I asked.

"They're all over the place," Steven said. "We don't have to go very far to get 'em. Sometimes we'll go in big circles for a while to give the tourists their money's worth. People lock their kids indoors at night. Out on the golf course—"

"A *golf course?*" asked Lyons.

"Yeah, one of them sand jobs. Surprised you never heard of it. There're so many bears around that people take a rifle when they play golf."

"Who needs a rifle?" yelled Gabe. "If they give you any lip, just club 'em over the head with a nine iron."

Steven chuckled. "They don't like to shoot 'em. Around town, I mean. It's bad for business."

"What do you mean?" Mom asked.

"Spoils the hunt," he said.

Lyons waited to see if Steven would explain but he had lost himself in a third croissant. "You see, Carole, every polar bear shot in self-defense is one less bear that tourists can harvest during the hunting season. The bear quota goes down, local guides get upset, the community loses income."

Steven pointed a jam-smeared thumb at Lyons, "Yeah. What he said."

"So what about Raymond's bear?" asked Mom, who finally sat down with a coffee for the first time today. "Do you really think he *saw* one?"

Lyons took a thoughtful sip. "Like Steven said, maybe so, maybe not. This blizzard sure isn't helping us answer that question."

Mother Nature, in her usual playful timing, chose that moment to knock out the power for the third time that day.

"Heavens!" Mom said. "Where did I put those matches?"

I thought I heard a chuckle from Steven.

As usual in these situations, Gabe came to our rescue, pulling matches out of the darkness he always lives in. Nobody was in a hurry to go anywhere—to do so was life-threatening. Professor Lyons and my supposed cousin ended up staying for caribou stew and bannock. Our bear chat carried on well into the night under the warm glow of a kerosene lamp.

"It's finally letting up," announced Mom after shining a flashlight out the bathroom window. Steven and I stuck our heads out the back door. All I could see was a light from Dad's office over at the station. He'd phoned earlier to say he would spend the night over there to keep an eye on the emergency generator.

"There's enough busted equipment over here already," he said. "A freeze up in here would shut us down for good." Dad seemed to thrive on worst-case scenarios.

Lord Gord's house stood in total darkness. The rest of the town might as well have blown away for all we could see. A few stars twinkled merrily above a flying carpet of blowing snow.

"Lousy night for golf," I said.

"In the summer we tee off at midnight," said Steven turning his face my way. I watched his eyes sweep across the stars like he was reading a book. "The tourists get a bang out of it. Stick a rifle in their golf bag. Tell 'em a few bear stories. You can make some big tips."

"All true stories?"

Steven thrust his open hand out into the wind and drew a slow circle in the air. "Maybe so. Doesn't seem to matter to them."

I glanced at his face but it had fallen into darkness. The kerosene lamp behind us painted an amber light around his shadowed form. "You going to go for it?"

"Might as well. I seen worse than this."

Steven disappeared completely as a shadow plugged the light from inside.

"What's the word, Steven?" It was Lyons. He'd made himself pretty much at home on the couch by the woodstove all evening. A tempting place to crash for the night compared to their drafty old warehouse. It wouldn't surprise me if they got there and found the roof blown off. It sounded like he was leaving this decision up to Steven.

"Looks okay to me," Steven said without turning around.

"All right then. We're off."

After they left Mom filled in a few gaps about Steven's life. It turned out he'd dropped out of school at age twelve. Kicked out actually, after lighting a roaring good bonfire under the gym. He hung out with the druggie crowd for a while, experimenting with everything from sniffing gas to snorting crack, became something of a local pusher at age thirteen, then vanished before the cops could nail him and ship him off to some reform school down south. As far as Mom was concerned, he'd fallen off the family tree until he showed up on our doorstep with the professor.

"Imagine, Dr. Lyons with three or four degrees and Steven barely finishing grade five. I wonder if the boy can read."

"He seems to have some bear smarts," I said, surprising myself at how quickly I jumped to his defense. "It's almost like Lyons depends on him."

"In more ways than one. Lord Gord has Dr. Lyons pinned under a microscope, watching his every move. Unless he hires locals like Steven, the mayor could pull the plug on his research permit in a blink and throw him out of town. On the other hand, Lyons can help Steven stay out of jail."

"So they sort of keep each other out of trouble."

"Uh-huh. Like Lyons said in the paper, they may have much to learn from each other."

Everyone else had hit the sack. Mom took another peek out the window. "Thank God, it's dying. Go to bed, Ashley. I just want to get a few more goodies in the oven."

State of Emergency

Ashley's house
Tuesday, January 10th, 11:18 a.m.

It was only a bluff. By midnight the blizzard seemed to have doubled its strength. It pounded against my bedroom all night like a big fist trying to get in. The log walls shook all through the next day. But, unlike some of our neighbors, we had food and we had heat. Despite all the driftwood lying along the shore, few people in town had woodstoves and nobody had a wood-fueled oven like Mom's. In spite of Dad's protests, she'd insisted on barging it in from Inniturliq when we moved here. The blizzard brought out the wisdom in her weirdness. Since day one of the blizzard she'd been baking almost twenty-four-seven, pulling comfort food out of that oven for a growing horde of visitors.

By day three nobody was talking much about polar bears. Dad fired up the generator at the station for everyone with portable radios. The phones still worked. But that was about it. Lord Gord had declared a state of emergency. "It will take tens of thousands of dollars to do the necessary cleanup and repairs after this storm," he announced over the air waves. "We will be entirely dependent on government funds to help us recover from this disaster since this is money we just don't have."

"Just listen to him," hooted Gabe. "You can almost hear him rubbing his hands."

Gabe had an edge to his voice that told me he was entering the first stages of cabin fever. For me, cabin fever means I develop an acute allergy to people generally and I'll go on a drawing binge in my room. For Gabe, it means hard-core shouting, breaking things, or maybe a string of seizures. "If you're sick of Lord Gord's voice," I said, "why don't go over to the station and grab the mike from his well-greased hands." That was my way of giving some air to Gabe—literally. He was a total ham on radio and there was nothing he loved more than to take over the studio for a good "jaw-wag and jam" as he called it.

"By Jiminy, that's a good idea, Ash," he yelled. "I'm going bananas in this joint. Stick your head in a hornet's nest. Let's get the show on the road!"

I bundled Gabe up as if he was setting out for the North Pole, then led him by the hand across the street to Dad's station. While the storm blew its stack, Gabe did his best to lift the town's spirits for the next two hours, with his goofy unscripted banter and plenty of old-time fiddle jigs.

After eight blackouts, a crew of sixteen power boys working double shifts had given up trying to fix the wind-shredded lines. "Thank goodness," Mom said, relighting the kerosene lamps that night. "Somebody's going to get electrocuted out there."

Every street in town was plugged solid. The town's entire fleet of snow removal vehicles was stuck in the snow. I'm talking four road-graders, six plow trucks, one bulldozer, and two front-end loaders. Of course the water truck was stuck too and people were beginning to run out of water. Rumor had it that there were twenty-foot drifts out at the runway and even bigger ones plugging mile after mile of the ice road. Somebody reported seeing a fishing boat actually *floating* near the shore where water had gushed up through fresh cracks in the storm-battered sea ice. Snow had crept down the chimneys of the town's diesel power plant and basically snuffed it out. With no road or air access there was talk of military airdrops or bulldozer trains bringing in food and emergency supplies once the blizzard let up.

In the meantime pipes were bursting all over town, including in the school which had been without power only hours into the storm. The word was that some kind of weird surge had fried its whole electrical system, including the backup generator. It could be weeks before the school would be fit for student occupation. Like I say, there's a definite up side to blizzards.

Our house had become a kind of refugee camp for people whose homes had frozen up. Rosie, Courtney, and Courtney's older sister Becca moved in with sleeping bags tucked under one arm and caribou drums under the other. "We're gonna beat this blizzard to a pulp," Rosie said as we warmed up our drums in my room. I never did ask her what shape her Pink Palace was in. I imagined the wind screaming right through that shack up on Rainbow Ridge. Warm or not, Rosie always jumped at any excuse to get out of there.

We raised a lot of hell with our drums and our whoops but failed to beat down the storm. We emerged from my room two hours later to learn that the wind was stronger than ever and that a dozen more refugees had moved in. The table was covered in cards, sewing projects, and comic books. The air was filled with town gossip, quiet laughter, and the sweet scent of wood smoke and wet dogs. *Star Wars* was back in the VCR. Mom busied herself with non-stop rounds of hot chocolate and cranberry bannock for everyone. Even Dad had come home to relax and refuel between his vigils at the station. At first I thought he was asleep the way he was draped over Gabe's couch with his ball cap pulled to his chin. Then I noticed his thumb hooked around Jacques's collar and his fingers gently stroking the sweet spot behind his floppy black ears. Such was the state of emergency in our house.

Chaos

Ashley's house
Thursday, January 12th, 7:32 a.m.

I lay in bed all night wondering which was more likely to raise the roof, the blizzard or the snoring. As soon as it felt a teeny bit like morning, I hopped out of bed without bothering to open the curtains. What was the point? The pounding on my bedroom wall told me not much had changed overnight. Rosie and her crew slept on the muskox rug covering my floor. I stepped over them on my way downstairs, wondering if they were throat singing in their dreams.

I sucked in my breath at the number of sleeping bagged forms that greeted me. They were splayed out in front of the woodstove and on just about every other flat surface in the house. I even noticed someone curled up on Uncle Jonah's floor, though he probably never knew it.

Mom was the only one awake. She had the oven fully stoked with driftwood and was rolling out a big slab of dough on the counter. She looked wrecked. Maybe it was the flour in her hair or the purple sacks under her eyes or the way she hefted the rolling pin around like it weighed twenty pounds. I leaned my elbows on the counter across from her. She still hadn't seen me. A rank halo of cigarettes leaked from her housecoat. For all her devotion to New Age health kicks and wholesome living, Mom still loved her smokes. But she rarely took a puff in sight of anyone and never, ever indoors. While everyone slept, she must have ducked outside to blow smoke rings into the storm.

"Have you been working *all night?*" I asked.

"What? Oh, Ashley. What are you doing up so early?"

"I couldn't sleep through the earthquake upstairs. What are you making now?"

"Blueberry pie."

"Blueberry pie. For breakfast. Ah . . . Mom, isn't that going a little overboard? You look half-baked yourself."

"Just let me get these into the oven. Give me a hand, would you."

She surprised me. I realized that it had been years since I last helped Mom with any baking chores. I used to be right in there with her when I was a little kid—sifting, pouring, stirring, testing. She was so damned good at it. I used to really stress out if I burned a tray of muffins or forgot the sugar in the brownies. I felt clumsy beside her and always broke things. I became known as "The Kitchen Klutz." Eventually I threw in the dish towel. My specialty in the kitchen became washing dishes.

But this morning was different. Mom was beyond burnout and we had starving refugees to feed. So I gave her a hand, working shoulder to shoulder, rolling dough and shaping it onto four big pie plates. A few toots from Gabe's harmonica told me he was awake and that he'd be craving his coffee real quick. We filled those pies with berries, popped them in the oven, put on enough coffee to supply a small army, then plunked down at the table with a tub of potatoes to peel.

"Can never have enough caribou stew around, you know," Mom said.

I heard some pounding above me, not the wind this time but Rosie and company. A few minutes later they came stomping downstairs.

Mom shook her head at them and lifted a finger to her lips.

"Storm's letting up," Rosie whispered, filling her pockets with yesterday's bannock on her way through the kitchen. "Gotta see if anyone's still alive at my house. Call me later, Ash, okay?"

"Roger."

"Thanks, Carole," Courtney said, scooping up the last of the bannock.

"Rosie's house must have been warm after all," Mom said after easing the door closed behind them.

"You really should screen your refugees more carefully before you let them in," I said.

"A little break never hurts. It's chaos over there most of the time." Mom stopped peeling and shot an anxious look at something behind me.

I turned around to see Gabe march out of his room straight for us. "Speaking of chaos," I muttered. I could tell he'd forgotten our floor was carpeted with bodies.

"Gabe, freeze!" I snapped. Too late, he'd already stepped on somebody's dog. The yelp got a few people squirming in their bags. Somebody across the room cracked a ripping fart. Gabe stood on one leg with his arms above his head like he'd been caught in a prison spotlight.

"Don't shoot," he said. "I'm unarmed!"

I grabbed his hand and we picked our way through the bodies to the table. Mom sprang up to fetch him a coffee.

Gabe whipped out his harmonica. "How about a little lullaby to put everybody back to sleep," Gabe said in his polished radio voice. He started playing "Hobo's Lullaby." I put my hand on his arm to shut him up but heard the room fill again with snoring.

"Not bad, Gabe," I said. "It worked."

He just flashed his sightless eyes at me and kept playing softly.

Mom savored her coffee with long, slow sips. Her body seemed looser and her head rolled slightly to Gabe's music. She pushed a dog-eared article clipped from the *New Age Times* towards me. She had to be the only person north of sixty who subscribed to it. Dad called it expensive fire starter.

"You want to talk about chaos," she said, "read this."

I tore into a potato with fresh gusto. "No thanks, Mom." I didn't dare encourage her.

Mom pushed the article closer. Its title: "Flapping to a better world."

I flicked a few potato peels on it.

"Ever heard of the butterfly effect?" she asked, slipping on the skinny reading glasses that always hung around her neck.

"We got enough weird insects up here already."

"The idea is that every little thing we do has an impact on our world."

"A lot of them don't belong here."

"Who doesn't belong?"

"Bugs. New ones pop up every year."

"I'm talking about the vibrations we send out into the world."

It was too early in the morning for me to even *pretend* to humor her. My bullshit alarm was already clanging. I kept peeling and played dumb. "I saw a bumblebee last summer the size of a golf ball. Weird butterflies too."

"Listen to this, Ash," Mom said, brushing my peels off her article. "'When a single butterfly in China flaps its wing, it produces a tiny change in the air around it. Though very small, this triggers a different chain of atmospheric events to unfold. Since our weather is connected in one dynamic system, this change can spread to the other side of the planet. So, a month later, a tornado devastates a town in Oklahoma—because a Chinese butterfly flapped its wing.'"

"What happens when it farts?" asked Gabe. "A tidal wave mashes Nanurtalik?"

I threw a potato peel at Gabe. For a moment it hung on his harmonica until he blindly flicked it away. The peel landed on one of the sleepers—who jerked and kicked a dog who stood up and shook which knocked over a floor lamp which fell on Mom's favorite prayer plant which tipped over and spilled soil all over the floor.

"See what I mean," Mom said in an I-told-you-so voice as she leapt for a broom. "Everything's connected."

"Every little thing, eh, Mom?" I said. "So a few puffs from your cigarette could bring London Bridge tumbling down?"

Mom was too wiped to open up the smoking thing again and dove right back into her article. "Listen to this, Ash. 'The idea of chaos theory comes from the fact that large, seemingly random systems are actually controlled by minuscule factors that can drastically change how the larger system operates—'"

"I don't know how you can believe this wacky stuff," I said, "but not that smoking will kill you."

Mom didn't even look up. "'Chaos shows up everywhere in our world, from ocean currents and tree branches to the effects of a butterfly flap on our weather—'"

"So what *does* happen when it farts?" Gabe asked again.

"'It is likely that the brain itself is organized according to the laws of chaos—'"

"That is, if it's not starved for oxygen by cigarette smoke," I said. "Did you smoke when you were pregnant with me?"

She looked up and I caught a shadow of guilt in her tired eyes. "Don't be silly," she said. "Hear me out, Ash. It gets better." She kept reading. "'Perhaps the most exciting application of chaos theory is that its central principle—that tiny influences can have gigantic consequences—applies as much to butterfly flaps as our personal thoughts, words, and actions.'"

Somehow I knew this was coming. "Like smoking?" I said flatly, trying to take the wind out of her sails. Sometimes I wondered why I was so hard on Mom. I knew that smoking was the soft underbelly in her armor of perfection. She'd stay up all night obsessing over kooky articles like this or surfing the Internet for salvation. Then she'd smoke her head off the next day to try and feel better. Nicotine and New Age schlock. Mom's addictions. Vicious vices crawled the streets of this town and I'd do whatever I could to keep them from our door.

As the sleepers shook our walls with snores, Mom pulled out another article. "Here's a perfect example of what I'm talking about: 'The Water of Life—Changing the molecular structure of water with our words, prayers, and music.'"

"Aw, come on, Mom."

"No, listen, Ash. This is really interesting.

"Yeah, Ash," Gabe said. "Give her some air time. The world's going to hell in a handcart. Time to start swimming against the current."

"'We have the power, each and everyone of us," continued Mom, "to change not only ourselves but the entire future of this beautiful planet we all share—'"

on thin ice

"You really should take up knitting, Mom. Put your energy into something concrete."

"Forget knitting," Gabe said. "Heck, you could teach her to draw, Ash. Help you wrestle some of your ghost bears onto the page."

"Like, I need help?"

Mom ignored us. "The whole point is we can make real physical changes to the world around us just with our thoughts."

"And music too?" Gabe said. "I heard you say music, didn't you? Music, Carole? *MUSIC?*"

"That too, Gabe. There's no need to shout, dear."

"Awright!"

Mom ran her finger down the page. "Some Japanese guy studied this effect. Dr. . . . ah, here it is. Dr. Masaru Emoto. A doctor of alternative medicine."

Gabe clapped. "A witch doctor! A medicine man! Bring him up here and he'll be as busy as a one-armed paperhanger."

"Forget it, Gabe," I blurted. "What you've got is incurable." I instantly wished I hadn't said that. Blind, autistic, a victim of fetal alcohol syndrome. How *dare* I say that? But Mom's New Age mumbo jumbo really had me steamed.

"The planet's sick too, Ash." Mom gestured to the window without looking up. "Our climate's sick. Dr. Emoto says we can help it. Listen to this—"

"Mom, please. You'll rot Gabe's gullible mind."

"Gullible schmullible, Ash," barked Gabe.

"Hear me out this time, Ashley. If music sends out good vibes why not your art?" Mom lowered her glasses and looked at me. "Or those lively dreams of yours?"

I looked up from the potatoes. I hadn't thought of that.

"What's gullible mean, Ash?"

"Just eat up her words, Gabe, and you'll know exactly what I mean."

"Hear me out," continued Mom. "'Using a powerful microscope in a very cold laboratory, Dr. Emoto photographed newly formed ice crystals after exposing them to different kinds of words, thoughts, and music. He discovered that water exposed to positive energy showed brilliant crystal patterns with exquisite symmetry. Water exposed to negative energy produced crystals that were lop-sided and dull. His work gives tangible expression to the truth that the vibrations from our inner world have a direct impact on the outer world around us.'"

"Sounds positively dangerous," I said.

"I don't get it," Gabe said. "What's gullible, Ash? Gullible, *GULLIBLE!*"

"Be patient, Gabe. I don't think she's done yet. Not nearly, I'm afraid."

"'Since water covers much of the planet, controls our climate, and makes up over eighty percent of our bodies, the impact of our words and thoughts can play a large part in healing our global and personal environments.'"

"You better stick to recipe books, Mom," I said. "I think your personal environment is coming undone." My mouth kept up the battle of mind over magic. But another part of me that spins my dreams and drawings seemed to sit up and listen with all ears.

Mom kept reading. "'One way to do this would be to take a rock from your local water supply and engrave positive words or images on it, then return it to the water. Based on his research, Dr. Emoto suggests 'Love and Thanks' can form the most beautiful water crystals. In controlled laboratory experiments, prayerful songs delivered over a water body created the same kinds of molecular changes in water.'"

"Awright!" exclaimed Gabe and he ran into his bedroom.

Bizarre. I had this image of some Buddhist monk singing into a wired-up fishbowl while men in white coats hovered bug-eyed over their computers.

Gabe ran into the bathroom with his fiddle. He leaned over the toilet bowl and started playing "Drowsey Maggie."

"What the—" Then it struck me what he was doing. "Hey, Gabe. You better at least lift the lid."

"Keep it down, Gabe," Mom said.

"What?" he asked. "The toilet seat?"

"The music. It's still early." Mom interrupted her New Age newscast to watch the performance. She and Dad had adopted Gabe as a toddler. When I was a baby my *tiguaq* used to hum songs to me before he could even talk. "I can think of better ways to use his musical gifts," she said.

"Gifted *and* gullible," I said.

The newscast continued. "Dr. Emoto believes that what we think has an impact on all the water locked in our atmosphere," Mom said, waving her article at me like a courtroom exhibit.

"You mean . . . like *clouds?*" I asked.

"Like whole weather systems. Stormy thoughts, stormy weather. We shouldn't be surprised that our climate is going crazy."

I gave her an overdone nod like she'd converted me. "Be careful when you flush that, Gabe," I said. "You don't want to upset any blissed-out bubbles."

Gabe leaned closer to the toilet bowl, almost poking it with his bow.

As he bent over I glanced out the bathroom window. I could actually see the sky.

"I think the storm might be finally dying," I said.

"A six-day storm, Ash? Now *that's* what I call chaos."

"I call it a blizzard."

"You want to talk about chaos," she said, pulling out another article.

"No, actually. I'd rather—"

"Then how about *this.*"

"Really, Mom. You should go to bed. You look wrecked. I can finish these spuds."

"Get this. 'Backyard astronomer, John Pugsley, from Boulder, Colorado stumbled on a huge supernova while doing a routine search for asteroids. The explosion, named 1101PX, was discovered on New Year's Day.' That's just last week, Ash!"

"What do I do with all these peels?"

"The yellow compost bucket under the sink," she said without looking up. "You really *are* lost in the kitchen."

"And you're lost in space, Mom."

She continued. "'A supernova is a large star that collapses on itself, triggering a titanic explosion powerful enough to consume whole solar systems.'" Mom looked up to see if I was listening.

I was.

"*Mon Dieu,* Ashley. Whole *solar systems!*" She pulled the article closer. "'In the case of 1101PX, the star in question was a white dwarf, a type of burned-out star—'"

"Burned-out is right, Mom. You're going to collapse too if you're not careful."

"'NASA scientists determined that the supernova was five hundred million light years away—'"

"So," I said, "the thing blew up five hundred million years ago?"

Mom took off her glasses. "Well . . . yes. I guess it took that long for the light to reach us."

"Just a harmless blast from the past," I said. "What's the big deal? We're safe, Mom. Our solar system is in no danger of vaporizing anytime soon. The sky isn't going to fall tomorrow. There're more important things to worry about." I waved my potato peeler around the room. "Like, will our sewage tank explode when all these people wake up and have to hit the john?"

Mom would not be deterred by reality. "There's more, Ash. 'NASA reports that a supernova this large has not likely been seen from Earth for the past two thousand years.'"

"Uh-huh." I smacked my lips. "Sort of like that Christmas star."

"Well . . . yes. That might be the supernova they're talking about."

"Okay." I looked over at Gabe, then broke into my off-key yodeling. "Ohh-ohh . . . Star of wonder, star of light. Star with royal beauty bright . . ." The Christmas spirit had pretty much fizzled in our house but I'd try anything to get Mom to change channels. I knew Gabe couldn't resist and he stumbled out of the bathroom to join me in the chorus. ". . . Westward leading, still proceeding, Guide us to thy perfect light."

Mom waved her finger around the room then put it to her lips. "Shhhh!"

But there was no stopping Gabe. He had perfect pitch and an incredible memory for lyrics. Once he started a song, he had to take it the bitter end. He backed up and started "We Three Kings" all over, singing every verse to the final "Alleluia!" Gabe loved any devotional ditty, as he called them. He ended with an ear-to-ear smile and a long-drawn-out "Ahh-men."

No one stirred. Most people around here slept in church.

I looked back at Mom to see her staring out the kitchen window. The clouds were blacker than black but at least there was nothing coming down. I figured we'd derailed her thought train until she spoke again.

"Those poor bears," she said.

"Huh?"

"Think of those bears."

"What do exploding stars have to do with polar bears?"

"It has *everything* to do with them, Ash. Don't you see the connection?"

"Ah . . . I must've missed it somewhere, Mom." I tried to change the subject. "You wanted these mashed, right?"

"You have to boil them first."

"Ah, right. This potato peeler sucks."

"Just hold it more sidewise. Really, Ash, whether it's a butterfly flap, or a supernova, it's all connected. Everything we think, say, or do has an impact somewhere."

"You mean, in other galaxies too, I suppose?"

She pointed out the kitchen window. "Just look at this weather, will you? Where did *this* come from? Or the Labor Day storm? And why are polar bears suddenly scratching around our back doors looking for food? It's all connected, Ash. We have to take some responsibility for these things."

A little dam burst in my brain and I didn't like where my thoughts began to flow. I had an innocent little nightmare about our town getting flooded and that's exactly what happened the next day. I dreamt about a blizzard that swallowed an iceberg and a few days later one swallowed our house. Were my inner and outer storms somehow connected?

Mom must have seen the brooding look on my face and took it as a sign of victory. "There're big changes happening all around us, Ash, and we can't ignore the roar of the waterfall that we're paddling toward. Polar bears could be the first over the brink."

"Here we go again, folks," piped in Gabe. "Up the creek without a bloody paddle!"

I thought of the Suluk River, how one day it squirmed from bank to bank like a fire hose out of control and the next it was a

on thin ice

lazy, brown snake slinking towards the sea. I thought of Crab Bay, carpeted with house-sized waves battering the shore or locked tight as a drum under six feet of ice. "Really, Mom, it's no big deal. Change is natural. It's how you read the—what do you call them?—the *signs*. Those three king dudes didn't run for the hills when they saw a little supernova two thousand years ago. They kind of . . . welcomed it, wouldn't you say?"

"But—"

"All change isn't evil, Mom. It's how you look at it. How you *adapt.*" I plunked my potato pot in the sink and started filling it with water. "Like, you could look at this blizzard as the end of the world or simply a great chance to cozy up with the neighbors."

"But think of the *pace* of change, Ash, the *kinds* of change, like nobody's ever seen before."

I noticed beads of sweat on Mom's forehead.

"This is pandemonium, I tell you," she said, pulling a cigarette out of her apron pocket. "We've entered the Great Chaos!"

Mom's old-fashioned baking timer went off with a clang.

"Saved by the bell!" shouted Gabe.

"Pie's ready, Mom," I said with equal gusto.

Mom sprang up and flipped the timer off. "Shhh, you guys. Let folks sleep."

"*PIE IS REA-DY!*" I sang out.

That did the trick. People started rolling around in their sleeping bags or sitting up and rubbing their eyes. I pulled all five pies out of the oven. The lip-smacking smell of fresh blueberry pie soon woke the rest of them. Mom finally descended to earth and made ready to care for all her needy flock.

Ajai jaa Song

ROSIE'S HOUSE

THURSDAY, JANUARY 12TH, 1:15 P.M.

Blah-blah-blah. I'd had enough soul-searching chats about how the world was about to go spinning off into another solar system or break up into mosquito-sized crumbs. All the talk about blizzards and bears, chaos and catastrophes, had shaken my brain loose. Book me a bed in the intensive care unit. I had a bad case of cabin fever. Instead of beating my head against the wall, I decided it was time to go beat the drum at Rosie's place.

The treasure Rosie had given me that morning last fall out on the tundra, calling the caribou with her invisible drum, was way better than anything we'd ever hauled home from the dump. She'd been wrong. Drumming *was* in my blood. Over the next few months, I had joined Rosie, Courtney, and Becca, practicing every Saturday afternoon, no matter what was happening in the Toonoo house. We'd even landed some gigs at school talent shows and basketball games. By December we'd become a local institution and had been asked by Lord Gord himself to perform at the community Christmas party.

Mom had declared that this was my destiny unfolding and decided to sew some outfits for us. They were red and white, designed like a traditional woman's parka complete with an *amauti* pouch in the back and a long tuxedo-like tail. Aana made us all some amazing sealskin *kamiiks* with a flock of ravens flying up the sides. We decided to crown our costumes with homemade headbands that sent rainbow beads trickling down the sides of our faces as we swayed back and forth. At first I felt like an imposter wearing this outfit in public. But after a while it felt like a second skin, something I could hide in like a custom-made Halloween costume.

We were the Dream Drummers—the name was my idea—and we were good. Rosie and her cousins let me drum. They let me dance. They even got me singing—throat singing, that is. Lucky for them throat singing had nothing to do with holding a tune. Two of us would stand facing each other, pulling nature sounds from deep in our throats—loons, geese, sled dogs, rivers, the wind. We'd go at it, eyeball to eyeball, until somebody broke up laughing. That's how it worked. It was all a blast. Most of the time.

"Oh God, not again!" yelled Rosie's father when he saw me walk through the kitchen with my drum under my arm. He was lying on the couch with a spilled beer on the floor beside him. I gave him a friendly nod on my way to Rosie's room. I never knocked when I went to Rosie's house. She advised me to just barge in and not to talk to her parents. I slammed her bedroom door behind me.

"'Bout time," she said. "I was getting a bad case of the fever."

"Me too. It's going around town."

"Let me show you something while your drum warms up."

We played modern drums made from hoops of laminated wood and stretched blue nylon. Rosie's Uncle Pete had made one for me soon after I joined the group. I propped it against the radiator as Rosie rummaged for something in her tiny closet.

"Ah, here it is," she said, pulling an old drum out of a garbage bag.

It was a traditional Inuit *qilauti,* a wide, flat drum made from driftwood and caribou skin. It was the last thing she rescued before her old house collapsed in the flood.

"*Ittuq's* drum," she said, gently stroking the brittle drumhead.

"Your rock star grandfather."

"That's the guy. It's an ancient thing. Probably a hundred years old. Sure glad we saved this from the Labor Day storm."

"Yeah, risked your life for it, is more like it," I added.

I could tell it was priceless to Rosie by the way she cradled it. A short antler handle stuck off the bottom like the stick on a giant lollipop. A thick wooden drumstick, wrapped in walrus skin, dangled over it from a piece of caribou rawhide. I stroked the drumhead. The skin was peppered with little brown welts where a bunch of warble fly larvae had burrowed into the caribou's back and hitched a ride one winter long ago. A big split now ran through the center of the skin.

"Boy, if this drum could talk," I said, almost in a whisper.

"Yeah, really. Lots of stories, eh?"

I imagined Rosie's ancestors, huddled in an iglu, grooving to the beat of that drum as it swayed back and forth in the skilled hands of her grandfather and his father or maybe his grandfather before that. Who knew how old it really was? How many songs had been danced to this drum before it fell silent? The story Rosie told was that her grandfather died while pounding the drum's last song. She said that was precisely when the skin cracked open—the moment his heart stopped. Rosie liked to believe these kinds of stories. No harm in that, I guess.

She stuck a big tack in her wall and hung the *qilauti* right beside a shocking pink poster of American Hi-Fi that featured one of their smash hits, "The Geeks Get the Girls." That was Rosie, one foot in the iglu, the other in a rock concert.

Drumming was good medicine for me. It tamed my hamster mind. It stopped time. Like Rosie promised, it could drown out the world. Next to sketching, it became my favorite thing to do. But sometimes it got out of hand. Like today.

We hadn't practiced since Christmas, and our next gig—playing for a wedding feast—was still a month away. But I needed to beat something and, like Rosie said, a drum was better than a window. That iceberg dream had cracked up my insides and, days later, I could still feel something leaking out. Something volcanic. I thought a little drumming would throw some water on whatever was brewing inside me. I was wrong. It only got worse. Much worse.

I wasn't even drumming when things went off the rails. Rosie wanted to play me her *ajai jaa* song. I'd heard about this before. In the old days, everyone had their own *ajai jaa* song, which was supposed to be as unique to a person as a fingerprint, capturing the nuggets of their life experience. I'd always thought you had to be really old before you could hear your *ajai jaa* song, let alone play it for anyone. But Rosie liked surprises. She liked gags too, but I could tell by the concentration on her face as she tightened the skin of her drum over an electric heater that this was no gag. It struck me that maybe she'd lived a lot more than I had. I asked how she learned her song.

"It came to me in a *dream,*" she said with a spooky voice and a bug-eyed face. As usual I couldn't tell if Rosie was pulling my leg. She knew damn well that I took dreams seriously—sometimes too seriously in her opinion.

I heard a thump against the wall, then shouting in the next room. Her mom and dad were at it again. To Rosie it might have been a mosquito in her ear.

"We're safe with my door closed," she said without looking up from her drum. "Nobody dares cross that line."

Rosie started beating her drum softly, like she was waking it up. I sat cross-legged on her bed and listened. The drum spoke. Rosie sang. Her body swiveled like a drunken top. I knew something was going on when my breathing got all sped up and I felt like I'd sprung an air leak out the top of my head. Something hot crept across my chest and reached inside.

I opened my eyes wide. I'd felt this before. Last November in Tuktu Hall when Tuurngaq the Ghost Man had knocked the stuffing out of me with his drum.

I dropped both hands to the bed and clutched Rosie's quilt as if to stop me from levitating. Rosie's eyes were closed. Her song rose like a loon in flight, hung in the air like a cirrus cloud, fell like spring snow, then rose again to new heights. I hardly recognized her voice.

I heard shouting from the kitchen and something crashed on the floor. Rosie played on, drowning out one world, opening another.

My fingers tightened around Rosie's quilt. Her flying drumstick struck me hard. My chest became the drumhead. With every beat, that sucking wound opened wider until I felt each breath go right through me like I wasn't even there. Like someone or something else was breathing just under my skin. I wondered if I might still be wearing the bearskin suit of my dream.

My eyes refused to open.

I must have blacked out. The next thing I knew I was face down on her bed. My face was wet like I'd been crying. Rosie played on with eyes still closed, her drumstick pounding me into pemmican. Another second in her tiny bedroom and I would have suffocated.

Without a word I flung Rosie's door open and ran through her house. Her mother was slumped over the dining room table with an empty bottle of Scotch at her elbow. She didn't even look up when I snatched my parka from the chair beside her. The outside door was wide open and a ribbon of windblown snow stretched across the kitchen floor, creating toe-high drifts around a pile of broken china. Her father was nowhere in sight. I slammed the door behind me and ran headlong into the wind, gasping for air. My chest rang with the lingering throb of Rosie's drum.

Victims

THE SPIT

THURSDAY, JANUARY 12TH, 4:25 P.M.

To try and calm the storm inside me, where else could I go but the Spit? A brisk walk on the Spit on a windy day usually drove my blues away, like flicking the dust from a doormat with a few quick shakes. But gusts of panic followed me to the very tip of the Spit, nipping at my heels, squeezing the air out of my chest, smothering my brain. I was escaping from something bigger than this town. Stepping off land onto the frozen Arctic Ocean felt a bit like walking the plank.

The blizzard's rear flank of stratus clouds hung in tatters near the eastern horizon. I turned my face to the sun but there was no hint of warmth in it. All I could hear was the hiss of shattered snow crystals streaming over the rock-hard snow. I squinted. Backlit by the late afternoon sunshine, the rivers of blowing snow looked like orange steam venting through volcanic fissures. As I plodded away from shore I saw that the sea ice had buckled in the storm creating fresh cracks so deep that water had gushed up through them creating a thick film of frozen spray.

Where the snow wasn't iced over, the blizzard had carved it into mini mountain ranges of diamond-shaped peaks and twisted valleys, all leaning towards the northwest wind. I knew there was a name for these kinds of drifts. Rosie says her grandfather *Ittuq* had different names for snowdrifts formed by winds from just about every point of the compass. He had a word for the best kind of snow to chink cracks in drafty iglus and another word for the clumps of snow that form around animal tracks blasted clean by blizzard winds. He even had different names for snow depending on the sound it makes when you step on it. Today it made a whiny squeak under my boots but don't ask me what you call it. Nobody taught me those names in school, even though I'd spent my whole life in the Arctic. I called it snow.

I hadn't thought much at all about the bear until I turned my back on the Spit. Something else had been here a few hours ago. A trail of animal tracks wove around a big snow-covered boulder beyond the Spit which the locals call Blood Rock. I could see a patch of reddish soapstone peeking out from under the snow. That color might be how the rock got its name. Or maybe because, in the summer, this was a favorite target for drunken boaters to slam into. Some of them had ended up dead.

Blotches of yellow snow all around the base of Blood Rock told me that at least one fox had trotted by recently, but I could find no prints in the hard snow. A splash of crimson just beyond the rock caught my eye. Blood. I figured a fox must have cut its paw on the glassy crust. I picked up a set of tracks leading to and from the rock made by a much heavier animal.

The wind had messed up the tracks, sculpting them into ridge-backed mounds. Here and there I caught the deep imprint of claws and figured it had to be either a polar bear or wolverine. The naturalist in me got an idea. Though the tracks were all deformed, the pattern of foot placement was still in pretty good shape. I bent over, stretched out my gloved hands and placed them in two of the prints. I planted my boots in two more tracks behind me. This was a big animal. I started to walk on all fours, locking on to the prints as I moved. First I swung my left leg forward, then, to stay true to the prints, I had to move my arm on the same side. Next I moved the right leg, followed by the right arm. With each step I had to turn my fingers and toes in to match the angle of the tracks. I was swinging my limbs much like a giant caterpillar.

I jumped out of the tracks like they were red hot. Polar bear! No other big animal moved like that. I looked out to the frozen sea, expecting to spot an iceberg on the horizon. I took a fearful look at the tracks to see if, as in my dream, I might detect a human footprint with claws. The veil between my dreams and the world of bread and butter had thinned to the breaking point. As in my latest blockbuster, my feet decided what happened next. It seemed I had no choice but to follow the polar bear tracks to see what story they could tell me.

The bear's path was patchy, the wind having smothered its tracks with snow in some spots and obliterated them in others. Wherever I lost its trail, I just kept walking in the same direction and could usually pick it up again after a few paces. The bear took a curving route along Crab Bay more or less paralleling the shore. It occasionally deked closer to town as if looking for the best way in. I found a shallow depression in some softer snow, as if the bear had sat down here to size us up. The snow on one edge of the depression was streaked red. Maybe it wasn't fox blood I'd seen after all.

At one point I lost the trail and was about to give up when I spotted something fishy behind Vince's shack.

Though I'd never seen Vince out dogsledding, he always kept a bunch of malamutes chained up down by the shore. About five of them, I thought, not counting the puppies which had been born a couple of weeks before. His malamutes had to be the scrawniest dogs in town, always yelping and whining. Vince had trouble saving money from his odd jobs. "It just slips from my fingers," he said. Guzzled down his throat is more like it. Most of the time Vince had barely enough to feed himself, let alone his dogs. But they were his only family and thanks to occasional handouts of caribou ribs or fish from his neighbors, those starving, yapping dogs were a permanent fixture of this part of town. At least, they used to be.

I heard no dogs. I saw no dogs. Just a pile of fish guts and stripped ribs behind the sheltered side of one doghouse. Today the doghouses looked different. Bigger somehow and all shiny. I took a deep breath and walked over to investigate. The ice by Vince's place had buckled even worse than by the Spit. I had to step over big chunks that had ridden up over each other like derailed train cars. The terrific stresses from the blizzard had created fresh cracks here too and it looked like a lot of seawater had gushed through. Amazing. Something the Elders claim they'd never seen before. Seawater sloshing onto the shore in January. That's what made the doghouses so weird looking. The ones closest to shore were coated with so much ice it looked like somebody had turned a fire hose on them, then walked away.

But where were Vince's dogs? Where were the puppies that Rosie and I had visited the week before? The roof of one doghouse was missing. Probably torn off by the wind, or the bear? I looked down into the plywood shell and gasped. There were the puppies, all six of them, curled together in a huddle of frozen fur. Buckets of salt-water spray had surged through the doorway and entombed them all in ice. I stared in fascination at the lifeless bodies. The sight was awful and beautiful, like the marvel of seeing ants or ladybugs locked forever in a death pose in the heart of an amber jewel.

Maybe Vince had forgotten about the puppies and gathered the rest of his four-legged family into his tiny shack to wait out the storm. But that ended hours ago and by now his dogs would be going wrangy in there. It was getting dark but I saw no light in the window. No smoke rose from his chimney—which was rimmed by a rat's nest of grimy yellow icicles. The blizzard had plastered snow against his back wall, draping it in the shape of a mermaid kissing a dead fish.

Vince was like a ghost. He could disappear for days and no one had a clue where he was. Then you'd see him down here on the shore, sitting just out of reach of his dogs, with a beer in his hand, staring out to sea. Wherever he went, though, he never took his dogs.

Had the polar bear dined on them? Poking around the other doghouses, I found no blood, no signs of a struggle, no bits and pieces of husky dog.

My toes were getting cold and my stomach was grumbling. The shadows that had chased me to the Spit had blown away and my head was clear enough for me to go home. It was a short but steep climb to Vince's shack and I kept slipping backwards on the ice-encrusted snow. After one great lunge I managed to scramble to the top of the bank. I took one last look at the dogless shore. That's when I noticed the dog chains. From up here I could see that all them had been stretched tight, away from the shore, and disappeared under the frozen bank I'd just climbed.

"No way," I said to myself. "God, no!"

Without thinking I dropped to my bum and slid back down the bank, almost cracking my skull as I smashed into an iced-up doghouse that offered all the resistance of a brick wall. I jumped up and tugged on one chain, then another. Every one was locked solid into the ice.

"Sorry, pups," I said as I wrestled a two-by-four from the frame of their roofless home. I started whacking at the spot where a chain disappeared into the ice. In no time I was panting and sweating like a rescue worker at the scene of an avalanche where every second counts. It was tough going at first but got easier once I broke through the thick outer layer of ice. Below that, the layers alternated between icy crusts and wind-packed snow, recording the shifting patterns of the blizzard's temper tantrums over the past six days. As the light failed, I tossed the stick away and started digging with my hands until I saw . . . fangs. The long, ice-coated canine teeth of a dead malamute, their length exaggerated by the dog's frozen lips which were curled back into a grotesque grin. Like the puppies, all the other dogs must have been buried alive in a quick-freezing shroud of seawater.

I turned my head away and gazed at the southwestern sky now glowing a muddy orange where the sun went down. I thought about the bear, the blizzard, the poor dogs drowned in the middle of winter. I closed my eyes. "What *is* happening here?" I said out loud.

I turned back to the dead dog, about to start hacking the rest of it out of the ice—like I was really angry at something—when I heard a rifle shot ring out.

BLAM!

My stomach clenched. The bear was back! Again I scrambled up the icy bank. I ran, ducking low through the back lanes of Nanurtalik like a commando dodging sniper fire.

BLAM! A second shot rang out. I ducked lower, almost crawling.

As I puffed up Heartbreak Hill, I stopped for a moment to take in the sight of Eddy's Place silhouetted against a sky now drained of all color except for an orange crescent moon. The blizzard had transformed our log palace into a roasted marshmallow, golden brown on one side where bare logs stuck out and creamy white on the other where snow had engulfed half the house. On the snowy side I couldn't tell where the roof ended and drifts began. The south deck had been swallowed whole and both glass doors behind it were caked in white. Tentacles of snow reached even up to my dormer window, smothering my view of the Spit.

We normally had to climb up a small flight of stairs to reach the back door. So much snow had piled up that I had to climb *down* to it through a narrow tunnel that Dad had carved out this morning. It was our only escape hatch. Mom's rowboat archway was mostly buried, along with the thorny bust of Jesus. But in the dim light I could still read the painted church plaque that hung from the bow: *He maketh the storms to cease.*

"Sure," I muttered as I turned the doorknob. It was locked.

Thunk. The tunnel fell dark as something large moved in front of the opening. The sound of labored breathing filled my ears and I could feel warm steam on my neck. A sharp jab to my back released a seismic wave of terror through my body. My heart refused to beat.

Sila's All Screwy

ASHLEY'S HOUSE
THURSDAY, JANUARY 12TH, 6:55 P.M.

"Move it, Ash, I'm freezin'."

"Pauloosie! What the—"

"Ya gotta try it, Ash. The tobogganing off the roof is awesome."

"You scared the crap out of me. Didn't you hear the gunshots? That bear is back."

"No bear's gonna find me on the roof. Come on, open it. My toes! I can't feel 'em."

I jiggled the doorknob. "It's locked. Who the hell would—"

"It's just frozen. Give the door a good bash."

I went at the door with my shoulder, once, twice, three times. "Help me, kid."

Paulooise twisted the knob while I threw myself at the door for all I was worth. It gave. We both flopped onto the entryway floor like sacks of potatoes.

I hopped up and slammed the door behind us just as another shot rang out.

BLAM!

"*Mon Dieu,* Ash!" cried Mom, running over to me with open arms. "Where were you?"

I could see by the wild look in her eyes that her nerves had already come undone. I let her hug me. I let her hold on as long as she liked. Her hand was warm on my cheek and she smelled of cinnamon. While she made soft, cooing noises in my ear, I noticed her apron was all dusted with flour. A pan of fresh baked sticky buns sat on a cooling rack beside the oven. Just hours after a freak blizzard buried most of Nanurtalik, Mom is merrily making sticky buns to cheer up her flock. God love her.

Before I could open my mouth—*BLAM!*

"Hit the deck!" yelled Mom.

"Hit the deck!" echoed Gabe. "We're under fire again, boys! Run for the trenches!"

I didn't know a blind person could run so fast, straight for the bathroom and—*Thud!*—into the empty bathtub. Maybe he thought it was bullet-proof.

Mom tried to stuff Aana and Pauloosie under the dining table. Pauloosie ended up yanking Mom off her feet on his way down. Aana, who is certainly no gymnast, sputtered some colorful Inuktitut as I tried to fold her frail body into a low squat to shield her from the bullets.

Wiggins kept opening and closing his wings as if deciding whether to fly or not.

Jacques ran several times around the dining table, doing his trampoline bounce with every step. Then he dove into our huddle, like a caribou squeezing into a herd to escape from bugs. It takes a lot to get Jacques to say anything but he started howling right in our faces, pawing the air, obviously freaked about something.

"Is *this* what you call pandemonium, Mom?" I asked.

Mom just opened her eyes even wider, then gasped, realizing that we were all crammed up against Uncle Jonah's scrawny legs.

I noticed a nasty bruise on his ankle where the skin had rolled back like wax paper on a greasy hamburger. "Uncle, get down here quick!"

I heard another shot—*BLAM!*—and jumped up to help bring him to his knees. It was like trying to move the statue of Mary in front of the church. I thought maybe his hearing aid was on the fritz again. "Get down, *Akkak!*" I yelled. "Can't you hear them? There're bullets flying all over the place again!"

He just stared into that old stained coffee cup of his like it was whispering to him. Pauloosie calls it his personal crystal ball.

BLAM!

I ducked back under the table. "You try, Mom. He won't budge!"

"Sonly dos," Jonah said, in a slurred whisper.

"*What?*" Mom and I said together.

"It's only dogs," he said without looking up. "Charlie's shootin' all his sled dogs."

I popped my head above the table even as another shot rang out.

BLAM!

"You're kidding! How could you know that?"

Uncle Jonah just nodded his head slightly and tightened his lips.

"Why would Charlie kill all his dogs?" I demanded.

"Didn't have much choice," he said. "It's gotten too risky."

"What's got too risky?" asked Mom.

BLAM!

Wiggins picked up on the boost in Mom's blood pressure. "*Awhk! Awhk! Game ovah! Game ovah!*"

"Shut up, Wiggins," she snapped.

"*Awhk! Shuh-op Wiggin!*" he shrieked while flapping up a storm. "*Shuh-op Wiggin!*"

Mom waited for the feather thwacking to die down, then asked again. "What's too risky, Uncle?"

Uncle Jonah seemed to be enjoying the attention, purposely dragging out the suspense. He started spinning his soapstone cup with one finger.

"*What,* Uncle?"

"Sleddin'," he said. "Can't take dogs over the ice no more."

BLAM!

"Do get down, Uncle!" Mom implored.

The frozen snarl of that dog by the shore rose up in my mind. "What do you mean, Akkak, about the dogs?"

"The ice lies," he muttered. "Can't trust it like we used to."

"What do you mean?"

"What's on the surface doesn't tell you how safe it is. Just can't tell any more." Uncle Jonah started fiddling with his hearing aid, causing it to whistle and wail. He was unusually talkative, all charged up by something. His eyes kept darting to the door, like he was expecting that phantom bear to come knocking.

Mom grabbed his limp arm but he shook her hand off with surprising strength. "Please, Uncle, get down," she said.

Aana clapped her hands as if summoning a house pet. "*Ai, Ikuma. Qaigit!* Come now!"

Uncle Jonah ignored her. "Can't trust the ice no more. Charlie's dogs won't touch it. Sila's all screwy. Can't even trust your eyes no more."

Jacques let fly another great howl.

"What good are dogs anyways?" he asked. He scowled at Jacques who always avoided him like the plague. "'Specially a crazy one like that. Alls you can do is burn your sled. Shoot your dogs."

"How many dogs has Charlie got these days?" asked Mom.

"Lessee," he said, staring at the living room window now taped over where Raymond's bullet went through. It was totally caked in snow. The few teeth he had looked extra long and yellow, almost like the frozen fangs on Vince's dog. His glinting eyes were stoked with fire, locked in place like they were carved out of soapstone. They didn't even twitch when the final shot rang out.

BLAM!

"Must be ten or so," Uncle Jonah said nonchalantly.

"You mean how many dogs *did* Charlie have, Mom," I said, ducking back under. "I counted ten shots."

"Seems like a silly time to put down his dogs," Mom said. "I mean, the storm's barely over."

"That storm must'a been the last straw for Charlie," said Jonah. "Who the hell heard of water comin' up through the ice like that in January?"

It seemed we all held our breaths under that table for about five minutes until Mom broke the silence. "No wonder Jacques was so upset."

Pauloosie sat up, hugging Jacques' head to his chest. "How did he know, Mom?"

"Dogs know these things, Pauloosie. Don't ask me how they know, but they know all right."

No Calling Sound

On the sea ice west of Nanurtalik
Thursday, January 12th, 6:55 p.m.

You dream of a fat seal that slips from your teeth and disappears down a breathing hole with a loud splash.

A distant crack draws you out of the dream. Then another. You remember that sound. It is dangerous. Not shifting ice. Not rocks splitting open in the cold. You feel a twinge in your stomach. A mix of hunger and fear. Your nostrils flare. The air is close and stale. You can't tell if your eyes are open or closed. You squeeze your furry eyelids shut, then fling them open. Still you see no difference in the light. You are buried in snow.

Then you remember. Walking into the storm. Moving into those strange orange lights. Listening for the calling sound. You find good smells. Fish guts. Caribou meat. Other sweet scents you've never known. Some bad scents too. Smoke, oil, plastic. Humans.

But no calling sound.

You remember hearing that same sharp crack. Lots of them. Seeing puffs of snow fly up in your face. Panicking as some stinging thing pierces your butt. Feeling fire shoot to your brain. Running blind into the sideways snow. Away from the lights, from the human smells.

Still buried in snow, you cautiously wiggle your paws. No pain. You gently flex your forelegs. Everything is all right. You ease your massive hind legs towards your chest. The fire returns. You wince and throw your head high. A heavy crust of wind-packed snow breaks open above you. Your nostrils fill with ice-cold air. Your eyes fix on a sliver of pale light near the horizon. The setting moon.

Again, you remember those smells. Those sweet scents drifting from the human place. You swing your thick neck to look over your shoulder. You see the small orange lights far away near the ground. They twinkle like stars through streams of windblown snow.

For a moment, you forget your wound and spring to a stand. Thick clods of snow fly off your fur. You let out a bellowing roar. The pain from the stinging thing burns. You collapse on your side trying to lick your wound but it is too far back. You angrily crunch and swallow your frozen blood from the snow pit where you slept.

You know you will never go back there.

It is too dangerous. Humans always mean trouble.

Except the ones with power like your own. But the calling sound has died. Did you ever really hear it?

You rise to all fours, this time very slowly. You turn your back on the human place and limp towards the moon along an unknown shore, sniffing for seals.

The Bear Shaman's Song

Part IV
Chasing the Bear

With raised harpoon,
I struggle to catch up to her,
Nanurluk's great power is too much for me.
She charges into the high mountains above the clouds,
or disappears into a misty crack of open water.

Hunting Plans

You can imagine the talk around town after Raymond thought he shot a polar bear in the January blizzard. News of the tracks I'd discovered spread like wildfire. Some believed me. Some didn't. Dad sat on the fence at first but when Lyons suggested they team up on a bear hunt, Dad jumped into the believers' camp. Dad's work at the station had been limping along at half speed since Vince totaled the big dish. Barge delivery of a new one was still months away. Dad was always looking for new ways to pay the bills and he thought maybe it was time to try out the polar bear hunting business.

Right after the blizzard, on the advice of local hunters, Lyons drew a fifty-mile circle on his helicopter survey map with Nanurtalik in the center. He'd flown most of this area over the past couple of months, looking for bears, and hadn't spotted one. But hunters on the ground had seen enough tracks and seal kills to know they were moving this way.

Lyons wanted to hunt down any nearby bears, tranquilize them, and slap on a fancy satellite transmitter so he could monitor their movements. He believed bears were trickling in from the east because unstable ice conditions had upset their usual seal hunting activities. Dad told him this matched perfectly with what the Elders had predicted years ago. High tech science and traditional Inuit knowledge were now working off the same page.

"Sometimes you've got to get out of your chopper and sniff around," Dad had told Lyons when they started kicking ideas around for a bear hunt. Over many cups of tea around our dining table, they carved out a plan—head east along the coast until they picked up any bear sign, then head north to look for open water where bears would most likely be hunting. Lyons stressed they weren't after skins, meat, or trophies. He called it a "reconnaissance hunt" to live-capture a bear for scientific purposes. Dad on the other hand wanted to do what he called "a dress rehearsal" for a real bear hunt, using sled dogs, eating only traditional foods, entertaining rich tourists, the whole bit.

As it turned out, there was a tourist in town with lots of cash in his pocket. Don Smithers was a retired banker from Texas who'd flown to Inniturliq on a whim to visit the northernmost town on the continent. When he heard about the ice road to Nanurtalik, he hopped in a rented pickup truck and drove the hundred and fifty miles to town—"because it was there," he told us later. Word spread that banker Don wanted to get out on the land and see a polar bear. This was good news for Lyons who'd just dumped a big pile of research money into helicopter pilots. He wanted Dad to organize a bear hunt. Dad wanted decent money for the job. And Don had the dollars to pull it all together.

Lord Gord almost torpedoed the whole expedition when he publicly accused Lyons of stealing work from local people and demanded a huge cut of the profits for the community's local development fund. But Dad somehow convinced him that this was a low-budget research trip that would gather useful information for real polar hunts down the road. Besides, Lyons had hired only locals, including me.

I'd been suffering from the winter blahs lately, something Mom liked to call SAD, short for "seasonal affective disorder." She said it had something to do with a shortage of natural light that screwed up people's hormone balance. One morning I came down to breakfast and she had a fancy full-spectrum lamp set up on the table for me to stare at while I ate my toast. I humored her for a couple of mornings, bugging my eyes at the lamp whenever she was in sight. Then I quietly ditched it in a dark cupboard and we both forgot about it. That wasn't the medicine I needed.

Our drumming group had been mothballed for a while, with no gigs since Christmas, and Rosie had stopped calling around for practices, probably because of mounting crap at home. My artistic well had dried up lately and my dream life had gone stale. A long string of dreamless nights would be followed by a spurt of silly sideshows as thrilling as Saturday morning cartoons. No bears starred in any of them and I felt strangely lost and alone. This bear hunt couldn't have come at a better time.

Lyons hired me as camp cook, which I thought was pretty funny considering my reputation as Kitchen Klutz. But I figured I was up to it after Mom announced she would pre-fab most of our meals. We packed some country foods like *mipku* and *maktaaq*. But Steven was big on pizza and doughnuts, so we compromised with what Mom called a twenty-first century bush menu. We ended up packing everything from apple pie to Malaysian garlic shrimp, all frozen rock hard. I was supposed to make all the meals but Mom said it would mostly be a case of *thawing* instead of cooking. That suited me fine.

Our hunting party consisted of Lyons, Dad, Don, Steven, and me, plus thirteen yelping dogs. Dad had scrounged the dogs around town after Lyons agreed to pay their owners a wage of twenty bucks a day. We had enough food for twelve days.

Mom wasn't uptight about all the school I'd miss. We both knew I'd learn way more on the land than sitting in a stuffy classroom under brain-numbing fluorescent lights. It was the ice Mom was worried about. She figured it was getting a bit "chaotic" with all our weird weather. Dad assured her he would keep me in the rear to avoid any unplanned dips in the Arctic Ocean.

I'd been out on the land around Inniturliq with Dad and Mom many times before, goose hunting, ice fishing, caribou hunting, whatever the flavor of the month was.

But I'd never been on a real bear hunt.

Cutting Loose

On the sea ice northeast of Nanurtalik
Thursday, March 23rd, 3:05 p.m.

We left Nanurtalik with the sun behind us and a spring-like breeze coming off the ice. We took off with five snowmobiles each pulling a sled. I had the lightest load and so had been given the least powerful machine, a beat-up Tundra Ski-Doo with about as much suspension as a wheelbarrow. My butt would never be the same, but I wasn't complaining.

As we turned our backs on the town and blasted off the Spit, I gulped at the cool wind rushing past me like a drowning person coming up for air. I tipped my beaver hat way back and drank in the Arctic sunshine. I breathed easier with each passing mile along the frozen shore, away from the prison walls and choking air of town. God, it felt good to cut loose! I was bear-woman shedding her fur. I imagined huge, hairy clumps of it falling onto the swirling snow behind me.

I quickly learned that job descriptions on a polar bear hunt are pretty flexible. When I wasn't on food duty, I ended up doing a lot of pushing and pulling, packing and unpacking. My other main job was to keep the sled dogs from killing each other.

The last thing we'd done before leaving town was put the thirteen dogs into Dad's sled. What a cramped ride they had, stuffed in a big plywood box with no lid. Five of them had never been towed in a sled before and at first they kept jumping out. This was definitely not a good idea given that the dogs' harnesses were tied to the bottom of the sled. I traveled behind so, as soon as I saw one go over the side, bouncing along like a sack of potatoes, I'd bomb up to Dad and report an attempted suicide. One by one, the dogs finally learned what a stupid game this was and, by the time we were about five miles out, they all stayed curled in the box on top each other—until it was time to do a number. I saw one suddenly stick its head out of the box and look around anxiously. I figured it needed to go bad but I didn't know if this was something worth bothering Dad about, so I took a wait and see approach. The dog climbed over his growling teammates to the back of the box, balanced himself very carefully with his butt over the edge, then let go right on cue. I was so fascinated by this process that I almost got smeared by the fallout. But I veered off at the last moment, sparing my windshield and parka the insult. By the looks and smell of it he must have had fish for supper the night before. Whew! And so the dogs survived.

The ride was incredibly rough. There were lots of tilted slabs of ice leaning towards the shore, most of which had been upchucked last fall as the ice formed. The thicker, sharper ones probably busted out during that freak blizzard in January. There was little relief between slabs where the surface was covered by humps of frozen spray and buckled ice. After twenty miles of this I'd developed the backside of a broncobuster. It got so rough that Lyons decided to cut north sooner than planned. For the last few miles Dad had been pointing out ribbons of smooth ice that led away from the shore. Lyons seemed more than happy to follow his advice, even though we'd seen no sign of bears.

We were headed out to nowhere with no landmarks to follow. All we knew was there should be open water ahead where seals could breathe and feed. And where there were seals there were bears—or so we hoped. We soon ran out of smooth ice and were back into the rough stuff, crawling along as we steered around chunk after chunk of ice.

By six that night, the sun had slipped below the horizon and our stomachs were grumbling. But Dad had a hunger for more miles before we camped. Far ahead, I could see huge walls of ice silhouetted against a purplish orange sky. This was the pressure ridge where Dad hoped to camp, a perfect lookout for spotting bears.

All I could do in the meantime was concentrate on the next ice chunk to avoid cracking up my snowmobile or sled. It helped keep my mind off my butt and my fear that a polar bear might leap into my path at any second. I stuck as close to Dad's sled as I could without smashing into it.

Dad had the heaviest load with all the dogs, so his wooden sled didn't do very well in the wicked ice. He got stuck more than anybody. I did what I could to help push him out but I needed a hundred more pounds and a lot more muscle to be of much use. As a paying tourist, Don wasn't supposed to lift a finger. On most polar bear hunts from other communities, tourist hunters would take a ski plane out to the base camp and avoid all the grunt work of getting out there. But Don had said he wanted to experience "the real Arctic" and didn't mind sharing the work. So, as Lyons and Steven went ahead to chop a path through the labyrinth of ice, Don was often there beside me, shoulder to shoulder, pushing Dad and his yelping dogs forward. Inch by inch, chunk by chunk, it was good, wholesome work.

We spotted our first polar bear tracks about the time I had to pee real bad. It had been over four hours since we'd left town and, after two breaks of bannock and tea, my well-jostled bladder was rebelling big time.

Steven had spotted a few clear prints in his snowmobile's headlight but couldn't put on the brakes before running over them. "All I know is they were pretty fresh," he said during yet another tea break. He took a long sip then turned to me. "And they were humongous."

I scalded my tongue with tea. "Humongous, eh?"

He nodded as he peered into the falling darkness behind me. "I've heard of bear tracks that size but never seen 'em myself."

It was getting too dark to see where the tracks led so, after packing up our thermoses, the men decided to move on.

"Wait!" I said, sounding a little too urgent.

All four of them looked at me.

"Ah, could you hang on a second? I have a . . . business appointment."

I ducked behind the nearest ice chunk, half expecting to share my outdoor bathroom with a giant bear.

Base Camp

PRESSURE RIDGE BASE CAMP
THURSDAY, MARCH 23RD, 11:48 P.M.

It was almost midnight before we reached the pressure ridge and found a patch of smooth ice big enough to set up camp. I stepped off my snowmobile and stretched my aching body from toes to fingertips. The ridge towered above me like a giant saw blade, its jagged teeth glowing green against a moonlit sky.

Time to unpack the sleds. We had hauled an entire camp on five sleds, something my ancestors did in one sled pulled by a small team of dogs. I felt somehow spoiled but glad to be born in the century I was. I had most of the light stuff like tarps, blankets, foam mattresses, and some food. Steven had the rest of the food, tents, cooking equipment, tools, folding tables, and caribou skins. Don pulled all the gas and propane in his sled. Lyons had the tent poles, bush radio, some scientific equipment, and a pile of frozen char for the dogs. And of course Dad had the dogs.

The first thing he did was free them, one dog at a time. He let them run around for a while, sniffing and peeing on unfamiliar chunks of ice. They seemed testier than ever in this new territory, constantly growling and snapping at each other. I wondered if it was because they smelled a bear but didn't say anything. Before they could rip out each other's throats, Dad strung out a long chain, anchored both ends to the ice, and tied them up. Each dog had its own measured space, but the fussing continued until Dad threw each of them a fish as a midnight snack. They shut up after that. Then we laid everything out on a big, blue tarp and went to work.

Setting up camp was another huge job. It was after 1:00 A.M., ten hours from the time we'd left town, that our canvas wall tent was up and organized and my official job as cook began. We had a nice little kitchen setup, with a two-burner stove, a Coleman lamp, and a propane heater which Steven called the microwave, since that's how we thawed most of the food. Steven helped me find just the right snow for drinking water and got things going in the kitchen for me. Soon the five of us were sitting down to steaming plates of pre-cooked chicken with a tomato-mushroom sauce and rice. We were all almost too tired to eat anything but after a couple of mouthfuls we were chowing down with as much gusto as the sled dogs. After a couple of warmed-up doughnuts, our tummies were happy and we were able to call it a night at 2:30 A.M.

Steven had set up a small dome tent for himself and disappeared after snarfing down the final doughnut. The last thing Dad did before bed was unlock his gun case, load his rifle, and prop it by the tent door. Then the four of us crashed along the back wall of our tent, with just enough room for a comfortable fit. I slept next to the wall with Dad right beside me.

It had been years since I'd spent this kind of quality time with him. He seemed like another man out here, so competent and calm. Though he still hadn't said much to me, I could tell he was glad to have me along. All his talk, weeks ago, about me putting my "artsy bears" aside and working more, and there I was, working shoulder to shoulder with him, for real money, in the heart of polar bear country. I had to chuckle as I nuzzled into my five-star sleeping bag. Lying there in a warm, protected cocoon, floating on the sea ice above an insulating cushion of caribou skins, listening to the gentle, snoring chorus of my fellow bear hunters beside me, I was happy.

Night Stalker

PRESSURE RIDGE BASE CAMP

FRIDAY, MARCH 24TH, 5:58 A.M.

I woke up a few hours later to the sound of barking dogs. Dad's sleeping bag was empty. I looked up just in time to see him duck out the tent door carrying his rifle. I heard him yell at the dogs and they clammed up right away. But something was scratching around near the other side of the tent. I could clearly make out the sound of sharp claws clicking on the ice.

"DON!" I yelled, without thinking.

Don rolled over in his sleeping bag, stopped snoring, but didn't wake.

"What is it, Ashley?" came Lyons' voice.

"There's a bear behind the tent!"

Lyons bolted upright and tipped one ear towards the back wall. I heard the cocking of a shotgun.

"Stay put!" whispered Lyons.

"DAD!" I yelled and jumped over to the door while still in my sleeping bag.

I heard Steven chuckle. Then Dad's voice. The two of them were having a moonlight chat, sounding as cool as cucumbers. A moment later, Steven stuck his head in the door. He calmly sized me up, still standing in my sleeping bag. "Where'd you ever learn to sleep like that?"

I was too wound up to say anything clever before he ducked out again.

A few minutes later Dad reappeared and quietly slipped back into his sleeping bag.

"What was it, Dad?" I had to ask.

He rolled over to face me and in the dim light I could see the whites of his eyes. "It's okay. You're safe now, Ash," he said in unusually soothing tones. "We shooed it away."

"What? What?"

He laughed. "It was a huge . . . hairy . . . white . . . Arctic fox."

Bear Lookouts

Before I even opened my eyes the next morning, my nose was twitching to the smell of cowboy coffee. Steven was first up and had whipped together a late breakfast of fried bannock, hash browns, and bacon. Before I could even pretend to help, he thrust a full plate under my nose.

"Hey, I thought that was my job," I said.

"Guess who's on dishes?"

We spent most of our second day sitting on our butts and, believe it or not, most of the third day too. We'd spotted some polar bear signs and found a high lookout point near some good seal habitat. As Dad had predicted, there was a sprawling stretch of thin, young ice about a mile beyond the ridge. Now all we had to do was wait for a bear to come waltzing into view, hitch up the dogs, and go after him. I quickly learned that hunting the great white bear was all about patience.

Dad, Don, and I took the first shift on the pressure ridge, while Steven and Lyons stayed in camp to organize the darting rifle and other scientific equipment. Lyons had big plans for our bear—tagging, satellite collaring, measuring this, sampling that—so he had lots of tools to get ready. Before making the climb, the three of us slipped white camouflage covers over our parkas which, to a bear, became instant cloaks of invisibility. It was quite the climb, almost forty feet to the top, with so many holes and pointy chunks of ice that I couldn't take my eyes off my feet for fear of breaking my leg or cracking my skull.

The view from the top of the ridge didn't surprise me: miles and miles of chunky, snow-caked ice, spreading out in all directions except to the north where the young ice lay not far away. It was like looking at the side of a huge, treeless mountain plastered in crushed white rubble. More than the view, what struck me up there was the sound: there wasn't any. No vehicles, no planes, no leaky taps, no hum of the fridge. If a polar bear sneezed a mile away, we'd hear it for sure.

We each found a roost on top of the ridge, spread out our caribou skins, and sat facing different directions to boost the odds of catching a bear in our binoculars. Nobody said much. If we could hear a bear sneeze, it would definitely hear any chatter from us. I sat way up there, sucking on sour candies and glassing around with a pair of high-powered binoculars that Lyons pulled from his box of tricks. My eyes soon wearied of staring at sunlit ice chunks and glaring snow, so I took a lot of breaks, relying more and more on wide-angle, naked-eye viewing. I saw all kinds of bears out there, even bursting out now and then with exclamations like, "There!" or "Look!" or "That's *gotta* be a bear!" But no one saw what I saw and they all chalked it up to hallucinations.

As much as I enjoyed the air, the light, and the peace, it wasn't glamorous work. I got pretty bored at one point and pulled out my sketch book. I figured this would be okay since I look at the landscape with extra sharp eyes whenever I draw. But I put it away real fast after Dad saw what I was doing and gave his head a quick shake. As chummy as we were out on the land, art, as usual, was still far off his radar.

My butt and legs kept falling asleep and, despite the caribou skin, the cold seeped into me wherever my body rested against the ice. Thank God it wasn't windy. That would have finished me off. The dogs started fighting and howling a few times and I welcomed the chance to scramble down the ridge and shut them up. It got my blood flowing again but I almost broke my neck more than once tripping over the jagged ice.

Nobody told me how long a shift would be. We must have been up there at least three hours when I saw Steven bounding up the ridge like he was skipping through a shopping mall.

"There's your bear, Don," he said coolly.

Don sprang up and glanced around. "Where? Where?"

"In your dreams," said Steven with a chuckle. "You were sleeping on the job."

Dad and Don had a good laugh over this. Steven's little joke made me realize I wouldn't settle for a dream bear out here. I wanted to see the real thing.

As Steven and I picked our way down the ridge we passed Lyons coming up. He was carrying a big spotting scope and tripod over his shoulder.

"Anything to increase our chances," Lyons said. He was breathing hard and in the cool, white sunlight he looked much grayer to me than when he first came to town last November. I wondered how long he would be running around the Arctic chasing bears. But I could see a boyish excitement in his eyes, which reflected a deep connection with bears that I could relate to.

I thawed some giant wedges of caribou pizza for lunch and delivered them to our ridge-top sentries.

"Hey, I thought we ordered Hawaiian," said Steven as I slipped a warm slice into his bare hands.

"Don't mess with the cook," I said, "or you'll be on dish duty for the rest of the trip."

We spent the next few hours playing non-stop cribbage while sipping tea and munching on Mom's famous oatmeal chocolate chip cookies. Then it was time for another shift on the ridge— equally fruitless, but I had no complaints. This pace of life suited me and just being on the polar bear's home turf was reward enough for now.

Sea Tunnel

I'm sitting alone on a pressure ridge looking for bears. My whole body is covered in caribou-skin clothing. Stuck in the ice beside me is my narwhal tusk harpoon. I'm faintly humming a song which flows out of me as easily as my breaths. Part of me finds this amusing—me, carrying a melody!—and I almost wake myself laughing.

At first the song comes in fragments but as it sharpens, so does my vision. It's like the song and my sight are somehow connected.

I spot a distant, white form whipping across the horizon. My humming quickens, and my eyes somehow zoom in on a huge, galloping polar bear. I grab my harpoon and run down the ice ridge without taking my eyes off the bear. My feet negotiate the jagged surface with miraculous ease and I realize I'm fast-tracking again.

I leave the rough ice behind me and shoot like an arrow over a vast plain of young ice. As I close the distance between us, I know I've met this bear before. It lurked in the shadows as Nanurtalik sank out of sight. It flattened the inuksuk *that was crowned with my head. It lured me to the iceberg where my skin sprouted fur. This bear has haunted me, torn me apart, almost transformed me into one of its own kind.*

With winged feet and eagle eyes I now feel ready to meet this giant, hungry for whatever challenge it might throw at me. As long as I keep that song in my heart and harpoon in my hand, I know I'll be shielded and safe.

Can this bear ever run! In a smooth, rolling gallop it flies towards a misty crack of open water. I know I must catch it before—

Too late. The giant bear stretches out its forelegs and dives into the lead like an Olympic swimmer.

I stop so fast the harpoon flies from my hand and slips into the water without a ripple.

The song dies.

I clench both fists, listening to bubbles of bear breath popping on the surface. My heartstrings stretch with an awful longing mixed with fear.

I almost turn back when I sense a dim pulsation in my inner ear. The pulses get stronger, louder, flowing together in tributaries of sound that merge into song. It erupts from my chest. The song sings me and I become the song. Pursuing the giant bear, I fall headlong through a doorway into the sea.

I've entered some kind of tunnel. I stretch out my arms and feel a strange vibration in my hands as I sink. The tunnel walls are ribbed like the windpipe of freshly butchered caribou. I move down the passageway with amazing ease. It's like I've been here before, returning home after a long journey.

All goes swimmingly—until my voice of reason declares, "Hey! You can't breathe underwater!"

The song dies again. A silent chill washes through me. The tunnel walls close in, trapping me in a net of icy tentacles.

The sensation is terribly familiar. My mind recoils at the memory of my plunge through the frosty teeth of the icehouse tunnel.

I wake up sweating in my sleeping bag. I open my eyes to see Dad wide awake and staring at me with obvious concern. I tell him it was just another crazy dream and he rolls over. Once I hear him snoring I try desperately to remember that song. Maybe it's my lousy musical ear or the terrifying end to my dream, but I just can't bring it back no matter how hard I try.

Baseball Bats

After a day of ridge duty and cribbage games, Lyons, who was used to bear hunting from helicopters, got a little antsy. So on our second morning he announced that he and Dad would take the dogs out on the young ice to look for more polar bear sign. The dogs were more than happy to go for a spin. Don chose to join the search party, leaving only Steven and me in camp.

After they left we dutifully climbed the ridge and took up our positions. An hour went by without a word until Steven turned to me with pursed lips and raised eyebrows.

"Guess what," he said.

"You're getting homesick?"

He laughed. "Don't really have a home. This is it, I guess," he said, sweeping his arm out in front of him. He sat for a while in silence, then added, "They took 'em both."

"Both what?"

"Both guns. The professor's tranquilizer thing and your Dad's rifle."

"Oh."

Our little cocoon suddenly didn't seem so safe. As this revelation sunk in, I discovered that my polar bear bravado was reserved mostly for my dreams. My mind chewed on various worst-case scenarios for the rest of the morning. I decided to raise the subject again during our lunch break when we could talk easier off the ridge. "So, what do you suggest we do if our luck changes and a bear shows up in camp?"

Steven shoveled down several steaming mouthfuls of caribou stew before answering. "Let's see," he said, enjoying the question as much as the stew. "No dogs in camp; they would'a been handy to keep him busy. No weapons." He pulled a large Buck knife from a sheath on his belt and flicked it open. "Unless you want to use this."

"You first."

"No, really. If he's coming at you, all you gotta to do is go for the face. That's their whatchimacallit, their Achilles heel. Go for the face. They really protect their face and head. Even better, if a bear twists its head around as it comes at you, smack him in the jaw or poke him in the neck. When you're used to handling a bear this way it's almost like handling a mean dog."

"You've done this?"

"Not yet. But I know hunters that have. One guy's been attacked a couple of times, but he hit him in the face and the bear backed off. Course, you don't have a chance with bare hands. If you don't have a *pana* or anything, you can always hit him in the face with a big stick or a baseball bat. He won't bother nobody after that."

"A baseball bat?" I said incredulously.

Steven took another quick gulp of stew, then walked out of the tent without a word. He came back a minute later carrying an aluminum baseball bat.

"Yeah, a baseball bat. Never leave home without it. I keep it warm in my sleeping bag."

"You sleep with a baseball bat."

"Safer than sleeping with a loaded rifle, ain't it?"

Images of man-against-bear wrestling matches swirled in my head during our next shift on the pressure ridge. I could already see the sketches I'd draw the next time I got a chance—hunters and bears circling each other like heavyweight boxers, bobbing and weaving, jabbing and blocking. The hunters that danced in my mind didn't wield Buck knives or baseball bats. They brandished a *pana* and *unaaq*—snow knife and harpoon. As much as I believed Steven about fighting bears, I had to break our watchers' silence at one point to ask why he didn't carry his own rifle.

Steven took a final drag on his rollie and flicked it off the ridge. "Let's just say it was confiscated."

"By who?"

"By someone who thought they needed it more than I did."

"I see," I said, though I really didn't.

"Some people need protection more than others."

"Huh?"

"Polar bears are smart. They treat people differently. Some people scare them. Others don't. They're the ones they'll attack."

"So . . . which are you?"

"They haven't bothered me yet."

"And you've seen a lot of bears?"

"Lots."

"And they don't scare you?"

"What's the point?"

"Of what?"

"Fear. Respect them, yes. But fear can get in the way. After going hunting with this one tourist, I saw that some people have a lot more to be scared about than me."

"What happened?"

"Me and my uncle took this New York hunter out from Suluk River. We'd gone scouting with the dogs and came back to camp to find all his stuff torn up by a bear."

"What kind of stuff?"

"His boots, sleeping bag, extra clothes. The bear hardly touched anything else."

"Could that have been a fluke?"

"I might'a thought so until we saw the bear a few minutes later. My uncle's rifle was still hooked on his Ski-Doo and the bear was coming back to camp real fast. He gunned it straight for the New Yorker, no question. So my uncle ran right up to that bear and hit him in the face."

"With a baseball bat?"

"What else? That's where I got the idea."

"And the bear took off?"

"Like a racehorse."

"And the New Yorker?"

"He had to change his pants pretty quick. Except the bear had ripped them up. So I gave him a pair of my jeans." Steven pushed back his muskrat hat and resumed scanning the ice for bears. "Never got 'em back, come to think of it. But the guy tipped us good. Real good."

Hateful Animals

OPEN WATER LEAD NORTH OF BASE CAMP
MONDAY, MARCH 27TH, 2:09 P.M.

Your hind legs trail behind you as you paddle down the middle of an open lead, hunting for seals. Your nose tells you one is near but you haven't spotted it yet. As the scent gets stronger, you lower your head in the water. Just your eyes and muzzle break the surface.

There it is, lying close to the water's edge. A nice, fat seal asleep in the spring sun. Its snores make your heart race and saliva pours into your mouth. You submerge completely. You slowly scull forward, keeping the seal's dark form in view while underwater. You swim within inches of the ice, then explode out of the water in one giant leap.

The startled seal turns in time to look you in the eye and give one frightful yowl. Its body instantly surrenders as you crush the life out of it with one mighty bite to its neck.

Your mouth delights to the satisfying tang of fresh blood. You flip your catch over on its back, cock one claw under its soft chin, then slit the seal open with one quick slash. The snow flushes red as you rip off a mouthful of succulent meat. It is sweet and tender. For you this is the taste of life.

You step on its head and start peeling back the skin and blubber. You eat this first, making satisfied grunts as you chew. As you start crunching into its flesh and bones, you stop in mid-chew and abruptly lift your head.

What is that sound?

Could it be wolves?

Not out here. Too far from land.

A bloody chunk of meat drops from your mouth as you spring up on your hind legs. You hear the yelping and barking of many animals. It is too low and rough to be foxes. You draw in a deep breath through your nose. Though you can't smell them or see them yet, you know what it must be.

Dogs.

You've seen them only a few times in your long life. Been chased by them twice. Eaten them once.

You despise dogs.

Without another glance at your prize, you fall to all fours and gallop away from the rising chorus of hateful animals.

Bad News

It was almost dark by the time the men got back to camp. I was getting worried and had convinced Steven to fire off a couple of red emergency flares in case they were looking for us.

"What's with the fireworks?" asked Dad once he got the dogs settled and fed.

"Ashley's idea," Steven said. "Thought she'd leave a candle burning in the window for you."

"Where *were* you, Dad?" I asked, feeling more angry than worried.

"Good news," he said. "Tons of tracks about fifteen miles due north. And a nice juicy lead for seals and bears to play in."

"*Big* tracks," Lyons said. "We even found a fresh seal kill. Only half eaten for some reason. We'll head out first thing in the morning."

Lyons looked tired but happy. He was on the trail of his beloved bears and would likely bag one tomorrow.

"Bad news," said Steven who stood with his arms folded, watching the full moon rise like a giant pumpkin over the ice. "Big north wind coming."

The rest of us looked mutely at the starlit sky, dappled green and yellow with the night's first northern lights. The heavens looked pretty stable to me.

"This moon won't help much either," Steven added.

"How come?" I asked, feeling more comfortable with Steven, having spent the day with him.

"My uncle used to tell us not to hunt bears right after the full moon."

"Why not, Steven?" asked Lyons.

"He never did tell me," said Steven as he lit up a rollie. He blew a smoke ring at the moon. "Maybe we'll find out tomorrow."

Surprise Attack

PRESSURE RIDGE BASE CAMP
TUESDAY, MARCH 28TH, 9:45 A.M.

It all happened so fast.

We'd woken early to the sound of big fists of wind pounding the north wall of our tent, just like Steven predicted. Nobody had slept much and we had a "quick and dirty breakfast," as Steven called it. I had insisted on making breakfast this morning but later regretted it. My supposed corned beef hash was either burned or barely thawed. The potatoes were one notch above raw, the coffee polluted with grinds.

"Keep trying," is all Dad said as he picked some charred beef from his teeth.

"There won't be much for those bears to chew on if you keep this up," Steven said with a grin as he pinched his lean belly.

I tried to put a simple lunch together but all I found was some caribou jerky and a few sorry looking doughnuts for lunch.

We pushed off with the dogs under sunny skies but a rising wind.

I was amazed at the strength of the dogs pulling all five of us on one sled. Steven and Lyons sat up front on a slab of plywood laid across the sled. Don and I squeezed in the empty grub box and Dad stood behind the backrest ready to toss out the anchor hook whenever we were about to crash into a big ice block. The dogs seemed especially snarly that morning, leap-frogging over each other and getting all tangled up. When the going got really tight or the sled pointed mostly to the sky, Steven and I would jump out and run along beside the sled, ready to push or pull our hearts out as needed. In spite of the biting wind in our faces, it was tough, sweaty work. It took us almost three hours before we finally broke out of the rough stuff onto a smooth open patch of young ice.

The sled tracks from the day before had been obliterated by the wind, but Dad was a skilled dog handler and his loud commands steered them directly to the lead in no time. Everyone piled out. Dad pulled the grub box and gear off the sled to make a temporary camp. Steven led the dogs well away from the open water so they wouldn't sink the sled if another riot broke out.

"Amazing, Moise," Lyons said pointing to a large snowdrift right beside the open water. "You nailed it."

"Surprised?" said Dad without looking up.

I turned to see what Lyons was pointing at, half expecting to see a polar bear. A bloody splotch was barely visible by the upwind tip of the drift. Lyons kicked at the snow to reveal the half-eaten carcass of a ringed seal. "This is the kill we found yesterday. Strange that a bear wouldn't finish him off." Lyons fiddled with his beard while surveying the ribbon of open water. "This lead's a lot narrower than yesterday wouldn't you say, Moise?"

"With this wind it could close up pretty quick," Dad said.

"Look," I said. "You can actually see it moving." The floe ice on the north side of the lead was much older and thicker than what we were standing on. It was moving straight for us.

"You're right, Ash," Dad said. "Could cause quite a ruckus when it closes up."

"How's that?" I asked.

"The power behind a moving ice floe like that is awesome, even if it's moving slowly. When it smacks into this young ice it'll turn it into tin foil."

The dogs started going crazy for some reason, growling and barking and going for each other's throats.

Dad spoke to the professor with a new tone of urgency in his voice. "How be I dig out the rifle and your dart gun so we can be ready if a bear shows up. Maybe you could help Steven settle the dogs. We shouldn't stick around here too long." Though this was a jointly planned trip, Dad was clearly in charge for now. He turned to Don and me. "And you guys keep your eyes peeled for large white mammals with claws."

"Right," I said.

Don and I stood beside the seal carcass automatically gazing off in different directions as we had for so many hours on the pressure ridge. I missed having a high perch overlooking this ice-scape and felt suddenly vulnerable out here in a way I never had before.

Given the lousy sleep we'd had and the work of getting here, neither of us stayed vigilant for long. Don had turned his face from the wind and seemed lost in his view of the setting full moon. I became distracted by the steadily dwindling lead. The deep, dark water seemed to swallow all light. I felt like I had walked into my dream from two nights ago. I even tried to remember that tune I'd been humming but all I got was static. I couldn't hear myself think above the incessant yelping of the dogs and the rush of wind against my parka hood. All I was aware of was the black water at my feet and this odd prickly sensation taking hold of my spine.

"Did y'all feel that?" asked Don out of the blue.

I pulled my parka hood back and looked at him sideways. He was still gazing at the moon but with a quizzical look in his eyes.

"Feel what?" I asked.

"Some kind'a tremor in the ice."

I instantly became aware of a drum-like vibration coming up through my boots, almost like the footfalls of a running animal. I looked up and down the lead. It seemed to be closing faster now. The wind was stronger than ever. "Must be the ice banging somewhere down the line."

"You just might be right," said Don, appearing to relax. "From what the professor was sayin' I guess we can expect a good fender bender pretty soon." Don turned to face me. "Don't you think we ought'a—"

Don's ruddy cheeks went pale and his mouth hung open like he'd turned to stone. I knew right away what he'd seen.

"Bear!" shouted Steven.

I turned to see a polar bear running straight for Dad. If I'd just walked into my dream, this bear had just run out of it. It was huge, galloping at full tilt with its head up and ears back.

"DAD!" I yelled.

He'd taken cover behind the grub box—as if a half inch of plywood was going to save him from those massive teeth and raking claws! He had a rifle in his lap and was struggling to load it. My eyes clamped onto the gun case which lay at his feet. The padlock was still firmly attached. Dad was clutching Lyons' dart gun, one of the few kinds of rifles he'd never fired before in his life.

I watched helplessly as he lifted his head above the flimsy box, took one look at the charging bear, then stood up tall. He grabbed the gun by its barrel and started swinging it threateningly in front of him.

"In the face, Dad!" I yelled. "Bop him in the face!"

The chaos of yelping behind me suddenly stopped as a blur of dogs tore past us straight for the bear. Steven had cut them loose. They circled the roaring bear like a pack of wolves, trying to nip at its heels while doing their best to dodge its flying claws. The bear stood up, snarled and slashed at the dogs, then bounded forward a few steps. It did this over and over without veering from its chosen prey which clearly seemed to be Dad. The bear managed to club one dog in the head, breaking its neck with one powerful blow. The dogs moved back from the limp body, giving the bear a chance to make its final lunge towards Dad.

Dad bravely raised the butt of the rifle above his head—and watched the bear run right past him. With one final roar, the great bear dove into a fast-shrinking sliver of water and disappeared in a storm of bubbles and foam.

Dad spun around so fast that he tripped on his gun case and fell into the water after the bear. The dart gun flew out of his hands and sank out of sight.

The dogs lined up along the ice edge barking in Dad's face. "Shut up!" he yelled even as he struggled to keep his head above water. That bear seemed to have something out for him and I wondered how long it would be before it returned to claim his prize. Dad's waterlogged parka must've weighed a ton and I knew swimming wasn't his forte, especially in ice water.

"Hang on, Dad!" I yelled. I kicked the dogs out of the way, so hard that two of them ended up in the lead clawing the water by Dad's face. I heard a yelp beside me as Lyons cleared a dog-free space, then lay down on the ice with both arms out to Dad.

"Just another foot," groaned Lyons.

I could see fear sweep over Dad's face as he flailed his arms towards Lyons. I kept looking beside him for a huge, white form that I knew had to surface at any second. Meanwhile the floe ice behind him seemed to be closing fast on his head.

"Wait! Don't go away!" I yelled as I sprang up and grabbed Dad's gun case. I shoved it into Lyons' hands. "Use this," I said.

"Sit on my legs!" ordered Lyons.

"*What?*" I said.

"My legs! Sit on them!" Lyons strained every inch of his arms as he thrust the heavy gun case towards Dad. He would have fallen in for sure if Don and I hadn't plunked ourselves down on his skinny legs. The dogs kept barking all around us. *Where's Steven?* I thought. I craned my neck around to see him pacing the ice edge as he scanned the water for a rising bear. He held a baseball bat over his shoulder like he was waiting for a pitch. I would have laughed out loud in any other circumstances.

There was no sign of the bear, but the lead was disappearing before our eyes—with Dad still in it. His head went under just as his mitt made contact with the gun case. Lyons made a great lunge forward and caught Dad's hand while letting the gun case go. It too sank out of sight. No tranquilizer gun. No rifle. With a polar bear swimming around somewhere just below our feet.

Above the barking dogs I could hear a new sound of ice against ice. The surface beneath us started trembling like Jello as shock waves from nearby collisions raced through it. Lyons struggled to haul Dad out of the water. I felt him slipping forward and it began to feel more like Dad was hauling Lyons in.

"Steven!" I shouted. Lyons was sliding out from under us. The ice floe was already scraping against Dad's back.

In the end it took all four of us to haul Dad out of the water. Before we could flop him onto the ice, the lead closed completely with his foot still in it. Luckily the young ice buckled and popped, spitting his foot out like a gnawed peach pit.

It could have been worse. Much worse. We saved Dad from hypothermia by getting him in dry clothes and tucked into three sleeping bags. We saved the sled and extra gear by dragging it all behind us as we ran like hell from the exploding ice. We lost one dog, one bear and both guns.

Once we were at a safe distance and the remaining dogs were hitched up, Lyons checked on Dad one last time before heading back to our base camp. "You lost my gun, I lost yours," he said. "I guess we're even, partner."

Dad just smiled weakly and gave him two thumbs up.

"We still have a baseball bat," I said, grinning at Steven. "Just in case."

Hunkering Down

Pressure ridge base camp
Tuesday, March 28th, 2:15 p.m.

"Well, that was quite the adventure," Lyons said after we finally got settled back at camp.

Steven held out his empty cup to Lyons who filled it to the brim with hot coffee. "Not quite mission accomplished, eh, professor?"

"At least we've confirmed the bears are coming back to this region."

"At least one bear," Steven said.

"One *hell* of a big one," Don added.

"What I find most scientifically interesting," Lyons mused, "is how long that bear stayed underwater. Polar bears are not known to hold their breath for longer than two minutes."

"Maybe that bear hasn't read the same textbooks as you," Steven suggested.

The professor laughed. "Perhaps not. But we couldn't have missed him rising in that shrinking lead."

"We were kinda busy," Steven said.

"True, but once the ice closed behind Moise there was no visible means for that bear to escape. It's not improbable that it may have drowned."

"Bears are unpredictable," Steven said.

Lyons laid a hand on Steven's shoulder. "You know, after studying them for thirty-five years, that's the only thing about these bears that I'm certain of."

Lyons pulled out his notebook and scribbled away for a few minutes, then closed it with a decisive slap. "So, what would you say, gents," he turned to me like he almost forgot, "—*and* fair lady—about hitting the road?"

"This afternoon?" I said.

"What's the rush?" Steven asked. He was casually rolling yet another cigarette.

"No rush, really," Lyons said. "It's just that I thought a doctor should look at Moise's ankle as soon as possible and I have a conference call scheduled for the day after tomorrow."

"Don't worry about me," Dad said, hobbling over to the stove for more coffee. "And anyways, I thought we scheduled twelve days for this hunt."

"True, this phone call can proceed without me. But I thought if we covered some ground today we might—"

"What's that old saying?" Steven interrupted. "White men have the watches, we have the time."

That slowed Lyons down a notch and he smiled at Steven, almost like a proud father. He watched him in silence as he folded the cigarette paper around a tidy wad of tobacco with the same care that one might pack a bullet casing. "You told me you quit smoking."

"Yep," Steven said, firing the finished cigarette between his lips. "That was yesterday."

I stood up and hovered near the tent door. My asthma couldn't handle another one of Steven's rollies. "Would you mind quitting today *too?* I really am allergic to smoke."

With an extremely pained look on his face, Steven tucked the cigarette behind his ear. "All right. You take pity on me and I'll take pity on you."

"Besides," Lyons said revving up again. "It really is time we started packing up."

"No point in that," said Steven casually.

Lyons had already started dismantling the propane heater. "Pardon?"

"Whiteout's coming. Time to hunker down."

Lyons gave him a blank look and walked over to the tent door. We both stuck our heads out to have a peek at the weather. A sideways cylinder of dark clouds was rolling down on us from the north. In front of it, about as high as our cook tent, was a churning wall of kicked up snow. Lyons leaned back into the tent and stared at Steven incredulously.

"It's the oldest story in the book," said Steven without looking up. "People push the limit against crappy weather 'cause they have a bad case of hurry sickness. Then, *poof,* they disappear. Specially these days when the weather's so wonky."

Lyons sat down across from him. "We've been out here four days and you've *nailed* the weather every single day. How do you do it?"

"It's easy," said Steven with his typically straight face. "I just walk over to my tent and listen to the seven o'clock forecast on *KBRA.*"

Nanurluk

There was nothing to do but wait. We had tons of food and fuel, a sturdy shelter against the wind, a Coleman lamp that more or less worked, and dry sleeping bags. What more could you want in a whiteout? Dad and Don played cards on the folding plastic picnic table while Lyons, Steven, and I sat around the card table sipping hot chocolate and shooting the bull. Steven seemed more talkative than usual as he idly sharpened his Buck knife on a whetstone. I was full of questions about polar bear hunts.

"So this must be, what, your twentieth bear hunt?" I asked Steven. "Your hundredth maybe?"

"Yeah, that'd be about right," he said.

"So what makes all these guys fork out twenty grand to shoot a bear?"

"It's an act of God," said Don, who I'd thought wasn't listening.

"You're different, Don," I said.

"Like some fishermen, I s'pose," said Don. "If they don't catch a fish, the world doesn't end. It's all about getting out on the land. We saw the backside of a wild polar bear. I drove myself over that ice garden a few days back. We've seen some mind-blowing northern lights. A good catch so far, I'd say. I really came to get my feet wet in the Arctic."

Dad threw a marshmallow at Don. "I didn't see you swimming yesterday."

"I didn't see that in the brochure," Don said, ducking his head.

"You're a freak, Don," said Steven, chuckling. "I seen all kinds of big, white hunters from all over the world. For most of them it's some kind of crazy mind game, to fly up here and bag a bear come hell or high water. They take a skin home, then hang it on their living room wall. They don't even use it for a rug or nothing. Pretty pricey wall hanging if you ask me."

"Do they ever talk about their hunts in other places," I asked, "like Botswana or Borneo?"

"Some do. Rhinos, tigers, elephants. It sounds too easy. All you gotta do is drive up to them in a jeep and blast away. The worst that can happen over there is they don't get their animal. Here you die."

"What are you most afraid of out here?"

Steven stopped sharpening his knife "Who's sayin' I'm afraid?"

"I mean, you must have had some close calls in all those hunts you've been on. Even closer than this morning."

Steven looked at me with a sudden terror in his eyes and his knife raised in self-defense. He looked downright ghoulish in the flickering lamplight. "I been scared all right. *Freakin'* scared!" He slowly leaned across the card table towards me. "That I wouldn't get paid!" He flopped back against his chair. "It's just a job. Keeps me out of trouble, eh, professor?"

Lyons gave him a friendly nod. "That's for sure."

"But you wouldn't catch me hunting elephants. No way. Too big. My snow machine couldn't hack it. And besides, where're you gonna stash all that meat?"

"So, what's the biggest bear you've seen?" I asked.

Steven shifted in his chair and glanced at Lyons who sat with his hands folded loosely across his stomach. He'd slowed right down and seemed to be enjoying Steven's stories.

"I've seen a few bears over a thousand pounds. Like that one today probably. A couple broke nine feet. But nothing like a *Nanurluk.*"

Lyons unfolded his hands and placed them on the arms of his lawn chair. Dad looked up from his cards. Steven spit on the whetstone and scraped his knife blade over it.

"Nanwhat?" I said.

"*Nanurluk.* Ain't you never heard of them when you were a kid?"

"Rings a faint bell," I said, feeling a tiny door in my childhood memory bank creaking open.

"There's an old guy I met in Suluk River who says he's seen one, a couple maybe."

"Who was that, Steven?" asked Lyons as he pulled a pen and notepad out of his down vest.

"One of the Jaypetee brothers. Billy, I think it was. I know his house. I'll take you there next time we're in Suluk."

"I'd like that, Steven."

Don and Dad lay their cards down and pulled their chairs up to our table.

"How big did he say this bear was?" asked Dad.

"Maybe ten feet tall. Maybe twelve. I don't know. He just called it a giant."

"Did he ever catch one?" asked Don.

"They're supposed to be pretty slippery. Billy said nothing about catching one himself, but he told me a story about some guy seeing a giant bear lying on the bottom of the sea. Sleeping or something. He could see it through some thin ice and figured it was a *Nanurluk.* Huge. He hurried back to his iglu and dumped loose snow and water all over it, to stiffen it up in case the bear followed him home. Then he grabbed his harpoon and went after him. He tried to sneak up on the bear but the sun was behind the hunter and his shadow woke it up." Steven paused to test the knife edge against his thumb. "Getting there."

"And . . ." I said, having been totally sucked into his story.

"Seems this giant bear had a breathing hole, just like a seal. When it saw the man's shadow it started biting and scratching away at the ice like he was gonna tear it open. When the hole was big enough to push its head through, the hunter stuck his knife in the bear's eyes and cut off its nose."

"Can't see, can't smell," said Don. "That's one dead bear."

"Hang on," Steven said. "Blood spouted out of the bear's nose all over the place. So much blood that the hunter got scared and ran back to his iglu to hide. He waited for a long time but the bear didn't show up so he hitched up his dogs and went back to see what happened." Steven held up his knife and tested it again. "Almost," he said and stroked the blade against the stone, slower than ever.

With his head bent low and face in shadow, Steven could have been an old man. My spine tingled. Somehow I knew in my guts that I was hearing a story that was thousands of years old. The only sounds were the grinding of metal on stone, the broken hiss of the Coleman lamp, and the wind pounding on the north side of our wall tent.

I was about to prod Steven again when Don jumped in ahead of me. "Okay, so the hunter sneaks up on the wounded bear and—"

"Toast."

"Who?" asked Don and I together.

"The giant bear. The guy actually killed a *Nanurluk*. Can you believe it?"

From the change in Steven's voice I got the feeling that at least *he* believed it.

"What about the giant bear sleeping underwater?" I asked. "Do you believe that bit?"

"They hardly ever leave the water. They dive deeper than normal bears, right to the bottom. And they can run like hell. They'll swallow you whole if they catch you."

Now Steven was a little boy. He wasn't telling Billy's story anymore. He was telling us about *Nanurluit* like he'd just been sitting on someone's knee and heard it all fresh. Like the story itself had brought them alive. For Steven these enormous, magical polar bears were real.

For Don too, apparently. "So what happened to the giant?" he asked.

"The hunter found it lying dead on the ice, half out of the water. He tied a caribou rope around it and tried dragging it with his dogs but it was too heavy. So he skinned it right there and just took half the skin home and only about a quarter of the meat. That was all he could carry. That's how big this sucker was. The hunter lived on that bear meat for the rest of the winter. That's the way Billy tells it anyway."

Dad settled back in his chair and pushed his ball cap back. He seemed deep in thought, something he never has time for in town. "Did Billy ever say anything to you about the connection between *Nanurluit* and shamans?"

"Like, medicine power and all that?"

"Yeah."

"I remember him saying that if someone manages to kill a *Nanurluk*, its spirit moves into the harpoon for a few days."

I shivered as images of my glowing dream harpoon popped into my head.

"You don't want to mess with the bear's spirit when it's hanging around in that harpoon 'cause any little thing you might do or say, even *think*, that ticks off the bear and you're dead meat. So they used to call in the shaman to keep an eye on the hunter's family and make sure everybody followed all these fancy rules."

"Like what?" I asked, feeling suddenly breathless.

"I don't know, like standing the dead bear on its back feet, propping its mouth open with a stick, storing your weapons near the body, that kinda' stuff."

My brain went on red alert, struggling to hotwire a connection in the tangled pathways of my memory.

Steven looked up from his knife for a moment and stared out the flapping tent door. "Billy said something else about shamans. They kind of needed each other."

Lyons pushed his gold-rimmed glasses up the bridge of his nose. "Who, Steven?"

"Them and the *Nanurluit*. The bears helped the shamans do shaman stuff. The shamans helped the bears do bear stuff. Billy said sometimes they'd even trade places." Steven glanced at Lyons like maybe he'd said too much. "What the hell do I know? You could go ask Billy yourself next time we're in Suluk River."

Lyons nodded and started scribbling in his little notebook.

Steven gave his knife a final thumb test. I saw a tiny ribbon of blood race behind the blade.

"Ouch," he said, giving his thumb a lick. "I guess it's ready."

"For what?" I asked, trying to sound like I was joking.

He slipped the knife into his belt sheath. "You never know out here," he said, poker-faced as always.

Then it hit me. I remembered the giant ice-bear. Someone had stored a *Nanurluk* deep beneath the town. Someone who knew the shaman's rules and played them well.

The Bear Shaman's Song

Part V
Calling for Strength

I stagger and fall.
Nanurluk has stolen my power.
Ai! Ai! I call for strength.
My mind grows dizzy
As I stretch my limbs out on the ice.
While my teeth chatter
And eyes close,
I wonder—
Whose blood is this on the snow?

Nanurluk's Face

I can't do this. I can't write about this dream. I wouldn't dare sketch it.
Maybe later.

All I'll say is the sea tunnel ends. Can slow down by pressing against
the walls with my elbows and knees. Brightens up and widens near the
end. Big bright space. Can swim in it. Feels good. Like flying.
Happy.
Then something swims up from deep below me.
Nanurluk!
Chomps on my hand. My drawing hand.
Hauls me down.
I see her true face. Horrible! HORRIBLE!
All fangs and blood. . . .
I can't do this.
Not now.

Crazy Bear

Long after settling back home from our hunting trip, a giant polar
bear still chased me, night and day. My artist's fingers had taken off
on their own again, this time while I sat by the kitchen counter

talking to Rosie on the phone. She'd called about some ridiculous math problem, but my fingers were struggling with another, let's say, more gripping subject.

I wasn't even aware that I'd been doodling until I heard a gruff chuckle over my shoulder and turned to see Uncle Jonah staring down at my frantic scribbles. I slapped my hand over the drawing like he'd caught me writing a poison-pen letter. His coal-black eyes seemed bigger than ever behind his thick, square glasses. "Crazy bear," he said. "Lucky you."

"*Lucky?* What do you mean?"

Aana was bringing Uncle Jonah a fresh pot of tea from the kitchen and nudged him towards the table so she could see what had captured his attention.

"Show me, Ash," she said, pulling my hand away. Her grip on my hand tightened when she saw my scribbled nightmare. With a half-chewed, red pencil crayon I happened to find beside the phone, I'd drawn a female polar bear with blood-drenched fangs, raking claws, and a hideous, mocking grin. She wore a garland of freshly cut human heads and stood victoriously on a dismembered human torso. Somehow I knew that, if she chose, her fiery eyes could reduce home, family, mountains—even planets—to ashes. Everything about this bear screamed of death, destruction, and, for good measure, cosmic annihilation. And to think all this was innocently drawn by my doodling hand.

Aana sucked a sharp gust of air through her teeth. "How do you know this bear?" she asked, looking horrified.

"A dream, Aana. That's all. A silly nightmare." I didn't sound too convincing.

Aana pursed her lips tight and shook her head. "*Maiksuk!*"

Uncle Jonah picked at the grime on the lip of his bear cup. "Not such a bad thing, *Najak.*"

I leaned forward over the counter and tried to catch his eye. "What's that, Uncle?"

He stared more intently into his cup like a gypsy reading tea leaves. "Crazy bear does that all the time. She's testing you."

"Testing me? What do you . . ." It dawned on me that either his dreams had conjured up the same monstrous bear or—and this sent prickles up my spine—he had somehow tapped into *my* dream. Come to think of it, nobody really knew where he went during his many tizzy fits.

"Just tuck him in tighter," old nurse Mary Jane would always say when Mom called her in a panic. "And make sure he takes his nerve pills."

Shocked that Uncle Jonah seemed to know all about my nightmare bear, it occurred to me that maybe, just maybe, he went cruising during his comatose catnaps. Maybe he shook off his feeble, old body and enjoyed some weird out-of-body experience. Maybe he went zipping around in other people's heads—my head!

"How would *you* know who's been stomping through my dreams?" I demanded.

Another faint chuckle leaked out from his thin, unsmiling lips. "Did you look behind her?"

"*What?*"

"You gotta sneak behind that crazy bear and have a look."

Aana brought her hand to her mouth and made soft, clicking noises behind her teeth.

I couldn't say anything. I couldn't think anything.

Uncle Jonah cocked his head at me and threw sparks in my face. "She's telling you somethin'," he said, thumping his limp arm against his side, "but you only got half the story. She's two-faced, that one. You gotta get behind her."

"How am I supposed to do *that?*"

"You'll figger it out next time."

"What do you mean, next time?"

Uncle Jonah withdrew back into his cup, like a genie slipping into his lamp. Like he'd already said too much. "She'll be back," he muttered. "That one, for sure."

"But. . . ."

Aana sniffed at Uncle Jonah and lightly slapped the back of his withered hand. "Show her, Jonah."

"It's none of my business anymore, *Najak*. I can't poke my nose down there."

I stared at Aana for some clue. "Show me what? Poke his nose down where?"

Aana glanced at me with unusual firmness. "The church, *Uitajuq*. We have to go under the church."

"What the—"

"Come on, *Ikuma*," Aana said, now cooing like an eider duck.

Uncle Jonah reluctantly let her clasp his hand.

"Help little *Uitajuq*," she said. "Who knows how long before that nasty bear starts dancing around in her head again?"

Uncle Jonah Escapes

BACKYARD OF OUR LADY OF THE SEA CHURCH
SATURDAY, APRIL 1ST, 11:45 P.M.

It was a strange time and place to gather for a bear hunt—late on a stormy evening behind the church. But Aana insisted we go right away. I got the funny feeling that she felt another night's sleep might be too dangerous for me without making the link between my blood-drenched dream bear and Uncle Jonah's knowing chuckles.

"Come on," she said to Pauloosie who was half asleep in front of the TV. "Go get a shovel. We're going to dig out *Nanurluk's* den."

I didn't have a clue what she was talking about. But like her brother Jonah, Aana could be a real bulldozer sometimes and I wasn't about to get in her way.

Half an hour later, Aana, Father Ungali, Mom, Gabe, and I sat in the warm pickup while Pauloosie attacked a big drift behind the church with his snow shovel. Somehow, Aana had managed to drag Uncle Jonah out of the house but he refused to stay in the truck. As soon as we pulled up behind the church he announced that he was walking home in spite of the sideways snow plastering the town.

"You just stay put, *Ikuma,*" Aana said. "We need you down there."

"Hell, no," he said as he struggled with the door handle. "Nobody's shovin' me down there."

With that, he pushed against the door so hard that he ended up falling out onto the snow.

"Uncle!" I cried and jumped out to pick him up.

"I found something!" shouted Pauloosie, waving his shovel high.

Uncle Jonah shot him a piercing look, then pushed me away with one quick shove. I'd never sensed such strength in him. Or such fear.

He stuck his head back in the truck and scowled at Aana. "I'm through with all that!" he shouted, pointing his good arm at the church.

Aana crinkled her nose. "It's still in you, *Ikuma.*"

"It's over. Forget it."

"Don't give up on little *Uitajuq.* She saw *Nanurluk's* face in her dreams. Now you know for sure she has *nakuusiaq.* Just like you. Just like *Anaana.*"

"Has what, Aana?" I asked

"The gift. The gift."

"What gift? What are you talking about?"

"Wait and see, *Uitajuq.* You'll find it." Aana thrust a gloved finger under Uncle Jonah's nose. "With Uncle's help."

Uncle Jonah wheeled around, gave me a long, anxious stare, and shook his head.

"It's over, I tell you!" he said to Aana. Then he leaned into the wind and set a beeline course for Heartbreak Hill.

I was about to run after him when somebody pulled up on a snowmobile. I recognized the beaver hat adorned with a big, shiny badge. It belonged to Raymond Arseneau.

Raymond glanced into our crowded pickup, then over to Pauloosie who was still waving his shovel in the air. "What the *hell* are you guys doing out here?"

"Just a late night church picnic," I shouted.

"Who the hell's that?" he asked pointing at the trudging figure just beyond the glare of the truck's headlights.

"Uncle Jonah. Would you mind giving him a lift home?"

"Right," said Raymond who seemed happy to take part in a real rescue mission. Apparently his victim took some convincing. Raymond had to cruise beside Uncle Jonah for a while and almost cut him off until he finally stopped. Uncle reluctantly allowed himself to be folded onto the seat behind Raymond and they roared back to town.

Everyone piled out of the truck to inspect Pauloosie's work. He'd uncovered a ground level set of hurricane doors that I never knew existed. I looked at Aana who had covered her mouth with her kerchief to protect it from the wind. "This is *really* important, right?"

She pointed to the doors. "Down there," is all she said.

"This has something to do with bears, right?"

"Down there."

"If you say so," I said and yanked on the door's wooden handle. It tore off in my hand and blew away. I grabbed the shovel from Pauloosie, pried it under one door, and heaved. The wind caught the door and flung it open with enough force to rip it right off its hinges.

"Good Lord," said Father Ungali. "Another thing to fix."

"Sorry about that," I said.

The six of us stood staring down a short flight of stairs that disappeared into darkness.

My chest went tight, as if squeezed by frozen hands. I could feel an asthma attack coming on. I started breathing like I'd just run a marathon.

"Ash, are you all right?" asked Mom.

"It's the dust," I said. "It must be the dust."

"There's no dust here, Ash. Everything's frozen. But let's get you out of here quick." She grabbed my arm and tried to pull me away from the stairs.

I yanked my arm back. "No, Mom. I'm okay. Really. I'm fine." I spun around to look at her as if somebody else had spoken those words. Somebody who wanted me to go down that tunnel. All my instincts said: turn around. Go back to the light. Run for your life. But something drew me forward and I almost fell down the stairs like I'd been pushed.

Underworld

CRAWL SPACE OF OUR LADY OF THE SEA CHURCH
SUNDAY, APRIL 2ND, 12:05 A.M.
I peered into the gloom. "There's another door down here."

"You first," Pauloosie said.

I could see it wasn't far down and there was enough light from a nearby streetlight to allow me to navigate the final steps without breaking my neck. I was walking a razor's edge, fighting an inner tug-of-war that, at the same moment, pulled me up towards the lit street and down into darkness.

The lower path won. I took a deep breath and marched down the final stairs. Five steps, six, seven. That was it. Then bare dirt. After bashing my forehead on the door frame, I fumbled for the knob. It was much lower than I expected, like the door was designed for hobbits. I gave it a sharp twist. "Damn! It's locked."

"Please, girl," said Father Ungali. "Mind your language in this place."

He'd made a very good point. This place was charged and I could feel angry sparks flying in my head.

"Where's the light switch, Father?" asked Mom.

"Don't ask me, Ms. LeBeau. I've never been down here."

"But I thought this was your church."

"This is God's church, Madam."

"Of course, but what about the keys to God's house? Surely he entrusts you with them?"

"Yes, he does, I mean—I'm not sure which you need." Father Ungali pulled out a fistful of keys on a silver chain. "It must be one of these. I just arrived and—"

"Last *June,* Father," Mom said as kindly as possible.

"Yes, but the bishop had some travel plans for me and I haven't had time to sort all the stuff in the rectory, let alone this—this— what would you call it? A basement?"

"A bingo basement!" shouted Gabe.

Pauloosie plugged his ears. "Stop yelling, Gabe. We can hear ya."

"We'd call this a crawl space by the looks of that door," Mom said.

"I see," he said. "I read in Father Broussard's journal that the church builders tried to build a basement—"

"That's the way they built churches in France in those days," Mom shouted above the wind, "so of course that's the way they built churches in the Arctic, for God's sake."

Gabe clapped his hands. "I'll say, for God's sake! For Pete's sake too. F-f-for the love of Mike too." Gabe's stuttering told me something was upsetting him.

"Who's Mike?" asked Pauloosie.

"Forget it, Paulie," Mom said. "Gabe watches too much TV."

"Father Broussard said that they only got down a foot before they hit ice," said Father Ungali.

"Permafrost," corrected Mom as she dug around in the deep pockets of her parka.

"Yes, of course. So they decided to jack the church floor five feet off the ground." Father Ungali chuckled weakly. "Father Broussard used to say this brought his people five feet closer to God."

"No b-b-bingo tonight, boys!" exclaimed Gabe "I'm climbin' the church beh-beh-bell tower."

"Nix that, Gabe," I said. "It got torched by lightning, remember?"

"A true act of God," said Father Ungali, trying to be funny. "No insurance for that."

Nobody laughed.

I'd had enough chitchat. "The keys please, Father," I said. He dropped the whole tangled mess in my hand. "What are all these for?"

"I don't have the foggiest. There're a lot of things to lock up in an old church like this, but, as I say, I haven't had a chance to go through them all yet."

I should have had Gabe open the crawl space door. He's pretty handy in the dark. But I knew he was too upset to be of any help right now. It took me five minutes to find the keyhole and another ten to find the right key. "There we go," I said as the tiny door creaked open.

A waft of cold air filled my nostrils. It was stale and sickly sweet, as if a family of stray cats had died down there a long time ago. In spite of the smell, the blackness seemed strangely welcoming to me, almost familiar. I felt like I'd fallen into one of my dreams.

From the heavy breathing around me, I couldn't tell who was more nervous, Gabe or Father Ungali. Mom kept rummaging through her pockets. "What *are* you looking for, Mom?" I asked.

She dug out a handful of stuff, holding things up towards the streetlight: an empty cigarette box, half an Eat-More bar, a polished quartz crystal, a Swiss Army knife, a deck of Chinese I-Ching cards, a broken pair of sunglasses from last spring's fish camp. Mom's life in a pocket. "Ah, here it is." She flicked on a tiny penlight.

Pauloosie plucked the Eat-More bar out of her other hand and stuffed it in his jeans. "Thanks, Mom. I'll guard the emergency food in case we get stuck in this dungeon."

Mom took one baby step forward into the crawl space. Like scared sheep, everyone but Aana moved with her—just one step. Aana had sat down on the bottom step, looking stone-faced and clicking her tongue against the roof of her mouth.

Mom slowly swung the flashlight from side to side. Its feeble beam caught a scattered mound of book-sized golden crosses stacked on the frozen ground. We shuffled, en masse, towards them. "Heavens," she said. "These must be worth a fortune."

"Buried treasure!" whispered Pauloosie as Mom tightened her beam on glittering crosses.

"Gold spray-paint," I said. I could see they were made of wood with rusty screws sticking out the back. "Must've been attached to the church pews or something."

Mom swung her flashlight around. The original wooden beams below the church floor were all cracked and sagging, propped up here and there by skinny metal pipes that stood on blocks of buckling two-by-fours. Those little pipes were basically holding up the whole church. Any wood touching the ground was rotten with mildew and mould. It struck me that the next good storm would knock this old church right off its flimsy foundations.

Mom focused the beam of her flashlight "What the . . . ?"

Everyone froze, squinting into the shadows, trying to make some sense out of the twisted shapes she'd stopped upon.

Everyone except Gabe, of course. "What? What? What is it?"

The Trunk

Crawl space of Our Lady of the Sea church
Sunday, April 2nd, 12:25 a.m.

Father Ungali was the first to figure it out. "Lord help me!" he whispered.

"*What?!*" shouted Gabe.

"Angel wings."

The wings were made of cardboard, now green and gray with mold from years of neglect in this wet musty place. I shivered in my parka. "Probably used in some kids' Christmas play," I suggested. "Who knows how long ago?"

The sparks in my head were dying. I felt like my brain was being freeze-dried. I reached for Mom's free hand as she steered the flashlight beam towards some round, pale thing off in a corner.

"What's that?" gasped Pauloosie. "It's—it's a skull!"

"I knew it!" shouted Gabe. "Cannibals!" He tugged on my arm and squeezed my fingers like he does when he's about to lose it.

"We got you covered, Gabe, " I said as calmly as I could. "Hold your horses." I grabbed the flashlight and thrust it forward. "It's only lichen," I said. "An old shriveled up patch of lichen. Must be a hundred years old."

"Our Lady was built in 1926," said Father Ungali.

That's how he talked about this place, as if it was alive. Our Lady.

Something orange caught my eye. It was a patch of bald rock where the soil had been dug up, probably by the original French Brothers who tried to build a basement. "Some kind of weird rock," I said.

"Our Lady is built on a foundation of solid rock," said Father Ungali proudly. "One would expect nothing less for a House of God. Father Broussard called it the Rock of Ages. He had another name for it—what was it?" Father Ungali put his fingers to his lips. "Oh yes, I remember now. Firestone. You can see how it almost glows."

Firestone. The very name gave me goose bumps. I had seen this strange rock before. Then it came to me. Blood Rock off the tip of the Spit. But I couldn't remember where else.

"Mind your heads," Father said as we ventured further into the darkness. "It's frightfully dark." He placed a protective hand over the crown of Gabe's head as if granting a papal blessing.

"Bless you too, Father," Gabe said in a churchy tone. "It's like the dark side of the moon down here."

Pauloosie giggled while clinging to my parka. "How the heck would you know, Gabe?"

"You're the one who should be leading us through here," I said.

"Yes," said Father Ungali. "The blind leading the blind."

"It's darker than dark, I tell you," Gabe said in a trembly voice. "There's nothing coming up on my radar screen."

I noticed that Gabe was breathing hard in short, gaspy breaths, like just before one of his seizures. Please, not now, Gabe. Not here.

He sucked in his breath like he was choking. "I'm way out of my comfort zone down here."

Father Ungali got distracted by the pile of fallen angels for a moment, just long enough for Gabe to crack his forehead against a rotten beam. He stumbled over a couple of golden crosses that split apart like matchsticks. "*Ouch!* Oh, hells' bells! Protect me, Father! I can't see the forest for the trees."

"What *are* you talking about?" asked Pauloosie. "Trees?"

I heard a sharp hiss behind us.

"The trunk," Aana barked. "It's in the trunk."

I swung the light around to see Aana pointing with her chin towards a dark, square shape we'd just walked past. I shone the light on a grand, old railway trunk that was rimmed in solid brass.

"In there," Aana said. "It's in there."

"What? *What?*" Gabe said. He was picking up some vibes in here that rubbed him the wrong way.

"We'll know soon enough," I said as I leaned forward for a closer look. The trunk was in amazing shape compared to the holy debris we'd found all around us. It looked like it had come off a barge just yesterday. There wasn't a hint of mold on it. This discovery gave me more chills. I got the strong impression that there was something alive in there that was immune to decay.

Still, I knew that I absolutely had to see what it was. I shone the light along the top edge and found a latch on each side that flipped open with ease. The big central latch was locked. I tugged at it, hoping it would fly apart like the door handle. It was rock solid. While examining the keyhole I noticed two initials carefully inscribed above it in some Gothic hand: P.B.

"P.B.," I whispered.

"P.B., P.B." said Father Ungali.

"*Bien sur,*" Mom said. "Pierre Broussard!"

"Ah, this is the good father's trunk," said Father Ungali. He paused, then shook his head. "Hmmm. But this is very strange."

"What? *What?*" Gabe said.

"Father Broussard was very meticulous about Our Lady's assets. He left a detailed inventory. I knew right away those were angel wings because he'd even put them on it. Every cross was counted. But the good Father made no mention of this elegant trunk."

"So . . . you wouldn't likely have a key for it," I said.

"Well, let's have a look," he said as he again dropped all his keys in my hand.

I shone the light in Gabe's sightless face. He hadn't exactly calmed down but we were running low on batteries and I wasn't about to leave at this point. "How'd you like to give it a try, Gabe, while we save some flashlight juice?"

"Forget the keys, Ash. Gimmee a crowbar. That's what we need. A c-c-crowbar. Have you s-s-s-seen any down here, Ash? Ash? Are you there?"

"I'm here, Gabe. Do you think you could—"

"Bust and run, Ash. B-bust that thing open and clear the decks, Ash. Run for the hills!"

Mom's flashlight was fading fast. I reached for Gabe's hand, nested the keys in it, and guided his other hand to the big latch. "I promise we won't stay long, Gabe. Aana is hell-bent on us seeing something in this trunk. I'm sure she wouldn't bring us here if there was any danger." I could feel my stomach tightening even as I spoke. "There's nothing to be afraid of, Gabe. Can you just give it a try?"

"O-okay Ash. But d-d-don't blame me if we can't stuff the genie b-back in the bottle."

I watched Gabe's finely tuned fingers set to work on the lock, testing one key, flipping it over, and testing the next. After the third key, I switched off the light to save power and we were plunged into darkness except for the faint, backlit silhouette of Aana sitting at the bottom of the stairs. Gabe quickened his pace, like he was getting into the groove of some new musical instrument.

My heart flipped into overdrive, not so much from the total darkness—it felt oddly comforting—but from the grinding suspense over what was in that trunk. I was glad when Mom started up some nervous banter.

"So, Father, why do you think Broussard had so many keys?"

"Well, Our Lady had many things to lock up."

"Like what?"

"Oh, like the communion tabernacle, the pump organ, the cupboard for the holy chalice, the vestments locker, the—"

"But surely the locals wouldn't steal things like that."

"Yes, surely. Of course not. But I have heard that the good father grew up in a rough part of Paris. Maybe it was just his habit to lock everything up."

I would have laughed if it weren't for my frozen jaw. Everything about me felt cold. Something in me had iced up and was about to split apart with the opening of that trunk. I could hear Gabe flipping through the keys with amazing speed. Every flip was like a clanging countdown to that moment. Yet I had to know what was in there. The tug-of-war continued.

Then, silence.

"Gabe?" I fumbled with the flashlight but couldn't find the switch. I heard the keys drop on the frozen floor. "Gabe? What are you doing, Gabe?"

"You were right, Ash," he said. "No key. Let's get outta here."

"Somebody must've stolen it," Pauloosie said. "Where's your light?"

222   on thin ice

"Can you try again, Gabe?" I asked.

"I tried 'em all. Three times. I tried 'em all three times, Ash."

"Maybe we could drag the sucker out of here," I suggested. I groped for a handle and tugged. "It's like it's full of rocks."

I heard shuffling behind us and a sound like Aana giggling. "Full of rocks," she echoed.

"Yeah, we could pick the lock sitting round the fire," Pauloosie said.

That image appealed to me. Toss the trunk in the pickup and snoop through it in a warm safe place, not this stuffy, frozen dungeon. I turned around to look at Aana. "Maybe open it back home, eh Aana?"

Aana threw her arm forward and pointed rigidly to the trunk. "Now, *Uitajuq*. No more dreams till *Uitajuq* sees it!"

I turned the light back on and swung it towards her. She was already headed our way. "See what Aana? *What?*"

Mom reached for her hand to guide her to us but she pulled it back. She had her caribou mitts off and her hand was clasped tight like she was holding something very precious.

"What's up, Aana? What?" Gabe said between heavy breaths. Without a task to focus on, he was beginning to come apart again. I wondered who would be first, him or me.

Aana held her clenched hand out for me. I hastily shook off my glove and she pressed something metallic into my palm. "Try this," she said.

It was another key, made from the same kind of brass that edged the trunk. "Where did you get—"

"Try it." Aana planted her knuckles on her hips and leaned towards the trunk.

I slipped the key into the center latch. It fit perfectly. I gave it a lively twist and the latch sprang open. I handed the flashlight to Mom, took a deep breath, and threw open the lid.

Newspapers. Old, scrunched up newspapers. I poked them with a bare finger like a cobra might be hiding just below them.

"*Zut alors!*" Mom said. "They're all in French." She plucked out a page, smoothed it on the front of her parka and held it close to her face. "A pity I don't have my reading glasses. Ash, what does it say?"

I was hardly in the mood for catching up on French news but I thought the distraction might allow me to regain my breath and my brain. "Yeah, it's—oh, look: 1966. The Paris edition of *Le Monde.*"

"Father Broussard's native place," said Father Ungali. "The good father loved his newspapers. I found some of his old boots and every one was burnt at the heels. They tell me he would spend hours reading the paper, puffing away on his pipe, with his boots on the woodstove until they started smoking."

"What a packrat," Pauloosie said. "Hanging on to old newspapers."

"Yeah, a real packrat," Gabe said. "Now can we get p-p-packing outta here? Like, n-n-now already?"

"Very soon, Gabe," Mom said. "What's it say, Ash?"

"Let's see. How's this for headlines: 'Ronald Reagan landslides into California's governor seat.' 'Russia makes first planet landing as Venera III touches down on Venus.' 'Ancient Egyptian Temples of Abu Simba drowned by Aswan Dam'. . . ."

"Excuse me," Pauloosie said. "That's all very thrilling but I thought you said your flashlight was dying. Like, we didn't come down here to read the paper, did we?" With that he thrust his hand into the trunk. "There's gotta be something a little more exciting in here."

I shrank back as he groped around deep inside the trunk.

"There's something really hard." He thrust in his other arm. "Really heavy." He pulled out a loaf-sized object wrapped in newspaper and presented it to me. "Here, you should get the prize."

Mom shone the fading light on me as I gingerly removed the paper. There was no turning back now. I felt like I was holding a piece of fate in my hands.

"Some kind of Christmas present?" said Pauloosie as he watched me peel off the last layer of newspaper to reveal a wrapping of exotic gold cloth.

I looked up at Aana who shot me a quick nod. Like the trunk, the shining cloth was in mint condition, as if whatever it concealed had been wrapped hours ago. I peeled back the cloth to reveal something smooth and shiny. It was soapstone. Even in this faint light it seemed to glow. It had that reddish orange hue, exactly the same color as Blood Rock, Uncle Jonah's cup, and—I remembered now—the eerie underground quarry guarded by the icehouse bear.

Firestone.

That One

CRAWL SPACE OF OUR LADY OF THE SEA CHURCH

SUNDAY, APRIL 2ND, 12:40 A.M.

I removed the last of the gold cloth covering the firestone. Cradled in my trembling hands was a dancing polar bear. It stood on one leg with its forepaws raised high, its neck thrown back, and its muzzle pointed skyward.

I looked again at Aana. Her eyes darted from me to the bear and back to me as if testing my response. I was numb. I was speechless. All I could say was, "Who?"

Mom gently lifted the dancing bear from my hands, like I was about to drop it.

Aana just sniffed and elbowed Pauloosie. He dove his hands back into the trunk and felt around. "Yep, there's lots more where that came from," he said.

I unwrapped three more carvings, all bears, all exquisite, all cut from firestone. A hunting bear, crouched over a seal hole—all patience. A running bear, its muscles rippling with power—all strength. A drumming bear, with mouth open wide as if singing— all joy. They were almost too beautiful to look at. Too real. I half expected them to flush purple in my hands, like the harpoon of my dreams. My fears fell away, and I was left beyond the reach of words and thoughts.

My spell was broken by a hiss from Aana. "Keep looking," she said. "It must be in there somewhere."

"Hey, Ash, I got a b-b-b-better idea. Wh-wh-why don't you hit the p-p-pause button, Ash," Gabe said. "I say let's get outta here n-n-now!"

"He's right, Aana," Mom said. "It's getting very late. We can come back tomorrow when there's some daylight—"

"That one," Aana said. "It's in there."

The ice returned. My whole spine twinged. "You don't mean—?"

Aana flicked her lower jaw towards the trunk. "That one *Uitajuq* saw."

"I guess this is some kind of scavenger hunt," Pauloosie said. "She's gonna hold us hostage down here until we find whatever. Can you squeeze any more juice out of that light, Mom? I can barely see the trunk."

Gabe muscled between Pauloosie and me. "Who needs light? L-lemmee have a look-see. N-n-nobody's g-gonna keep me hostage d-d-down here."

With that he felt around the edge of the trunk then stuck both hands in deep. "Got a b-b-b-big one! Wh-where are you, Ash?" he shouted as he lifted out another package, twice the size of any of the others.

I took it from him and had torn down to the gold cloth layer when Mom's flashlight finally gave out.

"God help us," came Father Ungali's voice out of the darkness.

"Don't worry, Father," Mom said. "I've got a lighter. Like you say, God helps those who help themselves." She got it going after a dozen desperate flicks. "Hah-hah. You see, Ash. One of the rare benefits of smoking."

Mom's voice seemed blurred and far away, like I'd heard it in a dream. I cradled the heavy package in one arm while my fingers went back to work, moving at an almost frantic pace. With my heart in my throat, I stripped off the last bit of cloth. Under the feeble glow of Mom's lighter, all I could make out was the shape of a standing bear. The carving's finer details were in shadow. My hand shook. "Closer, Mom. I need more light."

"God help us," repeated Father Ungali, this time in a mere whisper.

The boundary between my worlds dissolved. The Earth stopped spinning. There was no past or future. No inside or out-side. No dreaming or waking. Only—this face. "It's her!" I said, not moving my lips. Looking back at me was the ghastly she-bear of my nightmare.

"That one," said Aana nodding slowly. "*Nanurluk.* Uncle's favorite."

My head reeled. "What? You mean, *Uncle Jonah* carved this?"

"*Suukiaq,*" she said. "Jonah, for sure."

"*All* of them?"

"All."

"But they're so incredible. So *alive*. They seem to glow with life."

"*Ikuma,*" she said. "That's why everybody called him that. The fireman. They said he could light the stone on fire."

"Yeah, sure," Gabe said. "Until he got his fingers b-b-burnt playing with fire. Firewater, eh, Uncle? Eh, Uncle—Uncle?"

"Uncle Jonah's not here, Gabe," Mom said. "He went home with Raymond, remember?"

"No, he didn't."

Mom held her lighter up to his face. His brow was a mess of wrinkles and his head tottered on his neck like a drunken puppeteer was in control. "He did, Gabe," she said. "It's okay. He's back home."

"He m-m-musta come back then," Gabe said. "As sure as sh-sh-sh-shootin'. He's here all right. I can f-f-feel him. He's—he's hiding over there someplace—in a c-c-corner someplace!"

Gabe was coming to a boil, breathing hard and fast. He stuck an arm out, stiff as a board and waved it around. "He's d-d-down here all right, playing c-c-cat and m-mouse with us."

Aana smacked her lips loudly. "Hush, Gabe. Jonah's gone to bed."

My eyes made a cautious sweep of the darkness. "But how could Uncle have known about—about my bear?"

Aana chuckled softly. "He carved this a long time ago. How could *you* know about *his?*"

The carving seemed to gain weight as my mind squirmed. I couldn't hold it much longer. "Here, Gabe. You feel it."

"Maybe, Gabe, you've seen this bear too?" Mom asked.

I shuddered as I carefully placed it into his open hands. Now Mom was really stretching the envelope.

Gabe ran his probing fingers over the carving the way he explores an unfamiliar face. His fingers danced over every detail of the bear's satin smooth surface: her piercing, blood-red eyes and leering grin. Her dagger fangs and terrible claws. Her swollen nipples and the garland of severed human heads that adorned her neck. In the flickering light I watched Gabe's face twist into weird contortions in response to the message of his fingers, as if mirroring the bear's grotesque face. He yanked his hand away making a sizzling noise between his teeth. "Holy! I w-wouldn't want to m-m-meet her in a d-dark alley."

Pauloosie's hand reached out of the darkness. "Lemee see too." He tried to touch the bear but Gabe pushed his hand away.

"N-n-no, wait," Gabe said. "I'm not f-f-finished." His fingers slid back to the severed heads for a moment, then he turned the carving over. I'd forgotten to do that. I heard the echo of Uncle Jonah's words, like he was whispering in my ear: *You gotta sneak behind that crazy bear.*

"Wow!" Gabe exclaimed. "What's *this* all about?"

I grabbed the lighter from Mom and held it close to the stone. A second face looked back at me, this one almost human. A soft, tender face that reminded me of the Madonna in front of the church. Her eyes were almond-shaped sapphires that seemed to pour out kindness. Her mouth was poised in a subtle smile. She held one sheltering paw above four young humans who suckled at her chest. Her other paw lay flat upon an icepan, grounding her to the Earth. Instead of mutilation and death, her garland from this side showed nodding Arctic poppies carved by none other than a master. This sculpture was a miracle.

"Cosmic!" Gabe said as his fingers explored every delicate flower.

Something blew up above our heads. *BOOM!*

"What the hell?" cried Gabe. That's when he let the bear slip out of his hands.

I lunged for the carving, breaking its fall to the rock-hard floor. It dropped like a ton of bricks on the fingers of my right hand, my drawing hand. I heard the bones crack.

"*Aamittara!*" cried Aana. "Be careful with that!"

"Earthquake!" shouted Gabe. "We're d-d-done and dusted now, b-b-boys. I'm outta here!"

BOOM! BOOM!

I impulsively shoved my wounded hand into my parka. "Aaagh!"

"Are you okay, Ash?" asked Mom.

"Don't think so. My fingers—"

BOOM!

Gabe lunged into the darkness only to bash his head again on a low beam. Father Ungali went after him. "Nothing to worry about, Gabriel. It's only the furnace going on. I know that much."

"Sounds like a dinosaur waking up," Pauloosie said.

The old, tin air vents hanging from the floor started trembling like distant thunder as the main fan kicked in.

"Don't b-b-be too sure," Gabe said. "It's n-n-never the first b-blast that gets you. It's the aftershocks. Let's scram before this house of G-G-God comes a-tumblin' down!"

The Bear Shaman's Song

Part VI
Dreaming the Bear

On the wind
I smell the breath of seal.
Its breathing hole is near
And I can hear the sea calling me—
Ha-jai-jaa, ha-jai-jaa!
With flippered hands
I slide towards a circle of dark water.
A trap!
Through my leathery skin
Nanurluk crunches my skull.

Trapped

I'm frantic to find the tunnel. I know that Nanurluk *lives below it. I've seen her mysterious face in firestone—benevolent, bewitching, almost holy—and now I'm obsessed to see the real thing. There's something I must learn from her. I want this so bad I'm willing to gamble she'll spare my eyes from her other side—that face of unspeakable terror.*

The melting sea ice is covered in puddles and ponds that block my route. I can hear meltwater draining away all around me. I fix my eyes on a fat cloud far ahead. Its belly shows a dark smear, telling me there's open water below.

I feel certain that's where the tunnel lies.

I can't fast-track through this mush. I instinctively stop and raise both arms with palms downward, like I've done this a thousand times before. My chest begins to pulse with energy surging up from the bottom of the sea.

I feel a faint vibration in the back of my throat. I begin to hum.

It's that song. Again it comes to me in bits and pieces. Frustrating! I capture what power I can and run, sending up a fine spray of meltwater beside me.

The swirling, black cloud seems to suck all light from the sky. A roaring sound drops from the cloud. Looking down on me is the swollen, black eye of a hurricane. As a ferocious wind wraps around me, I spot a circle of dark water ahead of me—the door to the sea tunnel!

My joy flicks to alarm when I see it's shrinking fast, and with it, my only chance to enter Nanurluk's *domain.*

I leap with outstretched arms toward the tunnel entrance. Its open-
ing is no bigger than a seal hole and only my hands fit through. My
face and chest smash against the ice.

The hurricane rings in my ears. Icy jaws clamp around my hands.
My mind reels in confusion and regret.

The ice starts trembling beneath my battered body. The sensation is
terribly familiar, like what I felt moments before my father was attacked.
With my hands still pinned in the ice, I struggle to roll onto my back and
look up into the snarling, blood-drenched face of a giant polar bear.

My gamble is lost.

I've fallen into Nanurluk's *trap!*

Claiming a Seal

MOISE'S POLAR BEAR HUNT CAMP

SATURDAY, APRIL 22ND, 10:15 A.M.

You can smell your next meal. You lift your whole head out of the
water and sniff deeply. A dead seal.

There is another scent from some animal you don't recognize.
A strong, greasy smell. A good smell.

You silently place your front paws on the edge of the ice and
peer ahead. A human is kneeling beside your seal. He seems to
be eating it. Behind him, far away, you can see two small human
dens on the ice. A faint purple glow from the den mouth tells you
there is another human inside.

The wind is blowing from the humans to you. They won't smell
you. If you are quiet, they won't hear you.

You smell dogs. You lift your head higher and look over both
shoulders. You see no dogs.

The kneeling human has his back to you. If you sneak up on him you can claim your seal without any trouble.

If he turns around he might spray you with his firestick.

You watch him for a long time until hunger pushes you up and out of the water.

You are very hungry for seal but the human is in the way.

You jump on him before he sees you. He makes frightening mouth sounds. You stop the sounds by biting his head and clawing his back. You jump on him till he stops moving.

Then you take your seal.

Dream Epilogue

ASHLEY'S BEDROOM
SATURDAY, APRIL 22ND, 11:19 A.M.

When I opened my eyes that morning my head lay at the wrong end of the bed with my face scrunched up against the rough log wall of my bedroom. My blankets and sheets were all twisted around my legs. I must have been thrashing around all night like an angry char caught in a fish net. I'd opened my window a little too wide before I went to bed and now a dusting of spring snow covered my pjs. I pushed myself away from the wall forgetting about my broken fingers.

"Yeeouch!" Fire surged through my right hand and up my arm. A vision of my hands clamped in the ice flashed into my half-awake brain. Then the whole crazy dream spilled out and I scribbled it into my journal as fast as I could in spite of the pain in my right hand. It had been in a cast since that night below the church when Uncle Jonah's *Nanurluk* carving broke my artist's fingers.

I laid my journal on my stomach and closed my eyes, replaying the dream in detail. There was much to learn from it.

I must have dozed off again because moments later, *Nanurluk's* terrible face rose up again, this time with my father's mangled head in its jaws.

I jerked awake to the shrill ring of a telephone below me.

Something Awful

ASHLEY'S HOME
SATURDAY, APRIL 22ND, 11:45 P.M.

I heard a long silence after somebody picked up the phone. Then Mom's voice broke in. She sounded hysterical, shouting one minute, sobbing the next like I'd never heard before. I kicked off the knot of blankets, brushed the snow from my pjs and ran downstairs. Mom was pacing the kitchen with the phone to her ear, tugging at her hair. Her face was pale and streaked with tears. Gabe rocked on the couch, wrenching his hands together. Pauloosie and Aana sat with their eyes locked on Mom as she marched back and forth.

"What is it?" I asked.

"Something awful," Gabe said. "You can bet on that. Something awful!"

"*Ahfull! Ahfull!*" shrieked Wiggins.

I could see that plainly enough. I tugged at Mom's housecoat. "What is it, Mom?"

"It's Dad," she sobbed. "A bear got him."

"*What?*"

"I knew it!" shouted Gabe. "It had to be a bear. We told him it was a harebrained idea. He wouldn't listen. Bears like to pick on Moise. They want to pick on his bones! Pick on his bones!"

I put my nose in Mom's face. "Is he—"

Mom shook her head. "They radioed a chopper and medevaced him straight to Inniturliq."

"How bad?"

Mom raised a hand. I could hear a male voice at the other end. It sounded like Steven. "How much blood?" she asked, then, "Good Lord."

Blackout

INNITURLIQ REGIONAL HOSPITAL

SUNDAY, APRIL 23RD, 10:48 A.M.

Thanks to more freaky warm weather, the ice road to Inniturliq was already closed. The next sked flight out was three days away, but Mom couldn't wait. Like the big guns from Empire Oil, Mom decided to charter a plane. Twenty hours after Dad was mauled by a polar bear, Mom, Pauloosie, Gabe, and I were standing by his bed in the intensive care ward of the Inniturliq regional hospital.

Dad was asleep on his stomach, snoring gently like he always does, only with a bubbly interlude between breaths caused by the oxygen tubes shoved up his nose. His head was wrapped in square bandages held in place by an elastic hairnet like they wear in fast food restaurants down south.

"The bear tore his scalp to shreds," said the nurse. "It was quite the sewing job. Three hundred and twenty-eight stitches. I believe that's a record for this hospital."

He had more bandages stuck to his neck and shoulders. His back was bare, covered with a railway yard's worth of claw marks, puncture wounds, and stitches.

Mom pointed to his back. "Why no bandages?"

"The surgeon wants to air those wounds to accelerate healing," the nurse explained. "It's all right. He doesn't move around much. In fact, he's hardly lifted a toe since he got here."

"Is he . . . paralyzed?" asked Mom in a trembly voice.

"We don't think so but—"

"Coma?"

"That's always a possibility but we'll have to wait and see. He did receive several bites to the head and one along his spine. But they didn't seem too awfully deep. On the other hand—"

"What do you mean, wait and see?" asked Mom, hardly reassured by the nurse's clinical bedside manner. "How long do we have to wait?"

"He may just be in a restorative sleep." The nurse pointed to a heart monitor machine. "He's showing strong vital signs and the only internal injuries we can detect are six broken ribs." She checked the clipboard hanging off the end of Dad's bed. "No, sorry, make that seven. There may of course be some cranial maladjustments that—"

"What?" I said.

"Forgive me. Brain damage. But we won't know that, will we, until he wakes up."

"The rest'll d-do him g-good," Gabe said. "L-let him sleep off any more c-c-crazy ideas about guiding p-polar bear hunts."

Two hunts, two attacks on Dad. I wondered if it was the same giant bear. I felt anger rising in me as we stepped out of the hospital into the noise and congestion of downtown Inniturliq.

Bear Bait

After our aborted hunt with Lyons when Dad almost got eaten by a bear, drowned in the Arctic Ocean, *and* consumed by hypothermia, he got it into his head that Nanurtalik was now ready to get into the business of guided polar bear hunts. It took some time clearing the legal hoops, getting the local wildlife council's blessing, snagging another rich hunter, and, trickiest of all, convincing Lord Gord that Dad was the man for the job.

Ever since Jimmy's death confirmed there were polar bears in the region, the mayor had often spoken of guiding the first hunt himself. But he claimed the timing was bad. He'd already booked a month-long tour of Japan supposedly to attract tourist dollars to Nanurtalik. After several squabbles, he and Dad negotiated a deal that would put money in both the town coffers and Dad's dwindling bank account. The last door swung open when a hunter from Wisconsin answered Dad's ad in the *New York Times* travel section. The guy flew up two weeks later and joined Dad, Steven, and twelve sled dogs on Nanurtalik's first real polar bear hunt in over thirty years.

The hunt was a disaster.

"When I found him I thought the bear had ripped half his face off," said Steven, tearing into a rib-eye steak at Inniturliq's Midnight Sun restaurant. "It was just a bloody blob of flesh. No eyes, nothing."

"N-n-nothing?" asked Gabe. "J-just a bloody b-b-blob, you say?"

Pauloosie's fork-load of French fries froze halfway to his mouth. "So . . . do you think that's really why they put him on his belly. So we couldn't see his—"

"Don't worry, Paulie," Steven said. "Moise's face is still in one piece. It took me a while to figure out I was looking at his scalp. That bear had ripped it clean over his eyes."

"Good Lord," Mom said.

"So tell us again what happened," I said. "I've only heard bits and pieces."

Steven took another big bite of steak. He attacked it like he was sitting in an iglu, stabbing a big piece with his fork, holding one end with his teeth, then sawing a knife through it to hack off a chewable chunk. "We'd been camped on the young ice near a good lookin' lead for over a week and seen only a few bear tracks. Your dad was pacing the tent floor pretty good, thinking that hunter from Wisconsin would want all his money back and tell everyone what a crappy time he'd had if we didn't cough up a bear. After a few days of pulling his hair out, Moise got an idea. He stole one of the seals from the dog food box and smeared it with bacon grease. Then he chucked it out on the ice a few hundred yards from camp." Steven sawed off another chunk of steak. "Bear bait," he said, chewing hard on the left side of his mouth. "I guess it worked pretty good."

"What did he do when the bear attacked?" I asked.

"What would you do? Scream, I guess. I wasn't in camp. The dogs had been going snaky, being tied up for so long, so I thought I'd hitch 'em up for a little spin. That left your dad and the hunter in camp."

"Did they have the rifle?" asked Mom.

"One each actually. I packed Lyons' shotgun on the sled, then took off down the lead lookin' for more bear sign."

"What did you find?" asked Pauloosie.

"All I picked up were a few blown-over tracks, humongous ones, like we saw out there with Lyons, and a couple of ravens picking on some old blood. I ran out of open water pretty soon so I spun around and headed back to camp. I was about half a mile out when I spotted Moise in my binoculars. He was lying face down in the snow. I guess he'd gone out to check his seal bait for any fresh sign. When I found him, his rifle was still slung over his shoulder. The bear must'a snuck up and jumped him from behind."

"Like, *stalked* him?" asked Pauloosie.

"Yeah, sure. Like, stalked him. Polar bears'll do that."

"And the seal bait?" I asked.

"Dragged a few feet away, then dumped, like the bear left in a hurry."

"What about the hunter?" asked Mom.

"I found him sleeping in his tent. Didn't hear a thing."

"Why do you think the bear took off?" I asked.

"The dogs probably. Some bears don't like dogs much." Steven struggled with a stringy part of his steak. He put the restaurant knife down and whipped out his Buck knife to finish the job. "Except to eat maybe."

"So you never saw the bear?" I asked.

"Nothing. All I saw was those same big tracks coming straight out of the water, then straight back in. That's it. Like a ghost." Steven finished off his steak with a contented belch. "So, I been meaning to ask how you guys got over here so fast. The next sked flight isn't till Monday."

"You didn't think we'd twiddle our thumbs at home after you called to tell us what happened. We chartered a Cessna of course."

Steven whistled. "That's the kinda news that could wake up Moise. He survives a polar bear attack, then you steal an arm and a leg from him while he's lying down."

Mom was not amused. "How *dare* you say. . . ."

Steven held up both palms. "Just kiddin', Carole. Just kiddin'."

"Besides," Gabe said. "Who says he *has* s-survived? They don't stick people in intensive c-c-are for a stubbed toe for G-God's sake. He m-might survive, all right. As a v-v-vegetable!"

Pauloosie leaned over his plate to catch Mom's eye. "He'll wake up okay, won't he, Mom?"

"I'm sure he'll be fine," Mom said, sounding not too persuasive. "He's a tough nut."

"That's *if* he wakes up," Gabe said. "By the looks of him I wouldn't c-count your ch-chickens yet. Not y-y-yet anyways!"

I abruptly turned to Gabe like he could see me. "How the hell would you know what he looks—" I cut myself short. Even a blind man could tell that Dad was in a very bad way.

Closing the Book

MIDNIGHT SUN HOTEL, INNITURLIQ
WEDNESDAY, APRIL 26TH, 2:54 A.M.

Steven flew back to Nanurtalik on the Monday sked flight. The rest of us ended up spending four long days in Inniturliq. Even though I'd grown up there and we had lots of friends in town, Mom insisted we stay in the Midnight Sun hotel across from the hospital. "I want to keep a round the clock vigil to support Dad, and the fewer interruptions the better," she'd said after we checked in. She had brought extra sleeping bags and, to save money, we all crashed in one room.

I didn't mind. I wasn't feeling too sociable and the town did-n't feel like home anymore. Some ass had set fire to my old school over the Christmas holidays and burned half of it down. Mrs. Beckwith, the only art teacher I'd ever connected with, had a nervous breakdown soon after and moved back south. Somebody had pulled the money plug from the Northern Lites Youth Center where we used to hold fiddle dances or play Arctic sports or just hang out, and now it stood dark and derelict. Holly, one of my best girlfriends, drank herself to death on Valentine's day. I was beginning to wonder, like, where *is* my home? And now this thing with Dad, thrashed by a phantom bear, vegetating in a hospital bed that he might never get up from.

Pauloosie and I did end up visiting some of our old buddies. Mom had coffee with a couple of hers. We took Gabe over to his old stomping grounds at the radio station. But we mostly hung around the hotel or camped out in the intensive care ward with Dad.

"Still stable," the nurse announced cheerfully every time we went over, which really meant: "He's still in a deep coma and we don't have a clue when the hell he'll snap out of it."

I hadn't slept much since we'd got here, thanks to the whine of the hotel room bar fridge, the slap of wires against the outside wall, and the thumps and shouts of drinking parties all around us. On our last night I got up in the middle of the night, having tossed and turned for hours on a floor that smelled like a cigarette factory.

Forgetting about my buggered right hand, I had brought my sketchbook along thinking we might have some time to kill in Inniturliq. I've got all night, I thought as I opened it to a fresh creamy page. I hadn't done one sketch since Uncle Jonah's *Nanurluk* carving fell on my fingers. I tried a few warm up sketches with my drawing hand—a close-up of a polar bear's paw, a standing silhouette against a rising moon. Enough of my fingers emerged from the cast for me to hold a charcoal pencil, but it caused too much pain.

Just for a lark I thought I'd try my left hand. I remember Yoshi had us do that once as an exercise to help us, as she said, "draw out of the box." The lines were childish but clear. I seemed to press harder with my left hand, like I was carving instead of drawing. It felt weird, but I could do it. What ended up on those pages was even weirder.

I drew a polar bear at the circus dressed in a clown suit and balancing on a beach ball. I drew one dancing in polka-dot shorts down a crowded highway as vehicles crashed all around it. I drew another pacing a heavily barred cage at the zoo as screaming kids threw apples and hot dogs at it. Waving from a fire truck in a fourth of July parade. Selling used cars. Adorning a can of pop. Drinking a bottle of beer. Spitting out great gobs of chewing tobacco. I drew a polar bear wearing a nurse's uniform pulling a sheet over my faceless father's head.

I folded my hands over my open sketchbook and turned to the hotel window. The wind had picked up and I watched the hospital across the street fade away behind a veil of blowing snow tinted orange in the streetlights. After sitting like that for about an hour, it dawned on me that I couldn't see the hospital anymore. It had vanished into the storm and with it, a part of me.

I looked down at the ridiculous sketches I'd just done. I flipped back through the pages, glancing numbly at hundreds of polar bear images. Undoubtedly some of my best artwork.

I stopped at the terrible face of *Nanurluk,* drawn from my dreams. I carefully studied its cruel smile, blood-drenched fangs, and garland of severed human heads. I thought about all the crazy bear dreams I'd had over the past few months. . . .

A door opened in my brain. Again I flipped back through my sketchbook, this time looking for the date when that bear-guy and his furry friends first showed up in my dreams. Last August, soon after we moved to Nanurtalik. Until now I hadn't thought much about what the name meant: the place with polar bears. There had to be a connection. My dreams had taken on a fever pitch and I didn't like where they were taking me. Troubles in my dreams had spilled out into my life—the flooded town, the blinding blizzard, my busted hand, and now this—Dad getting his face half ripped off by a giant bear. These were all bad dreams come true. And what about Uncle Jonah, with his spooky carvings, his mind-reading tricks, his odd chuckles and funny looks? What did he have to do with how these cards were dealt? I didn't care to find out.

A cold shudder gripped my worn-out heart, then fell away as something in me died.

I turned back to *Nanurluk's* ghastly face. Several timeless minutes passed. I realized that the fingers of my broken hand had been absently stroking my once precious polar bear toe bone that had tapped the center of my chest for years. I reached up with my good hand and pulled hard, snapping the caribou rawhide that held it around my neck. I dropped the cord and bone onto *Nanurluk's* face and closed the book. I put on my parka and boots, tucked my sketchbook under my arm, and slipped out of the room.

The wind was amazingly bitter for April but what did I care? No weather surprised me anymore. Peering through horizontal snow I found exactly what I was looking for in the parking lot behind the hotel. I walked up to a giant dumpster and lifted the lid. Something black flew up into my face and I fell backwards into the snow. I looked up to see a raven settle on top of a streetlight. I opened the dumpster again and winged my sketchbook into a sticky puddle of motor oil and what looked like frozen vomit.

A few hours later I woke up to the sound of a garbage truck tipping the dumpster's contents into its hold, then crushing everything into oblivion. I rolled over and dropped like a stone into a dry, dreamless sleep.

The Bear Shaman's Song

Part VII
Both Bear and Hunter Forgotten

Harpoon and snow knife,
Seal and seal hole,
Hunter and bear—
All are lost
In the crushing ice
In the hungry sea.
No traces remain
Except these prints on the beach
Blurring together.

Fallen Angel

I hadn't done one bear sketch since tossing my best artwork into the dumpster after Dad's attack. I'd almost burned my dream journal along with it but something bigger than anger stopped me. My dream machine had been going haywire lately, but I brushed it off as nothing more than mental static. When I heard the stone Angel up on the hill behind the church had fallen, my *inuksuk* dream came rushing back to me in living Technicolor. I felt like a seawall had burst in my brain, releasing a deluge of painful memories that I'd swept under the rug for months.

It happened on June tenth. A big windstorm hit, almost as big as last fall's Labor Day storm. I heard on the radio that the wind was gusting as high as eighty miles an hour over in Inniturliq. Crazy!

Luckily it was an offshore wind and we were spared another disastrous flood or stampede of ice. What set this storm apart from others is what it did to the rotting ice. We usually don't see much open water until well into July. But the south wind had blown so hard overnight, it tore the land-fast ice from the shore and created an open lead of water about a mile wide.

"Another surprise from the skies," was what Rosie called it, a weather fluke that nobody in town had ever seen before.

Like when lightning hit the church. Like when seawater crashed on the shore in January. Like when the Angel blew over— or so everybody said. I knew better.

From town, the Angel wasn't very big. You could hardly see it. But when it disappeared from the hill, everybody was talking about it.

"Our guardian Angel's bit the dust," announced Gabe over breakfast. He'd heard about it on the local 6:00 A.M. newscast.

Of course Mom got pretty excited over this one. "It's a sign!" she said, flinging open the curtains on the only window facing Anirniq Hill.

"Like, what else *could* it be, Mom?" I asked.

Mom and Wiggins seemed to be on the same wavelength and he immediately clicked into his *"Game ovah! Game ovah!"* routine.

I normally didn't give two hoots about Mom's signs and wonders. But after a recent string of chaotic dreams—none of which I'd recorded—I needed time to glue my inner world together. I could do without things falling apart in the outer world. There was something electric that hung in the air after that windstorm and I wasn't in the mood to get zapped.

The wind had died as quickly as it rose. I heard Rosie's shave-and-a-haircut knock on our door just before she swung it open and stomped into the living room with her gumboots on. "Morning, all. Hey, Ash, let's go check it out."

I knew exactly what she meant. "Check what out, Rosie?"

"The fallen Angel. We've got to put Humpty-Dumpty back together again. Who else is going to watch over all the sinners in this town?"

She was in the best of spirits. I was in the worst. "That's Father Ungali's job. He can handle it. You want to play cards or something? Scrabble maybe?"

Rosie made a big show of cleaning one ear out with her finger. "What? I'm hearing things. *You* want to stay inside after a storm like *that?*"

I love the freshness after a rain. What it does to those old lichens splattered on the rocks. Before a rain they're dry and crunchy like corn flakes. After, they get all soft and swollen like seaweed. I love how the rain brings out their colors—black lichens turn a dark olive, white ones go all powdery green, orange ones glow like hot coals. After a good rain, I sometimes spend hours up in the hills with my pastels, sketching away, sitting on a rain-soaked rock, oblivious to my wet bum. But that day, all I wanted to do was hide. I didn't want to go up there and look at it. I didn't want to fix the Angel. *Don't go up there. Don't disturb her. Let her rest in pieces.*

You see, I knew what knocked over the Angel. It wasn't the wind. The wind was just a cover. An alibi.

But of course Rosie hypnotized me into it. She just stood by the door, refusing to take off her jean jacket, saying, "*Atii, atii,* Ashley. Let's go!"

Rosie had this weird power over me and I usually did exactly what she wanted. Sometimes when I felt like crawling into a hole, she'd clamp a leash on my neck and drag me out somewhere—like the way sled dogs used to drag a dead polar bear out of its den. I was feeling steamed as I slipped on my boots and jacket and wanted to tell her, *Nothing personal, Rosie, but sometimes you make me feel like a bloody dead bear, dragging me around by the throat like this.* But something stopped me and the words choked in my throat.

Anyway, it wasn't her, it was me. Rosie's got no power over me. As Mom would say, I give it to her.

Whatever.

Somehow she got me out the door and climbing that hill.

Wounded Trail

I'll never tell her. Ever. That's what I told myself over and over as Rosie and I walked towards Anirniq Hill. *I'll never tell her about that dream. The one from last winter where the polar bear bowled over the* inuksuk, *then ripped my face off.*

I'd had enough bad dreams come true.

The trail up Anirniq Hill began just behind the church. It led right out of the cemetery. Mom called it a "spirit trail." Of course she would. And of course I had to bug her about that. "So, Mom, I suppose next Halloween you'll be on the lookout for a parade of skeletons running up and down that hill, maybe training for their marathon to the Promised Land?"

"Too late to train then," she had said, in all seriousness. "We've got to start here and now. That *is* the Promised Land."

"Whatever you say, Mom."

"Dead men tell no tales," piped up Gabe.

"Huh?" I said.

"Dead men don't run marathons either."

"Whatever you say, Gabe."

I wasn't in the mood for spirits or skeletons the day Rosie and I climbed Anirniq Hill. I'd been spooked enough as we walked past the church.

"Well, look at that," exclaimed Rosie, staring at the Madonna statue. "The poor kid's arm fell off."

A faint tremor went through me. The plaster arm that had dangled from the Christ child for as long as anybody knew had broken clean off. It lay in a dirty puddle of rainwater, his tiny hand opened to the sky in what looked like a gesture of pleading. "Do you think it was the wind?" I asked.

"Wow! Must've been. Scored a direct hit on one Angel and one baby Jesus." Rosie sort of chuckled but I think she was a bit shocked too. "That was some honkin' big wind."

We gawked at the broken statue for a while, then hoofed it through the cemetery, stepping around broken crosses and rock-piles that may or may not have marked graves.

Aana liked to say the trail up Anirniq Hill was ten thousand years old. Some people around here liked to believe her. My bull-shit alarm went off over that kind of stuff but, where Aana was concerned, I didn't say anything. I let her believe what she liked. Just last week in social studies, we'd heard that ten thousand years ago this part of the world was still locked in an ice age. No trail. No people. Just glacial ice.

Still, it must have been a pretty old trail. Aana said hunters used to climb up here in summer and watch for polar bears cruising the coastline, as they chased down crabs and dug up shelfish—that is, until bears disappeared from around here. "Don't know what happened to the polar bears," she once told me. "Maybe somebody said something bad about them and the bears said, 'Uh-uh, good-bye, Nanurtalik.'"

The trail was deadly slippery but there was no turning back. Though the rain had stopped long ago, all around us we could hear trickles of water hurrying down to the sea. Since we'd moved here last June, I must have been up it a hundred times. I knew this trail like the curve of my long fingers. But there was something weird about it today. Not the gurgling sounds. That was normal. Some people called this Whispering Hill. Not the rainbow sheen on the wet rocks. No. Something was weird with the ground. Something I'd never seen.

The trail had opened up overnight.

Rosie noticed it first. "What the—Was there an earthquake or something last night?"

"Fat chance. This place hasn't seen an earthquake in a million years. Looks like everything's melting, like the permafrost collapsed or something."

"Can't handle heat, I guess," Rosie said, trying to make sense of this mess.

We stood before a long, sneering gash in the hillside, big enough to swallow both of us whole. Clumps of soggy peat hung over a freshly exposed wedge of ground ice that peeked through the soil like rotting teeth. I decided then and there not to say anything about this to Mom. I could already hear her response. "You see, everything *is* falling apart. It's the Great Chaos unfolding in our own backyards."

We stared at the gash like southerners gawking at a traffic accident along a highway. It cut clean through Aana's ten-thousand-year-old trail. Clearly this sort of thing didn't happen every day. There was a new pain here I couldn't put my finger on but I think Rosie felt it too.

I wanted to spin on my heels and run as fast as I could out of that cemetery. But of course, we continued up the trail. I stole a final glance at the wounded ground as we climbed. I could see something bright poking through the peat. I squinted. It wasn't ice. Some kind of weird rock, nothing like the purplish brown shale that covered Anirniq Hill. It was a reddish orange color streaked with yellow.

The sight of it sent a cold tingle through a dusty corner of my brain and I abruptly turned my back on it.

Everything's Changing

CLIMBING ANIRNIQ HILL
SATURDAY, JUNE 10TH, 1:20 P.M.

The wounded trail seemed to open some sore spots in Rosie and she started rhyming off her family's latest tragedies while I trudged silently behind her. As usual, everything was falling apart there too.

Her older brother Jake had almost drunk himself to death on his eighteenth birthday. "The cops found him face down in a ditch at the edge of town," Rosie said. She hadn't seen her father in two days. "Sleeping off another bender in somebody's outhouse."

"I think these weird winds drive everybody a bit loony," I said, struggling to be helpful. But mostly I just listened. I felt like her psychotherapist sometimes.

Things must have been pretty bad for Rosie. I'd never seen my lion-hearted friend lose it like this. But I knew her family's chronic catastrophes could pull the plug on her power. I knew she'd gone over the edge when her voice went all squealy and she started waving her arms above her head as if protecting herself from a mob of angry ravens. I was about to break my gloomy silence again when she stumbled backwards on the loose shale and almost knocked me over.

"Hey, who's the tour guide here?" I said, throwing all compassion to the wind.

"Won't you please pardon my sins! It's a tricky trail."

"I can't believe it. You've lived here all your life and you still haven't learned this trail yet." I wasn't really mad at her. The rain-washed air had already flushed a lot of mud from my brain. I was more scared than mad, but sometimes fear comes out disguised that way. I pointed to the black rocks. "See how the lichens are worn off here. That's the one and only way to go."

She stepped aside with her hands on her hips. "Sorr-ree, ma'am! Like, this is my first time up the hill."

We'd been up here together countless times. I squeezed my lips shut, fearing I might say something even stupider.

"Why don't *you* go first, then?" Rosie grumbled.

I wasn't really mad at her. And she wasn't really mad at me. She was mad at life. Why do people take their personal stuff out on each other, especially when they're supposedly best friends? It was all a smokescreen for inner battles. I knew all this in my head. Still, the tension wouldn't blow away.

I sighed and fixed my eyes on the knobby summit of Anirniq Hill like we were tackling Everest. "This was *your* idea, remember."

I held my ground. She held hers. We just stood there not looking at each other, like two teed-off sled dogs. It was one of those stand-offs I hoped we could laugh about later. But she out-stubborned me again and I grudgingly took the lead, just like she wanted.

To move was healing. With each step, stiffness flowed out of my legs, my chest, my head. It poured out like water through a sieve. I could breathe again. I quickly forgot what we'd been arguing about. My dreams were dust in the wind. All that mattered was the next step. That was enough for now. In this simple act I found shelter. I clung to each step like they were solid rungs on a flimsy rope ladder swinging in the wind. Each step. Each breath. Each moment. Mom's words for the here and now came back to me: the Promised Land. A hokey idea but for once I agreed with her.

As we picked our way up through the loose rocks, my mind wandered backwards in time. I wondered how old this trail really was, how many Inuit feet had climbed Anirniq Hill—Angel Hill in English—and whose hands had built the Angel *Inuksuk* in the first place. This got me thinking about my *inuksuk* dream again, and I tilted my gaze up from the rocks to see who might be watching us, waiting to pounce. I looked over both shoulders. I scanned the whole hill. I suddenly felt small. Vulnerable.

My gumboot went down on a wet chunk of loose shale and I totally wiped out, almost cracking my skull on a big rock. "OOF!"

"What *are* you looking for?" demanded Rosie.

"Ah, snakes," I said, wiping mangled black lichens off my hands.

Rosie laughed. "So it's snakes now? Get serious. The nearest snake is a thousand miles from here."

"Can't be too sure these days."

"What do you mean?"

"Did you see that robin last week?"

"Who could miss it? Merrily singing on the roof of the post office all day long. Major weird, eh?"

"Freaked out Uncle Jonah when he heard it. Gabe too. He went out and recorded it with the radio station's shotgun mike, then broadcast it all over town."

"As if no one had heard it. That robin belongs here about as much as your Wiggins. Talk about oddball species!"

People liked to tease us about Wiggins. Lord Gord once told Dad that it was bad luck to keep a bird in the house. "Hey, don't you start picking on Wiggins too. So what if he comes from the Amazon? He's family. He belongs."

We started up the trail again, slower, closer. Something had thawed between us. "It was butterflies last summer," I said.

"What?"

Rosie's mind had darted off to more pressing matters. "Strange butterflies," I said.

"You mean those big yellow and black ones?"

"Nobody'd ever seen them up here either. Swallowtails."

"Swallow-whats?"

"Swallowtails. Eastern Tiger Swallowtails, officially known as *Papilio glaucus*," I added, with a thick, Italian accent.

"Oh-kay. If you say so."

I wasn't trying to show off. That's what they're called. I get a kick out of nature's scientific names. Besides, I think it's important to find out about these things. Figure out what the heck's going on. Everything's changing so fast. You gotta stay on top of it.

It was Rosie's turn to stop. As tough as she is. I'm convinced she can't walk and think at the same time. "So, what about the monster crab that washed up on the beach last fall."

"The furry one?"

"Yeah. All covered with pink fur with this humongous claw. Skinny legs as long as my arms. Like it dropped from outer space. Did you see that thing?"

"The dogs ripped it apart before I got a chance. I saw a photo at school. Some kind of deep-sea spider crab."

"*Bizz-arre.*"

"Supposed to be moving north as ocean currents warm up."

"It's like we're being invaded by aliens or something."

"Not far from the truth really. So why not snakes?" I asked.

"It'll be panda bears next."

"No bamboo."

Rosie tripped again, doing a face plant into my back. Maybe she was looking for snakes. "What?"

"No bamboo. That's what pandas eat."

"Okay. It's agreed. No pandas. How about . . . a giant anteater? Could be good eating."

"Not enough ants."

"A three-toed sloth?"

"Like, duh. No trees to hang around in."

"A pink flamingo?"

"Actually, there're a couple already in town, stuck on top of Vince's shack."

Rosie sniggered. "Almost got you there. Okay, how about koala bears?"

"No eucalyptus trees. Besides, they're not bears."

"Okay. What are they then?"

"Let's cut this crap, Rosie." I didn't want to talk. I needed all my concentration to keep on the lookout for—

"Whoah! *You* can sure be a bear sometimes."

I had to chuckle in spite of my woozy brain and wheezy chest. That happened all the time in my dreams. A polar bear would chase me, then all of a sudden I'd be chasing a bear. Then—this felt *so* weird—there'd be only one of us. It was like we shared the same body.

My chest hurt and I realized I'd been gulping air with each step. Something had triggered my asthma and I felt like an eighty-year-old climbing a ladder.

We walked on in a heavy silence until we crested the hill and spotted the pile of rubble that was once the Angel. I made a mental note to rip one particular dream out of my journal. Pretend it never happened.

My dream about *Nanurluk* knocking over the Angel.

Defining Ashley

Summit of Anirniq Hill
Saturday, June 10th, 2:10 p.m.

"You stuck?" asked Rosie.

Rosie sounded far away. I hadn't realized I'd stopped dead in my tracks when I'd seen the fallen Angel. I stared at that rock pile like it was a nest of seething vipers. I felt my lungs contract. My eyes hurt and the hill, the smashed *inuksuk*, Rosie—everything—went all swimmy, like I was underwater. For one sizzling moment, a door between worlds had been flung open and I didn't know which way to fall.

"Ash? You okay?"

"What? Yeah. Altitude sickness, I guess."

"Sure." Rosie bounded up to the mess of broken rocks like it was completely harmless. "Come on. Help me put the old girl back together."

"No, wait!" What was I saying? "Shouldn't we look for that bear first?" Clearly my mouth and brain had disconnected. "I mean, shouldn't we make sure the coast is clear before we—before we fix that thing." I squinted around, pretending to scan the coast for wandering bears. "We could see her pretty good from up here if she's still around. Aana told me they used to come up here to look for bears." Next thing you know I'd be telling her about that dream, the dream I felt I'd just walked into.

"So all that snake talk was just a crock. Come on, Ash, forget your old bear. She's halfway to Inniturliq by now. They got a way bigger dump than ours."

My head swirled. My boots filled with lead. A couple of snow buntings whizzed past my nose, drawing me back to a familiar, heather-scented world. With clearing eyes, I watched them swoop down on the fallen Angel, salute her death with a cheerless twitter, and shoot off down the hill. Then, out of nowhere, a cold fist of icy air hit me point-blank and my arms and legs flew out like a scared cat in midair.

It was my turn to lose it. I was floating, falling into darkness. I could feel a tremor going through me, cracking something tight and tired in me, like a second skin that no longer fit. From the deepest part of my belly I could feel a shriek welling up. It rose to the top of my throat like thick vomit.

Before I let go with both barrels, my fall was broken by Rosie's horsey laughter.

"Ash, are your planning to hang-glide your way home?"

The tremor subsided like a broken wave returning to the sea. I blinked hard. I realized that my arms and legs were still spread wide in a skydiver's pose. I yanked myself together, hugging my arms around me as if I stood naked against the wind.

Rosie found one of my hands and dragged me over to the fallen Angel. I could feel my eyelids tightening as if I was about to walk into a morgue. Would she notice my shattered face in those stones?

"You see?" she said, in almost motherly tones. "It's just a pile of rocks. Nothing to freak out over."

She kneeled over the jumbled stones. I could tell she was sizing them up, trying to piece the *inuksuk* together in her mind. All that was left of the original *inuksuk* were two stout legs and an almost perfectly rectangular capstone forming the waist. I saw nothing faintly resembling Ashley Anowiak. I stood up and looked out over the Spit far below. The air was as clean and fresh as air could be and I forced a bucket-load of it into my lungs.

"This was one fancy *inuksuk*," Rosie said thoughtfully. She picked up a long, smooth chunk, probably part of an arm. It looked like it had been sculpted. "You know what?"

My head hurt and I had no idea where she was going with this. "What, Rosie?"

"These structures are probably as close as our ancestors ever got to building pyramids or temples or whatever."

"Uh-huh," I said while double-checking all the rocks for toothy grins or eyes like mine.

"No, really. This lookout must have been some kind of—what would your mother call it?"

I looked up at her.

"A power spot?"

"Yeah, that's it. Whadya' think? Some kind of sacred site where shamans would come to hear their secret songs or go on a vision quest—"

"Or take a pee. Come on, Rosie, you're right, this *is* just a pile of rocks. And a pretty view." I bravely picked up what looked like the other arm. "So, do you want to rebuild the old girl or not?"

She stood up and put her hands on her hips. "Maybe there's a proper way to do this. I mean, this probably still *is* a power spot. What if we don't do it right and—"

"Mom's a sucker for all that power spot stuff. I'm afraid it doesn't run in the family."

"Why are you so hard on your mom?"

"I'm not."

"You are."

"Not."

"Are."

"You treat her as if she's committed some unforgivable thought crime or something."

"Hmph."

"At least she's home every night, unlike *some* mothers I know around here. Makes your meals, helps you with your homework—"

"Does my laundry. Yeah, like, I know already. I have the perfect mom."

"So?"

"So what?"

"So why do you always rag on her like that? Like she's a—"

"Voodoo priestess?"

"Well, yeah."

"She'd be the first to tell you that history's given voodoo a bum wrap. But that's her business, not mine. Trouble is, she'd like to convert me into her very own New Age princess." I slammed the arm-piece down on the *inuksuk*'s waist, almost breaking it in two.

"Watch it, Ash."

I steadied my rock as she set a big anchor stone on top of it.

"You don't really believe that," Rosie said. "About converting you, I mean."

"One space cowgirl in the house is more than enough, thanks. When she starts floating away into mumbo jumbo land I like to reel her in with a bit of common sense backtalk."

In spite of the cool wind, I was beginning to sweat with all the lifting. The biggest chunk was a busty torso piece that we hefted into place with much serious grunting. It melded with the rocks below like we'd glued them together.

"It's for her own good," I continued. "If you could see all those weird books she used to bring home from her flights south."

"I've seen some of them. Spooky stuff."

"Tarot and Tea. Talking with Nature. Everyday Shamans. Animal Medicine Cards. Witches I Have Known. How healthy is *that?*"

"She doesn't fly down there anymore, does she?"

"Hardly ever. Not since we moved here. She's kind of off the airline grid now. Good thing too. She used to go to all these creepy séances."

"To catch up with the relatives, I suppose?"

"Yeah. *Dead* relatives. Some strange family reunion."

"She could have worse hobbies, you know. Like booze or crack or . . ." Rosie sucked in her breath, "square dancing!" She was really trying to lighten me up but failing miserably.

"This New Age stuff's as addictive," I said, "and as dangerous. Sometimes I think she should be sent to some institution, you know, like where people get deprogrammed. Lock her up for a couple of weeks in a cozy, padded cell with some down-to-earth therapist. I bug her about it just to burst her bubble now and then. Keep her feet on the ground. Our little . . . chats, we'll say, help keep her brain rooted to her skull. Otherwise I'm convinced it would blow away into the clouds, like a balloon."

We both looked up as if following Mom's brain drifting off into the sky. A big chunk of blue was showing now, sliced through by the contrails of three high-flying jets.

"And crash into one of those jets up there," Rosie said. "Doesn't it seem to you like there're a lot more jets flying over us these days?"

"Mom says it's all part of the Great Chaos. She says it's a sign of too many confused, restless people in the world. They're all— how does she put it?—*hungry for meaning in life.* So they fly all over the place looking for happiness. Everything's a *sign* to her. I say bunk. It's only because the Russians opened up their air space and let a bunch more planes fly over the North Pole, that's all. I read about it in the *Tundra Times.*"

"Yeah, I saw something about that."

"I even showed her the article but she didn't believe it. As if it was a threat to her Great Chaos theory. She threw the newspaper into the woodstove like she was mad at it. Like she was just plain mad, I mean, like, *crazy* mad."

"Carole's one of the sanest people I know in this crazy cesspool of humanity. Just 'cause somebody thinks or acts a little different doesn't mean they're nuts. Look at Gabe."

"What about Gabe?"

"Well, he's a little . . . unpredictable sometimes. A little explosive maybe. If a person didn't know him or get his jokes they'd probably say he was a total fruitcake. But you'd be the first person to throw yourself in front of a bear to defend him."

"Yeah, so?"

"Gabe's got his problems all right. Besides his eyes, he couldn't give you change from a dollar if his life depended on it. And he's got the attention span of a lemming. But Gabe probably has a thousand fiddle tunes up his sleeve. And he's got to be the friendliest guy in Nanurtalik, hands down."

"What are you saying?"

Rosie stopped chinking the *inuksuk*'s armor with little rocks and leveled her deep brown eyes at me. "What I'm saying is your mom is no crazier than Gabe. Or you for that matter. A little different, maybe. But what's wrong with that? Gabe's got his jokes and his fiddle music. Your mom's got her signs and her stars. And you . . . well, you've got your art and your dreams. These are gifts, Ash, not curses. Everybody's got them."

My dreams were nobody's business but mine. "And you, Rosie?" I snapped. "What's *your* gift?" The edge in my voice surprised me.

Rosie dropped to her knees and stared up at the resurrected Angel. She stuck a flat stone into a narrow gap in its arm. "Oh, I don't know. How about bricklaying?"

Nothing came to me either for a moment until an image rose of her taking on Lord Gord at a public meeting or wrenching a fishhook out of the snapping jaws of a thrashing Arctic char or singing her heart out in front of the whole community. "You've got guts to spare, Rosie." As I realized this, something crusty in me softened. "That's what I like about you most."

Rosie laughed. "No, I know what it is. I'm a real good faker. That's all."

She was the last person to talk about herself and quickly turned the spotlight back on me. "You know, I read something in one of those trashy mags beside the grocery line that helped me figure you out."

"Oh, thanks a lot. And what *trash* did you discover?"

"There was this article that really got me nodding. Yep, I said to myself, that's Ash." Rosie paused, obviously enjoying the suspense. "I got so into it that I stepped out of line to finish the article. There's no way I'd buy that crap."

"So we've gone from trash to crap. Now you've really got my interest up. And what, pray tell, was this article about?"

"Well, funny you should ask." Rosie pulled some torn and crumpled pages from the back of her jeans. There was dark muck on them from her bum-slide on the hill and she brushed it off.

"I thought you said you didn't buy the magazine."

Rosie unfolded the pages with a criminal look in her eye. "Why pay for the whole thing when you only want one article? Like you said, fearless. Besides, I did it for you," she said, sticking it under my nose.

"Oh, great. So now I'm your accomplice in—" I ran out of air for a second, like somebody had clapped a hand over my mouth. I was looking at a blue-eyed, blonde-haired little girl with a puckish smile and a frizz of purplish light around her head. That glow, that color, just like the light that danced from my harpoon, that enveloped the bear of my deepest dreams. The article was titled "Krystal Kids." I pretended to be aloof. "This looks like that kid in *The Exorcist.*"

"Ever heard of an Indigo child?"

I hadn't but I didn't like the sound of it. "Remember Mom's Internet was down for most of last winter. We're a bit out of the loop." I tossed the pages back to Rosie. They almost blew off the hill but she managed to stomp on them with her boot. "And we don't subscribe to *Star News* magazine."

"I bet she's heard of it. There're supposed to be these special kids out there who. . . ." She ran her muddy fingers down the article. "Ah, here it is, 'who are gifted with a new and unusual set of psychological powers.'"

"I thought you said *everybody's* got gifts."

"Well, yeah, but they're buried in most people. Covered in dust and junk. You've dug through all that and found your treasure—just like we do at the dump—and you spread it around."

"Come on."

"No, really. Like, who in this town hasn't been bowled over by your bear sketches?"

"Big deal. It's a small town, Rosie. Starved for culture. My pictures are crumbs." We both knew I didn't mean this, but I was trying to throw cold water on her thought parade. It didn't work.

"No, listen to this. 'How to recognize an Indigo child'. . . ."

"You're not suggesting that—"

"Shut up and listen." Rosie leaned back against the Angel and propped the article on her lap. The Angel's head, which must have weighed thirty pounds, teetered on its rocky shoulders.

"Cripes, Rosie, go easy! That lady's gonna brain you if you snuggle up to her like that!"

"No worries, Ash," Rosie said without looking up from the article. "We've built this baby like a brick shithouse. It would take a hurricane to knock *her* down." Then she dove headlong into the article, dissecting quotes from it like a lawyer making her final pitch before the jury. "'Indigo children are now recognized as one of the most rapid advances in human evolution ever documented in the civilized world. These children of the new millennium are sensitive, gifted souls with an evolved consciousness. They have come here to help change the vibrations of our species. They are our bridge to the future. . . .'"

I grabbed my stomach with both hands. "Oh, Rosie, where's the barf bag?"

"Go with me on this, Ash. I'm getting to the good stuff."

"It's good you didn't pay for that."

"Come on, just listen. 'Born within the past fifteen years, these children demonstrate remarkable abilities in the area of clairvoyance, healing, memory, transpersonal communication, or—and get this, Ash—'profoundly creative expression in the areas of music or *art*.'" Rosie punched the word "art" as if shoving a long paintbrush in my face.

"They sound like aliens to me."

"Well . . . in fact they *are!*" Rosie's finger raced over the page. "Lemmee find that part."

"Huh?"

"Yeah, here it is. 'The Indigo child may seem antisocial or *alienated* when not with their own kind. If there are no others of like consciousness around them, they often turn inward, feeling like no other human understands them. Though school is generally not challenging for them academically, it is often extremely difficult for them socially.'" Rosie looked up from the page with a satisfied smile. "You see, Ash? You *are* an alien."

I just shook my head, jetting a great sigh through my nose.

"Still won't own up, eh? Okay, here's the clincher. 'Regardless of their specific gifts, these children are generally bright, independent thinkers who display amazing powers of memory. They share a strong desire to live intuitively, tapping into an inner wellspring of wisdom often expressed by a clear sense of purpose in life, a well-developed sense of morality, and an unusually fertile *dream life*.'"

"So what's this 'Indigo' bit," I asked, trying not to sound too curious.

Rosie held up the picture of the moonchild while straining her neck around to read the caption below. "'Indigos are easy to recognize by their unusually large, clear eyes, and, for those that can read them, a purplish-blue glow about their heads.'"

"Indigo. Like the paint covering the ceiling of the church?" I blurted. My curiosity had leaked out.

Rosie proudly folded the article and stuffed it back into her jeans. "Yeah, come to think of it. Maybe there's a connection there."

I just shrugged. I'd have to process all this later. Alone.

"I rest my case," Rosie said, rubbing her hands. She'd been watching me like the ball was now in my court.

I had a fierce allergic reaction to labels. They made me want to scream. Mom thought she had Gabe all figured out. Like discovering a new recipe, she one day announced that he showed all the classic symptoms of Williams Syndrome stirred in with a smidgen of Autistic Savantism and a sprinkling of Fetal Alcohol Syndrome. In her mind, Uncle Jonah was a bi-polar schizophrenic suffering from post-traumatic alcoholism and the gradual onset of class two Alzheimer's Disease. If she got wind of this Indigo stuff she'd soon have me all sorted out and safely tucked away in a bottle beside her treasured bear bones. "Indigo, schmindigo," I said, hoping to close the courtroom door.

"Don't you think the shoe fits rather well, Ash?"

"That's bullshit, Rosie. Like you said, everybody's got some kind of gift. I'll buy that. But a few bright kids out there doesn't mean there's some kind of New Age revolution going on. If anything, it's like these powers or whatever have been around for ages and we've just forgotten how to get at them. Maybe we're all born with this magic bank account inside but there's nobody around anymore to show us how to make withdrawals."

I was surprising myself again, like I actually knew what I was talking about.

"You mean, like . . . a shaman?"

I thought of *Tuurngaq* and his bear claw belt, of the singing shaman of my dreams, but I quickly pushed them out of view. "Sure, all right. But can you name one?"

"Well . . . there's Black Elk and—"

"No, I mean a *living* shaman."

Rosie gave me a vacant look. "I don't know. Certainly not in *this* town."

"In any Arctic town?"

"There used to be. My grandfather *Ittuq* told some pretty amazing stories. You know, people popping in and out of iglus without using the door. That sort of stuff."

"That was then. This is now."

Rosie shrugged. "I guess the missionary types snuffed out that part of our culture."

"Like I say. There's nobody left."

"Maybe these Indigo kids are sort of filling the gap."

"Can we drop the Indigo freaks for now?"

"Okay, then. You're not an Indigo child." Rosie stood up and arched her back into a giant stretch. It was time to go. "Then how about an S.I.T?"

"What?"

"An S.I.T."

"Lemmee guess . . . a Seriously Impaired Twit. How thoughtful of you, Rosie."

"A Shaman In Training."

"A *what?*" I said, laughing a little too hard.

"Why not?"

"You just said there's nobody out there."

"Maybe shamans don't need to live anywhere in particular."

"You mean, like they're floating around in cyberspace waiting for a collect call from one of your Indigo Girls?"

"Ever heard of *inner* space? Maybe that's where they're hiding."

I felt somehow violated. What could Rosie know of this world? That was my terrain. My home. When I saw it most clearly, it was a hundred times more real than the breeze on my face and the wet chunks of slate beneath my feet. "That's all history. Any shaman stuff we heard about in Northern Studies class happened eighty years ago. Remember? Those anthropologists like Ras . . . Rasmussen and Peary, was it?"

Rosie shrugged. "I might've missed that class.

"Anyway, they picked the old stories and songs right out of the Elders' heads. Picked them clean. Take nothing but culture, leave nothing but smallpox-laced blankets. That was the anthropologist's motto."

"Rasmussen was half Inuk like you."

I'd forgotten that, but I could feel a roll coming on. "Do you remember that other guy we heard about in class, the one who—"

"The grave-robber?"

"Yeah. He robbed a bunch of traditional graveyards over in Alaska and took a boat-load of heads back to some museum down south."

"What's-his-face—Icelandic family—Stefansson."

"That's him, Rosie. For ten points. First he picked their heads clean, then took them home in a box."

"Those anthropologist guys wrote down a lot of the old songs and stuff. If it weren't for them, we might have lost a lot more."

"It's all gone, Rosie. The magic's gone—if it ever *did* exist."

"What about your grandmother?"

"Aana? She might be smart. She might be full of tricks. Okay, like—she's got a few old tales and tunes up her sleeve."

on thin ice

Rosie folded her arms and nodded slowly.

"But that doesn't make her a closet shaman," I said. "No more than I am."

"I just wonder sometimes," Rosie said dreamily. "What if someone with your gifts had been born a hundred years ago?" She raised her eyebrows a hair or two and looked up at the clouds.

"Come off it, Rosie. A few wild dreams, a pretty picture or two, and you're ready to sign up for my levitation class."

"Something's in your blood, Ash. Something different."

"My blood is just a watered-down soup cast off by leprechauns, French voyageurs, and Iglu builders."

"What about old *Ikuma?*"

I choked. "Uncle Jonah?"

"Yeah. Think about it. Where does a guy like that get the smarts to carve statues that sizzle with life? Like his stash of bears under the church. They stare right back at you, Ash."

"God, Rosie. You don't really be—"

"With fire in their eyes. You've seen them."

You bet I'd seen them. Inside and out. That was my business, not hers. "That's a bit over the top, don't you think?"

She sat up and clapped her hands. "I just got it. *That's* why they call him *Ikuma,* the fire man. He draws fire out of stone."

I couldn't look at her. Scrambling for safety, my gaze locked on the Spit, curving out into Crab Bay like the tail of a fox. Huge swells from last night's storm broke over it. They stretched their foamy fingers clear across the runway. A sky-sized movie screen unfurled before my eyes, veiling the Spit. Up rose an image of my dream-shaman, dancing around a huge *Nanurluk* figure carved from glowing firestone. The shaman held a harpoon high above his head and kept playfully thrusting it towards the giant bear's chest as he sang his haunting song.

Could I really hear it? No, it was only the shrill laughter of a passing gull. I shook my head like I had water in my ears. I saw the frothy Spit again, clear as day.

"You okay, Ash?"

"Yeah, yeah . . . ah, what were you saying?"

"Jonah's carvings. I figure that old Father Broussard was *afraid* of Jonah's carvings, Ash. Why else would he stuff them in that trunk and deep-six them under the church?"

"Well, he might've been keeping them for—"

"That old priest must've felt threatened by them."

"I suppose they stole the priest's *power,* as Mom would say?"

"Stole it from him? Gave it to us? I don't know. He must've thought they were idols."

"You mean, like in the Old Testament?" I turned on my TV evangelist voice and raised my arms to the sky. " 'When men forsook God and sank into ignorance and moral corruption. When men fell to their knees before the birds of the air and beasts of the field.' "

"Exactly. You know, living idols worshiped by the local heathens. That's how they saw us."

I dropped my arms. "Speak for yourself."

"Those statues must've really messed up the priest's missionary work?"

I shrugged.

"That's why he scooped them up as fast as Jonah could make them and locked them in that trunk."

"Why didn't he just ditch them in the sea?"

"Maybe he was afraid to. You told me how they were all carefully wrapped up in gold cloth. It's like he was giving them a proper burial, like in the pyramids or something."

"You're nuts, Rosie. Jonah made some pretty carvings. The priest took a liking to them. He got a little carried away—"

"Didn't your grandmother tell you he bought every single one."

"Most of them, I guess. Except for that firestone cup of his. And maybe a couple in some museum down south. Okay, so old Father Broussard got a little obsessed. Then he forgot about them. Then he died. End of story."

"Remember, after you'd gone under the church that night? You told me Ungali said Father Broussard thought those carvings sucked some kind of weird energy out of the ground?"

"Direct from the underworld."

"Yeah."

"Like a reverse lightning rod."

"Something like that I guess."

"Yeah, right."

"No, really. Has your dad ever figured what it is around here that's jamming his air waves? Maybe it has something to do with Jonah's sculptures."

"Come on, Rosie. You're not suggesting—" I turned and looked down at the cemetery. Even from up here I could see the fresh gash that split open last night and the reddish orange rock poking through. Now I knew what it was. More firestone.

"What, Ash? *What?*"

I looked back at the half-built Angel. "Nothing."

"Face it, Ash. However you look at it, there's something special about Jonah's sculptures."

I picked up a long narrow rock that must have been the Angel's right arm. "There's something special about *any* decent sculpture. Jonah was a good artist. He knew his soapstone."

"I'm talking something more than art here, Ashley. You can see it in your drawings too. The same gift."

"Why don't you and Mom have a nice little séance over this."

"I'm not trying to be funny."

"Neither am I. Really. Maybe you two can contact the statue spirits and they'll tell you their whole story." Something dark squirmed inside me when I said this. Like it was waking up.

"Same gift, Ash."

I folded my arms tight across my chest. "Like, that was over thirty years ago. Jonah burned out in the seventies."

"Same blood, Ash. Same blood as yours." She gave my pale hand a quick poke with her index finger as if proving her point. My skin went all white underneath, then gradually regained its color as the blood flowed back in. "Yep. Your blood's a little thinner maybe. Some French spice stirred in. A pinch of Irish. But basically it's the same as his." Rosie leaned back and looked at me funny. "You know, I've never noticed this before, but you've got the same nose as Jonah."

"Come on!"

"No, seriously. The same wide nose." She laughed. "Like the snout of a polar bear."

I impulsively rubbed the flat bridge of my nose "What *are* you getting at?"

"Maybe Jonah's gift was too much to handle. Too much energy roaring through him. Maybe he didn't have the strength to handle it and he got torched from the inside out. You know. He is *Ikuma* after all."

Rosie was definitely sounding like Mom. Gifts, energy, fire, inner strength. All that New Age lingo. "And maybe you're hallucinating all this."

"Face it, Ash. You and Jonah must have some weird link. How else would he know all about your dream bears?"

"How should I know? Maybe he sneaks up to my room when I'm at school and rifles through my dream journal."

Rosie started chinking the gaps in the *inuksuk* with smaller rocks. "When you think about it, you're a lot like him actually. Both dreamers. Both artists."

As usual, I granted Rosie the last word. All I wanted to do was fix the Angel and get the heck off the hill. I breathed easier with every rock, enjoying the simple satisfaction of working with my hands, especially since my spinning head had shut down in defeat.

"There," Rosie said with a triumphant clap. "The Angel's reborn and nobody turned into a frog. We must have done it right."

I sprang to my feet and high-fived Rosie. "Hallelujah, sister!" I was glad to get moving and shake off the dust from my brain. But my body had other ideas. I'd been sitting so long on those damp rocks that my bum had gone fast asleep along with most of my right leg. On top of that, I stood up so fast, all the blood must have drained from my head making me super dizzy. I took a couple pathetic steps forward, then tumbled sideways, like a rotten tree, landing smack on top of the Angel.

Rosie caught me in her arms before I did too much damage— to me or the Angel. "Hey, ya drunkard!" she yelled. "Would you watch where you pass out!"

I'd managed to bonk the Angel's head off with my shoulder and it almost hamburgered Rosie's foot. Before I could collect myself she froze and almost squeezed the breath out of me.

"Ash, look!"

There was no hint of clowning in her voice. I peered over my shoulder at her face. She looked genuinely scared and had fixed her eyes on something in the sky. Still hanging in her arms, I turned to follow her gaze and saw a big jet falling out of the clouds, heading straight for the sea.

Nanurtalik's 9-11

SUMMIT OF ANIRNIQ HILL
SATURDAY, JUNE 10TH, 3:05 P.M.

Long before my bear dreams started, I used to have recurring nightmares about planes plummeting from the sky, slamming into the tundra with an earth-shaking boom. They sprang from my worries about all the flying Mom used to do as a stewardess with Arctic Airways. After each nightmare I'd grab crayons and frantically draw pilots stomping out a cockpit fire, screaming passengers with their arms in the air, or a raging fireball devouring the plane. Then I'd throw my pictures in the woodstove to burn the dream images from my mind.

But it hadn't worked completely. Those images came racing back to me as Rosie and I stood, riveted to the summit of Anirniq Hill, watching that plane come down.

It looked like the jet had completely lost control, the way it wobbled in the sky. It seemed to be falling more than flying. The lower it got the taller we stood, until we were both on our tiptoes, with bodies stretched to the breaking point. Rosie started sobbing, almost instantly, making a deep, throaty noise like an Arctic loon makes in flight. I kept rubbing my eyes, not for tears but because I couldn't believe what I was seeing.

Thanks to Mom's job with the airline, I knew a bit about planes, at least enough to know that this one was in big trouble. Back in Inniturliq, where there's a half decent runway, I'd waved hello or goodbye to countless jets that carried Mom across the continent. Never, except in my nightmares, had I seen a plane approach the earth so fast and at such a steep angle. And those wings kept wobbling as if some maniac monkey was at the wheel.

As it got closer, broken thunder filled the sky, like the sound a jet makes when it takes off.

"Must be giving 'er full throttle," I said in a hushed voice.

"What the *hell* for?" asked Rosie, like she was really angry.

"Maybe to pull out of the dive." Jet-fuelled horsepower versus gravity. By the angle of that dive, it looked like the odds were stacked in favor of gravity. But wait—the nose seemed to be inching up.

"Look!" I shouted. "She's pulling out!"

Rosie grabbed my arm and started shaking it like a cheerleader's pom-pom. "It worked! It worked!"

I wrenched my arm back and squinted hard at the falling plane. Had I imagined it? No. With painful slowness, the plane started to break its descent. I squeezed Rosie's hand. I imagined cheers ringing through the aircraft as the pilot regained some control and everyone felt themselves sink into their seats at the bottom of the dive. But then I realized that anyone looking out the window might not feel so jolly. Instead of heading for the sea, the plane was now aimed squarely at Nanurtalik. It could never pull up in time.

This was not some air show flyby with a friendly tip of the wings. This was the real thing. Nanurtalik's 9-11.

"Shit!" whispered Rosie. "It's headed right for my house!"

"It can't," I stated flatly. "It won't."

Down in the village we could see people popping out of their houses, looking up at the thundering jet headed straight for them. Like ants scattering before the footfall of a human, some of them started running like crazy, down the street, out to the coast, even up the hill where we stood. Others took one quick look, then dove back into their houses as if a flimsy wood and shingle roof could protect them from a huge plane dropping in at five hundred miles per hour.

Rosie started that sobbing again. My stomach clenched tight and hot as I felt all my fear about to come to a boil. I remember thinking, *No wonder people scream when they're terrified.* My scream was seconds away. Like I'd witnessed all this before, my brain fast-forwarded to the horrendous boom of the plane slamming into the village. In my mind I saw the flames and the blood and the splintered remains of houses spread along a giant ditch of destruction that sliced the town in half. My stomach was about to split open as if cut by a cleaver.

Fishtail

SUMMIT OF ANIRNIQ HILL
SATURDAY, JUNE 10TH, 3:11 P.M.

The scream never came. My stomach loosened, so fast I thought I might soil my jeans. With a maneuver you'd expect more from a fighter jet than a full size passenger carrier, the plane went into an abrupt banking climb. Its new flight path brought its nose more or less in line with the top of Anirniq Hill—or, in other words, with Rosie and me.

I ducked for cover behind the *inuksuk*.

"Are you nuts, Ashley?" yelled Rosie. "Let's get out of here!" She started running down the back side of the hill.

"No, wait," I yelled. The plane was still climbing. Turning and climbing. Turning and climbing. It would be a close call but it looked like it would clear the hill. Though still shaking, the plane now behaved as if under control, veering gradually away from us in a wide clockwise turn. The rising thunder told me the pilot still had the throttle wide open. Gravity had lost this game. So far so good.

As the plane got closer I realized what all the wobbling was about. The right wing seemed to be damaged and was shaking something awful, especially under the strain of a tight, full-power turn. The plane was only a couple of hundred feet off the ground as it swooped over the village. The sound was deafening. I had never seen an airborne jet up so close. As the wounded plane whipped past Anirniq Hill, almost level with our noses, I could clearly read the dark blue letters painted on its pure white body: *Air France.* I convinced myself that I could see pale frightened faces pressed against the windows. Without thinking, Rosie and I threw up both arms and waved, cheering them on to wherever the heck they might safely touch down. Inniturliq maybe. Or—

Our arms dropped when we heard a sharp bang audible even above the scream of the plane. A split second later, oily black smoke belched from the left engine.

"What next?" shouted Rosie.

"It looks bad," I said. "Left wing's on fire. Right wing's about to fall off. They'll never make it to Inniturliq."

"Where else *could* they land?" asked Rosie.

Before I could say anything three hatches swung open under the plane and something dark dropped from its belly. Wheels. The plane's landing gear locked neatly into position.

"Does that answer your question?" I asked.

"No way!"

"They're gonna try to land right here, on the Spit."

"That big thing? Impossible!"

Another deadly threat now lay directly in the path of the wounded Air France jet, that is of course if the left engine didn't blow up or the right wing didn't shake clean off. For a plane this size, the runway itself was a death trap. It would be madness trying to land there. The Arctic Ocean lay just a hop, skip, and a jump away from the end of the airstrip. But what choice did they have, now that everything was falling apart?

Jets don't land here. Never have. The biggest thing to ever touch down on the Nanurtalik runway was a forty-four passenger Hawker-Siddeley 748, a clunky two-engine prop plane built around the time my dad wore moss diapers, probably in the fifties. The one that flew us here last summer smelled like a gas station and most of the ceiling light fixtures were cracked or half melted. Now how safe do you think *that* made me feel? But at least the thing fit the runway. I mean, *just* fit. There's a red fox den right off the end of the runway that we almost creamed after skidding to a long, jerky stop. Single-engine Beavers, Cessnas, and the odd Twin Otter were the standard traffic on our dinky little runway. Not humongous jets from France.

The plane now taking a wobbly aim at the same strip looked to me like an Airbus A320. I knew from pouring over Mom's in-flight magazines that this plane had ten times the horsepower of the 748, twice its length, and three times its carrying capacity. I figured there must have been maybe a hundred and fifty souls on board. "God bless them all," I cried, sounding an awful lot like my mother, as we watched that plane circle behind Anirniq Hill and make its final descent to the wave-washed mud of the Spit.

More people started streaming out of their houses. Anybody who'd been running in panic now stopped and turned to see what would happen next. Like Rosie and I, the whole town seemed to freeze, holding its breath.

As the jet swooped low over the village, almost grazing the church's burned-out bell tower, there was another loud crack and the smoke from the right engine doubled. Once the fire reached a fuel tank that plane would be toast for sure. The pilot obviously wasn't about to fool around with a couple of landing attempts. It was now or never. There was no time to get perfectly aligned with the runway. From where we stood it looked like it was on a direct collision course with Nanurtalik's one and only telecommunications tower. Most planes wouldn't even come near it.

"After all this!" yelled Rosie. "The tower!"

Save the jet from crashing into the sea, smashing into a village, bonking a hill, or blowing up in mid-air, and now this: a measly spike of red and white metal brings it down. There's no justice in plane crashes.

It must have been an optical illusion. We braced ourselves for the impact but somehow the plane squeaked right past the tower. It went into a final white-knuckle bank, then somehow leveled off, coming in straight and true as if giant Airbuses landed here every day.

"What a pilot!" I said.

"What a hero!" Rosie said.

When the big wheels hit the dirt, the back half of the jet disappeared in a cloud of kicked up sand and flying rocks. I imagined the runway, designed for planes with a fraction the weight, cleaving apart like a cornfield under a farmer's plow. There was a final roar as the pilot cranked the back-thrusters to full power. In a matter of seconds the jet closed the gap between it and the end of the runway. Even with over a hundred human lives at stake, I felt a sudden stab of pain in my chest for those red foxes which, if still hanging around their den, would be plowed under by the plane's slashing tires. I became aware of another sharp pain, this one in my right hand which I realized had been caught in a vice grip by Rosie—and tightening fast. I squeezed back. The final moment of truth was approaching at lightning speed.

Besides the fox den and a couple rows of red landing lights, there's not much at all beyond the end of the runway. The land gets much rockier, then angles off to the north in a sharp curve. Except for its sandy tip, much of the Spit is lined with jagged boulders that slope steeply into the water. It would be a very rough ride until it slammed into the sea.

My mind raced through every possible scenario. I wondered how the plane would move across the water—like a giant skipping stone or a rotten log being sucked under by powerful rapids? How long could a big stressed-out plane like that stay afloat? How many people would scramble out of the plane only to drown in the frigid Arctic waters? How many would go down with the airship when it finally sank?

The right wing of the plane couldn't have fallen off at a better time. What unfolded was a fluky scenario that never occurred to me—grinding to a stop on *land*. As soon as the jet left the runway it started bouncing like crazy, still screaming towards the sea. It might have been airborne for a second or two—we couldn't tell because of all the dust and smoke and crap in the air. Whatever happened down there, it must have caused enough stress in the plane's structure to snap off the damaged wing. It fell onto a patch of grass, bending backwards and acting like a rudder which steered the plane along a path that exactly mirrored the curve of the Spit. The extra drag of the wing slowed the plane down just enough to park its nose within a stone's throw of the uttermost end of the Spit. But the rest of the plane was still in motion, fishtailing towards the sea.

Ring of Fire

SUMMIT OF ANIRNIQ HILL

SATURDAY, JUNE 10TH, 3:18 P.M.

The wheels must have snapped off when the plane left the runway and now it slid sideways on its belly, swiveling around its nose. When the dust finally settled, all that ended up in the drink was a bit of the plane's left wing, just enough to douse the smoking engine and send up a billowing cloud of saltwater steam.

Air France had dropped in for a visit.

Rosie stuck two fingers in her mouth and let fly a long, piercing wolf whistle. "Incredible! Ab-so-lutely incredible!"

I just shook my head. "It's a miracle, Rosie. A miracle."

"That was one *hell* of an air show," Rosie said, half giggling, half crying.

"Yeah. You couldn't ask for better seats."

The show didn't end there however. If Mom was watching, she'd be mighty impressed by the crew of that plane. Seconds after it came to rest, they'd kicked out the fore and aft doors on the right side and unrolled yellow emergency slides for the passengers to escape. The plane sat on a funny angle, dipping towards the sea and, once inflated, the slides didn't quite touch the ground. Instead they flapped around in the wind, hardly offering a safe glide to safety. If the flight crew opened doors on the other side, they ran the risk of filling the plane with seawater since a few big waves already clawed to get in.

"Forget the slides," I said, as if in radio contact with the flight crew. "Wait for someone to bring a ladder."

"Yeah. What's the rush? That plane's not going anywhere soon."

"Yeah. And the fire's ou—"

Even as I said these words I spotted a new wisp of smoke rising from the crash site. Then flames. But not from the plane. From the grass torn up by the broken wing. A spark from the engine fire must have got it going. But—after all that rain last night?

"Oh-oh," I said.

"What? What?"

"Don't you see it?"

"Oh. Smoke. It's only grass."

"Maybe," I said, not liking what I saw. I watched the growing columns of smoke. I could see flashes of orange between them. "Afraid not, Rosie. Grass doesn't burn black like that. That's jet fuel."

Like a giant bellows, the wind off the sea fanned the flames into a lively blaze that raced through the grass and then over the bald sand.

"Yep. That's fuel for sure. What else could burn a beach."

"But it'll be okay. The wind's blowing away from the plane."

"Tell that to the fuel."

Everything happened so fast. A big chunk of the Spit, between the end of the runway and the plane, leapt into flames. Regardless of the wind, restless tongues of fire spread willy-nilly, the biggest marching straight for the starboard wing.

"This is not good," I said absently, feeling the space between my ears go numb.

"Where's all the fuel coming from?"

When Mom first started flying all over the place I really got into airplanes, reading up on different kinds, learning the basic principles of flight, even building one from scratch. For my grade six science fair project I built a scale model Boeing 747 from scratch out of play-dough, popsicle sticks, and Saran wrap. It was a see-through model that showed the guts of the plane in different colors. I remember squishing a lot of orange play-dough into the wings—fuel tanks. There were times I wished I didn't read so much. This was one of them. "It must have leaked out when the wing snapped off. The fuel tanks in there musta got pretty banged up."

"So—now they're dumping their load big time?"

I just nodded, watching the rising flames through fingers that now covered my face.

"Look, people!" Rosie said.

I lowered my hands. There was a flurry of activity around the double-wide trailer that everybody calls Terminal Two—there's never been a Terminal One, unless they mean the old log outhouse beside the runway. The red and white postal truck was parked beside the terminal and I saw what must have been Annie run outside, jump in, and tear full blast down the road to town. A handful of other workers piled into two pickups, skidded across the parking lot, then booted out of there fast.

"What chickens!" I said.

"Maybe they're going for help," offered Rosie.

I didn't think so. More likely scramming from the fire or a plane about to explode. Even from way up here I could see a couple of long ladders in the back of one of the trucks. They should've headed the other way, *towards* the plane.

"Or maybe they're getting the fire truck?" Rosie said, not sounding very hopeful.

The fire hall sat at the other end of town from the airport. If there was anybody in there they must have been sound asleep or hung over. I could see that both of the yellow garage doors were still shut tight. There was no sign or sound of a fire truck.

One vehicle remained in the terminal parking lot. The water truck, finishing its daily rounds.

"There's still somebody in there," I said. "I wonder who. . . ." I saw movement by the truck. Somebody had just unscrewed the water hose from the terminal building and was madly reeling it back into the truck. He was either going to clear out like the others or. . . .

"Who's on water delivery today?" asked Rosie.

"Don't know, but I sure hope he's got more balls than those other guys."

The ring of fire still danced across the Spit. It wouldn't take long before it reached the starboard wing and licked the puddles of fuel that I knew must now lie below it.

The driver jumped in and took off faster than I thought that old water truck could go. He kept accelerating through the parking lot and drove right past the road to town.

"Where the hell's he going?" Rosie said.

"Looks like the runway," I said, shielding my eyes against the sun which had now broken out of the clouds. A narrow, dirt track branched off from the south end of the strip which Annie and I sometimes used as a shortcut back to town when no planes were coming or going. I thought maybe that was the guy's plan.

I was wrong. As soon as he hit the runway, he spun the truck due north, towards the plane, turning so fast I thought the thing was going to flip over.

"All right!" I said.

I noticed he'd turned on his revolving orange hazard light just like an emergency vehicle screaming down the runway at some big international airport. It flashed bravely on the roof of his cab sending out a beacon of hope to the passengers trapped on the listing plane. Some of them waved bright red blankets at him from both doorways.

"Go get 'em!" yelled Rosie, now back in her cheerleader mode. It had been quite a morning for mood swings.

At first it looked like he was going to drive right into the fire. He was still accelerating and I hated to think what would happen when he hit the rocky stretch at the end of the runway, let alone the flames. The guy must have known the airport property pretty well because, just before the strip ended, he veered left onto another dirt track that had yet to catch fire. He was able to circle around the worst of the flames, though he must have been flying around the cab like crazy the way that truck bounced. The smoke was thick and the flames were high and we lost the truck for a few long seconds. Then it reappeared, stopping abruptly in the fast shrinking gap between the fire and the plane.

"What's he gonna do?" asked Rosie.

I shrugged, leaving my shoulders propped around my ears. It was then that I remembered the binoculars around my neck. I raised them to my eyes and dropped my jaw.

I saw the driver jump out of the cab but I couldn't identify him. Heat waves from the fire broke his body into weirdly jiggling pieces.

"He's going for the hose."

The truck too was all jiggly and I couldn't see exactly what he was doing. A curving burst of white told me he'd managed to turn the water on. That old truck had a powerful pump. Ask anyone in town whose household water tank had exploded from too much pressure. But could it defeat a firestorm of jet-B fuel?

A high fountain of water sprang above the smoke and opened a small gap in the flames. The heat waves cleared for a moment and the driver's body glued back together. I recognized his twisted posture and that ratty tweed cap.

"Can you believe it?" I said, handing the binoculars to Rosie. "That's Vince."

"Come on—no way." Rosie adjusted the binoculars for her eyes. "God. It *is* him."

Vince was working the leading edge of the fire, whacking it down with a wide jet of water any firefighter would be proud of.

He seemed to be gaining the upper hand, dispersing the fuel while snuffing out the flames closest to the broken wing. It would take a while for the rest of the fuel to burn off but if his water supply held up, he could probably hold it back long enough to stop any further advances towards the plane. I could see more red blankets flapping by the doorways. What a buzz Vince must've created in that plane.

The standoff lasted about five minutes before Vince's water ran out. The fountain fell, shot up a couple times, then dribbled down to nothing. Terminal Two is the last stop on the water delivery rounds and usually sucks the truck dry. Vince was lucky to have a drop in there when he took off down the runway.

I was afraid the fire might be flexing its muscles again when I heard a siren coming from town. The fire truck boys had finally got their act together. It took them another five minutes to reach the plane, having bumbled back and forth at the end of the runway looking for the track that Vince found in seconds. The fire had started advancing toward the plane again but the fire crew sprayed some red gooey stuff all over it. Soon all we could see was a few pillars of black smoke being ripped apart by the wind.

As the smoke cleared completely, the Air France jet gleamed white in the sunshine, looking like a giant beluga whale sunning itself on the beach.

Rosie looked at me with a goofy grin on her face. "Cripes!" she said, pointing to the resurrected Angel. "After all that we never screwed her head back on." We laughed so hard I thought I was going to puke.

When we could stand again, we shared a wild whirling hug, then took off down the hill leaving the headless Angel mutely pointing at the downed plane.

The Healing

The crash of Flight 1772 from Paris to Hawaii had quite an impact on Nanurtalik—and I don't mean just on the Spit. The newspapers said it was more weird weather that brought the plane down. Some kind of bizarre temperature inversion left over from the previous night's storm had created an air pocket the size of the Grand Canyon. The plane drove right into it and dropped into an invisible pit of weak air resistance that was over a mile deep. When it finally hit bottom, the stress was so great that one engine almost fell off. That's when everything started falling apart.

A smoking piece of the outside world dropped into ours and everybody—I mean *everybody*—had to look beyond their own little melodramas and give a hand to the Frenchies, as Gabe called them. Uninvited visitors from the other side of the planet needed help and there was no one else to give it but us. During the two days it took to organize enough planes to fly everyone out, these people had nothing, not even their hand luggage, since the RCMP wouldn't let anyone back on the wrecked plane. We had to take care of all their needs—and I'm talking real basics here: food, water, shelter, clothes. It was all up to us. Everybody said the plane crash was one of the best things to happen to Nanurtalik in a long time, maybe ever.

The crash had a tremendous healing effect on all of us. Vince was the first of course. He'd leapt from the shadows of his bruised and boozy existence by saving the lives of all 154 passengers and crew. Mom said that nobody could have survived the blast if that wing tank had ignited. Vince became an instant hero across the country, at least for a day or two.

Raymond, who seemed happiest during emergencies, found his new niche as Mr. Organizer, making elaborate lists and official announcements to match every stranded passenger with volunteer billets across town. He even set up some people in Empire Oil's fancy trailer, thanks to a little help from Lord Gord who pulled out his secret keys to the place.

Mom organized a small army of cooks to feed the Frenchies down at Tuktu hall. Rosie and I were drafted into this army and put in a couple of eighteen-hour days keeping everyone alive. It was like a non-stop sweat lodge in there, but I have to say my kitchen skills went up a notch or two. Even more incredible was the fact that Rosie's mother appeared out of nowhere on the second day, stone-cold sober, wearing a blue and white checkered apron. I wasn't too busy to stop and stare as she walked into the kitchen and sidled up to Rosie asking for instructions. Within minutes they were working side by side over a stove, a sight I wouldn't have dreamed of under normal circumstances.

Gabe seemed more stable than I'd ever seen him while he and his musical buddies organized and presented a fiddle dance one night for our guests. Steven and Pauloosie started up what they called the Kiq-ass Committee for the kids on the plane, organizing games of indoor soccer and volleyball in the school gym. They hardly needed a word of French. They found that, like art and music, sports seem to have a universal language that anyone could understand.

Professor Lyons, who had a very basic grasp of French, toured people around his polar bear lab, showing them skulls and bones he'd found on the land, videos of him and his crew taking measurements from drugged bears, photos of his climate monitoring stations, even pictures he'd taken on our aborted polar bear hunt when we sent two rifles into the drink. He said afterwards that it was good for him to try and explain his research work in the simplest words possible, since that's all he had to draw on anyway.

Even Dad's bear wounds seemed to heal faster during those two days. We'd all agonized over his recovery until he snapped out of his coma ten days after the attack and asked for a cup of strong tea. Five weeks later he was still in a lot of pain, so I was amazed when he announced that he wanted to take the Air France people out on the land for a quick tour. He asked me to come along as translator in the school bus and, with Mom's blessing, I ducked out of kitchen duty for a couple of hours. Minutes after Dad pulled up to Tuktu Hall, the bus was jam-packed. As he pulled the bus door shut I asked him where he would take them.

"You tell me," he said. "I'm just the driver."

"But—this isn't even my town," I protested, turning to see all the eager faces looking at me.

"Who says it isn't?" asked Dad as he handed me the bus microphone "You can at least pretend."

Dad revved the motor and looked up at me, obviously waiting for instructions. I was trapped. There was only one place to start.

"To the Spit," I said. "And make it snappy, "I added with a nervous laugh.

Call it beginner's luck but, after my initial butterflies, I got into the tour guide groove like I'd done it for years. There was no time to think about my French. I clicked right into it, the way Dad or Steven seamlessly flip in and out of Inuktitut when talking to the Elders. I never knew I was a ham but found myself telling Eskimo jokes and stirring in a few tall tales along the way just for laughs.

I had Dad drive to the end of the runway and down the Spit track as far as he could. Of course everybody wanted to take pictures of each other in front of the trashed plane, which had been decorated in miles of yellow police tape. Then I took them for a stroll on the beach and soon had most of them, from grandmothers in tennis shoes to toddlers in diapers, down on their hands and knees digging in the sand for polar bear toe bones. It didn't take long to find a couple of bones plus an amazingly well preserved copper spear-point. A silver-haired Muslim woman came up to me cradling something in her palm like she'd found a rare emerald.

"Qu'est-ce que c'est?" she asked.

I gasped. It was a delicate caribou bone sewing needle. Its tiny drilled hole was still intact and the business end was sharp as a tack. Though it must have been over a hundred years old, Aana could have added this to her sewing kit beside the best of her hand-picked needles. Dad whispered in my ear that these artifacts should stay in the community. I explained this in French and met no resistance from anyone. They seemed to understand right away that these were home-grown treasures found in a very a special place. *Wait till Mom sees these,* I thought as I carefully wrapped them in a Kleenex and handed them over to Dad.

Next stop: Anirniq Hill. Not everyone was keen on going up the trail so I set the others loose in the cemetery. Less than twenty-four hours had passed since Rosie and I had gone up here to rebuild the Angel, but it seemed like weeks ago. The ground had dried out and, with a troupe of French hikers behind me, it was an easy climb to the top. I felt a surprising stir of pride as we beheld the view below—the rolling tundra wearing a lime-green coat of spring colors, the graceful arc of the Spit, the Arctic Ocean still capped in shimmering ice with a broad, blue smile along the shore, and the compact island of humanity called Nanurtalik.

"Grandiose!" someone shouted.

"C'est si beau!" cried another.

"Trés sauvage!"

"Incroyable!"

Again all the cameras came out and by this time everyone wanted me in their photos. As my face grew sore from smiling, it occurred to me that all of these nice people came very close to being drowned or blown up or spread across the melting sea ice like so many fallen leaves. But no, here they were on Anirniq Hill, laughing and shouting and celebrating a world that, hours ago, had been as foreign to them as the moon. Before leaving the hill, I took a moment to ask for help in putting the Angel's head back on. A dozen people stepped forward and we almost dropped it on our toes amidst the laughter and, in my case, tears.

Our final stop: Our Lady of the Sea. Everyone got a kick out of the fact that the church had been designed, built, and ruled by Frenchmen for over eighty years. The wild exuberance of our hilltop visit was countered here by a hushed joy and reverence shared by everyone from the moment we set foot into the church. It was only in walking people around the building that I realized that the words below the fourteen stations of the cross were written in French. For some reason, I paused in front of the fourth station, *Jésus rencontre sa mère*—Jesus meets his mother.

I moved to my favorite pew and motioned for everyone to sit. For several timeless moments, we stared in silence at the ceiling's glittering artwork.

"*Trés inspirant!*"

"*Charmant!*"

"*Merveilleuse!*"

"*Quelle église!*"

Then out came the cameras one last time, flashing as they might if a bunch of Nanurtalikians were standing before the Eiffel Tower.

On the way back to Tuktu Hall, one man asked me if we could stop at the icehouse. My neck hairs bristled. I asked him how he'd heard about it and he said it seemed to be a rumor going around town. Nobody he'd talked to had actually seen it. "They seemed almost afraid to talk about it," he told me in French.

All I did was smile and shrug. That was one place these people didn't need to know about.

None of the Frenchies got to know Uncle Jonah either. He seemed to burrow deeper into his room while everyone else seemed to be coming out of their closets. Miracles do have their limits. His healing time would just have to wait.

As for me, whatever was broken in my dream machine seemed to fix itself the night after all the Frenchies left. I hadn't had any big dreams since before Dad was attacked, just a bunch of surface static that occasionally stole my sleep away. Though my fingers had sprung back to life weeks ago, I still couldn't bring myself to draw. The thought of it actually frightened me.

Nanurluk's Cave

ASHLEY'S DREAM JOURNAL
TUESDAY, JUNE 13TH, 3:58 A.M.
I've been here before. I've seen that swirling black cloud. I've felt this wind wrap around me.

Nothing can touch me this time.

I raise my hands above the ice and pull the song from the seabed. My inner ear patiently waits.

Silence.

I raise my hands higher, breathe deeper.

A ripple of sound becomes a trickle, and soon, a torrent. My song swells in my chest. I wait until it fills every cell, then release it into my dream-world.

This time it doesn't break up. I won't let it.

*This time I won't get stuck in the tunnel. I won't let it close on me.
I know who waits for me at the other end. Let* Nanurluk *show me any
face. I'm ready for the hunt.*

*My song is soft but steady. Even as I dream, I'm amazed at my fast-
tracking skill, controlling the pace, stopping at will. But the very whiff
of pride weakens the song and slows me down.*

I watch for Nanurluk's *traps.*

*Again, the cloud spins above me like a black rose. Again, I spot the tun-
nel gate below it. Now I know it could close in an instant. I move quickly
but cautiously towards the water's edge. The wind dies the moment I reach
it. Mist rises from water that's blacker than black. I stare forward at nothing. For a moment I'm lost in fear. The song fades to a whisper and with it,
my heartbeat. Somehow I know that this time, if I let the song go, I'm dead.*

*I've never had to cross this threshold before. With a slight tip of my
head I could look at my dream-face in the mirror calm surface. I want
to skip this step in the journey and enter the tunnel. I want to dive in
with eyes closed so I don't have to see who I am.*

The song fades. My legs weaken. I drop to my knees.

*Still looking forward, I open my eyes wide. A white figure races
towards me from across the lead. I steady myself. The song gains
strength. My vision sharpens. It's my bear shaman, dressed in polar
bear skins and a loon skin cap. As always, his face is hidden by the*
qilauti *he beats.*

*My heart leaps to the sound of his song. Our songs meet over the
still water, weaving their colors together like smoke from two fires.*

I'm ready to look.

*I tip my gaze downwards to see a young woman's face with Aana's
smile, my father's sloping brow, and Uncle Jonah's wide bear-like nose.
Long black braids hang in two silky loops, almost touching the water.
Below her collarbone I see a bear claw birthmark.*

Like the shaman, my body is covered in polar bear skins. I hold both arms out to admire them—only to discover two bear paws before my face.

The whole world stops. I feel this is the challenge I've resisted all my life. How long can I deny my true nature—part woman, part bear?

No more.

I examine my dark paws and flex my claws. I stare at them, not with terror but with acceptance, gratitude, and awe. I look up at the drummer, my teacher, who helped open my eyes.

I plunge headfirst into the dark water. My journey leads downward, through the tunnel to Nanurluk's domain. My song courses through my bones and blood.

I free-fall like a skydiver, arms stretched out behind me. My claws click against the ribbed walls of the tunnel as I plummet towards a fast-widening light. In the rush of flight my song falters once or twice and instantly I notice the light fading, the tunnel walls squeezing in on me. But I pull the song together and pop out into a watery realm of purplish light.

I'm a space traveler stepping through the throat of a wormhole into another universe. I'm a goldfish released from a jam jar into a vast sea. I can swim anywhere I please with perfect control. I'm filled with an almost overwhelming sense of joy and freedom.

Then I remember Nanurluk's terrible form reaching out for me in this very realm. Again my song slips away and, for a moment, I sink help-lessly out of control—until I hear faint drumming drifting down through the tunnel. The shaman's song rescues me. Soon I'm swimming like a bear, paddling with my forelegs as my rear legs trail behind as rudders.

There are strong currents down here and I choose one that angles steeply towards the bottom. That's where I'll find her.

The seabed looms up before me. The bottom is rich with starfish and sea urchins, mussels and kelp, all softly glowing purple like the water itself. I skim just above the bottom, looking for signs.

A shaft of intense light sticks out of the soft mud ahead of me. My harpoon! As I clutch it, a surge of warmth channels directly from the seabed into my body and energizes my song.

Now, I'm invincible.

I swim on, my prize held close. I find a network of markings criss-crossing the mud. Polar bear tracks! I follow the biggest set to the mouth of a colossal cave. As I approach its mouth, a giant bear swims towards me at lightning speed and thrusts its bloodied face into mine.

I've drawn this face a hundred times. I know it well but haven't tamed the terror. With my song pulsing weakly in my heart, I raise my harpoon and speak to the biggest, baddest bear there ever was.

"You have torn me apart enough times already, Nanurluk. You have reshaped me into the form now before you. I greet you with the respect you deserve and ask only to see your other face."

Nanurluk's crimson eyes lock onto mine. The hold on my song frays to a feeble thread. Even underwater I see blood dripping from her long fangs. I detect the sickly sweet scent of death hanging around her neck. I keep my gaze fixed on her terrible face, waiting for her next move.

She raises one paw high above my head, as if to knock it off—then propels her massive body around, to reveal the beloved face I thought I would never live to see. Four young humans, attached to her in a suckling pose, wave their free arms to invite me into the cave.

The Source

ASHLEY'S HOUSE
TUESDAY, JUNE 13TH, 9:22 A.M.

I can't say exactly what went on down in that seabed cave. As much as I'd like to, I can't draw it either. What happened in there was beyond words, beyond forms. It was all song. I seemed to have plugged into the very source of my song, everyone's song. The echoes in that cave were incredible, as if every *ajai jaa* song ever sung in the Arctic had been bouncing off its walls for thousands of years. Yet I could still hear mine through all the hubbub. Even more amazing is that I was able to carry it across into my waking world, without the guidance of any giant bears or bear-skinned shamans.

As I woke up it was still singing inside me. I could feel it tickling the back of my throat all day long. Before I hit the hay that night I quietly tried to sing it out loud and, in spite of my voice, it didn't come out half bad. Given a choice, I'd take the inner version hands down.

The next morning, the song was gone. Try as I might, I couldn't get it back. I stayed in bed until noon sleeping fitfully on a pillow soaked by tears.

The Bear Shaman's Song

Part VIII
Returning Home

Tired and hungry,
I return from the hunt
Hands empty
And heart full.
My footsteps are light,
Padding softly through the thawing snow.
I know these mountains,
Now glowing above me.
The sky is clear.

Cold Turkey

It took four Hawker-Siddeley 748 loads to fly all the Air France folks and their luggage out of town. They must have tuckered old Mary Jane right out because the day after they left she decided to hand in her nurse's lunch pail for good. She liked to think of herself as a kind of Arctic Florence Nightingale, having moved to Nanurtalik over twenty years before—about the time Ingrid, her replacement, was born. Through that whole time, she had tackled more medical emergencies and saved more lives than most doctors would in a southern town ten times bigger. She had no time for "magic potions or witch doctors." Mary Jane preferred a nuts and bolts approach to health care. "There's a pill for every ill," was Mary Jane's favorite motto.

Ingrid, on the other hand, was fresh out of nursing school and took a "less is more" approach to doling out drugs. Amazingly, the two nurses got along well and I guess Mary Jane felt okay about passing the lives of all one thousand and one of us into Ingrid's hands. Now it was Ingrid's job to take care of Uncle Jonah's medical calamities.

During Ingrid's first home care visit, she was propping up Uncle Jonah with some newfangled therapeutic pillow shaped like the head of an ax—"This'll help take the crimps out of your back"— when she spotted a big, brown bottle of pills behind the headboard of his bed. "What on earth are *these?*" she asked, holding the bottle high and giving it a shake like it was full of mouse turds.

"Those are Uncle's pills," Mom said, defensively. "He has such *awful* fits."

"Fits?" asked Ingrid. "What kind of fits?"

"Oh, he'll shiver and shake all over, then slip into some kind of coma, usually for an hour or so at least."

"A coma?"

"Just a benign coma. That's what Mary Jane called them."

"A *benign* coma?"

"Yes, a bit frightening at first. But Mary Jane said that we had nothing to worry about, as long as he was tucked in tight and took these nerve pills."

Ingrid's forehead went all crinkly. "Nerve pills, you say. Hmmm. What on earth are nerve pills?"

"I really don't know. But that's what—"

"—Mary Jane called them," Ingrid said with narrowing eyes. "Right."

"Well, yes. She'd keep filling up the same bottle whenever it got low. Didn't charge Uncle a cent. She liked to reuse things, I guess. No harm in that. That bottle's probably at least ten years old."

"Ten years, you say?" Ingrid took back the bottle and held it close to her nose. "The label's all worn off. Wait a minute. There *is* something here. I can just make it out." She squinted at the oil-smeared label. "Tri . . . az . . . o . . . lam. Triazolam." She shook her head slightly and made a faint whistling noise. Then she abruptly looked up at Carole with wide unblinking eyes. "Do you mean to say that this man has been taking a steady diet of Triazolam for *ten* years?"

Ask Mom about herbal remedies or aromatherapy scents and she could go on for hours. But when it came to prescription drugs, she was way out of her element. "I'm not sure," she said sheepishly. "We just moved here a year ago. Mary Jane said those pills would—how did she put it?—take the *sting* out of his comas."

Ingrid's eyes opened wider.

Mom reached for the bottle and dumped a few pink pills into her hand. "Some people need to take tranquilizers for a long time, don't they? I mean, forever?"

"Ten years?" asked Ingrid in disbelief.

"It might have been longer. Like I say we've only lived here since—"

"How many pills does he take a day?"

"Two, I believe. Maybe more. He won't let us—"

"Do you know what Triazolam is?"

"Well, Mary Jane said it was some kind of long-term tranq—"

"These are *sleeping pills!*"

I looked over at Uncle Jonah to see if he was taking all this in but, sure enough, he was fast asleep, snoring sideways on his fancy, new pillow. Aana caught my eye and raised a finger to her lips. I guess she figured this was none of his business.

"He does seem to sleep a lot," Mom said. "But Mary Jane said—"

"Mary Jane is a sweetheart," Ingrid interrupted. "Delivered lots of babies, saved lots of limbs. But she wasn't exactly up to speed on the side effects of all the wonder drugs she doled out."

I wondered how much of the real Uncle Jonah was buried under an internal smog of chemicals. "So what's wrong with this triazo-whatchamahcallit stuff?" I asked.

"Well, there's a time and a place for sleeping pills," Ingrid said, "like if somebody suffers from occasional attacks of insomnia. But these kinds of drugs shouldn't be taken for more than a *few weeks* without careful supervision." She gave the bottle another disdainful shake, then chucked it into the garbage bag she'd brought the pillow in. She held the bag wide open for Mom who looked at the pills in her hand as if they were cyanide, then tossed them in with the rest.

"Triazolam can have some very serious side effects," Ingrid said while tying a tight double knot in the bag. "How's Jonah's breathing? Does he suffer from respiratory problems, for instance?"

"He gets pretty wheezy just walking to the kitchen sometimes," Mom said. "And wait until you witness one of his coughing fits. You know, it hurts my throat just to hear it. We always thought it was from smoking those awful rollies."

Ingrid held up the garbage bag like a fisherman showing off his catch. "Combine drugs like this with existing chest problems and you've got a recipe for respiratory failure."

"What's that mean?" I asked.

"Basically, your brain forgets how to control your lungs and you can't breathe. That's it. Game over."

"*Game-ovah! Game-ovah!*" came Wiggins's shrieking call from the next room. That bird had amazing ears. I had to laugh but Ingrid's face only got darker.

"Your great uncle must be one tough nut. Years of unbroken Triazolam use would kill a normal man half his age."

"He's one tough nut!" shouted Gabe. "Tough nut!" Gabe couldn't resist company and had plunked himself down on Uncle Jonah's greasy old sofa.

"What about those comas?" asked Mom. "Surely this drug must have helped control them?"

"It probably *caused* the comas. Comas are one of the well-documented side effects of this drug. . . ." She sniffed the air like a narcotics agent. The smell of cheap wine oozed from the walls. "Especially when combined with alcohol or other drugs."

Aana chose this moment to nudge an empty wine bottle under the bed with her toe.

"My goodness!" Mom said. "The poor man's lucky to be alive."

"*Tuff nut!*" shrieked Wiggins. "*Tuff nut!*"

Gabe clapped his hands and let out a hoot. Even Ingrid found this funny and a fleeting smile thawed the lines on her face.

"So how do you think Uncle will react to going off that nasty drug after so many years?" I asked. "Like, don't you go through cold turkey when you're hooked on stuff like this?"

"It's cold turkey time, folks!" shouted Gabe. "Cold turkey!"

"It's very possible," Ingrid said, slinging the garbage bag over her shoulder. "His body won't like this at all. But consider the alternative. It could be a rough ride for a few days but he might just emerge a new man once it's all over."

"A new, *old* man, you mean," I said.

Ingrid nodded. "Or an old, new man. Whichever way you look at it, cutting him off quick can only do him good in the long run." Ingrid looked down at Jonah, who was now snoring like a trooper. "Who knows what stories he might tell after being half asleep for ten years?"

"Our very own Rip Van Wrinkle!" exclaimed Gabe as he leapt off the couch and sidled up to Uncle Jonah's bed. Gabe felt around for the old man's face. He straightened his glasses, tickled his Fu Manchu beard, then planted a couple of quick pats on his greasy white hair. "Sweet dreams, Rip old boy!"

Uncle Jonah coughed a wretched cough, blinked twice, then his eyelids slammed shut like they were made of lead.

Mom escorted Ingrid out the door like she was a visiting dignitary. "Please come again soon," she said. "Uncle may need your help. Drug free help, I mean."

"There's a lot you can do for him," Ingrid said. "But don't hesitate to call if you think you can't handle something."

The moment Ingrid passed in front of Wiggins' cage, he added his final two bits to the afternoon's drama. "*Cold turkey! Cold turkey!*" he shrieked, more or less in Ingrid's ear.

Awakening

Uncle Jonah's tizzy fits ended the day Ingrid chucked his so-called nerve pills in the garbage. So did his comas, benign or otherwise. He seemed pretty normal—listless, hanging out in the shadows—until the cold turkey stage kicked in a few days later. The first sign of trouble was when his withered right arm started to shake. It would flop around on the table like a fish out of water, often so bad that he had to pin it down with his good arm. Sometimes the shaking spread to his other arm or to his head or torso. When it took over his legs, he'd grab onto a chair or counter while his feet danced like he was clowning around in a vaudeville comedy act.

When the tremors got really bad, he'd refuse to sit down or accept a helping hand, even from Aana. It was like there was a lightning storm roaring through him, trying to escape, and he was determined to face it alone, on two feet, head on. He'd stand there, panting and shaking with his eyes scrunched tight and his knuckles all white. These spells weren't at all like his tizzy fits. You could see that Uncle Jonah was conscious through them all. He seemed to be trying to harness a gale of energy now waking up in him after years of being half asleep. When each storm passed, he'd open his eyes, growl for another cup of tea, then go stand by the picture window facing the Spit. He'd spend long, silent minutes there, clutching his bear cup and staring down at the Spit. Then another round of tremors would hit and Uncle Jonah would be back on the vaudeville stage.

I figured the tremors would eventually tear him apart. He looked scrawnier than ever, losing weight from a body that was already skin and bones before he went off those pills. I gave him a month to live, tops. After a week of cold turkey tremors, I seriously considered asking Mom to put him back on the pills. Give him his old slothful self back, and maybe a couple more years of shoddiness.

The shaking spells stopped before I found the nerve to suggest more nerve pills. His appetite seemed to double overnight as did his daily ration of tea—from about ten cups to twenty. Instead of lying in bed or on his couch all day, he became incredibly restless, getting up every five minutes and stomping around his room like a caged bear. When he got sick of that he'd storm into the living room and stand in front of the window again, shuffling from one foot to the next, with his arms pressed tightly across his chest, his eyes burning up the Spit.

Uncle Jonah must have gained fifteen pounds in two weeks and now moved like someone half his age. Even his withered arm seemed to have more oomph. But boy, was he grumpy! Mom had kept him prisoner indoors under the guise of what she called medical observation. She wanted to wring the old guy out completely. Throw out his sleeping pills. Cut out his cheap wine. Snuff out his cigarettes. The more Mom took away, the more he wailed and banged the table with his cup. He was like a little kid who'd thrown so many wild tantrums over something he wanted that he forgot what it was. But Mom held the food lever and had a hot-blooded will in her that could take on Uncle Jonah's. Beats me what plans she had for him. Get him carving again. Dredge his pickled brain for stories of the old days. Save his soul. Teach him the ukulele. I don't know. Mom never did say exactly.

But it seems Uncle Jonah had his own plans. His hibernation was over. Whatever fountain of energy he'd unbottled was too powerful to be contained by four walls and a roof. Instead of recommending a steady diet of nerve pills, I suggested to Mom that she unlock Uncle Jonah's prison. It was plain to me that he had to get outside, get his feet reconnected with the ground. I could see in his eyes that something out there was calling him and a hundred sled dogs couldn't keep this bear cornered much longer.

Mom must have bought my prescription. "Back to your old playful self, eh, Uncle?" she said one day, when she caught him trying to climb out the bathroom window after trashing the screen with his narwhal cane. "How about a stroll on the Spit to burn up some of that excess energy?"

"'S 'bout time you asked," is all he said and, with a new spring to his step, he made a beeline for the back door. On the way out he stopped in front of Mom's bomber jacket and pulled out a pack of smokes and a lighter.

Mom looked at me with a shrug. "Well, two out of three vices ain't bad." She sprang up and gave a pan of rising dough a light tap with her fingers.

"Ah-hah!" I said. "My mother, the drug pusher. Feeding nicotine to innocent old men."

As usual, she ignored my jabs about her smoking. "You go with him, Ash."

"Excuse me. *What?* Just me and him?"

"I have to get this bread in the oven and Gabe's still at the station. He'll be on the air for another hour at least."

"And Pauloosie?"

"He's helping Steven finish the skateboard park, so you'll just have to—"

"But how are we supposed to get down there?"

"Well, just out our door you'll find a well-defined trail leading directly to the Spit, worn down by your feet, I believe."

"Duh, Mom, but I'm not in the habit of strolling there hand in hand with *Uncle*. You have to drive us."

"Ash, you've seen how he stares at that Spit all day. And remember this was *your* idea. He's got enough momentum to carry you there on his shoulders, like he did when we used to visit from Inniturliq."

I looked at the old man already trotting, almost jogging down the trail. His gumboots barely touched the ground. I shook my head in disbelief. The way he moved reminded me of the fast-tracking I did all the time now, but only in my dreams. I'd never seen him move like that. His shoulders were hunched but square. I sat there once? Impossible. "No. Did he really carry me?"

"I have a picture somewhere," Mom said. "I'll try and dig it out for you later. Go ahead, Ash. It'll be good for you both."

The sight of him moving like that gave me the chills. I felt like he was testing me or something. For some reason I was nervous about being alone with him out on the land. "What about you, Aana?"

Aana shook her head. "I'm busy." She was focused on her latest sewing project, my mishmash coat again. Even though I'd never worn it, she would dig it out occasionally to fix a minor tear or reinforce a zipper. It was like she put it on display to see if I was ready to wear it. I paused to examine this gift from my mother that I'd chucked away, deep in a closet, after little more than a glance. Now I felt I was seeing it for the first time. I ran my *doigts d'une artiste* over the luxuriant beaver sleeves, the natural sunburst pattern of the *siksik* fur, the striped tail of a raccoon. "It's nice, Aana." I meant it this time. "Thanks."

Aana nodded with an approving grunt. "Take his cane," she said.

"Huh? Oh, his cane. I don't think so." I swung the back door wide open. "Look at him go, Aana. He's kicked the cane habit along with drugs and booze. He doesn't need it anymore."

Aana looked at me with a funny twinkle in her eye. "Take it," she said firmly. "He'll need it down on the Spit."

"What?

Aana clucked and swung her chin towards his room.

I found Uncle's narwhal cane crammed diagonally inside the frame of his north-facing window. It struck me as an odd place to store it, like he was purposely exposing it to the summer sun that shone from that direction. Recharging it or something, like a solar-powered radio. I stared at it, remembering how, out on our hunt, Dr. Lyons had explained that nobody really knows the purpose of a narwhal's tusk. "It could be some sort of acoustic or electromagnetic antenna to allow the whales to communicate in ways we can't even imagine. It's one of those mysteries of nature that science may never crack."

Uncle Jonah's cane seemed to glow in the sunshine and I hesitated to touch it, half expecting it to turn purple in my hands. I gingerly wrapped one finger and thumb around it. No sparks. No tingles. "Get real," I said to myself with a nervous chuckle.

I snatched the cane from the window and held it in both hands. I'd never paid much attention to it before. The worn tip and dark, greasy handle told me it must have been very old. I ran my thumbnail over the handle and scraped off a patch of grime. I gasped. There was that same reddish orange rock streaked with lightning. Firestone! I held the cane at arm's length and slowly spun it around. Two hollows carved into the side of the stone looked like—eye sockets. The handle suggested some kind of skull. An animal skull. The front of it split and curved like two long fangs. It was a polar bear's skull. How could I have missed it?

I heard Aana shout from the next room. "*Uitajuq!* Get going!"

Aana tossed me my mishmash coat as I ran past. "*Uitajuq's* coat."

"Thanks again, Aana," I said as I slipped it on. I was surprised how well it fit.

Fast-Tracking

Trail to the Spit

Saturday, June 24th, 1:20 p.m.

Wiggins was flapping up a storm as I ran past him. "Outside, Wiggins? Outside?" I said while whacking my shoulder with my hand. He got the message and climbed on board. I wouldn't be alone with Uncle Jonah after all.

I didn't bother calling Jacques. I knew he wouldn't come. For some strange reason he'd been avoiding Uncle Jonah more than ever lately.

The sun smacked my face with a gush of molten gold. A cool breeze off the tundra carried the scent of blooming Labrador tea and last fall's bearberries. A mixed flock of snow buntings and Lapland longspurs exploded from a grassy patch ahead of me, filling the air with their tinkling calls. I zipped up my mishmash coat. As oddball as it was, I felt quite at home in it all of a sudden. "A good match," as Mom had said.

I glanced up Anirniq Hill to make sure the Angel Rosie and I had repaired was still standing. There she was, the First Lady of Nanurtalik, her stone arms stretched due north and south, like she was blessing everything in between. I knew the sky wouldn't fall on a beautiful day like this. My universe seemed in pretty good order. Except I'd lost Uncle Jonah.

Wiggins leaped from my shoulder the moment we left the road and struck off down the trail. "Go find Uncle," I said. "Go find Uncle." And Wiggins shot ahead like a retriever after a duck, flying just above the trail and calling for Uncle with non-stop squawks. I waved Uncle's cane in the air, amazed that an eighty-nine-year-old semi-invalid hermit could explode out of the house so fast and disappear. I was a little amazed too at my urgent need to find him. Like, there was some ache in me that only he could heal. For sure, this was an about-face for me. Very weird. But there was no denying it. Something bigger than Aana's orders made me break into a run.

I caught my toe on a rock and wiped out, crashing into a clump of dwarf willows. When I stood up, laughing, I spotted Wiggins, circling high over the trail. I ran a few more paces and spotted Uncle Jonah right below him. He hadn't slowed down one bit since he left the house. If anything, he was booting it even faster. All I could see were his head and shoulders bobbing above the curving lip of Heartbreak Hill.

My artist eye clicked on, creating an image that begged to be drawn: Uncle Jonah wore the tundra landscape like some grand flowing cape. From where I stood, it looked as if he was sinking into the ground, moving through it along some magical cleavage in the Earth's skin that led straight to the underworld. And the Earth welcomed him—her cushiony plants and mosses, the shattered chunks of shale, the sweet smelling peat, the clay soil, the thick lenses of ground ice, and, below that, the firestone.

There was firestone under the church, behind the cemetery, below the community icehouse, and beyond the Spit at Blood Rock. It dawned on me that the whole town rested on a rare bed of firestone.

Mom liked to go on about how rocks give off different kinds of energy, some good, some bad. Dad talked about something weird in the ground around here that screwed up his telecommunications signals. Uncle Jonah had carved with nothing but firestone. As I watched him merge with the Earth, it hit me that this was why Uncle Jonah could never leave Nanurtalik. There was something special in the firestone that fed the flames of his power.

And that power was back—in his legs at least. Man, was Uncle Jonah flying down that trail! I shook my head. "Wait a sec!" I said to myself. "What am I *thinking?* The guy's gonna crack his skull open if he doesn't slow down." My artist eye fell shut and my feet went into overdrive.

I usually sauntered down this trail, sucking what I could out of each step, each plant, each view, as I escaped from some craziness at school, at home, or in my darker dreams. Now I was sprinting faster than I'd ever run before. The faster I went, the more I got this feeling that I was leaving something behind. Not just ho-hum fears and frets this time, but something bigger. I felt lighter. I felt safe.

The trail was anything but straight and smooth, but somehow my feet knew just where to plant themselves. Without thinking, I had been rapping the ground with Uncle Jonah's narwhal cane as I sped along. It seemed to guide me and I felt that I could have run just as fast with my eyes closed. I realized the sensation was thrillingly familiar. Exactly like fast-tracking! My feet had sprouted wings. Only this time I was awake.

Seconds later, I pulled up to Uncle Jonah and we were fast-tracking side by side towards the Spit. He didn't even look at me but made a satisfying grunt that sounded like approval. It was exhilarating.

Until I turned to offer him the cane and tripped again.

This time I skidded to a stop in a patch of squirrel-tail grass. If I'd landed on rocks, I might not be here to tell my story since I bonked my head pretty good. I had the wind knocked out of me and felt like a cherry bomb went off between my ears. Before I could open my eyes, a pair of claws clamped onto my shoulder. I cracked my eyes a slit to see Wiggins's horny black beak snapping the air an inch from my nose. He seemed really worked up over something and started squawking in my face and swinging his wings high above his head. A shadow fell over us from behind and Wiggins took off like a rocket. I turned around to see a huge, hairy form reaching out for my head.

Uncle Jonah's Discovery

The Spit

Saturday, June 24th, 2:05 p.m.

Uncle Jonah had this ratty, old bathrobe that he wore night and day, rain or shine, sleet or snow. This thing looked like he'd worn it non-stop for the past ten years at least. Since we moved into Eddy's Place last summer, Mom had managed to peel it off him just once during one of his deeper comas. Holding it at arms length, she chucked it into the wash along with half a bottle of bleach. In theory it was a white bathrobe, but after a few days hanging loosely off Uncle Jonah's wiry frame, it took on a yellowish tinge like you might see in the fur of an old polar bear.

That's the color I saw after my second wipeout on the Spit trail. I opened my eyes and saw a polar bear standing over me with its raised paw about to knock my head off. A scream welled up but choked in my throat. I watched the giant figure change shape, its edges rippling and shrinking, revealing a thinner, more human outline. My bear turned out to be Uncle Jonah in his bathrobe that flapped harmlessly in the breeze.

Wiggins seemed less convinced he'd only seen an illusion and kept bouncing around like the rocks he tried to perch on were nests of stinging bees.

Uncle held an arm out to me. If this gesture of help wasn't surprising enough, I realized he was offering me his gammy right arm.

"Uncle! You looked like a—"

He gave a snort that could have passed for a laugh and waved a couple of fingers in the air. I reached for his hand but he shook mine off.

"My cane," he said in a hoarse whisper. "I need it back."

In spite of my ass-over-tea-kettle spill, I had managed to keep a firm grip on his narwhal cane. I thrust it towards him like I'd fallen in a relay race. "That's *some* cane, Uncle."

He grabbed the cane as a soldier would take up his sword. It was then I realized that, after sprinting from the house to here, the old guy wasn't even breathing hard. Neither was I, come to think of it.

My head had cleared enough for me to get up on my feet and look around. "Holy! How did we do that?"

Another snort.

We had covered the last half mile of trail in what seemed like seconds and were already well past the airstrip and onto the grassy area where the Air France jet crashed. The smell of jet-B fuel still hung in the air. There were deep furrows in the peat where the plane's landing gear had slashed the ground before it snapped off. Except for a few miles of yellow police tape draped around it, the plane wreckage lay untouched, waiting for government inspectors to crawl all over it and decide what went wrong. Uncle ignored the plane. His mission had nothing to do with it.

"I thought you didn't need your cane, Uncle," I called as he marched straight for a big gash in the ground.

"I do now," he shouted gruffly.

But he didn't use it for support. He stopped at the furrow and started waving his cane over the dug up peat like he had a fire hose in his hands, moving it around just like Vince did when he was out here making a hero of himself. He held it steady and flat at waist height, moving slowly above the furrow like he was divining for water. Every motion seemed purposeful, almost like a dance—the way he held that cane, moved his feet, and rocked his head. I detected a faint song on the wind. It sounded like the kind Aana sings, ancient, haunting, yet somehow familiar. Like Rosie's *ajai jaa* song, I knew it belonged to this land as much as caribou and bearberries. That was the first time I'd ever heard Uncle Jonah sing. But, as it turned out, it wouldn't be my last.

I hadn't a clue what Uncle Jonah was looking for. Whatever it was, I knew this must have been what got him climbing the walls for so many days, then, when Mom set him free, booting down the hill like a madman. I decided to keep a respectful distance, finding a dry, flat rock to sit on and watch what treasures he might dig up. Wiggins was still agitated, so I tried to console him by offering my shoulder and a honey stick.

It didn't take long for Uncle Jonah to find what he was looking for. I'd drifted into a mood where nothing he could pull out of the ground could surprise me. A human skull, my dream harpoon, a box of jelly donuts—I was ready for anything. What he eventually found was a bit of an anticlimax until I realized what it was. I knew he was on to something when he let out a whoop, threw down his cane, and started scratching at the stirred-up peat like a dog going for a bone. I ran over to help and was soon down on my knees beside him, clawing at the cold ground.

It turns out it *was* a bone he was after, a hot dog-shaped thing that was slightly tapered at one end and had a crude hole drilled in the other with a rotten piece of caribou hide hanging from it. The bone nested comfortably in Uncle Jonah's hand—his right hand—like it was an extension of his body. It had been carved from the thigh bone of a very large animal, probably a polar bear.

The instant he twirled it around under my nose I knew what it was. A stick for beating a *qilauti*, a traditional Inuit drum. He started waving it in the air while slowly flipping an imaginary drum in his other hand. A genuine smile grew on his face—though, because he was so out of practice, it had a twisted, almost gruesome look to it. His body started swaying like a teenager's. I could see that, behind the thick lenses of his glasses, the fire burned brighter than ever. And then that song, that song, poured out again from his lips.

My breaths grew short. My chest resounded with each graceful swing of his drumstick. Fingers of wind off the tundra grew stronger, as if ready to pluck away anything in me that might resist the magic of my great uncle's song. I closed my eyes. His song filled my swelling heart. A voice deep within me cried out, *I know this song!* But the voice was smothered by a rising insect-like drone before I could identify it. My chest might have burst open and the whole sky poured in if it weren't for the arrival of the 4:40 sked flight from Inniturliq.

I opened my eyes to see an Arctic Air Twin Otter bearing down on us.

"We really should get out of here, Uncle," I said, sounding a bit like my mother.

He glanced at the plane, shoved his treasure deep in his bathrobe pocket as if hiding it from view, and started trudging back up the trail.

Wiggins squawked in the air above me, anxious to head home.

"Your cane!" I shouted, realizing Uncle had left it behind.

"You keep it," he shouted, without looking back. "Belongs to *Uitajuq* now."

It Can't Die

You let a big char drop from your blood-drenched mouth. It is still alive and swims downstream, out of sight, with a couple of flicks of its red-tipped tail. Something makes you lift your head and listen. Something far away, beyond the coastal plains and the big delta.

You don't want to leave this river. It is swollen with fish returning to the sea. But you know you must go.

The calling sound is back.

It didn't die.

It can't die.

Now you can forget about hunger. Forget about looking for seals and starfish, stranded whales and Arctic char. Other bears can have them.

Someone is calling you.

Calling you home.

A human with power like your own.

You turn towards the sound and run like a cub, barely touching the ground.

Swimming in Songs

"I didn't know you liked drumming, Uncle," Mom said after hearing my story of what happened on the Spit.

I didn't tell her about us fast-tracking together down the trail. I didn't tell her about my vision of Uncle Jonah wearing a tundra cape or a polar bear's body or about how he sang his drumstick out of the ground. I still had a lot to digest and I didn't want Mom dissecting everything to pieces.

"We'll have to get you a real drum," Mom said nodding to herself. "Yes, that would be a perfect way to burn up all the extra energy you seem to have these days. Keep you out of trouble, eh, Uncle?"

Uncle Jonah sat silently at the table with his bear cup and drumstick before him. I was struggling to concentrate on some boring math homework. I looked a few minutes later to see my great uncle with his right hand wrapped firmly around his drumstick, his eyes closed, a faint smile on his face.

Mom was in her people management mode. She now had a plan for Uncle and nothing would stop her from carrying it out. For once, I thought she was on the right track. "What about it, Ash? Do you think we could find a spare drum in this town for Uncle?"

I looked up from my books at Uncle Jonah. His usually downcast eyes had been trained on me a lot since he went off his pills. I sensed he'd been staring my way for some time and now I was caught in the beam of a powerful searchlight. I felt oddly close to him since our adventure on the Spit, yet frightened at the same time, like that feeling you get just before walking into a final exam.

"Well, let's see. Rosie's got that old thing of her grandfather's hanging on the wall but it's in pretty bad shape."

Uncle Jonah shook his head without taking his eyes off me.

"Then there's old Tuurngaq. He might have an extra drum lying around."

Uncle shook his head again.

I almost asked him how the heck he would know when a simple solution occurred to me. "Look, Uncle, you can use my drum when I'm not rehearsing or at a gig or something."

Uncle nodded and the searchlight warmed.

I ran up to my room and fetched my drum for him. His fingers ran over the drum's stretched nylon surface and plastic rim, hardly what you could call traditional materials. To my surprise, he seemed quite satisfied with it. I couldn't tell whether it was the drum he was pleased with or the fact that I had offered it to him. Without a word, he scooped his drumstick off the table and ducked into his room.

I was honestly a little worried about what would happen when Uncle started to drum. Rosie almost split me in two with her *ajai jaa* song. But it was okay. With the first few beats of Uncle's song, I knew I was safe. In fact I felt safer than ever. I closed my math books, lay my head on my hands, and listened. I couldn't get enough of it, swimming in his song.

Uncle started with the song he'd shared with me down on the Spit, one he would come back to again and again over the next few days. He seemed to have dozens up his sleeve, some sharp and windy like a midwinter blizzard, others deep and mellow like a gently rolling sea under the midnight sun. His songs came out one after another, as if they'd flown a holding pattern in his head all these years, waiting for the pill-induced fog to lift. The discovery of his drumstick was the green light to bring them all back to earth.

Uitajuq's Song

The day after Jonah started drumming, we woke up to find his room empty and the back door flung open. He seemed to have left in a hurry, even neglecting to put on his bathrobe which Mom found stuffed in the bathtub. It wasn't until Rosie called that we had any idea where he'd gone.

"Hey, Ash, you wouldn't believe the racket that Jonah and Ghost Man are kicking up over here."

Tuurngaq lived alone in a tiny frame house across the street from Rosie. Though he and Uncle Jonah had known each other since they wore moss diapers, Uncle Jonah had never visited or spoken of him once in the year I'd lived here.

"They've been going at it since about four this morning," Rosie said, "and they're still going strong. Jonah's gonna beat the crap out of that drum of yours if you don't get it back soon."

"No sweat, Rosie," I said. "He knows what he's doing."

I ran over to Rosie's for a listen. We sat on her bed with the window open, rocking to the beat of my great uncle's garage band while leafing through old *Archie* comics.

"Jumpin' Jonah and the Ghost," Rosie said. "Playing all your favorite hits from the fifties."

"And beyond," I added.

"Yeah, I'd say *way* beyond by the sounds of it. These tunes must go back to the last ice age."

After a cycle of about ten songs, they always came back to the one Jonah sang on the Spit. One time round, Rosie plucked her grandfather's *qilauti* off the wall and started tapping it gently in time with this song. That gave me enough acoustical shield to slip in a bit of undercover humming. Rosie seemed to think my musical ear had improved lately but, until now, I'd never dared anything but throat singing outside of my own room—or my dreams. To my surprise, I found my voice could follow Jonah's closely, almost effortlessly, as if I'd sung it a thousand times. My humming rose, breaking into full-blown song. Words I didn't know came out of my mouth. A strong, quiet witness in me listened with the same contentment as it might watch a polar bear sketch flowing from my hands.

With eyes closed, I let the song go, releasing it like a bird that had been caged in my throat since the day I was born. I went from zero to sixty in a matter of seconds, throwing off my fear of singing and giving myself up to Jonah's song. Warm honey flowed from my open lungs to every cell of my body.

I don't know how long I went on like this. All I know is that, when I opened my eyes, the drumming had stopped across the street and there were tears streaming down Rosie's face.

"Ash, you found it," she whispered.

"What?" I said, as my brain slowly regained control of my lips.

"You found it," she repeated, grabbing my hands.

I looked at her, feeling my cheeks flush with embarrassment. "My voice? Yeah, well, let's keep this between you and me, okay?" Some fears take awhile to die.

Rosie laughed and wiped the tears away with her sleeve. "Nice, yeah. Now we have something we can work with. But I'm talking about your song, Ash. Your *ajai jaa* song!"

A truckload of bricks fell on my head. I remembered where I'd heard that song before. In the dreamy depths of the sea where I'd met *Nanurluk*, my guardian and guide, who had invited me into her cave.

I must have given Rosie a crazy look. "Don't you get it, Ash?"

I got it all right. I knew that she had nailed it again. I'd opened a great, shining gift—a *nakuusiaq*—with enough layers to unwrap for the rest of my life. What bamboozled me was how Uncle Jonah could have known that song, my song.

I stood up on Rosie's bed and looked out the window at Tuurngaq's house. No movement. No sound. Rosie told me later that she didn't hear a peep out of them for the rest of the day.

When Uncle Jonah finally came home around suppertime I asked him a question I'd rehearsed all afternoon, "That song of yours that you play over and over. How did you learn it, Uncle?"

He stopped on his way past the table and looked at me with eyes as piercing as harpoons. "Not my song. No. Belongs to Uitajuq."

The Bear Shaman's Song

Part IX
With My People

Wearing skins of nameless animals,
I find my people.
Though my *kamiiks* are ragged and torn,
My lungs fill with song.
The wind dies
And tundra flowers bloom
Before my open eyes,
My open eyes.
Ha-jai-jaa, ha-jai-jaa!
I am *Uitajuq!*

A Gift for Uncle Jonah

ASHLEY'S HOUSE

SUNDAY, JUNE 25TH, 7:40 P.M.

Uncle Jonah died on his ninetieth birthday. His nine lives were up. Exactly how and where he died, nobody knew. It was like he vaporized. The last time I saw him, I'd just come home from a summer solstice drumming gig at Tuktu Hall. It was the first time I'd played my new drum in public, the one Rosie had given me to celebrate my one year anniversary in Nanurtalik. "This makes it official," she'd said as she placed it into my open hands. "You have now been officially adopted as a true Nanurtalikian." It was a beautiful drum, a *qilauti,* made from caribou skin and driftwood by Tuurngaq himself. Some day I would ask him to make me a belt of polar bear claws to go with it.

I'd just set my new drum down by the door when Uncle Jonah almost sprinted through the kitchen and plucked it away. It seemed he needed a drumming fix in a bad way.

An impulse rose up in me from a deep, warm place. "Hey look, Uncle. You might as well keep that." I hoped Rosie would understand. I could always borrow it back now and then for gigs. Besides, it seemed like a fair trade for his narwhal cane.

Uncle Jonah stopped in his tracks just as he was about to close his bedroom door behind him. He stuck his head out and leveled his coal-black eyes at me, like he was hunting for something in my face. He slowly raised the drum. "This. For me?"

"Yeah, sure. You keep it. Ah . . . Happy Birthday and all that."

His eyes seemed to flash orange for a moment, then relax. His lips curled slightly into the shadow of a smile. "*Taima Uitajuq. Taima.*"

I nodded to him while wiping something from my eyes. I guess they were tears. When I looked up his door was closed.

The drumming started right away. It was quiet at first, rose to a fever pitch, then faded, only to rise again. He went on like this for hours. His voice followed the drumbeat's course, like it was falling into deep canyons, scaling mountains, then falling again. Mom and I stood by his door for a while, not daring to go in. We could tell by the shifting light under his door that he was on his feet, walking around as he drummed, maybe even dancing. I noticed with some embarrassment that we'd been holding hands and gently swaying together to Uncle Jonah's beat. But I didn't let go. At least, not until Rosie stormed in to have a listen.

"I heard old Jonah was singing up a storm," Rosie said. "What's got into him?"

"It's more what's coming *out* of him that counts," Mom said. "He's uncorked something rare here and it's lovely. *Mon Dieu,* so lovely."

Uncle Jonah carried on right through the special birthday supper Mom had prepared for him. Nobody said much around the table. I noticed that everyone, even Dad, was gently rocking and rolling to the beat, like we all should've been up dancing instead of eating Mom's five-star chocolate cake. I was just à la moding my piece with a scoop of homemade ice cream when Jonah reached a wild crescendo that ended with a weird, laughing scream. We all looked at each other without a word. Gabe leaned over his plate and cocked his ears. Then, another laugh followed by one ecstatic shout. "*Ha-jai-jaa!*"

Then silence.

By Aana's scrunched-up nose I could tell that even she was puzzled.

"Why don't you go check on him, Ash," Mom said.

"It's your turn."

Aana actually kicked my leg under the table and flipped her eyebrows at me. Mom pushed back her chair.

"Wait, Mom. I'll check. I'm sure he's—"

For a split second, I saw the crack of light under his door blaze lightning white.

Pauloosie saw it too. "What's he doing in there, flashing pictures?"

"He's up to something," Gabe said. "I can feel it! He's up to s-something! Some c-c-crazy birthday surprise!"

Wiggins was flapping something awful. Jacques started barking up a storm. Mom opened the kitchen door for him and he ran outside like a bat out of hell.

"It's okay, Gabe," I said reaching for Uncle Jonah's doorknob. Before I'd even touched it, a purple spark of static electricity jolted my fingers. It seemed to zoom up my arm and lodge itself into my chest, igniting a swarm of hot pins and needles in its wake. I held my breath and turned the knob.

My nostrils filled with the smell of ozone. It hung in the air like just after a thunderstorm. Uncle Jonah's bed, his ratty couch, his wooden rocker were empty. In the old days, when he still threw tizzy fits, I might have found him on the floor beside the bed. Maybe even under it. Not this time. There were no open windows. No busted screens. The old guy had simply vanished. And wherever he was, he'd taken my birthday present with him.

Merging

Usually Mom would wait two or three hours before calling the troops to look for my wandering great uncle. This time she ran to the phone before I'd even had a chance to look under his bed. Minutes after the lightning flash under his door, she'd put everyone on red alert—the RCMP, the Coast Guard, the Hunters and Trappers Council, all the deputy fire chiefs she could remember, even Raymond Arseneau, the safety guy who once fired six bullets into our house. Search parties fanned out over the tundra, along the shore, out on the sea, and in the air. Thanks to Gabe's birthday broadcast of a secret tape he'd made of Uncle's songs—by standing outside his window with a microphone while he drummed—everyone in town had been touched by the magic of Uncle's "rebirth," as Mom called it. Few people slept that night. There was a new buzz in town that fuelled an all-night search and rescue mission under the midnight sun.

They never did find Uncle's body. What they did find, the morning after he vanished, was a dead polar bear. Steven spotted it from Lyons' research helicopter which he'd donated for the man-hunt.

Naturally the whole town was talking about Uncle Jonah. Then, on the coattails of his disappearance, up pops Nanurtalik's first polar bear—I mean *confirmed* polar bear—in over thirty years. It was almost too much for the local grapevine to bear.

So Lord Gord called another meeting in Tuktu Hall. Rosie and I took up our usual positions along the west wall. You could almost hear the crackle of curiosity in the air. The meeting opened with a stirring prayer song from Tuurngaq who seemed two inches off the floor as he drummed. I could handle it this time. Instead of collapsing to the beat of his drum, I felt like leaping up there with him to dance.

As soon as Tuurngaq finished, the mayor cut to the quick and invited Steven and Lyons up to a floor mike to tell their story.

"Steven is still back at the lab, Gordon," Lyons said. "Perhaps we should wait until—"

The mayor sighed heavily. "Oh, go ahead,professor. We might as well hear your version. But *please,* stick to English. Or, if you like, Inuktitut."

Lyons shrugged. "Steven is a good language tutor but my English will have to do for now. It was yesterday around 7:00 A.M., as we returned from a final sweep above Crab Bay. Steven spotted the bear while we descended towards the airstrip. At first I thought it was a chunk of residual sea ice that got hung up off the Spit. But Steven knew better. We dropped lower and I saw clearly that it was a polar bear, a dead one, lying face up in the shallow water between the end of the Spit and Blood Rock."

"I understand you have taken charge of this bear, Professor?"

"Not at all, Gordon. We simply took the liberty of air-lifting it to the STRESS Center so we could conduct a full autopsy in our laboratory. Steven assisted closely with this operation and has since prepared and stored all of the meat for distribution to the community."

"And what did your autopsy reveal?"

"It was an exceptionally large, female bear."

"How large?"

Lyons pulled out a small notebook from his shirt pocket. "Yes, here it is. It measured ten feet, nine inches and weighed one thousand, five hundred, and ninety two pounds. This is most remarkable considering that males tend to be anywhere from one quarter to one third larger than females."

Lord Gord whistled, almost to himself. I could just imagine visions of trophy-sized bear rugs dancing in his head. "Do you mean to say there could be even *bigger* males roaming around out there?"

"It all depends on how unusual this female really is. All I can say is that, until June 26TH, the largest bear our team had tagged was a nine-foot-ten male just over fourteen hundred pounds. Let me tell you, that bear down on the Spit put quite a strain on our helicopter."

"What kind of shape was she in?" asked the mayor. "Hunters in other communities tell me even our biggest bears are wasting away because of the weird weather we're getting these days."

"Indeed, it has been irrefutably demonstrated that some polar bear populations have suffered significant weight loss and fat depletion due to climate-induced aberrations in regional ice patterns, thereby influencing their foraging strategies and—"

"Remember, Professor, you promised me English?"

"Forgive me, Gordon. Perhaps I'm a little too close to the subject."

"Just tell us: was that bear killed by climate change or wasn't it?" asked Gord with no little hint of sarcasm.

Lyons paused to stroke his beard. I could tell he was choosing his words carefully here. "I'm afraid I couldn't really answer that question since we have very little data to draw from in your region. You see, since they're opportunistic feeders, the health of polar bears can vary widely from week to week or season to season. This can be a hungry time of year for certain populations of polar bears when access to seals dwindles with the melting sea ice. The bear we found off the Spit did show some signs of chronic nutritional stress. But its stomach contents suggested that over the past few days it had been feasting on Arctic char. In fact this bear was in remarkably good shape, considering her advanced age."

"And how old was it, Professor?"

"The bear had lost several teeth, including a top and bottom canine, but fortunately she'd retained the standard premolar that we use for aging bears. We pulled this tooth, then cut and stained it to enable us to see the annular growth rings which—"

"Professor, how *old?*"

"Ah, sorry. Thirty-three years." Lyons fixed his eyes on the row of white-haired Elders sitting up front. "Quite a remarkable bear, really," he said in unusually dreamy tones. "An Elder giant among giants. I believe in your language you would call her a *Nanurluk?*"

My eyes narrowed as the memory of our last night on the sea ice came rushing back to me, listening to Steven's stories around the flickering lamplight as the wind pounded on our tent.

"Maybe just stick to the science side of this, Professor. Most of us grew up on a steady diet of *Nanurluit* stories. They're said to be so big and powerful that no ordinary person can hunt them. But they, in turn, like to hunt *us.*" The mayor paused. "Do you suppose this was the bear that attacked Moise?"

"Nobody got a good look at it," Lyons said. "Not even Moise. But that's entirely possible. He seems to attract bears that way."

"And do you suppose there are more jumbo-sized bears nearby?"

"I suspect a bear like her is relatively rare. But your people would know best, Gordon. It's questions like this that make it so important for us to keep working together."

"This bear was thirty-three, you say."

"That's correct. Quite a ripe old age for a free-ranging bear."

"What would that amount to in human terms?"

"I would say roughly ninety years old."

Rosie elbowed me. "How old did Jonah turn the day he evaporated?"

"Ah, ninety, I think. Why do you—"

"Uh-huh," she said like she was on to something.

Lord Gord wanted clear-cut answers. "Isn't the purpose of an autopsy to figure out how something died?"

"Of course."

"So?"

"In this case it's rather difficult."

"But you're a professional, *aren't you,* Professor."

"Of course, but—"

"So?"

"It might have simply been old age, a condition that doesn't show up well on the autopsy table. However we did discover an old wound in the bear's left *gluteus maximus.*"

"English, please."

Lyons stepped closer to the microphone. "Ah, its *butt.*"

A low giggle rippled through the crowd.

"We suspected infection, so we opened the wound to investigate and found a .45 magnum bullet lodged in the deep cutaneous layers. Judging by the thick scar tissue around it, the bear must have been shot several months ago. Sometime last winter, I suspect."

Lord Gord glanced around the hall until his eyes landed on Raymond Arseneau. "That would be *your* bullet, Raymond? I can't think of anyone else in town who packs that kind of pistol."

Raymond just waved his hand as if bidding at an auction.

"So it *was* a bear in that blizzard," Rosie said slapping my knee. "I thought Raymond hallucinated all that."

"We discovered another wound in the bear's chest," continued Lyons, "a most peculiar wound that appeared singed around the edges."

"*Singed?*" asked the mayor, incredulous. "You mean like . . . burnt?"

"I believe so. Some of the fur in that area showed signs of combustion."

"*Ikuma,*" Rosie said under her breath.

"What?" I said.

"The fireman." Rosie grabbed my chin and turned my face toward hers. "Join the dots, Ashley."

I stared at Tuurngaq as if he might know the meaning of this. He was already looking at me, like he had been for a long time. He flashed a toothless grin at me. With that one look the dots started streaming together. I stared straight ahead, speechless. I could feel some vital fact seeping into me. But it hadn't yet hit my brain. I knew then without a doubt that this bear and my great uncle were somehow linked.

Lord Gord had lost the edge to his voice and now sounded just plain curious. "And the wound? What did you find there. More bullets?"

"No bullets. It was a clean slit in the middle of her chest, like the bear had been recently jabbed by a very sharp harpoon."

"A harpoon, you say. How recently?"

"Just hours before we found her."

The mayor's mouth opened but no words came out.

"The wound led to the central chest cavity but, curiously enough, it was quite clean. There was no evidence of bleeding or clotting. All vital organs were intact. More than intact, actually."

"What on earth do you mean?"

Lyons looked over at Steven Allooloo who had just walked in carrying an orange garbage bag under one arm. They exchanged knowing nods. "Even more curious was the fact that this polar bear appeared to have two hearts."

Lord Gord grabbed the front edge of the podium and sprang to his tiptoes. "*Two hearts?*"

"We have retained the heart—or should I say, hearts—to see if it might represent some kind of congenital deformity. I have read reports of three kidneys occurring in an isolated population of black bears in northern Mexico. And there's one documented case from China of a panda bear having an extra liver. But two hearts?" Lyons shook his head. "This is unheard of in the scientific literature. As I say, quite a remarkable bear."

The mayor tugged on his ear, brought his heels back to earth, then, in a hushed voice, translated Lyons's story for the Elders. This sure got the tongues wagging and the white heads bobbing.

After about fifteen minutes of this, Lord Gord straightened up and addressed Dr. Lyons once again.

"That's quite the story, Professor Lyons," he said, lifting his arm toward the exit, "but, if you don't mind, the Elders would prefer to discuss this matter in private—"

"I understand. But there's more actually."

"More about the bear? What, I suppose it woke up and cartwheeled out of your laboratory?"

Lyons smiled faintly. "It's about what we discovered near the bear."

Lord Gord lowered his arm and rose again to his tiptoes. "Go on, Professor."

"Of course these findings go beyond the scope of my autopsy report but they may shed light on the unusual circumstances surrounding the bear's death, and, possibly, that of Jonah Anowiak."

"I knew it!" shouted Rosie, so loud that everyone in the hall turned their heads our way. She ducked her face behind the collar of my mishmash coat.

"Knew *what?*" I whispered.

"Just listen."

I looked back to see Steven walk briskly up to Lyons's side. He had a tight grip on the bag as if it were full of treasure.

"I'll defer to Steven here," said Lyons, stepping aside, "since science has little to do with the rest of this story."

Steven gave him a slight nod and picked up the thread. "So, yeah, as our chopper was about to set down on the Spit, we saw some strange tracks all over the beach. Fresh boot tracks mixed with bear prints, all mixed together in a kind of circle. There was nothing leading to it, no tracks at all. That was it, just this weird circle in the sand."

"How" The mayor's voice faltered, ". . . how do you explain these tracks, Steven?"

"Beats me."

"But you've been on lots of bear hunts, seen a lot of bears."

"Sure. I think the Professor and I are about neck and neck in the bear department." Steven shot Lyons a tight-lipped grin. "But I've never seen anything like this. It's kinda' like . . . well—like they were dancing or something. I've seen carvings like that, you know, with the bear and the hunter, circling around, sparring each other, while kickin' up their heels in some kind of dance."

The hall fell silent.

Steven continued after a few moments. "We were so freaked by those tracks that we didn't think of asking the pilot to land somewhere else. The tracks got wiped out by prop wash. After our chopper landed I saw some stuff blowing all over the place."

"And?"

"After we hauled the bear to shore we fished around just off the beach and found this." Steven reached deep into the garbage bag, then held something high over his head for all to see.

Tuurngaq cried out when he saw it. His voice cut a path straight to my heart. It sounded like a cry of joy. Steven was holding Uncle Jonah's coke bottle glasses.

Lord Gord sucked in his breath. "Why, I'd recognize those glasses anywhere."

"You bet, good old Jonah Anowiak, big-time bear hunter."

"So . . . what do you suppose happened to him?"

"Beats me, Gordon. Maybe still dancing around out there somewhere." Steven carefully folded Uncle's glasses and walked them over to Tuurngaq. The old man stared at them with a big, toothless grin on his face, then thrust them above his head like a victory salute. The whole hall burst into applause.

I was too stunned to clap.

"You mentioned other things blowing away when you landed," said the mayor when the applause finally died down. "Did you find any more clues to this mystery?"

"Just more mystery. Look at this." Steven reached back into the bag and pulled out a pair of wolf mitts.

I pulled away from the wall. "Hey, those are . . ." I fell speechless, remembering where I'd left them. In the underground icehouse at the feet of a giant bear.

Steven wasn't finished. He reached again into the bag and pulled out the *qilauti* I had given to Uncle Jonah the day he vanished.

I almost blacked out. If Rosie hadn't grabbed my arm at that moment I would have fallen over.

Steven's voice came to me as if from a dream. I tried to clear the fog from my brain. He was holding the drum out to me.

"Lose something, Ashley? Sure looks like your style."

I looked at Rosie through bleary eyes as if waking from a dream. "Style? What's he mean?"

Before she could say anything, my feet started carrying me towards the drum. I shuffled across the hall, oblivious to everything else. Steven placed it in my hands, skin side down. It was the same drum all right.

"How—how did this end up on the Spit?" I asked in a slurred voice. The question seemed unimportant even as the words left my quivering lips.

Steven shrugged.

I turned the drum over and got the shock of my life.

Lyons leaned over Steven's shoulder. "That *is* done in your hand, isn't it?" he asked.

It was like holding up a mirror I'd never looked into before. Someone had drawn a polar bear on the drum's caribou skin. With my entire adopted community surrounding me in silent wonder, I ran my artist's fingers over the image. It wasn't rendered in any paint I'd ever seen before. It wasn't charcoal or pencil. It seemed to have been *burned* into the canvas. I swear it was still warm under my fingers. There it was. The she-bear of my dreams. The she-bear Uncle Jonah had hunted down and captured in firestone. Whoever drew this bear had shown her protective side, that bewitching face so full of sacred power.

My bear. Uncle's bear. Our drum.

My vision cleared. The storm within me ceased. I fell, healed and whole, into a calm deep sea. I looked up at Lyons, his scientific eyes looking oddly puzzled behind his gold-rimmed glasses. "Yes," I said feeling stronger than I ever had before. "It's from my hand. I had a bit of help on this one."

Connecting the Dots

ASHLEY'S HOME
SATURDAY, JULY 1ST, 10:44 P.M.
The night after Nanurtalik paid its last respects to Uncle Jonah, I realized there was still an important piece missing from

the puzzle of his life. I knew Aana would be the one to fill in the blanks.

"You've never told me what happened to Uncle's right arm," I said to her over bedtime tea.

"You never asked."

"Well?"

"Too late to ask Jonah. Why didn't you ask him?"

"I never thought to ask, I guess. That gammy arm seemed as much a part of him as his big nose."

"I don't know anything about Jonah's nose."

"His *arm*, Aana. What happened to it?"

"What else? A bear."

"What?"

"A bear. They never liked him much. Always used to pick on him. Whenever he'd go hunting with anybody, it was always Uncle they'd go after."

"You mean like Dad?"

Aana pursed her lips and looked over at Dad who was snoring on the couch. "Yeah. Just like Moise, only worse."

"Worse!"

Aana nodded for a long time. "Jonah loved bears. Had a special thing with them. But he never had much luck hunting 'cause they always gave him a rough time. That's why he took up carving. Thought he'd hunt them in stone." Aana laughed. "A lot safer anyway."

"Did he have any successful bear hunts?"

"You saw his carvings. Caught them pretty good, eh?"

"Come on, Aana."

She chuckled, then took a thoughtful sip of tea. "He got a few bears."

"What did he use?"

"Harpoon mostly. In those days a lot used harpoons. You could hunt bears in their dens. He learned that from your grandfather." Aana jutted her chin towards the narwhal cane hanging above Uncle Jonah's door. Dad had hung it there after all the search parties finally gave up. "That's all that's left of those days."

"You mean *that* was his harpoon?"

Aana chuckled. "Whittled down a bit. It was his first carving."

I plucked his cane off the wall and stroked its narwhal shaft. Memories of the firestone-tipped harpoon of my dreams flooded back to me: glowing purple in my hands, leading me up an iceberg, piercing the sea tunnel, protecting me as I dared to enter *Nanurluk's* cave. I remembered fast-tracking down to the Spit with his cane in hand, how Uncle Jonah had used it to find his beloved drumstick, and how he'd given it to me like all his work was over.

I gently set the cane on the table before Aana. "So what about his arm?"

Aana shook her head. "*Maiksuk.*"

"What, Aana?"

"Bad thing, to go bear hunting with the full moon. That's what he did."

"Why is it a bad thing, Aana?"

"The moon brings the bears up."

"What do you mean, up?"

"In their dens. When the moon's bright they scrape the roof of their dens." Aana shrugged. "Don't know why but that's what they do. You don't want to walk around on thin roofs. That's what Jonah did. Fell right in on a giant bear."

"A giant bear? You mean like a *Nanurluk?*"

Aana shot me an odd glance. "Call it what you like. It was big enough. He fell right in there with it. His harpoon got stuck in the snow. All he had was his hands. He wrestled around in there for a bit, then remembered the way puppies can't bite down hard with something jammed between their jaws. So he shoved his arm as far back as he could into the bear's mouth."

"On purpose?"

"That's the way he told it. While the bear chewed on his arm he managed to grab the harpoon with his other arm and kill the bear."

"What did he do with the bear?"

"Some people said he hauled it down into the icehouse, but he never talked about it."

My jaw dropped. This was the same bear that spooked me thirty years later. There was no doubt in my mind that its power lived on.

Aana got up from the table and stretched. "That big bear finished Uncle's hunting days."

"And started his drinking days?" I asked.

"I guess so. Real bears or stone bears. Didn't matter which. He couldn't hunt either with that arm of his."

I abruptly turned to look at Uncle Jonah's *Nanurluk* carving now parked in an elegant display cabinet that Dad had made. "Pretty *artsy* case, Dad," I'd said when he unveiled it one night after dinner. We'd all had a good laugh over that.

Today, *Nanurluk's* kindly face was turned outward. Gabe had gotten into the habit of alternating its faces now and then, always taking time to run his magic fingers over the entire sculpture before turning it around.

"Ever been down in the icehouse, Aana?" I asked while wiping another day's crumbs off the dining table with a damp cloth.

"No, thanks. I leave bears alone. Especially *Nanurluk.*"

"So you do believe there's a giant bear prowling around down there."

Aana shook her head. "I don't know about that. But one got away on Jonah that night."

I stopped wiping. "Huh?"

"There was another bear in the den. He said it was a female, maybe three years old."

That eerie ring of tracks in the sand stole into my mind. I straightened up and stared at her. "You don't think . . . that was the dancing bear on the Spit? The one with two hearts?"

Aana made a soft, clucking noise, then smiled at me. I had seen that smile reflected up at me from the still black waters of my dream. "What does your professor friend always say? There's a lot we don't know about bears. Sure. Okay. But *Ikuma*, he knew a lot more about bears than your professor. More than anybody." Aana peered at me, moving her head slightly like she was looking for someone behind my eyes. "Except maybe Anaana, our mother."

"You mean *Uitajuq?* That was her name too, right?"

Aana nodded with great satisfaction. "Boy, did *she* know about bears! Just like you."

It would take me a while to sift through the meaning of all my bear adventures, both inside and out. I knew sketching would help. A bunch of sizzling images hovered restlessly in my brain. Maybe I could put an art show together at Tuktu Hall or teach an art class. Maybe I could visit the Singing Drum Elders' Home and gather more polar bear stories and songs for a school project. Yeah, and Rosie could help translate. Maybe I could assist Lyons and Steven in their polar bear research and keep tabs on the impacts of this crazy weather. But somehow I knew all this would only be a sideshow unless I tackled what had become my most important job: find out everything I could about my namesake who, according to Aana, knew more about polar bears than anybody.

"I'd like to hear more *Uitajuq* stories sometime," I said. "She sounds like a pretty cool lady."

Aana brushed some crumbs I'd missed off the table and threw them at Jacques. "Not now, little *Uitajuq*. It's past my bedtime." Aana stood up and stretched. "You'll get to know her good no matter what I say."

"If you say so."

Aana slid Uncle Jonah's cane toward me. "Put this back. You won't need it."

I carefully picked the cane up and cradled it in my hands. "There must be a lot of bear power stored inside this thing."

"Like I say, you won't need it, *Uitajuq.*"

"What do you mean?"

Aana shuffled around the table and hooked a finger over my sweatshirt collar, exposing my bear claw birthmark. "Now you carry bear power inside you. Always remember that."

"At least tell me one thing," I said. "Did your mother have the same birthmark?"

My grandmother's ancient eyes brightened. "See what I mean? You already know all about her." Then she covered her mouth with her bony knuckles and her chest shook with a girlish laughter.

Open Eyes

ASHLEY'S DREAM JOURNAL
SUNDAY, JULY 2ND, 5:48 A.M.
It's springtime in Nanurtalik. The sun on my face, the warm flower-scented breeze, the tinkling of longspurs and horned larks, the chirping

of ground squirrels, the cushiony moss and lichens beneath my kami-
iks—I sense all this more vividly than when awake.

My eyes are clear. My breathing deep. My heart is full. My song is
strong. I'm at home in this place.

I stand behind the church looking up at the stone angel. I hear dis-
tant drumming from the hilltop. My ajai jaa song blends with each
beat, growing in volume, lifting my spirit. I close my dream-eyes for a
moment. When I open them, I'm on the summit, standing where the
angel was seconds ago.

Before me is a tall man dressed head to toe in polar bear skins and
wearing the loon skin cap of a shaman. His song and mine blend
together like smoke from two fires. His back is to me as he blesses the
town, the Spit, and the shining sea with his song. He ends with a
powerful whack on his drum and a great shout that seems to shake
the sky.

Ha-jai-jaa! Ha-jai-jaa!

He slowly turns to face me as he lowers his drum. I'm startled to
look right through him at the flash of waves below. He is disappearing
before my open eyes. Uitajuq's eyes.

Just before his face dissolves into the sea, I catch a flash of fire
behind his coal-black eyes and wide bear-like nose.

I blink hard and my dream-mouth falls open. A sudden tremor of
doubt shakes my insides.

"Uncle?"

I feel suddenly alone and afraid. The instant I recognize my
teacher, my own flesh and blood, he vanishes.

"Uncle!"

I cling to my song. I blink again and—I am awake, still standing on the summit of Anirniq Hill.

I open my hands and see long, slender *doigts d'une artiste*—
artist's fingers. I look down and see pale bare feet where sealskin

kamiiks had stood moments before. Caribou skin pants have been replaced with polar bear pajamas. I touch my face, Ashley's face.

"How the heck did I—?"

Then, with a shudder, I understand. The magic veil between waking and dreaming, between Ashley's world and *Uitajuq's* has been torn away. The sun, the breeze, the birds spill freely from her world into mine. Uncle Jonah's final *nakuusiaq*. A loving gift to the spirit of his mother in me.

I look down on my new home, Nanurtalik, the place of the polar bear. Now so precious to me, yet so small, so fragile. I think of how quickly its culture, climate—even the land itself—could crumble into chaos. My heart shrinks with the knowledge that another freak storm could wipe this tiny, troubled town clean off the map.

My song deepens, telling me to look below this fragile film. I sweep my gaze over Nanurtalik's crooked streets and jumbled neighborhoods. My new eyes lock on something bright floating above Tuurngaq's house. It's that light again. The purple glow that welcomed me into *Nanurluk's* cave. I bring the song to my lips and narrow my eyes. There! Across the street. A dim glow above Rosie's house. And another above the Singing Drum Elders' Home. My eyes dart to Heartbreak Hill. Our house glows as if sprayed with grape candy floss. As my eyes adjust to their new powers, I detect more scattered wisps of purple light hanging over the town.

Somehow I know that these are hopeful signs of a sleeping strength just waiting to be awakened. I also know that trying to do this in our crazy twenty-first century Arctic will be my supreme adventure!

I didn't ask for this job. I guess it was stuck on me when Aana gave me my Inuktitut name. For better or worse, Rosie was right. I am a shaman-in-training. But even now that Uncle Jonah is gone, I know I'll never train alone. How could I when Ashley and *Uitajuq* are one?

The Bear Shaman's Song

1. Searching for the Bear

    Watching the ground for her tracks,
    I search for the bear.
    Nameless rivers, distant mountains,
    My search seems endless.
    With strength drained and mind exhausted,
    I cannot find her.
    There is only the song of the sea—*Ha-jai-jaa, ha-jai-jaa!*
    And the thunder of crashing waves.

2. Finding the Bear's Tracks

    Along the jagged coast,
    leaning against the wind,
    I find her tracks!
    My warm snow-house far behind me,
    I study her claw marks—*Aja! Aja-wa!* So huge!
    Nanurluk's tracks,
    Suddenly as clear as young ice,
    Lead me down the endless shore.
    There is no place to hide.

3. Glimpsing the Bear

The cry of the raven
Echoes off the mountains.
I follow Nanurluk's tracks across the sea ice.
Here no bear can hide.
Look!
On an iceberg!
What artist can draw her proud head,
those massive paws?

4. Chasing the Bear

With raised harpoon,
I struggle to catch up to her,
Nanurluk's great power is too much for me.
She charges into the high mountains above the clouds,
or disappears into a misty crack of open water.

5. Calling for Strength

I stagger and fall.
Nanurluk has stolen my power.
Ai! Ai! I call for strength.
My mind grows dizzy
As I stretch my limbs out on the ice.
While my teeth chatter
And eyes close,
I wonder—
Whose blood is this on the snow?

6. Dreaming the Bear

On the wind
I smell the breath of seal.
Its breathing hole is near
And I can hear the sea calling me—
Ha-jai-jaa, ha-jai-jaa!
With flippered hands
I slide towards a circle of dark water.
A trap!
Through my leathery skin
Nanurluk crunches my skull.

7. Both Bear and Hunter Forgotten

Harpoon and snow knife,
Seal and seal hole,
Hunter and bear—
All are lost
In the crushing ice
In the hungry sea.
No traces remain
Except these prints on the beach
Blurring together.

8. Returning Home

Tired and hungry,
I return from the hunt
Hands empty
And heart full.
My footsteps are light,
Padding softly through the thawing snow.
I know these mountains,
Now glowing above me.
The sky is clear.

9. With My People

Wearing skins of nameless animals,
I find my people.
Though my *kamiiks* are ragged and torn,
My lungs fill with song.
The wind dies
And tundra flowers bloom
Before my open eyes,
My open eyes.
Ha-jai-jaa, ha-jai-jaa!
I am *Uitajuq!*

Glossary of Inuktitut Words

Aamittara—careful

Aana—paternal grandmother

Aassuuk—I don't know

Aglu—seal breathing hole

Ainnaa!—An expression of fear.

Ajai jaa—Personal song or chant telling of one's accomplishments in life. The words may not be understood at first, but later the song becomes meaningful as the person makes it their own. Often connected with a traditional name (like *Uitajuq*) that is passed through generations and gives the singer a sense of belonging in the family, community, and the world at large. Also known as *Pihiit*.

Akkak—uncle on father's side of the family

Amaruq—wolf

Amauti—Traditional woman's parka with a deep hood at the back in which babies and children are placed.

Anaana—mother

Anirniq—angel, spirit

Angakkuq—sorcerer, shaman

Auka—no

Igunaq—rotten meat; often referring to fermented walrus meat, a popular traditional food across the Arctic

Inniturliq—Old camping site used for a long time; fictional name of closest major town to *Nanurtalik*.

Ikuma—fire

Illaujaq—"candled" or rotten ice on freshwater lakes and rivers

Inullarik—a true Inuk; a capable and talented man

Ittuq—grandfather

Kamiik—Traditional Inuit footwear often made from seal or caribou skin

Quviasuktuq—happy

Maiksuk!—bad thing

Maktaaq—skin of beluga whale or narwhal

Mipku—dried meat, often caribou

Muktuk—whale blubber

Najak—sister for an Inuk man

Nakurmiik—Thanks.

Nanuq—polar bear

Nanurluk—1.) A giant bear featured in Inuit stories, art, and sculptures. It is said to live only in water, sleeping on the bottom of the sea and breathing through an ice hole or tunnel much like a seal. This kind of bear is extremely difficult to hunt though some have been reported caught within recent memory. It may, in turn, hunt people. It is said to be a fast runner and always attacks on the run, often swallowing people whole. Inuit shamans would often make use of these giant bears as helping spirits. (pl. *Nanurluit*). 2.) A giant polar bear that lives in the ocean and is said to be bigger than large ships. An appreciated spirit-helper of the *angakkuq*. 3.) The most powerful shamans had been visited, shivering in their iglus, by *Nanurluk,* the Spirit Bear. *Nanurluk* devoured the apprentice, who would emerge, reborn, as a shaman. No longer human but now part of *both* the world of humans and the world of animals, the shaman interpreted the narrow path that had to be followed to avoid offending the spirits of sea and air.

Nanjrmikangakkuq—bear shaman

Nanurtalik—fictional name of Ashley's Arctic hamlet, meaning "place with polar bears."

Nakuusiaq—loving gift

Pana—snow knife

Pihiit—see *Ajai jaa*

Qaigit—Come here!

Qaujimajatuqangit—traditional Inuit knowledge

Qilauti—Traditional Inuit drum made of driftwood and caribou skin. It is struck with a wooden mallet often wrapped in the skin of walrus or seal.

Sikuliaq—new, thin ice on which it is possible to walk

Sila—weather, climate, environment

Siksik—arctic ground squirrel (after the sound it makes when alarmed).

Siku—ice

Suluk—feather

Suluk River—fictional name of community east of *Nanurtalik* where polar bears are plentiful.

Suukiaq—Oh yes! It's certain!

Taima—That's it. That's all.

Tiguaq—adopted brother

Tiiturumaviit—Would you like some tea?

Tuullik—loon

Tuurngaq—ghost, spirit

Tuktu—caribou

Unaaq—harpoon

Uitajuq—His / her eyes are open and stay open. Inuktitut name for Ashley and her great-grandmother, Anaana, mother of Uncle Jonah and *Aana*. Pronounced "*U-tah-yuk.*"

Teacher's Guide

A companion Teacher's Guide, *Polar Bears in a Climate of Change*, which includes a complete novel study, is available through Red Deer Press or on-line at www.onthinice.ca

About the Author

Jamie Bastedo's work is all about taking science to the streets. Whether playing environmental songs around the campfire, hosting nature shows on CBC radio, performing as an arctic explorer, creating science videos, running outdoor education camps, leading eco-tours, or writing about some marvel of nature, Jamie spreads a catching love for the land. Jamie's passion for popularizing natural science brought him national honour in 2002 when he won Canada's Michael Smith Award for Science Promotion. His outstanding contributions to the conservation and promotion of northern nature also earned him Queen Elizabeth's Golden Jubilee Medal. When not out on the land, Jamie hangs his hat in Yellowknife, Northwest Territories, where he lives with his wife and two daughters.